SPANISH
CROSSINGS

SPANISH CROSSINGS

A NOVEL BY
JOHN SIMMONS

urbanepublications.com

First published in Great Britain in 2017 by Urbane Publications Ltd
Suite 3, Brown Europe House, 33/34 Gleaming Wood Drive, Chatham, Kent ME5 8RZ
Copyright ©John Simmons, 2017

The moral right of John Simmons to be identified as the author of this work has been
asserted in accordance with the Copyright, Designs and Patents Act of 1988.

A CIP catalogue record for this book is available from the British Library.

ISBN 978-1-911331-68-1
MOBI 978-1-911331-69-8
EPUB 978-1-911331-70-4

Design and Typeset by Julie Martin
Cover by David Carroll & Co
Cover image courtesy Wolf Suschitzsky

urbanepublications.com

MIX
Paper from
responsible sources
FSC® C013604

The publisher supports the Forest Stewardship Council® (FSC®), the leading international forest-certification
organisation. This book is made from acid-free paper from an FSC®-certified provider. FSC is the only forest-certification
scheme supported by the leading environmental organisations, including Greenpeace.

© Wolf Suschitzsky

For the Jessies

CONTENTS

"So we beat on, boats against the current, borne back ceaselessly into the past."
F Scott Fitzgerald, *The Great Gatsby*

"But she laughed and said: 'The thought of knowing everything about anybody gives me the horrors!'"
Patrick White, *The Vivisector*

"They said, 'You have a blue guitar,
You do not play things as they are.'

The man replied, 'Things as they are
Are changed upon the blue guitar.'"

Wallace Stevens, *The Man with the Blue Guitar*

September 1984, Spain

Mother declared herself happy. She had not liked Madrid. In her head it still rang with the steel clang of jackboots on the cobblestones. Standing in front of Picasso's newly installed painting *Guernica*, paying silent homage, had left her tearful. Now we had moved south to Seville, and her mood lifted.

Sometimes we rattled through the streets on trams but mostly we walked. Even in late September Seville was hot, the heat rising from the pavements as well as burning down from above. So our walking was strolling and our strolling was sitting in the gardens. Watching the world go by was what Mother did now, now that the world was passing her by. It seemed that way to me too, now that I was nearing my fortieth birthday.

I had been a disappointment to Mother and Spain had been the reason for her disappointment. In her youth, her beliefs and her friendships had been defined by the Spanish Civil War. In north London, particularly in Hampstead, the war had raged fiercely through the weapons of words. I wish I had heard her then, in her prime. I was left with the black and white photos of a young woman with dark hair tied back and a raised clenched fist. "*No paseran!*" she shouted from the centre of her eccentric group of comrades.

But I disappointed her. My political belief was warm *leche* compared to her hot *cortado*. What should I do with a degree in languages, with Spanish as my main study? Of course I came to Spain, and of course this was the 1970s with Franco still in power. I broke Mother's forty year boycott of this country that, unseen, unvisited, she had loved despite the way it had disappointed her. Perhaps I took heart from that. Disappointments can be overcome. They do not need to last a lifetime.

I came to Spain as a lowly link in the journalistic chain. I filed stories with a reporter's objectivity – how Mother hated that – but with increasing excitement as Franco's time also began to fade into the history of black and white photography. He died, I rejoiced, I held my breath. I joined the people on the streets as colour returned. I was there, with shots ringing out in parliament, watching the coup failing like a scene from an opera. Then I came home.

By this time, Mother was frail. My father had long disappeared from the scene, unmentioned, unmentionable. I took it into my head to take Mother to Spain for her first experience of this country that had shaped her life.

"That would be interesting," she said. I wasn't sure if this was a commitment.

"I'll pay," I said. "We'll stay at nice places and we can go at your pace."

Her eyes were filming with age but there was a glint of her old spirit.

"I'm not dead yet. And not planning to be. I would like to see Madrid – and Seville. Pepe came from there."

So he had been mentioned. Perhaps this gave me a reason, apart from filial duty, for such a trip. I could walk in my father's disappeared footsteps.

After Madrid we took the train to Seville. Despite Mother's rejection of the advance of age, there was no mistaking her frailty. She was in her seventies now, her skin wrinkled like overwashed fabric, her voice closer to a whisper than a shout, her gait hunched behind an invisible stick. I walked behind, to follow her pace and direction, not my own. And she gained energy day by day as we both orientated ourselves towards Seville.

We stayed in the Hotel Doña Maria near the Cathedral. The bells tolled through the night but Mother never mentioned them. Her room was rather grand, with antique dark-wood furniture and devotional paintings. Not her taste, nor mine, but she could rest in the afternoons. The idea of siesta made more sense here.

On our first morning we visited the cathedral. Mother was still shocked by its Catholicism, by the flaunting of its wealth through gold and silver. The statues of Christ, the paintings of the Virgin, allowed no questioning of faith.

"I hate this place," Mother whispered to herself, perhaps to me.

She gravitated towards *la juderia* and *Alcazar*, instinctively on the side of the suppressed. But Jews and Muslims were not really present there. Their people had been swallowed by the past.

She loved the *barrio*, wandering the narrow alleyways without fear while I looked shiftily over my shoulder in the gathering darkness. We could smell rather than see the oranges deep in the leaves. Sitting on a bench in Plaza Santa Cruz, among the rose bushes, she listened to the gypsy wails and rhythmic strumming of Flamenco players getting ready to perform. By daylight she inhaled the architecture of the tobacco factory, allowing herself a secret cigarette while humming songs from *Carmen*. Water trickled through the days, the trilling of fountains all over the city, the stifling air freshened by the wafting of a fan bought in a shop outside the Cathedral.

So the days drifted by. We had set no time limit on our visit but I sensed it was nearing our time to move on. Perhaps Bilbao could no longer be avoided?

It was in the *Jardines de Murillo*, outside the *Alcazar* walls, beneath the ancient, leafy trees, that Mother declared she was happy. It was a relief to me, more than I had expected.

We said good night and wished each other sleep. I listened to the Cathedral bells marking the hours. In the morning, when Mother did not appear for breakfast, I knocked on her door but there was only silence. So I had to ask the hotel manager to open her room door. Her sleep was profound but at least, I consoled myself, she died happy.

PART ONE:
1937

Across the sea

CHAPTER 1

There was still bright daylight over London that evening. The blue of the May sky was given a red rinse through the layers of clouds that were rising on the horizon towards the end of this hot day. From up there in Hampstead, at the top of London, you could see for miles in all directions.

Lorna Starling walked up the hill from Belsize Park station. Observing her, you would notice a determination in her walk, the steady strides in sensible shoes. Perhaps her fixed air was occasioned by a slight lateness – or perhaps even by a refusal to be intimidated by the prospect of the evening.

She was soon to be 24, an age to be young even in these times. But Lorna might not have cared too much about the demands of being young; it was better to try, at least, for independence. So she wore walking shoes that owed more to practicality than fashion. The depression and the threat of war cast shadows over fashionable thoughts. Nor was Lorna comfortable with the idea of dressing up to make an impression. She adopted austere clothing in sympathy, it seemed, with the austere times. She would be happy to merge with the crowd, content not to be noticed.

Of course, she did stand out. Her absence of attention to herself drew the attention of others. She moved through the crowd like a sheep dog.

Lorna was surprised at the number of people. It was a sticky evening of that early summer and the weather had enticed out many. There were groups and couples making their way along the fringes of Hampstead Heath, while Lorna cut her solitary path through the crowds. People were chattering, laughing, reluctant to give in to any sense of foreboding below the surface of the moving tide. They wanted to enjoy, even with a muted desperation, the snatched jollity of the moment, the glimpse of peace that was still in their view.

Peace. It was an important word to Lorna. She had been a member of the Peace Pledge Union, embracing the idea of pacifism. But it seemed to lead towards a tolerance of Europe's rising fascism, which she felt had to be resisted. In the previous year she had stood in Cable Street to oppose Oswald Mosley's Blackshirts. Now she was on her way to a meeting about the grim situation in Spain.

The meeting was at the house of Diana Seymour, a wealthy woman and a socialist. No, Lorna sighed in exasperation to herself, the two were not mutually exclusive. Although Diana's background placed her in the conservative establishment, her political conscience set her against her own upbringing. Her family could deny recognition to her but not the money she had inherited from her father. So, while her brother sat in the House of Commons as a Tory MP, she lent her support and often her money to the Labour Party. Tonight she was lending her house to the anti-fascist cause, hosting a meeting to rally support for the Spanish republicans.

It hurt her, and it hurt everyone in her spacious sitting room, that the Spanish war was going badly for the republicans. The initial optimism had dissipated soon after the first involvements of the International Brigade had brought the first casualties. Franco's fascist forces were winning most of the battles and a month earlier the war had taken a more brutal turn with the bombing of Guernica and its civilians by German planes. This intervention by foreign forces supporting Franco's nationalists tipped the balance of power even further, especially when the British government stuck stubbornly to its non-intervention pact. It tested the certainties of a pacifist, as Lorna had recently considered herself, when the reports were of thousands of women, men and children killed in the bombing of a defenceless town.

Lorna rang the doorbell of Number 5. It was a nineteenth century street of elegant houses beyond the means or even the aspiration of a young woman who worked to do good not to make money. At the end of a week she might count deeds rather than shillings, and this tonight counted as a deed – at least in prospect. But now she was here, there was a sudden shiver of doubt, the last-second impulse to turn away. Standing on the doorstep, under the porch with its columns, Lorna cleared her throat to prepare for the possibilities of entrance or escape, and she touched the unfamiliar pearl necklace that she was wearing. Her misgivings were coursing through her, creating a flush of anxiety. This, she feared, might be a social test, and a test she was likely to fail. What a wonderful house, she thought, despite herself, while realising that the size of the house was part of her anxiety. Yet she recognised that wealth was necessary to further the causes she believed in – and, yes, she told herself firmly, she did believe in them.

She brought a smile to her face as the door swung open. "I'm Lorna," she announced to the man who opened the door.

"Come in," the ragged clothes announced from somewhere deep inside a body or an entrance hall. "Archie Bruce," he held her arm. "We're nearly all here."

Lorna recognised the name of the writer. She had not expected to meet him in this setting but *why not?* she scolded herself inwardly. The war had a polarising effect, putting people on one side or the other, and the artists seemed to line up naturally against the industrialists. *Too crude a distinction*, Lorna told herself, *but true*, she responded. There was no possibility of neutrality, which made the concept of non-intervention a statement of bias.

In the room were a dozen people, most of them men. So it was easy to pick out the hostess. Lorna made her way towards the tall woman in the centre of the room.

"Pleased to meet you, Mrs Seymour."

"Oh, Diana – please! Only my opponents call me Mrs Seymour and I have more than enough of them. I trust I will not count you among their number. But you must be Lorna – Bryan has told me much about you."

"I am. Lorna, that is. And you can count on me. Diana," she added.

"Then we must get you a drink. What would you like? Wine? It's French, we cannot be sure of anything else but it is the best, of course."

Lorna sipped the white wine. She had tried but failed to read the label. Did she like it? She was more used to beer and looked a little enviously at the glass of stout in the chubby hand of the man who stood next to her. His tie was tight in a collar that seemed uncomfortable on such an ample neck.

"Lorna, this is George Robb, from the Basque Children's Committee. And a trade unionist, as you know of course."

"Of course."

"Diana, you mustn't. You know I don't need any flattery."

"George, I intended none. But" looking over his shoulder at the door to the sitting room "I see our speaker has arrived."

First Lorna noticed his hair. It was smooth, and light caught it like sun on the sea's waves. His trousers were wide and flapped a little as he walked. His brown leather jacket was short, reaching just to the waistband of his trousers. All in all he gave the appearance of someone wearing borrowed clothes. His boots, in particular, seemed not to belong to the feet inside them.

Diana fussed over him, asking him questions, making arrangements for a drink. His voice carried easily to Lorna's ears and she could tell he was that cherished rarity in these circles: a working-class Londoner.

"Whenever you're ready," he said, but not convincingly. He seemed nervous; Lorna felt nervous for him. She smiled, suppressing the twinge of envy as Diana took his arm to lead him to a spot before the empty fireplace, where a lectern stood. "Bloody hell, it's a bit grand," he laughed. "I'm not givin' a lecture."

Other conversations in the room had stopped, as people realised the evening was about to start properly.

"Comrades," smiled Diana. "It's my proud task to welcome Harry James here tonight – and to welcome him back to England. Until a couple of weeks ago Harry was in Spain with the International Brigade. It's good to see that he's survived and we're all, I'm sure, eager to hear his story."

"But let me preface it with another piece of news. Last night the refugee boat *Habana* landed in Portsmouth Harbour. On board were 4000 children, Spanish children whose parents are resisting the fascists in the war that Harry has been fighting. We have here representatives from the Basque Children's Committee – and should you feel moved, as I'm sure you will, to want to do something – even though you might not be able to fight, your support for the children will be welcome and practical."

The room murmured, a supportive hum. Then everyone clapped as Diana waved Harry forward to speak. He clenched his right fist, and others returned the gesture. He cleared his throat, then cleared it again before beginning hesitantly.

"Look, I'm not – whatever you think, I'm not. Well, I'm not a politician, and I'm not a soldier neither. I guess I learned to be a bit of a soldier but I'd never picked up a gun till I got to Spain. I just felt I had to be there. Didn't think I could ignore it. If we ignore it, it gets worse, and I don't mean Spain I mean everywhere. Including here.

"I'm not gonna lie. It's goin' badly out there. Franco's got more men, heavier weapons, and he's got the Germans and the Italians fightin' for him. Meanwhile our government sticks to a non-intervention pact that says to the fascists 'just help yourselves, we don't mind'. I wish I could tell you a better story but, well, there isn't one, is there? I just tell you that I've lost a lot of good comrades. And that hurts.

"I was there in Gernika a month ago. Nazi bombs destroyed the town. And they killed hundreds, could have been thousands, of men, women and children. Not soldiers. Just ordinary people who lived there. People who'd come into town for the market that day. There was no real warnin', the bombers just flew in, dropped their bombs. I'd been in the war for six months, seen some terrible things. But I'd never seen anythin' like it – the people didn't have a chance."

Lorna stared at Harry, willing him on, a ringside spectator. His style was not polished, he was not a practised speaker. *Neither am I*, she thought. Looking around the room, Lorna saw that everyone was listening intently, like herself willing him on, recognising that this was difficult for him to do. But it was not a problem with public speaking, she sensed, there was something deeper, a wish to hide something from them, even from himself.

"Know what?" he said. "I'm not gonna talk about Gernika. I can't. I haven't sorted it out yet in my head. It's just too much and it was too terrible. One day, one day soon, I'll write it down so it's not lost. But it's off limits for now. Too much death, the kid I held in my arms as he died. That's what they're doin'. It's children they're killin'. So do what Diana says – give your money for the children. If it saves some of them, that's good. But soldiers should be fighting soldiers, not planes bombing children."

He looked around the room. His eyes challenged them as if they might disagree, but no one would dare push him further. There was a grim silence, like a fog descended over them all.

"Anyone got a question?" Harry asked.

CHAPTER 2

There had been questions and Harry had answered them more easily than he had spoken before, but his answers were quick, almost dismissive. People wanted to know about the International Brigade and what his fellow soldiers were like. *All sorts.* Can you tell us a bit about the bombing? *Rather not.* Will you go back? *I have to.*

Diana decided to move the meeting on by asking George Robb to speak about the Spanish children who had just arrived on the boat from Bilbao. Unlike Harry, George was not embarrassed by the sound of his own voice speaking in public. He explained that the children were in a holding camp run by the Basque Children's Committee. The camp was in a field outside Portsmouth donated by a local farmer. North Stoneham was well-enough equipped with tents, and the children were safe and being fed. The plan was to disperse them around the country to 'colonies'. The colonies might be run by churches, unions, groups of different kinds but, of course, it all took money. The children might be here for only three months and they could return home once the fighting was over. While they waited, they needed to be fed and looked after – their parents and families were back in Spain, many of them fighting for the Republicans, most of them threatened by fascist reprisals. After all, in the first month of the war 100,000 people were killed on their doorsteps, not on the battlefield. It's a nation that fears the knock on the door and these children, for the first time away from their home and their country without the comfort of their parents, were also living in fear.

"Will you help them? Will your organisations help them? We can take personal contributions or, if you're able to, from organisations you represent. Ten shillings, just ten bob a week, will pay for a Spanish boy or girl, to provide them with enough to live. Otherwise, well, otherwise I don't know. They'll end up on a boat being sent back where they came but I think we're better than that, don't you?"

The audience did not need much persuading. Diana led the way with a five pound note, then one by one people signed the form, handed over money and got a receipt. Even Archie, who looked in need of new clothes himself, handed over money.

Lorna found herself in the queue. It gave her time to think and work out her weekly budget. She did not earn much as a legal secretary but at least, she told herself, she had no one else relying on her money. She hardly saw her parents in Kent these days; she had no real wish to, she had left her suburban upbringing behind her.

"Put me down for ten shillings," she said to George Robb.

"That's very good of you, my dear. Is that all right? Takes a chunk out of your weekly purse, doesn't it? But no doubting it's a good cause."

"No doubt it is."

Her fingers trembled a little with the enormity of the commitment – not just the money but the fact that, as she saw it, she was adopting a Spanish child. She felt herself redden with the heat and the pressure of commitment.

"You're at Thomas Brothers, aren't you? I know Bryan well, he's a good man. I'll have a word with him, see if he can help out at all with the collecting."

"I don't think you need to."

"Well, if we're collecting weekly, it will make it easier if Bryan organises things."

She hated to have her personal life organised for her but she had to see it as paying her union dues. She got on well with her boss so it was not a matter of confidentiality – in fact she had planned to tell him about the meeting the following day at work. She knew he would be pleased. Bryan Thomas was a well-known figure in left-wing circles as the senior partner in the law firm Thomas Brothers that handled trade union work, took on cases to represent working people without wealth and stood defence against the establishment generally. Lorna could picture his raised eyebrow swiftly followed by a smile on his florid face. But was she being patronised in some way? It would be silly to protest but she felt resentment inside, the wish to stand up for herself as a woman.

She stood aside as the next person in the queue gave his contribution. Lorna's agitation fumbled inside her handbag, simply looking for something to do.

"Don't know about you, but I could do with a drink."

Lorna looked up and saw Harry James. "Me too," she said.

"Shall we sneak out? There's a pub down the hill."

She felt like a naughty schoolgirl – 'hopping the wag' as Harry put it. She liked him for that. At least he seemed to understand some of what she was feeling.

"Had we better say Good Night to Diana?" asked Lorna.

"Whatever for? Don't suppose I'll see her again – unless we tell her we're going down the pub and she joins us. Not likely. So – let's go."

They slipped out. On a warm summer evening they had no coats to put on, so they stepped down the stairs and out through the front door into the gas-lit twilight. Lorna smiled, thinking she might be on a secret mission. But with no idea what she might be trying to achieve, willing to go wherever this strange turn of events might take her.

In the first place it did not take her far. Just down the road, at the bottom of the hill, they walked into the saloon bar of *The Freemasons*. While Harry waited at the bar for Lorna's Guinness, she looked around the pub. It looked new, lacking that feeling of being lived in by local regulars. Most of the people seemed to have dropped in from outside the area. Like herself. Like Harry.

"The beer's a bit flat," he said about his own pint. "But I'm parched."

Lorna watched him down half the beer in one gulp. She was more inclined to take her Guinness, like life, in wary sips.

"Glad that's done," said Harry. "Didn't really want to do it but they told me I had to. Paying my dues. Said the story needed to be heard."

"I'm glad you did. But it must have been hard for you. Have you done that kind of thing before?"

Harry stared into his beer. Did he find answers there? He shook his head.

"Course not. First time for everything. You could tell. I didn't know – least, not till I started – that I'd find it so hard. Can you imagine?" He looked at her as if challenging her to find something lost. "Can you imagine what it was like with the bombs falling, with the women and children screaming?"

Lorna shook her head. "But you can tell me, if it helps."

"Don't know if talking's the help I need. A bit of not talking might do me good."

Lorna was not, at least not yet, ready to offer help that she might regret. The Guinness, sip by sip, offered a tactic in the situation while she sized up this man a bit more. Did she like him? *I think so. But can I be sure?*

"Another?"

"Let me get it, Harry."

"Not cleaned out by the committee then?"

She had forgotten the ten shillings she had given. A look into her purse confirmed its emptiness apart from some coins.

"I'm sorry. You're right, I haven't got enough."

Harry put his hand up in a 'don't worry' gesture. "It's OK, my union paid me. I've got money."

Lorna did worry. She was used to paying her way in pubs. Not that she was a big drinker but she needed to show what she was not. In thinking what she was not, Lorna had her mother in mind, a Kent housewife of the most suburban kind. *Not like her.*

"You OK? You look a bit cross."

She was not ready for honesty. In her experience that takes time. Honesty might drive him away, and now she was thinking that she might need him to stay with her, at least for a while, at least for this night.

"I'm fine. I was just wondering so many things about you, about what you've been through. But then I'm not sure if I can ask. You don't seem prepared to tell anything about what happened to you. And I don't need to know, but I'd like to know."

Their eyes locked, each unwilling to give way. Harry blinked, then put his hand over Lorna's hand.

"I can't. Don't know why but I can't. I'm going to write it down, just like I said I would. I'll do that before I go back to Spain. Like I said I would.

"But for now…for now let me say this. I knew nothing

of Gernika till I got there. On that first day they took me to the oak in the centre of town. Proud to show it. An old oak, just a stump left, but been there for centuries. It's right by the assembly, the place where the parliament meets. These are people who love democracy. That's why the fascists hate them so much, why they wanted to wipe them out. They did, the people were killed, nearly all of them. But that oak survived, I sat right by it while the bombs dropped. So did the assembly building. It was a bit of a miracle next day, walking through bombed streets and buildings, but these things survived. Symbols can survive, even when people don't. It's hope. It's why I have to go back."

Lorna put her left hand over his hand that was squeezing her uncomfortably tight. She lifted his hand off hers but did not let go. There was an intensity between them that seemed like a new experience.

"What shall we do?" Harry asked.

Lorna kept holding his hand. "Where do you live?"

Harry explained that he was staying in a house in Camden Town. It was empty for a few days while its owner was away. It was simply a bolt hole offered by a sympathiser.

They left the pub and started walking. Lorna's step was brisk, she was well-equipped for walking but Harry stopped at South End Green. They had walked, arm in arm, no more than two hundred yards.

"I can't." He grimaced, anger and pain on his face. Lorna's heart sank. She felt tears forming in her eyes.

"Why not?" her voice trembled, her chin too but, to her shock, Harry began laughing.

"Bloody boots! These boots are killing me. They just don't fit. They're not mine, you see? None of this clobber's mine."

Was it relief that made Lorna laugh too? Or was there something genuinely funny in a war hero brought to a standstill by oversized boots? Particularly at a time when their thoughts were on the absence of clothes. But it made their coming together in an embrace so natural that they kissed and held each other without worrying who might be watching.

"Sod walking," said Harry. "Let's grab this cab."

He hailed the taxi that had slowed to turn the corner. They clambered inside, falling into the back seat while the driver set the meter. They arrived at Delancey Street in ten minutes. There were stone steps up to the front door, with iron railings on either side. Harry stooped to pick the key up from under the door mat. "They trust me," he said. "Not just you," she added, following him through the door.

Fumbling to turn on the light in the hall revealed their discomfort. Suddenly they were clearly strangers who did not yet know each other. Would there be time for such knowledge? There were details that can take a lifetime to absorb: the feel of a hand, the tilt of a head, even the colour and texture of hair.

Lorna felt Harry's hand on her hair, his fingers stroking with what might have been curiosity in a better light. She never cared much for her hair; she kept it in a style that went with the flow of its natural waves, but it was designed for easy maintenance. She wanted to move out of this harsh hall light but did not know the layout of the house.

"I like your hair. There's no fuss to it, like a country girl." The cracking in his voice suggested he was not used to giving personal compliments. No more than Lorna was used to receiving them.

"Why fuss? Hair's not worth it," she said.

They had moved through into a room with a table and

chairs. It was sparsely furnished, though, linoleum on the floor, lacking the feel of a family home.

"Who lives here?" she asked.

"Someone I've never met. Don't suppose I will. I was just sent here last week, told the place was mine to use as the chap was away. They said he's a painter. But I'll be gone before he gets back."

Lorna looked at him, hesitating to find an answer she might not wish for. "So, you are going back?" A nod. "You are going back to Spain? Even after what you've seen?"

Harry's stare took him away from the room where he was standing, seeking a way to tell himself not just Lorna.

"I can't see what else to do. I've got to live with myself."

Lorna drew closer in sympathy. She folded her arms around him in an embrace meant to comfort. Harry bent his head down and his lips sought hers. It should not have been a shock because they had already kissed but she was surprised at least by the head-on assault of the kiss, accompanied by what seemed like a sob of yearning or grief, a sound that was animal yet deeply human. His tongue thrust deeply into her mouth and she felt her breath pushed back inside her. It took some seconds to respond but she withdrew, and turned her face away.

"Hold on, Harry, let's take it more slowly."

His eyes held hers, glistening a little. There was a yearning there and she was not sure she could satisfy it.

"Sorry," he mumbled. "Sorry. I've turned into a soldier."

"No need for sorry. But let's sit down."

They sat on the wooden chairs at the rectangular table covered with oilcloth. It was a bleak light under the naked electric bulb; it flattered neither of them. Lorna's skin had a ghostly pallor; Harry's, burnt by the Spanish sun, took on an orange glow. But there was something calming in the absence of flattery, enabling that calm to turn again towards attraction. Lorna took Harry's hand, kissed it gently, then placed it against her cheek. She sensed their mutual inexperience, but felt it might now be for her to take the lead.

"Upstairs?" He nodded. She led him by the hand. Their feet clomped on the bare wood of the stairs.

Inside the bedroom, despite the unfamiliarity of the situation, they recognised what each wanted to do in sequence. Boots and shoes were discarded first. Harry smiled with what might have been simply relief from discomfort. He was released to move more easily, so was she, removing each other's clothes with increasing eagerness until they were gazing at each other naked. There was a shiver of embarrassment that was soon stifled by an embrace. The touch of skin on skin along their bodies became not just real but natural. Finally Lorna took off the necklace of artificial pearls that she had decided at the last minute to wear that evening.

Their lovemaking was short and urgent. But they felt satisfied with each other, satisfied enough to lie in each other's arms, their faces turned together, breath mingling, lips still seeking the touch of the other's skin. They said nothing to each other, feeling no need, allowing their hands to shape the familiarity between them until, unaware who was the first to succumb, they surrendered themselves to sleep.

The morning sun came streaming through the curtains at 5 o'clock. Now they could look at each other with pleasure and curiosity, holding each other in the grip of their arms and this narrow bed. They talked, discovering more about their lives until this brought an awareness of the world beyond the room, with the outside noises reaching their ears of a city going to work, intent upon the need to do whatever it took to survive.

"Are you happy?" he asked her.

"I would be if you didn't go back to Spain."

Silence fell between them. It was difficult to say anything.

"I must get to work," said Lorna, disentangling herself from Harry's arms, from the sheets that were twined around. She looked down, seeing stains on the sheet. "What can we do about these?"

"Nothing to do but leave 'em."

"We can't. They're a mess. I'm going to have to wash them and bring them back another day."

Harry was quiet. He had not anticipated domestic concerns and wished such trifles would go away. But they were in a home, however uncared-for in appearance; its neglect was apparent, inescapable.

In the kitchen downstairs, Lorna put the kettle on and placed the teapot on the wooden table. She scooped a couple of spoonfuls of tea into the pot then poured boiling water on top. Placing the tea cosy over the pot made her smile. Knitted into a pattern of red and blue, it fitted snugly and added an unexpected domesticity to this least domestic of houses.

"When are you leaving, Harry?"

It was a blow to discover that he would be catching a train to Dover that afternoon. This gave an unwelcome urgency to their preparations. There was no time for lingering over the tea and toast. Lorna found the canvas bag for the bagwash so she could get the sheets washed. Harry would be gone when she returned later in the week but she knew how to let herself in.

"Sorry. I've not done this well, have I? I wish I had more time but I've got to meet the others."

"I know that. There's nothing to be done about it. But I can't just do the stiff upper lip. I know I'm not being fair but….Just *but*. But I thought a love affair would last more than one night."

"It will, honest it will. You were – you are – lovely. It's you I'll want to come back for. I don't want it to end with this either."

Lorna drank her tea. She might have cried but found herself laughing instead.

"The English find tea's the cure for all ills. If you're not happy, have a cup of tea. If you're really not happy, have another spoonful of sugar in your tea. Come on, Harry, drink up, there's a war to go to."

"Lorna, look. Or listen. I can't offer anything. It's not a time for thinking further than what's right in front of us. War. There's going to be more war. It's not just Spain, it's bigger than that, but I don't know how it'll work out. So I promise nothing but that doesn't mean that this meant nothing. I aim to be back. I will be back."

Lorna saw that she would gain nothing by prolonging this leave-taking. She wrote her address on a scrap of paper, then added her work address 'just in case'. Where Harry was going, there were no postal addresses. So they embraced like old friends going off on separate journeys.

Lorna's journey took her to work by way of the laundry where she dropped in her bagwash to collect next day.

CHAPTER 3

Lorna decided to carry on walking to work that morning on the blustery streets leading towards the centre. She needed to clear her head before work, so she headed south past Euston Station, then past Tavistock Square. She ignored passing buses, watching as people scrambled on board to sit on the top deck. She saw Russell Square on her right, noticing its trees that were now dense with leaves, and crossed the road to walk through it. In Russell Square, fallen blossom and seeds from the trees lay like brown snow, drifting when caught by the breeze. It accentuated the feeling that today, in response to whatever promptings of her moods, nature was displaying its full range of the seasons. Her emotions were changeable, so was the weather, and rain was now spitting from black clouds. She longed for the sun to break through again and allow her to see the world in a better light.

Russell Square had been a lunchtime refuge for her when she had been at Pitman College learning to type and take shorthand. As she passed the Pitman building now, memories of the people on the course occupied her thoughts, an imaginary pencil jotting down names and speculating on their subsequent stories. Nora – back up north by now. Jessie – into the papers, *News Chronicle*? Biddy – found a man, married. These people had been her first London friends after arriving from Kent but now, as London does, they had dispersed in different directions, making their own ways and lives, perhaps taking notes, perhaps not.

At the Kingsway Tunnel she caught a tram. It rattled and clanged underground through the darkness, sending her into what seemed, this morning at least, like the comfort of anonymity. The light in the tram half-illuminated faces, concealed lives. Lorna listened, with just a twinge of jealousy, to the young couple chatting on the seat next to her, making plans for later.

What might Lorna's plans be? Not in the years ahead, but that day, how to get through the day that suddenly loomed as full of difficulty? The sound of metal on metal signalled the tram's arrival at Embankment, and Lorna stepped down onto the pavement. From here it was just a two-minute walk to her work.

Lorna sat on a bench in Embankment Gardens to collect her thoughts. She was uncomfortably aware that she was in yesterday's clothes but reasoned that this would not be noticed. She spent little on clothes, and her wardrobe was restricted by lack of money and a wish to keep things simple. Her standard issue, to herself, was a grey skirt and white blouse, with only slight colour variations day by day. It seemed a waste of time to increase those choices.

Having set aside that concern, reaching into her handbag to dab a little scent onto her wrists and neck, she knew she could not avoid the meeting with her boss. Bryan Thomas would sense something different about her; it was a skill of his. He was the senior partner and the firm's figurehead, intimidating only in his shrewdness and understanding. Lorna had started two years ago at Thomas Brothers as a typist, then had been spotted by Bryan to become his secretary. She enjoyed the contact this gave her with the people and causes that the firm represented.

She liked to meet people. She was at her best when she sensed a vulnerability in others that she could help relieve, understanding the shared feeling. Generosity was important to her; she gave freely. She gave affection and friendship because they came naturally to her, but she had never forged a special relationship with anyone. Lorna had many friends but not one particular friend. She found giving easier than taking, but neither made her happy, there was always a fragility to any sense of contentment she felt.

She feared loneliness as a result. She feared that none were as lonely as those who feared loneliness, so she made an effort not to feel that way. This was one reason why she volunteered to do things for others – though, mainly, it was what she felt people ought to do. It shaped her politics too. She had joined the Labour Party to help others, not to change the very structure of the world. In her internal debate this was where she drew the line between socialism and communism. Would it be a line between herself and Harry? She might not get the chance to discover, much as she might want to. A flush of anger rushed through her.

Before meeting Harry she had been fatalistic about being alone. She knew people, mixed with people, but there was not one person who mattered more than anyone else. Harry had been that person, fleetingly, for one night. He offered a tantalising hope of a more enduring connection. But he also brought a greater fear that hope might be snatched away. She dared not hope, not for herself. She needed distraction, she needed to plunge herself into a new cause.

Arriving at work, she opened the sliding metal gate of the lift, and took it up to the second floor. She went into the cubby hole that was her office, containing a wooden desk, a chair and shelves holding files and books. Through the frosted glass she could see that Bryan Thomas was already at work.

She suppressed the slight bubble of irritation that rose inside her, almost like heartburn. She always tried to be first at her desk but this morning the change of routine had made that impossible.

A shadow passed across the glass panel, like a memory of her father. There were things she absorbed from her father although she would always be reluctant to admit this. Being first to the office was one. Giving up your seat to someone older on a bus was another. *It's a matter of respect*, he would say. They channelled their respect in different ways but agreed on the principle. *Little things matter, don't forget.* She didn't.

Lorna tapped on the glass of the office door and went in. "Would you like a cup of tea, Bryan?"

"That would be nice." He hardly looked up from the file he was reading, half-moon glasses perched on the end of his nose, his hair thick and white.

Making tea felt like a refuge this morning. She was not quite ready yet for the normality of office life. Too much had happened since she had been at her desk the previous day.

For no reason that was clear to her, her parents were in her thoughts this morning. Usually she tried not to think too much about her parents, not from malice or bitterness or disappointment, but because they drained confidence from her. She had left home to escape them, to become herself, and she bore them no grudge. Why should she? They had done her no harm. But she dreaded that she might become like them or, worse, that she might become them.

I exasperate people, said Lorna to herself, *just like my mother. Oh God, let me not be my mother.* Doris Starling wore a sense of nervousness, making her too eager in company. Perhaps it was simply a lack of practice because she had never had to work and do things for anyone other than her husband. George Starling, an accountant, was happy reading balance sheets and avoiding social occasions. Doris had married George with eagerness too; an eagerness that had flattered him and persuaded him that this feeling must be love. It did not take long for habit to wear away the edges of feeling, for balance to reassert itself even between the sheets. Lorna was the only child.

Doris could not match her husband's equanimity, she tipped the scales up and down to the constant consternation of others. Of course, Lorna loved her mother and all her vulnerability – much more than her cold fish of a father, but now she was relieved to see so little of both of them. Her father stagnated in the depths of small business in Orpington, seldom surfacing. Her mother took the train occasionally, venturing to London where she would take tea with Lorna in Lyons Corner House.

"You all right, Lo?" asked Bernie, the office boy. His familiarity always grated. Lorna excused him for being only fifteen but suspected that he would be no different at thirty or sixty. Some people seem set for life before they have lived. "Looks like you're still dreamin'."

"Perhaps I am, Bernie, perhaps I am." She carried the teapot on a tray into Bryan Thomas's office. Bryan looked up, stared at her like a doctor assessing a patient, then suggested that she should bring a cup and saucer for herself.

"How was it last night?" he asked as she poured out the tea.

"Last night? How do you mean?"

"I mean the talk I sent you along to listen to – and to report back on anything interesting that came up." He motioned her to sit down.

"Oh, I see what you mean." Sipping tea filled a gap, not for the first time that day. "A lot of people you know. Diana Seymour. George Robb. The speaker was Harry James."

"How was he?"

"I liked him. Terrible time he must have had in Spain. Was at Guernica when it was bombed."

"I heard that. Must have been bad. Did he open up about it?"

"Not as much as you might expect. I don't think he's used to public speaking."

"He'll get better, I expect. He's a communist. They'll want him to do more. It's part of the contract."

"He won't for a while. He's heading back to Spain."

Bryan's eyebrows raised. "Really? Already? I thought you might have persuaded him otherwise."

Lorna felt the blush on her neck, suddenly feeling the absence of her necklace. Had Bryan noticed this? Did he know? How did he know? She felt as if she had been watched yet she felt lightened by her secret's glimpse of daylight. Could she bring it into the open?

"He's a good man," Lorna said, emboldened by embarrassment. "At least I thought so. We look after a lot of communists."

"Indeed we do. It goes with our territory. But you have to watch them. They're not straightforward like our Labour friends in the unions."

"What's straightforward about George Robb?"

Bryan laughed. "You're right. He's a devious devil. Don't think I trust him further than I can throw him. And I hear he extracted some money from you too?"

"How d'you know?"

They looked at each other warily, neither sure if a mark had been overstepped.

"Diana rang me last night. Not to inform. Just to say she liked you."

Lorna's head was spinning. She was relieved to be sitting down. She hadn't taken account of the telephone spreading news – though it was part of her job, she still did not feel accustomed to it as part of life not work. There was a silence in the room, settling between them like a morning mist. Lorna shivered, feeling a premonition or was it simply the draft from an open window?

"I don't understand," she said. "It feels like you were spying on me."

"Not at all. Just looking after your interests."

"That's what I don't understand. What are my interests?"

"Did you like the young man?"

"I did."

"Best forget him. Chances are he won't come back from Spain. The odds are stacked against him. There are other ways to help, better ways. You found one of them – those children need our help."

"You know I'm helping. Diana told you that."

"She did. And I admire you for it. Your example meant I couldn't refuse Diana's request. I agreed that the firm would pay a fiver a week – on top of your ten bob. You've become an expensive woman."

There was smile on his face. It was almost below the surface, there but difficult to be sure of. A winter bulb just breaking the ground.

"There's more," he went on. "I said we'd provide *pro bono* legal service to the committee – no harm in doing George

Robb a favour. The work should be straightforward. They say it will only be for three months, then the children will go back. A weekly meeting, probably a bit boring. But you'll learn a lot, you might even enjoy it."

The smile was more noticeable. He was savouring her puzzlement.

"What are you saying?" she asked. "I'm not understanding what you're saying."

"I'm saying that we want you to represent the firm on the Basque Children's Committee. Will that be acceptable?"

"But I'm not trained for that."

"You'll be trained on the job, by the job. Lorna, I'm saying I think you're better than just a secretary. I want you to do more in the firm because I think you can. So add this to what you already do, and let's see how it goes."

She gazed at him, defiance pushing back tears.

"Of course I can. And what will I get for my trouble?"

Bryan laughed. Lorna joined his laughter. It seemed almost companionable.

"Ten bob a week on your wages. I thought you could use that."

CHAPTER 4

That day and the next went by in a blur for Lorna. When she got home to her flat in Highgate she found a postcard from her mother suggesting tea in town next Tuesday. She would need to have a late lunch to fit it in. She relished the thought that she might be busy with her new responsibilities.

Lorna spent some time reading the papers about the Basque children. Already she felt for them, and now she found her feelings deepening as she got closer to them through their family details. Strangely it had the effect of compensating for Harry's absence.

She was not used to thinking about herself, but the last couple of days had forced introspection on her. What would she do? Not just for the coming day but for the rest of her life? She had been gifted an unexpected opportunity at work, like a coin spotted on the pavement. She had gained and perhaps immediately lost a lover. Life seemed to be playing tricks with her in a way it had not done before. She had not previously felt the absence of these possibilities in her life but now they changed everything. Did this mean that she would change too? Her only definite thought was a trivial one, one that exasperated her a little with herself. The thought was about her hair, her hair that made no fuss, short and dark and crinkled so she only needed to brush it once or twice a day. Lorna decided to grow her hair until Harry returned.

She tried not to think about him, for there was nothing she could do. She did not even have an address to write to him. But Harry kept coming back inescapably to her thoughts as she stared out the window down to the coal barges on the river or into the files about the children who had crossed the sea. Harry and the children were moving in opposite directions.

Lorna got Bryan's permission to leave work early 'for family reasons'. She needed to collect the clean sheets from the bagwash shop before it closed at 5. She managed that with minutes to spare then set off to Delancey Street around the corner. She followed a man on the pavement who was strolling along with a swagger and whistling as he walked. The whistling was tuneful enough but she wondered what the song might be. She waited for him to walk ahead before going up the steps to the front door.

At the door she found the key tucked away where she had been told it would be. She was a little dubious about this, feeling too close to being a burglar – but what was there to steal in this house? Her memories from the other visit did not suggest a house that held great wealth. Once inside she was free to see if this were true or not because curiosity led her from room to room.

The surprise was the large room at the back of the house, leading on to a small garden. There were large windows that allowed light to stream in so there was no need to turn on the light switch. Even before she entered the room there was something strange about it, a particular smell or mingling of smells, as if the room had been recently painted, a smell of paint and turpentine. As she went in, the reason for the smell became obvious. This was an artist's studio. There were canvases stretched and waiting for paint, contributing their own fabric smell to the mix. Perhaps too the sweaty canvas of pairs of plimsoles underneath an easel.

Lorna took tentative steps inside, drawn by the paintings

but fearful to step inside not just a room but a mind. There was a canvas leaning against one wall, a large canvas that reached up to the ceiling and the skylight window, and it was covered with layer upon layer, swirls and swirls, of paint. Deep reds stood out as highlights on a background of blues that suggested both sky and sea, with blocks of earthy umber and green foliage. But it would be impossible for Lorna to say with any certainty that she was looking at anything as definite as a tree or even a fragment of leaf. She stood in front of the picture with a sense of awe and perhaps of doubt. She had not seen anything like this before. Was it good? Was it the work of a skilled artist or the daubs of a madman?

Her inclinations towards the former were reinforced by a bronze bust that stood on a work table. The dark metallic mass was that of a woman's face. The more she looked at it, the more recognisable it was, the more beautiful it was. She placed her hands gently upon its surface, enjoying the cool touch of the sculpture as her fingers traced its surface.

Then she saw the photograph on the mantelpiece. It leaned against the wall, a black and white image alongside colour postcards and scraps torn from magazines. The photo was the only framed item there, suggesting it had an intended permanence that the other objects would not match. It showed a group of half a dozen men in ill-assorted uniforms, each wearing a dark beret, each with a rifle slung over a shoulder. The man at the centre, the tallest of the group, stared at the unseen photographer with a challenging, half-smiling gaze, while raising his right hand in a clenched fist salute.

Realising that she had spent too much time in this exploration, and recalling that she had a practical task to perform, Lorna made her way back to the hall then up the bare wooden stairs. The walls were rough and uncared for, without any hint of the artist's work that seemed confined to the studio.

She hesitated to go into the bedroom where she and Harry had slept. The house felt strange in the daylight, and suddenly this seemed like an intrusion. She looked down at the sheets and pillowcases across her arm, feeling a slight dampness there. She pushed at the door and it swung open to reveal the unmade bed with its blankets in a heap on the mattress. There was no option but to resort to domestic practicality, so she pushed the blankets to the floor and stretched the sheet across the bed, smoothing it and memories away, tucking it in at the corners where thoughts of that night must remain.

Any intentions she may have harboured to forget Harry were dispelled by what she now saw on the table next to the window. There was a typewriter and she realised that it had been recently used to type the pages that lay across it. Picking up the pages she noticed a faintness in the typing caused by a worn ribbon, but it was clear enough to read even with its frequent deletions with rows of x's. It was clear that Harry had written this, presumably yesterday morning before setting off by train to the continent. She would need time and a calmness of mind to read the pages but was unsure that she had either.

She saw the envelope at the side of the typewriter, and her heart beat fast when she saw her name written in ink on the sealed envelope. She tore it open and took out the paper that was covered in blue ink. She had to read it, greedily, devouring its neatly-formed words, sinking down to sit on the bed.

My darling Lorna
For you are that to me, even though we hardly know each other, even

though I didn't have the courage to say that word when we were together. There's so much we didn't get a chance to say, my darling, but a time will come when we can say everything that wants to be said. Even me, your tongue-tied soldier.

The truth is, I don't want to go to Spain but the truth also is, I have to. I knew this since I was there in Cable Street. We fought Mosley's fascists. We used our fists, our muscles, to kick them out. We did it, it worked, it was right. We can't just let brute force have its way against those who need protecting. We resist it or it wins.

Same thing in Spain. We have to fight to kick the fascists out. If we don't they'll carry on and get stronger, not just there but everywhere. So I have to do what I can, even if this comes at the worst possible moment for me.

If we win, we can have a life, you and me. We can be happy together. But first I have to do this.

I think you know it in your heart. I hope you do. You are a clever woman, I know that, and you have deep feelings. Please believe I have such feelings too and they are for my cause <u>and</u> for you.

With all my love, until I see you next, take care, my darling.

Your Harry

PS I have spent some hours on the typewriter that was here. This is about my time in Gernika. It might explain a bit more. It's what I could not say the other night, at that meeting with all those people, it was too hard. But now I've done it. You might know how to make it useful.

CHAPTER 5

Lorna folded the letter back into its envelope, and tucked it into her handbag. Emotion roared through her in the silence of the empty house. She went down the stairs to the studio at the back of the house to read what Harry had typed. Her gaze took in the row of books on a shelf, most with the orange covers of the Left Book Club: *The Ragged-Trousered Philanthropists, The People of the Abyss*. These were books that she had read in a spirit of self-education, and she knew that Harry had experienced something similar, training himself to read and to write as authors read and write because that was the way to win your arguments.

Through the glass window overhead, blackening skies were threatening heavy rain but Lorna, despite instinctively turning on the electric light, was not thinking about storms outside. She settled in a wooden chair at a paint-covered table to read the top copy, setting aside the carbon copy typed on tissue-thin paper.

"To those who care
27 May 1937
My name is Harry James. I am a British member of the International Brigades. I am just an ordinary chap from London, someone not used to writing. My job is in the print, working as a compositor, putting the writing of others into metal type – but never my own words. I am not used to fighting either, and I became a soldier in Spain, learning what I could on the job, as we might say. Someone who felt he had to fight in Spain to stop the spread of fascism. We have seen

what happened in Germany and Italy, and now Spain, and we have our own fascists in England who have to be resisted. The failure to resist will lead to a dark world, and I have now seen just how dark that world can be.

I write this eye witness testimony from the war, in particular to describe the terrible events in Gernika, a town in northern Spain where I was a month ago. Where I was lucky to survive and write this account that can be read by anyone who wishes to know the truth.

At the end of April I was sent with a couple of comrades to the town of Gernika in the Basque country. We had been fighting against the advance of Franco's forces on the front line a dozen or so miles from there. We were sent there to make some local contacts but, honestly, it was a cushy mission, just meant to give us a bit of a break as we had been a long time in the battles. But it gave us no rest. To be honest it felt like a retreat; the town was filling with refugees fleeing from the fighting, and we became like refugees too.

I did not know much about Gernika. People said it was a small town but important to the Basques. A symbol of democracy, they said. A town of seven thousand people but now there might be more because of refugees. They said it was where the Basque parliament met and there was a famous oak tree where people talked about politics. Even the Spanish kings came here to swear solemnly to keep Basque rights in the church called Santa Maria.

That much I knew but it did not amount to much. Particularly as I do not know much Spanish and that might not even be the language people spoke there. Anyway I was with Ramon who is Mexican, and Nacho who's a local. We thought we would get by, meet some people, have some hot food and perhaps we would get drunk. We did not set our sights high.

We had entered the town on Monday afternoon, coming in by train, discovering that it had been market day. Stallholders were packing away onto carts, unless in some cases they were desperate to sell everything they had. It was a long way from Covent Garden market but not unlike in many ways. People were selling without trying to sell, or not wanting to be seen as trying. I wished I could have bought more but there was not much to do with green beans and potatoes. We planned to eat somewhere later, and Ramon and Nacho went off wandering in search of a bar. I thought they would not have to search too hard.

As for me, I wanted to see some things I had heard about, mainly the town square where the parliament building was, the church and the oak tree. I thought, if I am here, I want to make the most of it. I headed a little up the hill away from the centre.

I thought it would be more, the oak that is. The parliament looked grand, but I could not go in. The church, Santa Maria, had a wedding going on, or at least I think so. I did not want to go in carrying a rifle. So all I could do was go to the oak. When I say that, you might imagine a tall tree, with dense green leaves providing shade, as I myself imagined it. But it was no more than a stump, and from the stump sprang a few small saplings. If this was a symbol of something, liberty, say, then it did not say anything to lift the spirits in my heart. Yet it stood there, it survived, perhaps that was its message.

Sitting next to it was a woman. I could not tell her age; she looked old and weathered, like an ancient tree herself, but she might have been young, just ground down by her life. She had two children with her, one sitting in her lap, the other by her left side. In front of them was a cloth on which were set a dozen oranges.

I went over to them and the woman held out her hand, waving to the oranges, inviting me to buy. Her eyes held a deep sense of resignation. I looked into them but my gaze seemed to hurt her. *Cuanto*, I asked. She shrugged, simply gesturing at the baby in her arms, the young boy at her side. I put some coins in her cupped hand and sat down to peel and eat the orange.

Breaking the orange into segments, with the sharp smell of the fruit between us, I offered them in my hand. The mother shook her head but the boy was interested, though careful. I held the orange segments out again and handed him one that he put into his mouth. While he chewed and swallowed he used his fingers to draw in the sandy earth around the tree stump.

He made a simple drawing, a childlike drawing as you would expect. At first I thought he was just drawing patterns but then the shape formed into something I thought I could recognise.

"*Caballo?*" I asked and he nodded, shy but proud.

The church bell began ringing. At first nothing strange in that. But it kept on and people began streaming out of the church, looking up at the sky. The ringing of the bells turned into the wail of air raid sirens. There is nothing that freezes your heart as fast as that high-pitched scream of a siren. I was stuck paralysed sitting in the sand, doing no more than lift up my rifle, but the woman scooped up her children and ran off into one of the side streets, running down the hill. I suppose she was seeking shelter in one of the houses.

Perhaps I should have done the same but I did not know where to run and I thought there would be no safety in a building. There were also the oranges, abandoned on the cloth at my feet. I was now, it seemed to me, the custodian of the oranges, and I needed to guard them for the woman. Perhaps she depended on selling them, to get the next meal for herself and her children, and she would be back after the sirens finished wailing.

The roaring of the plane's engine was unmistakable now, getting louder and closer, like thunder rumbling in the distance. You could see the big plane clearly in the blue sky, heading from the direction of the coast down the valley towards us. It seemed to cast a shadow. But it was just one plane, it did not look like a big raid. I was still hoping and expecting that it would just fly past the town on a recce. That's what it did; it banked and headed north again, and I felt relieved it had gone. But then it circled above the mountain that was covered in forest, it seemed to gather itself, it roared like an animal and picked up speed as it flew low towards the town.

So I was not prepared for the bombs that dropped. I had heard about the bombing of Durango a month before, they said it had been German bombers, the Condor Legion, that destroyed that town. But there was still a part of me that, despite everything, despite the reason why I was there, did not believe the fascists could be that barbarous. This was just a little town on a market day, there were no soldiers apart from me, no defences, just ordinary people. The bomber droned, you could see it seem to steady, see the bombs drop, they fell on the other side of the houses in front of me, where the railway station was.

A cloud of dust rose above the red roofs of the houses. After the deep loud boom of the explosions there was a silence, a silence only broken by the sound of human voices. Shouts, screams, people calling to each other. Curses, pleas, survivors asking about each other's safety, cries of pain and of fear. It was a strange, eery sensation and I did not know what it was best for me to do. I gathered the oranges, wrapped them in the cloth, tying the cloth with trembling fingers so that I could carry this parcel of precious fruit. Because that is how the oranges seemed to me.

I decided to head towards the station where the bombs had exploded, thinking that I must try to help. There had been many bombs dropped, all close together in that first cluster. I suddenly knew that this would not be all, there would be more to come, and if there were more to come they would set their sights by that first bombing. It was true, I looked up and there in the sky, gathering like a flock of birds, the bombers were flying in formation above the river that was gleaming in the evening sunshine. Closer they flew, flying at speed and flying lower than I had seen planes fly before. This time there really was a shadow cast by the bombers, seven or eight of them now dropping their loads of heavy bombs on the red tiles of the houses below.

None of them landed near me, they were further into the centre of town. Where I was it was up a slope away from the narrow streets where people lived crowded together. Those people had no chance. The bombs fell, with a noise like coal poured from a sack into the hole below, disappearing into the holes that they made in the streets, the squares, the buildings. It was slaughter. Slaughter in this first wave of bombing but then I looked out towards where the bombers had come in. A feeling of horror flooded through me as I realised that another wave of bombers was heading this way and within seconds another scuttle of bombs were released from above.

This continued. It continued beyond endurance. I could do nothing but watch in horror as bombs rained down from wave after wave of bombers. Who were these people? How could they be so precise and relentless and without emotion as they destroyed the lives below? They were close enough to see the people they were killing. One plane flew overhead and I swear I could see the pilot's face with his goggles over his eyes. I lifted my rifle and fired at him. Hopeless. A waste of a bullet.

How long did this go on? I cannot say. Later I heard that the bombing lasted four hours, start to finish, but what I have described so far was simply the first phase. There was more to come, much more. But there was a lull in the bombing, the deep percussion of the bombs stopped for a while as if they were having a breather, perhaps sitting back to have a smoke. At that thought I cursed them, I hated them as I have never hated before but at the same time I was numb, my feelings had been blasted out of me. I sat at the foot of the tree stump, with the parliament building in front of me, and, miraculously it seemed, nothing in this courtyard had been touched. As I looked around I was the only person in sight, everyone else had fled into the streets and houses, perhaps, I hoped, into the makeshift shelters that I had seen earlier.

But the town was changed beyond recognition in those few minutes. Where the houses had stood, now there was just rubble. The rubble was made of bricks and timber and tiles and stone and, venturing closer in a daze, I saw that bodies were part of this bomb-made rubbish heap. To enter the first street I had to edge my way around a deep crater and beyond the crater there was a scene of devastation like none I had ever seen before. Not a single house was standing. Bodies and parts of bodies were scattered everywhere. One or two people emerged from underground where they had been sheltering, among them a priest who made his way through the rubble seeking any signs of human life, ready to give absolution. Over everything was a cloud of dust that choked your throat, blinded your eyes.

Impossible to imagine, things then got worse. More planes appeared on the skyline, a really thick cluster. If the first planes had been ominous as crows these were smaller, faster, like starlings. But even more merciless because these pilots were ready to look into the eyes of their victims as they fired on them with machine guns. They flew low, very low, over the town just as people were desperately running away to escape further bombing. Their bullets strafed the ground, chasing the running people below. Most of those people were women, many of them holding the hands of young children, but they had to perform a mad dance in vain attempts to avoid the bullets. Not just terrified people but animals too because this had been market day and the town was a transit place for sheep and horses and cows.

I retreated back uphill, to the oak tree, stopping to attempt the shelter of playing dead whenever the fighter planes screamed overhead shooting their rapid volleys of gunfire into the rubble around me and at any people who were running. They ran so fast those women but they could not run fast enough to save their lives, they were mown down in mid-stride.

Reaching the oak tree again, it remained untouched, as were the buildings around, saved perhaps by being halfway up the slope, making it more difficult for the planes to follow the ground below. Or perhaps it was simply luck. Looking down over the centre of the town the bombs had concentrated on that area, later bombs attracted by the earlier ones, making deeper and deeper craters till the centre of town was like one massive crater, a volcano without lava. Screams and wails drifted towards me on the air and the acrid dust, it was filthy, stinging my eyes, hard to see, so the sounds seemed even more intense. And the smell, the dryness of the shattered materials filling my nostrils, even though I wore a bandana across my nose and mouth.

When you think this is hell, it cannot get any worse, that's when you discover that it can. The planes this time were high in the darkening sky. Was the sky dark because of the clouds of debris or because evening was advancing? Perhaps there was hope in darkness because the planes would not be able to fly, they would not be able to see where to drop their bombs. So I thought that the planes high in the sky were returning to the air fields behind their own lines, perhaps deep into the central lands where they were strongest. Perhaps they were returning to Germany, training mission completed.

This delusion did not last long. Even in the fading light you could see the bombs falling from these planes, these explosive bird droppings that splattered when they reached the ground. Hundreds of them fell. They seemed to do less harm than the first round of bombing, perhaps they were smaller, perhaps they had exhausted their supply of big bombs. They fell onto tinder, the dry, flattened ground levelled by the first destruction. This was something different but I was slow to realise what it was.

The darkness seemed to be lifting, illuminated by outbreaks

of bright light, orange glow through clouds of dust. Looking across the flat landscape before me, I saw fires flaring up in the rubble. These incendiary bombs, for now I realised what they were, were the next stage in this military plan: bomb, strafe, burn. Kill. Destroy. Spare no-one. Spare nothing. The scene now really was like hell.

I am not a coward. I did nothing, but I am not a coward. I survived but I would not if I had been foolish in my bravery. My comrades Ramon and Nacho I never saw again. I grieve for them, I mourn them for taking the bomb or the bullet that could have been meant for me. I did not rush to help. But I am not a coward. Those fires were like funeral pyres, each one marking the deaths of many innocent people. I could not have helped by throwing myself on the pyre. Even so the thought haunts me, the guilt that I am alive.

At last, and in the blackness of a night sky, the assault stopped. The drone of the bombers went over the mountains, went along the coast or down the river, leaving an impression of silence. That is all it was, an impression. When you listened the night was full of noises: voices contorted by anger and pain, the cracking of timbers falling to ground as fires burned, the rumble of crashing masonry as buildings were stripped by flames of their last supports. Bells, absurdly bells, why were people ringing bells?

The bells, it seemed, were firemen arriving from outside town. They must have come from Bilbao, because the town's own fire-fighters, if there were any, would have been destroyed. But firemen need water and the bombs had destroyed the water mains too; trickles of water ran through the shattered storm drains, the trickles were dark with dirt and blood. The firemen were desperately searching for water, not looking for fires because they were all around, and ringing their bells as if to vent their frustration.

The time passed. The night was horrific. I curled up beside the stump of the oak tree, certain that this must be the safest place after what I had experienced in the last few hours. I was unscathed, so was the oak, so was the parliament. The courtyard remained quiet and deserted. I swear I did not sleep, I could not on the edge of that inferno, but I lost awareness of time and place. I became unconscious but it was not sleep.

Eventually the sky began to lighten. It was a grey morning, or it was just the greyness of a dawn in which the earth was smoking, puffing out smoke in shades of black and white from fires still burning bright orange. My throat was so dry, I found it hard to swallow the last swig of water in my canteen. The strangest light, unnatural, and the strangest feeling, disconnected from my self and from everything I saw around me. Seeing things through a murkiness that could have been smoke or drizzle or fog. With a smell every so often that was like Sunday dinner at home, a smell of roast lamb, a treat if ever we could afford it but now twisted by this human and animal destruction, a sacrifice imposed by bombs from the sky.

They had called it a sacred town, that is how they described it to me before I set foot there. Sacred enough now to have made a blood sacrifice. How many were dead? Hundreds, thousands. The numbers could not be counted but in a way they did not matter. For those carrying this out, and I knew by instinct that these were not just Franco's fascists, they were despatched there by Hitler and Mussolini, this was just a training exercise. For them these were not real people. While the British and French governments stood by, in their remote places of safety, sticking to the non-intervention pact they had proudly signed, pleased to avoid war at all cost. This was the cost. A town reduced to rubble and now in flames, its civilian citizens murdered without warning.

Ahead I could see the outline of what had been a street, stretching straight in front, with flattened houses on either side. There was a redness to the rubble, the redness of broken brickwork and the colour of all the tiles on all the roofs in this town, this town now without a roof. Fanciful, no doubt, to say it was also blood but that was how it seemed as I scrambled over the debris in this forsaken place. With a start, I saw a stiff arm sticking out of the rubble, an arm raised in defiant salute, fist clenched and raised to the sky. But stiff with the stiffness of death.

Hardly a house remained. Even those that still stood were now burning as the incendiaries burst into belated life. As they burst they burnt the beams and timbers and they crackled, as they crackled they cracked, and floorboards fell in flames, masonry crashed to the crowded ground.

It began to rain. Rain was always welcome when planes were a threat, they could not do their work properly. But their work was already done. The drizzle would do little to dampen the flames. I stumbled on, meeting other stumblers who crossed my path. They talked to me, really talking to themselves, but making no sense to me. None of this made sense. The children huddled together in a tight-knit group, holding each other in comfort, but dead as I realised from touching one of them. Wisps of wool blew in the wind, some of it burning like matches, some of it charred black by fire. Market produce lay all around, vegetables recognisable but burnt to charcoal. I knelt down to open one piece of sacking and inside was an oozing blackened mess of oranges turned to marmalade by the heat and the still burning flames. I stamped down on the parcel with the heel of my boot but as I did so I felt ashamed that I had abandoned my own parcel – the poor mother's parcel – of oranges that I had been guarding. I started to sob, the memory was raw.

A man in a dark suit and tie, wearing a trilby hat, was talking to me. He was jabbering away in Spanish but I had no clue what he was saying. He was a strange sight, here among the debris, dressed for a night out at a gentleman's club in London. *What are you doing here, who are you?* I wondered or perhaps I spoke. In any event he then stopped gabbling in Spanish and walked towards me. He put his hands on my shoulders, shook me as if to make sure I was real, then asked "Are you British?"

I nodded. It seemed the natural thing to do, to nod and to hold out my hand for shaking.

"Good God, man, what are you doing here?"

"I could ask the same of you." I could but I am not sure if I did. It was like being awake in a dream. He started telling me things but I could not take them in and besides, the noise was deafening. I could hardly hear as buildings kept collapsing, as fires blazed and the rain streamed down my face. I wiped it and recoiled from the muddy, bloody grime that now covered the back of my hand.

Later I pieced together what he had been saying. His name was Stevenson. He worked in the British Embassy that had been in Bilbao but most of the staff had now moved for safety into France, just across the border in Hendaye. He was one of the last ones left in Bilbao. He had driven to Gernika to see what had happened with his own eyes.

"But my own eyes can scarcely believe," he admitted. "I had not imagined it would be so bad."

By now we were in his car at the edge of town, ready to head for France. I was a willing refugee from this place of destruction, sitting in the front of the car while Stevenson drove. On the back seat he had placed two bombs – "safe" he said.

"I want to take them with us. Don't worry, old chap, they won't go off, they're duds. But they're German, you can see, and they're evidence I need to show Sir Henry. He won't be inclined to believe otherwise."

It was slow progress as we dodged around craters and bombed vehicles, but we joined the slow procession of sand trucks heading east out of Gernika. The trucks were full of bodies, taken who knows where to be buried. Looking back the town lay below me, still blazing in pockets, but seeming absolutely still and lifeless as a corpse. We drove their sharp mountains, densely covered in trees, woods that might be refuge or a threat but we kept going. In a few hours we crossed the bridge of a wide river, from Spain into France, pulling into the drive of the residence that was now the British Embassy for Spain, presided over by Sir Henry Chilton.

There is, of course, much more I could write about the days that followed. But I have a train to catch, and I must go, back to Spain, back to the war, for I have no other choice."

CHAPTER 6

Lorna sat in the smell of turpentine, with the imagined smell of cordite in her nostrils. She felt deeply for the people who had died. She felt even more deeply for Harry who had survived. Longing to see him again, wanting to talk to him but not knowing what she might say, she closed her eyes.

In the darkness behind her eyelids she felt the burning light of a town in flames. In the silence of the room she heard the booming of the bombs, the rattle of machine gun fire. Slowly her thoughts returned to the artificial light of the studio's electric bulb hanging on its flex, the white flashes of lightning seen through the skylight above, the crashing of thunder rolling overhead, the rat-a-tat of rapid raindrops on the roof and windows.

The storm was so loud that she did not hear him enter. The first she knew was a voice behind her, deep and almost aristocratic, startling her into consciousness.

"Have you been here long? I was expecting a man not a woman. I knocked, even though it's my own house, but I received no answer."

As he spoke, speaking as if to allow time to pass and accustom her to the situation, he came around the table and stood in front of her. She saw a heavily built, tall man of middle age, with a cravat worn at the neck inside a brown jacket.

"I'm sorry. I shouldn't really be here." Lorna started to gather things together, collecting the pages of Harry's letter, stuffing both copies inside the foolscap envelope. Feeling flustered at being discovered in a place where she did not belong, torn between fear and embarrassment.

"Cigarette?" The man offered the pack of Senior Service towards her. She shook her head.

"Are you spying on me?" he asked.

Lorna was surprised by the question. Espionage had not been in her thoughts. She might more readily have expected a question about burglary. She realised that she had to explain her presence with as much honesty as she could summon to her aid.

"You must find this strange, in your own house. I am not a spy, no, certainly not. My name is Lorna, I am a friend of Harry James, he asked me to retrieve some things he had left here. Because Harry, you see, has now gone back to Spain."

"Vincent," he replied. "Vincent Hillyer. Artist. My house, open to the right sort of people."

The man's face showed no emotion, no sense of being part of a conversation. He simply stared without expression, as if evaluating her, seeking a truth that might lie beneath the skin. Then he reached out slowly, without aggression so she did not flinch, to hold her chin between the fingers of his right hand. His fingers lifted her face towards his gaze.

"Good face," he stated, as a matter of observation. "Cheek bones are rather fine." He looked her up and down, his assessment seeming to penetrate the layers of clothing. "Have you ever modelled?"

"Modelled? How do you mean?"

He waved his hand around the room, so that she would see all the drawings and paintings. He pulled out one canvas from behind the main work that had previously attracted most of her attention, exposing the image of a nude woman whose shape was built up in layers of oil paint. She looked further, noticing more portraits of people, mostly women, mostly pencil sketches of heads and shoulders and parts of bodies, many more than she had first noticed. At first the room had seemed dominated by abstract paintings filled with colour, but now she saw that these were less abstract than first realised, her gaze was returned by eyes in charcoal, ink, paint and pencil.

"Oh no, I never have. And I don't think I could." She felt herself blushing under his examination. "These women have more to offer an artist like you."

His wordless exclamation showed disagreement without attempting to argue. "You might change your mind. At least you know that I'm an artist and at least you haven't scurried out the door."

Lorna got to her feet. She now wanted to leave as soon as she could, with the minimum awkwardness. Yet the situation remained inherently awkward. She tried to manoeuvre her words closer to an exit.

"I will think about it. I do like your work. Though I don't really know much about modern art. I like colour. But I like this too, can I touch it? This is very striking."

Permitted by his nod, she laid a hand on the dark-brown bronze head of a woman that she had noticed at first when alone in the house. She smoothed her fingers over the hard, unyielding hair that had been sculpted into waves, laid hands on the swelling cheeks and the downward sweep of the nose. It was true, it was to be admired, something beyond her previous understanding.

"Ah well," he said, "you show taste. That's Kitty, I know her. It's a bust by Epstein and I will never come up to his standard. An apprentice at best, to the master."

"I thought it was yours."

"I own it. But I did not make it. Sculpture's not for me, I

simply paint and draw. Clever of you, though, to pick out the only work here not by me."

"I'm sorry."

"No need to be. I know my limits even if I try to stretch them."

She was expected to answer but she could not find the right words to say. Eventually she asked "What are you working on now?"

He untied the cardboard portfolio that he had laid against the wall, taking out sheets of paper that he spread across the floor.

"This is what I've been doing for a couple of days. I wanted to help the Spanish war effort but I'm not up to the heroics of people like Harry. So I offered myself as an artist."

Lorna studied the pencil sketches that now covered much of the floor. They were mainly of children, boys and girls. She held up one of a young boy making a clenched fist salute, wearing a beret and boots. Then a row of boys making the same salute.

"Where did you do these?"

Vincent explained that he had been to the camp near Portsmouth that was providing refuge for 4000 Spanish children. He had been invited there to make drawings as part of the effort to spread information about the children and the war in their homeland.

"How strange," said Lorna. "I'm now on the committee that's supporting the children."

"It seems, then, that we share the same cause. We have already joined forces, without knowing it. Perhaps we will find other ways to do so."

He said this with a sparkle in his eyes, teasing her, it

seemed. But, feeling no threat, curiosity made her explore a little further.

"Can you tell me a little – what was it like?"

"You should go and see. You cannot be on the committee and not understand it first hand. The children are just children, as innocent and vulnerable as children anywhere. But without their parents. Without their country. They will not wish to stay, so go and see them soon."

Lorna nodded. This seemed the moment for her to leave without further fuss. She picked up the envelope with Harry's letters and, mumbling, excused herself to go upstairs where she had left her handbag. While in the bedroom she smoothed the sheet a little more, relieved to feel less dampness under her fingers. She noticed that Harry had left the boots, the ill-fitting boots that had caused him such discomfort. He would not want them but Lorna decided that she would take them.

A minute later, with a business-like handshake, she left Vincent alone in the house.

CHAPTER 7

Hot weather, as so often, ended in thunderstorms. That was to be expected but the violence of the storms took everyone by surprise. Torrential rain fell, and the storms kept returning with swollen black clouds, and they brought even heavier downpours from the sky.

Lorna took Vincent's advice to heart. She arranged an early visit to the North Stoneham camp in Hampshire, a generous farmer's field where tents had been erected for the Basque children. Diana, as another member of the committee, volunteered to go with her. Lorna had no idea what to expect, and she had never been to that part of the country, so she welcomed Diana's presence – even though she found her a little intimidating. *It's what I need to do*, she told herself, swallowing her anxiety in another cup of tea as she sat at home preparing for the following day.

Waterloo Station the next morning was dark, with the grey clouds overhead now threatening drizzle not storms. Electric trains were outnumbered and steam billowed all around from the metal engines arriving and departing with the greatest possible fuss. Travelling by train excited Lorna but she felt this was not something she should confess to Diana. They had arranged to meet in the ticket office twenty minutes before the train's departure time.

"It's me," Diana greeted her with a kiss on her cheek "and look, I already have the tickets."

Lorna smiled her "thank you".

"So," asked Diana "are you excited? I am. I love a railway journey. And now I've done my bit, now I'm in your hands for the rest of the day."

Diana demonstrated this by grasping Lorna's hands and squeezing them with her white-gloved fingers.

"Oh I say, I think I can dispense with these, don't you? Gloves will not be right in a rough and ready camp."

"I'm sure they will be glad to see you with or without gloves."

"I expect you're right," squeezing hands, now with gloves removed. "Though I expect I am wrongly dressed for our little adventure. These shoes, for example, I see you are much better prepared."

Diana's heels clicked on the stones as they walked to the platform. She breezed her way through the throng heading in the opposite direction towards work in London, elegant in her rose-patterned dress and a white hat with a wide brim. She might have been on her way to Ascot. Lorna, by contrast, was dressed more pragmatically, her flat shoes and grey suit showing her determination to do a professional job. *But I will learn from this,* thought Lorna.

Diana opened the door to the compartment and sat next to the window on one of the six numbered seats.

"Sit here, my dear," she said, patting the seat next to her. "You can put that away on the luggage rack," motioning with her eyes to the netted shelf above them. Within seconds she had taken command of the space, making Lorna a guest needing to respect house rules.

Lorna's canvas bag had been a last-minute choice. She had thought of all the things that might come in handy and one of these, a blanket, needed to be carried in a bag. Hidden even, for Lorna was not quite sure if it was appropriate. She explained this a little apologetically to Diana.

"Splendid idea. Get it out, we can cover our legs as we sit. It's none too warm today."

The need for warmth seemed to be contradicted by Diana's request to slide open the window as the train clanked out of the station. *Yes, I will learn from this*, thought Lorna. Diana's every action conveyed a certainty that Lorna might envy and, possibly, in time, imitate.

No one else had entered their compartment as a passenger. Their gender and lack of smoke suggested the need to respect privacy. The ticket collector gave a friendly "good morning" as he pulled open the door from the corridor alongside. On his way out he remarked "You look as snug as two bugs in a rug".

The blanket was tucked in loosely on both sides and Lorna felt pleased that she had brought it, winning Diana's approval. She was eager to impress on this first assignment outside the firm.

They talked about what they would do at the camp. Lorna was eager to learn and help in whatever way she could, so she looked to Diana for guidance.

"Oh, I'm sure we'll find out," said Diana. "In a funny way it's our camp, so let's see how well they're running it. A bit of common sense is often lacking in these situations. After all it's your money, my money, the money of trade union members that's making this possible. We want to make sure it's money well spent."

Outside the window the green English countryside slipped by, looking sodden from too much rain. Cows chewed vacantly as the train chugged past, standing on the higher ground away from the marshy areas.

"It really has rained," said Lorna. "I hope the camp is dry enough."

"Apparently the farmer who gave it said it was on gravel soil and it could rain night and day without causing any problem. We will soon find out."

"Will we have to do anything with the children?"

"How do you mean? Inspect their teeth?"

Lorna was starting to understand that Diana had a sense of humour. Not everyone did in these earnest political circles. Beliefs needed to be worn seriously, in dark sober suits, but Diana favoured a lighter and brighter touch. Lorna found herself warming towards Diana's approach.

"Do you think I'm naughty?" Diana asked.

"No, of course not."

"Oh, but I am. I can't help it."

Diana's hand patted Lorna's under the blanket, and it rested there as if finding it comfortable.

"There is one thing," said Diana. "The children will be dispersed. We're not expecting them to stay long in the camp."

"Yes, I read that."

"Some of them, poor dears, will go off to be looked after by nuns. I don't envy them the nunneries but it's better than a bombed house in Bilbao. Others, the luckier ones, will be sent to houses around the country. Well, we hope they are lucky. Not sure how Mrs B in Batley will cope with Maria from the Basque country."

"Perhaps they'll be good friends."

"Perhaps they will. You see some unlikely friendships. Some times opposites attract. Anyway children will be sent to these houses they're calling colonies. The colonial instinct runs deep in the British."

"Where will these colonies be?"

"They could be anywhere. Some will be in London. The

children will need to be visited when they're in these new places, have to make sure things are above board. So, I hope you don't mind, I suggested you could be put down as a visitor to one of them. Somewhere near you. And you will be able to develop a nice relationship with one or two of the children because that's the idea. To get to know them better, to show them places while they're here."

"Take them on trips, do you mean?"

"Only if you wish. It's more about having a friend, an English person they can ask about things, learn a little of the language. We all need friends," Diana's hand squeezed more tightly on Lorna's beneath the blanket.

"Of course," Lorna responded, if a little reluctantly.

They settled into a silence made comfortable by the rhythm of the train. It was now on an open stretch of countryside and there was little to distract them outside. Lorna's eyes closed and she might have dozed off had she not felt Diana's hand stroking hers then moving gently onto her thigh. Opening her eyes fully, she saw that Diana's eyes were shut and her face was set into a peaceful smile. She lifted Diana's hand away from her, raising the blanket and repositioning it around Diana, like tucking a child into bed. She felt hot, a flush brought on by the fumblings more than the blanket.

"Sorry," said Diana, her eyes still closed, as if in sleep. A few moments later she asked: "By the way, I meant to ask, did you and Harry hit it off the other night?"

Lorna blushed even deeper but she answered rapidly, spontaneously. "Yes, we did."

Silence fell again. Some minutes later Diana said: "He's a good boy. I'm pleased to have put you in touch with each other." She laughed, as if she had made a really good joke.

"Not for long," said Lorna, biting back her irritation. "I expect he's now back in Spain. But I haven't heard for sure."

Lorna missed Harry. She tried to block him out of her everyday thinking, if only to save herself anxiety, but he kept coming back into her thoughts. She could not forget him, certainly not here on this train alongside Diana, because that inevitably stirred the memory of their meeting. In reflective moments elsewhere, at home or in her work cubby hole, she stared into the depths of her tea, as if to see what he might be doing at that moment. She swallowed the tea in thirsty gulps, with his image in her head, the smell of his hair cream in her nostrils, the smoky taste of his lips on hers. She swallowed Harry, taking him and the memory of him inside her with a bitterness sweetened by pleasure in its vividness.

"A penny for them," said Diana. "You look as if your thoughts are far away."

The hiss of steam and the slowing of the train's rhythm spared Lorna the need to reply. She preferred to keep her thoughts to herself, they were safer there, under her control. The guard slid the door open: "Southampton in two minutes, ladies." It was easy for Lorna to hide her emotion in the bustle of getting ready, folding and packing away the blanket, making sure she had the paper handy with its names, titles and addresses.

Outside the station, Lorna realised that the arrangements were not clear. She looked around for someone to greet them because she had been assured that a car would be there waiting. But no one came forward, no one seemed to be on the lookout for them. Lorna was eager to find the shortest route to the camp or, even more eagerly, to Diana's approval.

She asked a taxi-driver if he knew the North Stoneham children's camp. He shook his head and turned away.

"I say we go this way," Diana smiled, happy to take Lorna by the arm, gropings below the blanket seemingly forgotten. *Perhaps I imagined it*, thought Lorna, walking along the pavement with Diana towards a car that was just pulling in. A Bible-black Austin drew up and the driver's hand waved inside the front rectangular window.

"I'm awfully sorry to be late," said the man hauling himself out of the driver's seat. "At least, I presume you are the two ladies from the committee and that it's you who will be visiting our Basque children's camp. If so, I am your driver."

They shook hands with the man who, they now saw, was wearing a black suit and clerical collar. His handshake was firm but his manner was friendly. Lorna cautioned herself to put aside her suspicion of church people. They stepped into the back seat of the car, ready to be driven to North Stoneham.

73

"Sorry, terribly rude of me. I'm Father Chambers. I should have said but was a little flustered by being so late. I should have explained my lateness too. Afraid the camp's got very wet. All that rain. Lots of mud."

He seemed to time his phrases according to the movements he made to the steering wheel. His driving did not fill the passengers with confidence. There seemed to be too many turns involved as he made his way through the outskirts of Southampton.

"So are the children washed away?" asked Diana, with a hint of mischief.

"Gracious, no. A few soggy tents but they'll survive. It just made it hard to get the car out."

As they drove along, there were flags and bunting hanging from the windows, lining the route. The King's coronation celebrations, still recent, were looking a little bedraggled.

"Flags everywhere," said Diana. "Did you tell the children they were in their honour?"

"They're probably confused enough without me adding to it. I wish. I wish there was a better sense of welcome. Already" turning sharp left "already the Council is asking when the children will all be gone?"

"After a week?"

"Yes. Sad, isn't it? Having said that, many people have been kind. Very kind. And the Boy Scouts are marvellous."

Lorna wanted to know more. Was it right to ask this silver-haired clergyman? Her head was full of questions about how the camp operated, and the questions tumbled out before she could feel self-conscious. "Are they settled? Is there enough food? What do they sleep on?"

"I'll tell you everything you want to know once we're there. We'll have a sit-down and a cup of tea. Only five minutes away now. Afraid this business of driving takes most of my attention. But, in brief, yes, they've settled. No, there's not quite enough food. Expected 2000 children and 4000 turned up. And they sleep in tents – War Office issue – on mattresses they make themselves. Stuff straw into canvas sacks. Quite comfortable."

There in front of them now was a wide banner stretched between two poles that formed a gateway. The road led off into a field between the poles and the banner spelled out NATIONAL JOINT COMMITTEE FOR SPANISH RELIEF. Then in bigger capital letters BASQUE CHILDREN'S CAMP.

"Welcome to our camp," said Father Chambers, waving his hand at the people standing guard by the entrance. He stopped the car once through the entrance: "Better not go further. We might just sink into the mud."

Lorna had expected some challenges, even surprises, on this day. But she had not foreseen deep mud. She looked out of the car window, wondering how she might negotiate the next part of the journey on foot, looking at her own relatively sensible flat shoes and then at Diana's high heels.

"Father Chambers," said Diana, in a tone that had been practised on others over many years. "Would you be a dear and get us some wellington boots? I'm sure you must have such a thing. Otherwise I fear we will be stranded in the back of your car."

He returned a few minutes later carrying two pairs of boots. "I hope these will do. We don't have much of a choice."

The boots fitted well enough, at least as well as wellington boots ever do. Diana and Lorna clomped their way through the clinging mud, each step threatening to detach a boot from a foot. Eventually they made it to drier ground and into one of the canvas tents. The mustiness struck them as soon as they walked in, Diana at ease, Lorna disconcerted. It seemed to Lorna that Harry walked back into her thoughts, marching in step with her. *Is he somewhere like this? Like this but with explosions all around?*

The promised cup of tea was brought by Edith, a local volunteer. "Two spoonfuls of sugar?" she asked, as if hoping she might save a little expense. "The children like even more, but they're not used to tea. We have a Horlicks tent and they seem to enjoy that."

"*Leche malteada*," said Father Chambers, proud of his Spanish.

"Night starvation will not be an issue for our children then. I am so pleased."

Lorna smiled to herself but she was not sure the others appreciated Diana's irony. They sat at a trestle table in the tent, on a bench that was simply a plank laid across a number of crates.

"So tell us, what are the problems? Can we help with them?" asked Diana, adopting a more business-like tone.

Father Chambers was a volunteer from the anglo-catholic church. Perhaps he had hoped that gave him an ability to create a bridge between Spanish and English cultures. But some of the basics needed to be addressed first: more food needed, the latrines were now flooded, the camp was not well-organised, there had been too little time to prepare as the government had delayed so long in authorising the evacuation from Spain. The children had sailed in the *Habana* just two days after government approval came through. It had been a rough crossing, and that had not helped the children to feel settled. When they arrived and saw a field of tents, there was some resistance to the idea of living in this way.

"One girl said 'I'm not a gypsy'. They are surprisingly – not sure how to put it – they squabble a lot. They're children but they are political. They divide into different factions. No fascists, but Basque nationalists, socialists, communists, anarchists. It leads to tensions. We might have to rearrange the tents into the different groups."

They talked about the tentative plans to move the children on as soon as possible. Different organisations were taking responsibility. The Salvation Army would take a large number. Many would go to convents and catholic organisations. Many, perhaps most, would be placed in houses in different parts of the country. Some of these would be individual children but most would be in small groups, living in colonies, houses in towns. Some would be in London.

"We are hoping that people might 'adopt' a child. It costs ten shillings a week to feed one of the children, and I understand that you have both agreed to that."

"Not me," said Diana. "I will pay the money and more but I need to limit my personal involvement. Simply too many other commitments. But perhaps Lorna will be more amenable."

Lorna looked from Diana to the clergyman, seeking a more definite sign than the clamminess in her palms. Anxiety rose in her throat and she feared her words would croak. Would that croak sound true or false? She wanted to do the right thing, she wanted to do what Harry would want her to do.

"I would be happy to," she spoke in a voice that was sure,

without a trace of croakiness. "But I must know more what is involved."

Father Chambers was reassuring in stating the limits of the commitment. A child would be assigned to her, not for safe keeping nor for looking after in her own accommodation. She would simply have to visit the child, help with any practical matters, give them a treat by taking them out to see London. For example. Other examples would be best supplied by her. But it would not be an onerous commitment, simply an act of human kindness.

"That sounds something I cannot refuse then," said Lorna.

"Excellent. Actually we have a boy we thought would be ideal. His name is Pepe Calderon and he's one of the older boys, fourteen, nearly fifteen. His father is an English teacher back in Bilbao and Pepe speaks exceptionally good English. He wants to learn more. He's a bright boy and I'm sure you'll like him. He understands everything you say and, given time, he'll talk freely."

"We should meet then," said Lorna.

"But first," Diana intervened, "we really ought to look around. Otherwise our committee would think we failed to do our duty."

Looking around involved walking and, in mud and wellington boots, they made sticky progress. Lorna could not easily accustom herself to a role that seemed like the visiting inspector. She feared she might observe something that would put her in two minds, caught between scrutiny and concealment, turning a blind eye to the failures of good intentions, not least her own. Her boots squelched, a little like her conscience, but she entered the tent where equipment was stored as the flap was lifted for her.

"Boots," said Father Chambers, "have you ever seen so many boots? We have not yet had a chance to distribute them. These were contributed by the shoemakers' union. Very generous of them. Like elves," he laughed. "We are just not too sure how best to go about it."

"Does it not come down simply to feet? Size of feet matching size of boot?"

"Four thousand pairs of feet. Most of them smaller than these. At best one thousand pairs of shoes."

Walking on between the tents laid out in rows, down the muddy street that had been formed by the arrangement of tent pegs, they became the subject of excited attention. Small children called out in Spanish, one or two of the older ones attempting English words of greeting. 'Hello' established at least the attempt to reach out to strangers across the barriers of language. One girl curtsied the visitors, bowing among the giggles.

"She thinks you might be the Queen," said Father Chambers. "*No Reina*," he smiled at the children, then turned towards Diana. "A natural mistake."

Diana wondered for an instant if her own irony had been trumped. But then she took in the innocence of his expression. If forgiveness were needed, she gave it, with a regal gesture.

Further down the field they came upon a dozen women, each with a child as a helper. Gathered around water pumps they were scrubbing at clothes and sheets in tin tubs, then rinsing them. Facing each other they twisted sheets to wring out the moisture, then put them damp and crumpled into baskets. They shook wet blouses and skirts, making them snap in the breeze, droplets of water spraying off like a shower of rain. Even as they stood there watching, Lorna and Diana felt the touch of a warming sun on their water-sprinkled cheeks. The sun was breaking through the clouds, for the first time that overcast morning, encouraging thoughts of progress. They pressed on, their boots still clinging to the mud, while the girls, no more than eight years old, struggled to carry the baskets between them, heading towards the washing lines.

There was a determined cheerfulness to the girls' labour. Father Chambers explained that the women were the *senoritas* – young girls in their early twenties who had volunteered to accompany the children as companions, teachers, protectors. Or simply friendly faces with familiar words and accents. Lorna held their eyes, then turned away in embarrassment at the examination of her own immaturity. *Am I ready for this?*

The atmosphere changed from the practical jollity of the girls to an air of suspicion when they neared tents with young boys outside them. There was a tension as they approached. Lorna regarded the boys with wariness as they stood in their short trousers and caps. They had a hardened quality, a walnut exterior, that English boys of their age lacked. One boy, older and bolder than the rest, stared at them with a smile that hinted at challenge, and it was he who raised his arm in a clenched fist salute, yelling '*No paseran!*' The other boys responded quickly, following his lead and holding their fists steady beside their faces. '*No paseran!*' they repeated, until stony stares turned into broad grins. Lorna saw that Diana had mirrored their salute and belatedly followed suit. Her fist tailed off into an apologetic wave.

The English group moved on, now walking around the edge of the camp.

"By the way, the boy at the front," said Father Chambers, "the one who led the saluting. That was Pepe."

Lorna smiled, hiding relief and resentment. She might not forgive him the lack of communion, the withholding of what might have been a blessing. "I would love to meet him. Soon," she insisted.

"No fear, we shall arrange it. You will have time to get to know him. But first we should eat."

Inside the big tent long tables were arranged in lines. There was a smaller table set aside for the camp staff. Lorna's heart sank at the plate of stew placed in front of her. She had not felt hungry and any feeling of hunger was driven away completely by the appearance of the dinner before her. Knowing how her pickiness would be viewed she made an attempt, spurred on by Diana tucking into her meal with apparent gusto. Lorna's knife scraped the plate but left most of the food and all her anxiety untouched. She cut the carrots and potatoes into mouthfuls that she chewed but found hard to swallow.

"You should eat," whispered Diana, "but I see you cannot. Put some here onto my plate."

The knife scraped noisily again but they made the transfer with no one seeming to notice. Lorna felt a surge of gratitude towards Diana. When the plates were cleared away, there was an acceptably small amount left on hers.

"I will see about Pepe now," said Father Chambers. "If you go into the other tent I'll bring him to you. By the way, I hope you didn't mind him saluting like that?"

"Of course not," insisted Diana, "why would we object?"

"Well, I'm not really political myself. But I warmed to it when we met the children off the boat. They sang the *Internationale* and clenched their fists while they sang. But it seemed to me as much a gesture of courtesy, as if they were trying to recognise us for our supposed convictions. In my case I'm here for humanity not politics, but these gestures form a human connection. We share faith even if we don't share the same faith."

Diana acknowledged his words with a benign expression, not quite trusting her own words to say the right thing.

Ten minutes later Father Chambers returned with Pepe. A smile still played around his lips, as if eager to please. He took off his cap as he entered and stood facing them, almost at attention. His eyes seemed to hold an innocence tinged with the shadow of precocious experience. He seemed to know secrets beyond everyday imaginings. *But a child. He is just a child.*

"Good afternoon," he bowed. "My name is Pepe Calderon and I am very pleased to meet you."

"Hello, Pepe. I am Lorna and I hope we will be friends."

"I hope."

"Are you from Bilbao?"

"I have been living there for two years because my father is a teacher. Before that I was in Sevilla."

"Your father has taught you well. You speak English perfectly."

"No, not perfect. But I try and I try to be better at English. Perhaps then I stay here."

"Well, Pepe," said Father Chambers, "I'm not sure that is part of the plan. I think your mother and father would like to see you home after the war."

"Only, I think, if the war turns out well. If we lose, I do not want to live under the Falange."

"Quite right, Pepe," smiled Diana. "You have the right spirit."

Hearing his ease with English, they encouraged Pepe to talk, and he did. His voice had an accent that they would define as Spanish but neither Lorna nor Diana had much experience of talking to Spanish people. Put to it, they could no more have identified his accent than his hair with a nationality. His hair was dark, almost black, offering nothing more distinctive than the gloss of brilliantine. *Foreign* would have been the honest response but there was a formality in voice, appearance and clothing that surprised them a little with its sense of the alien. They had both attached so many of their hopes to a foreign country outside their acquaintance and understanding. They had made Spain their friend, given it a place in their hearts, without the usual process of familiarisation. With every word spoken by Pepe they felt more closely bound to the country and the cause, despite the strangeness of the heavy jacket he wore, the slight remoteness of his expression that was occasionally tempered by a smile.

He told them about the situation in Bilbao, where bombs had become more frequent and where people lived in growing fear. Franco's forces were closing on the city by land and sea. The sinking of a Nationalist submarine had led to reprisals in towns that had already fallen to Franco. News got through that over two hundred Basque people had been rounded up and executed. They were shot then buried in a mass grave. This had struck fear into the residents of Bilbao, particularly the parents of young children. An even greater urgency had arrived with these stories, because no one doubted they were true. There had been so many of them in every part of Spain; so many families had suffered losses in a short time. The families in Bilbao saw the need to evacuate children but where could they go? Then suddenly there was news that the British government had given permission for a ship to sail and for refugees to be received in England.

"We pack quick. It was a lovely weather, raining, we love rain because the bombers do not fly in rain. My mum and dad want to make sure I get on the boat. I do not even get the chance to say goodbye to my dad, no *adios*, no embrace, he is away, not at home, so my mum take me on the train from Portugalete station. It is a crowd, lots of children, most of them younger than me. So I have to be a man for them. When we arrive in the docks at Santurce, the boat is waiting. *Habana*. I see its name on the side."

Lorna wanted to ask Pepe about his father but felt it would be better to wait. She did not want to ask a question that might involve the telling of a secret in the company of strangers.

"Was there any problem with the boat leaving?" asked Diana.

"We know Franco's boats are out there but there are big British boats as well. They protect us. Franco might have shot and sunk us. It would be easy, the boat is so full, we are packed like sardines. But the boat go as fast as it can, soon we do not see the land, there is just the sea all around. And very grey. I thought the sea would be blue. It get stormy and the boat goes up and down. Terrible. I have never been on sea before. I do not like it. They give us food but it is impossible to eat. You eat and soon you vomit. Everywhere children being sick. The adults being sick. And the boat going up and down, side to side, with waves high as buildings. All that good food go to waste. The latrines can not take it, it is horrible."

But safe, at least, thought Lorna. *Even in a storm-tossed boat. Away from danger.*

"I would like to know about my mum and dad. But it is safer not to. I am here in England and that puts them in danger if the fascists win. I hope they do not."

"We all hope that, Pepe," said Diana. "But we are pleased that you are here and that we can welcome you. I hope you will enjoy your stay."

"It should only be three months," said Father Chambers. "Then we hope you will be reunited with your mother and father. Till then, as I explained, Miss Starling here has adopted you – your English mother, we might say."

Lorna felt the clamminess of panic on her skin, like the coming of another thunderstorm. The tension in her muscles, the dryness of her throat, the pallor of her complexion, were proof to her of maternal inadequacy.

"*Mi madre inglesa,*" Pepe smiled with a bowing of his head. "I am full of thanks to you, Miss Starling, and to you, madam, too."

"I am Diana, and this, your English mother, is Lorna." Diana almost chuckled as she spoke the words. "But tell us, how did it feel to arrive in England after such a difficult journey by sea?"

Pepe had a way of polite dismissal, far beyond his years. He spoke plainly, seeing no reason to conceal his feelings from people who claimed relationship with him. He now took their acceptance as his right, just as he would take the right to liberty.

"I do not like waiting," he said. "There is no need. All that time on ship then standing still outside England. Just looking at England from the boat but not standing in it. Why let us come but not let us in?"

"I suppose they had to do checks first," said Diana, an unlikely apologist for British bureaucracy. "Just to make sure. There are too many people wanting to find fault."

"I know. But anyway…" he dismissed his own complaints with a gesture. "Doctors, nurses, they come next day. We hear a band playing. That is good."

His intuition told him that he needed to play the child. So his cheeks puffed out, his lips trembled as he gave a rousing rendition of the band playing a hymn. When he finished, he laughed, and the others joined in.

"Ah, Christian soldiers," said Diana, "still going onward while your boat was firmly at anchor. The Salvation Army is everywhere. God help us, wouldn't you say, Father?"

While Father Chambers feigned deafness, Lorna imagined the scene on the quayside at Southampton, with the Spanish children leaning on the boat rail while the brass band played. The uniforms of war and religion, and their purposes, were not that different, nor were their songs. The musical road to war, sanctioned by God's army on a Sunday, could easily be confused with the military march to music.

"Are you religious, Pepe? I think we had you down as a catholic."

"I am a catholic. But first I am a socialist. So is my father. My mother, she is the religious one."

He looked at Father Chambers first, but then at Lorna with a gaze of defiance. Beliefs, or their absence, were not for concealing. Yet he was also at that age when the complexity of belief is starting to be revealed.

"I will be nothing like your mother, Pepe," Lorna stated, as if introducing a contract. "I cannot replace her and I will do everything I can to return you to her as soon as possible."

"I thank you, *mi madre inglesa*." Pepe bowed from his waist, one hand tucked behind his back, first to Lorna, then to Diana. "And thank you for coming, lady of the roses."

He walked out of the tent, acknowledging at the entrance that Lorna promised to visit next week. Afterwards, in the train travelling back to London, Diana said: "He's a young charmer, isn't he? Was he flirting with me? Or with you?"

CHAPTER 9

Lorna lived in Bonfield Court in Highgate, in flats built in the 1920s. it was an area she might not have considered, had the flat not been passed on to her by one of the partners at work who had outgrown the space. A single-bedroom flat suited her needs, she could not have filled more rooms. She loved the locality but could not quite feel that she fitted there. Her neighbours were rich or intellectual, sometimes both, and Lorna could flaunt neither wealth nor intellect. She came from a home background that put a high value on being undistinguished, but she increasingly questioned such pigeonholing. "You will be respected as a professional woman," Bryan had told her firmly when she had questioned her own status. Believing him seemed a matter of loyalty that she should not question openly, though it was impossible to suppress private doubts.

That morning was one to feel just one of a crowd, to be indistinguishable. From the heights of Highgate the city was a big animal stretched below, with millions of individual cells coursing through it, each focused on its purpose: to work. Lorna accepted that, it even made her content. There were moments when she did not aspire to more.

The day's work was daunting when she thought about it. She took the bus down the hill then descended the stairs from Archway Road to the Underground ticket office. Hundreds of people would pass through in the next hour. Few of them would be mixing with the kind of people that she would encounter that day. Something like pride stirred, tucked inside her like the envelope she had slipped into her handbag.

She had a meeting with Bryan Thomas most mornings when she arrived. Lorna always aimed to be early but Bryan was often there first. He had told her that it allowed him to indulge in the pleasure of a long lunch. Lorna could vouch for that, from looking after his diary, but she also knew that the lunches were never solitary and always had a purpose. Bryan would return afterwards flushed with wine and things to do. Many of the things to do were done by Lorna.

This morning Lorna needed to run through the agenda of the committee meeting that was the main focus of her day. A pot of tea lubricated their conversation, as it often did. They sat across the desk with their folders, sipping tea from their white china cups.

"Usual people expected?" asked Bryan.

"I think so. Only apology is from the Dean."

The main committee was chaired by a Duchess and included a Labour member of parliament, a cross-bench Lord, senior people from the British Legion, medical profession and the Church (Anglican and Catholic), as well as a Council leader, trade unionist and Diana Seymour. The reason for Diana's presence was not obvious but Lorna was becoming increasingly aware of the value of contacts, the need to make connections with people to get things done. Lorna attended the main committee as a minute-taker, but she sat on the sub-committee as a full participant. The sub-committee, of which Diana was chairman, did the real work.

"Just a tick," said Bryan, pulling open a desk drawer. He slid across some typed sheets in a binder towards Lorna. "You should have these."

Lorna saw that it was a list of the Basque children with scant details, mainly addresses.

"It's not complete so you'll have to fill the gaps gradually. But we need to know who they are. It might be useful. You never know if we might have to represent them."

Lorna felt she was being given intimate details in these names of people and unfamiliar places. She began thinking how to fill the gaps, from other organsations' records, from her next trip to North Stoneham.

"Keep them close. We wouldn't want them to fall into unfriendly hands. Not that Franco's reach stretches to England yet. But you might need it for this afternoon's meeting."

She felt a little anxious about the list and her hand reached for the pearls around her neck. She fingered the artificial pearls like a rosary, taking comfort from their touch on her fingers.

"You look jolly nice," said Bryan unexpectedly. "A necklace, new clothes. Are you growing your hair?"

The observation disconcerted her. She had wanted those changes to be noticed without being noticed, and she was still on a journey that she preferred to keep secret. The truth was that in these committee meetings she felt as fake as the artificial pearls around her neck. She was discovering, reluctantly, that appearance was more important than she had imagined. Harry had looked at her and what had he seen? She had not made it easy. She no longer wanted to be seen as the efficient but dowdy woman in office uniform. She was mixing with many people who dressed well, and she admired them. Diana had become a confidante but also a role model. Lorna knew that her wardrobe needed to improve but lack of money would make improvement a slow process. She had accepted Diana's gift of a hat and she would wear it to the meeting. She hoped it would increase her confidence but she could not quite shake off the feeling that she was here – wherever she might be – under false pretences.

After a morning typing letters and making notes on the papers for the meeting, she decided to take a lunchtime break. She enjoyed sitting in public gardens, watching the office workers stroll by while eating the frugal lunch she brought with her from home. An orange or an apple would do for her. She doubted if she would ever adopt Bryan's lunchtime customs. Without her hat, she made her way along the curve of Aldwych then turned left into Drury Lane.

Passing the school on her right, the discordant bird noise of children's voices twittered from the school roof. Looking up, she could see no children as the roof was four storeys above her. But she smiled to herself, imagining them at play. These English children were no different from the Spanish ones in the sounds they made underneath the same blue sky.

Lorna sat down in Spring Gardens to read her book. Here too she was changing. Or at least she was accelerating the change she had made when she decided to leave home for a life in London. Spurred by the need to show that she was different from her mother and father, Lorna strove for an air of efficiency that could become self-sufficiency, for a feeling of depth that might leave her parents floundering. Her reading now stretched beyond the confines of her family's acceptable reading. No longer content with romantic novels she strayed into the unconscious stream of Virginia Woolf, sticking at it, determined not to be left adrift in her own shallows. Dorothy Richardson and Jack London followed, a strange pairing as she acknowledged to herself. As her political awareness widened she sought books from the public library that suburban bookshops might frown upon. *The Ragged-Trousered*

Philanthropists became a favourite to read in the privacy of her room along with the newly acquired *Road to Wigan Pier.*

Shaken from her reverie by the rattling of a delivery lorry, she hurried back to the office to collect her papers for the meeting. She felt better equipped to hold her own in such company, and later Diana would whisper to her that she had done very well. Emboldened by her praise, Lorna passed the envelope with Harry's Gernika letter to Diana.

"I don't know what to do with this," she confessed to Diana. "But I believe it is important."

"Important enough to merit a drink?" asked Diana.

Three weeks earlier Lorna might have said No. Three weeks earlier Lorna had not met Harry or Diana. Life was moving very fast. Now she felt like a slow drink with this unusual friend. Thinking of her parents, as she was that day, she resented that the gentility of her upbringing had discouraged acceptance of what might be deemed 'eccentricity'; especially when there was a suspicion that more than friendship was being offered.

The drink with Diana was companionable. It was the first time since that evening with Harry that Lorna had been in a pub. They talked about the characters on the committee and washed down their words with Guinness and gin and tonic.

"My dear," said Diana, "I have to go. A tedious dinner this evening. But I want to say how pleased I am that we are friends." She laid her hands, without gloves, on Lorna's and squeezed. "And don't worry, I meant nothing more. My words have no hidden meaning. I respect your feelings for Harry and will read this with interest."

She thrust the envelope into her handbag – so much more elegant than her own, Lorna observed and envied.

They left the pub, heading in opposite directions. Waiting at a bus stop, the old woman's voice screeched as she sold the evening papers. "*Star, News, Standard!*" Lorna bought *The Star* to read on the bus. On the top deck of the bus, directed there as the lower deck was full, smoke drifted down the aisle while people seemed to hide behind their newspapers, not noticing the dinging of the bell before stops, paying no attention to the workers outside hurrying home down the grey pavements.

Stepping down from the bus, along with three or four other people at the top of Archway Road, Lorna suddenly felt that she was being watched. She stopped, pretending to adjust the contents of her handbag. This allowed people to pass her by, people whom she studied carefully. She looked around, over her shoulder. There was no obvious shadow, no one hanging back to follow her. But the feeling of anxiety remained. It puzzled her; she was not normally subject to paranoia.

She crossed the road at the traffic lights. Cars ticked over, waiting for the lights, as she crossed in the company of half a dozen people. She tried to memorise each of the faces of her fellow travellers, but there was nothing to suggest her suspicions were well-founded. Perhaps the man carrying a rolled-up newspaper had his hat pulled down too firmly over his eyes? But he veered left, striding up the hill towards Highgate Village while she continued straight ahead.

She was relieved to enter the ground floor lobby of her flats. She looked back through the oblong glass panels to the side of the main door. She saw no one and switched on the lights. As she started to walk up the stairs to her first floor flat, she thought she heard the sound of footsteps. Looking back, no one was there, but she remained uneasy as she unlocked her door.

CHAPTER 10

Next morning there was a knock on the door. Loud. Then another knocking. Louder. Opening her eyes Lorna saw that it was daylight but the watery light of a grey summer dawn. The clock on the bedside table showed 5.30. Not a time for visitors. Not a time when you would expect good news. *Brace yourself for bad news at such an hour.* Lorna thought of Harry and her heart felt heavy.

She opened the door in her nightdress. Two men stood there in suits and hats.

"Miss Starling. May we come in?"

Lorna stood aside to let them enter. *Is this what death looks like? Are these his messengers?* She closed the door gently, aware that neighbours might be sleeping or possibly listening, expecting to be told the how, when, where of Harry's fate, and wanting the moment to be private.

"I suggest you put a dressing gown on," said one of the men. They had not removed their hats on entering. *A strange lack of respect*, thought Lorna. *Were they not properly trained?* Lorna took a raincoat from her coat rail, pulling it on over her nightdress, shrinking from its cold fabric.

The darker hat was showing her something – a card, a letter, official marks. She thought it was odd to send the Special Branch on such a mission. *Would an ordinary policeman not do?* She felt she was being tormented by the delay in giving her the news she dreaded.

"Do you know this man?" She was shown a black and white photo of Harry. He was smiling and easily identifiable. She wondered where it was taken. Would they let her keep it because she did not have a photograph herself?

"Yes, I do."

"When did you last see him?"

"A few weeks ago."

"Where?"

"In London. Are you trying to tell me something?"

The darker hat looked at her disdainfully, the lighter hat impassively. They were curiously unsympathetic, Lorna thought, given the circumstances.

"It's you who needs to do the telling. Where is he now?"

The question brought relief, a release from rising panic. Harry must still be alive. Lorna had made the wrong assumption about their mission.

"I have no idea. Why do you think I would know?"

"What is your relationship with Harry James?"

"What gives you the right to ask?"

"We have rights and we will exercise them, miss. I advise you to co-operate. It will be better for you."

What would I tell a client to do? thought Lorna. *You have the right to silence.*

"What is your relationship with Harry James?" Lorna said nothing. "Are you friends? Are you sweet on him?"

Lorna spoke to stop their escalating insinuations. "Yes. He is my friend. But it is none of your business."

"Who says? Is your friend a British patriot?"

"Yes. I believe he is."

"We think he's a funny cove."

"What do you mean?"

"I mean he's fighting a war in a country that's not his."

Lorna went silent again. She realised it would be best to say nothing. She could take courage from the knowledge that Harry must be alive if these people were looking for him.

They looked everywhere. Not for him but for any signs of him. There were none as Harry had never set foot in this flat. There was not much of the flat to search, just one big room with sections for kitchen, sleeping and sitting. Suddenly it struck her as a lucky stroke that Lorna had handed over Harry's account of Guernica to Diana the previous evening. There was nothing incriminating in it, not in any normal person's view, but these people might pervert any evidence.

"What are these, miss?" One of the men held up a pair of black boots. An innocent trophy of Harry's time with her, the boots that did not fit him, that she had removed from the house in Camden Town. A shadow passed across the room.

"They are boots, of course."

"Whose?"

"I really don't know. I was given them as a donation to the Spanish children's camp."

"Do Spaniards have big feet? It would be a funny child that fitted them."

"It would. They did not fit so I brought them back."

They carried on searching, lifting clothes from drawers and dropping them back roughly, pushing aside coats and jackets on the rail behind the curtain, feeling in the pockets, emptying cutlery from kitchen drawers and cups from sideboards.

"What about these?" He held up the documents from yesterday's committee meeting. He rifled through them but found nothing personal there.

"I am a lawyer," said Lorna. "Those are papers relating to my work on a committee chaired by Duchess Argyle. I am sure she will be interested when I tell her what is happening."

The men weighed up the information – true or false? They concluded that their visit represented enough of a warning.

"Our advice, miss, is to watch the company you keep. If you do, you'll stay out of trouble and we will have no cause to visit you again."

In a movement that seemed almost synchronised, they touched the brims of their hats and backed out of the door. Lorna leant back against the front door once she had closed it. The solid timber was reassuring. She looked around her little flat, reduced to an untidy mess but with nothing broken. The clock said 6.10.

Lorna knew she had to do something with her flat. First she needed to tidy everything away, return to an appearance of normality by putting back objects, clothes and papers that had been displaced. Then she would clean it because it felt dirtied. Afterwards, but as soon as she could, she would move. She no longer felt that this could be anything like home. Moving would take a little time to bring about but now she felt determined to find somewhere quickly.

Once she had restored everything to its place, she felt a little better. She felt the consolation of Harry's continuing presence in the world when she had feared his absence, disposed of like unwanted boots. She must do something about those boots too, but that now seemed a more difficult task than previously. To give away the boots might seem a betrayal.

She found it therapeutic to clean the flat. Hot water and detergent, spread by a mop, added a sheen and a pungent smell that might take away marks on the floor and even on her memory. She laid down sheets of the evening newspaper like stepping stones on the linoleum. Then she could tread her way around the room to dust and wipe the wooden surfaces with a cloth. She used vinegar to wet the cloth. Its acid smell rose in her nostrils, so she had to blow her nose. But the residual smell of the evaporating vinegar was as invigorating as a blast of fresh air. She lifted the damp sheets of newspaper behind her as she made her way back and forth across the room, opening windows to speed the drying.

There was a tiny bathroom with a bath but she was conscious of time pressing, so she washed herself as well as she could at the basin. Choosing clothes was difficult that day. They all felt soiled by the fingers of the intruders. She chose the brightest clothes she had in her new wardrobe, the blue suit and yellow silk blouse that she had bought on the previous weekend's shopping outing to Selfridge's. A special advance on wages to recognise her promotion had seen to that.

When she locked the front door she wondered if she would ever want to return. But she knew she would. She must. There was work to do, a cause to fight, and Lorna felt reinforced in that belief as she walked resolutely down the road with its bustle of people heading towards the city.

When she arrived at work, she immediately went to Bryan's office. Without the usual formalities of tea she told him that she had been raided by Special Branch that morning.

"Sorry to hear that, Lorna. It happens, I'm afraid. They've raided me a couple of times. I recognise their knock on the door now. Did they take anything?"

Lorna was surprised by his tone of indifference, almost acceptance. "They turned the place upside down. But of course they found nothing. They were looking for evidence of Harry, letters, that sort of thing."

"They rarely know what they are looking for. They are just as likely to overlook what their masters might want to see. I would protest but it would just draw more attention to you."

She went out of the room to the kettle so she could make tea. She had left home without eating or drinking anything; now she was still disturbed by what had happened, unable to shrug it off as Bryan did, not reassured by his insouciance. She returned with cups and a comment.

"It makes me uncomfortable to live in a police state."

"A police state? Not really. A police state kills its citizens. Ours doesn't do that. But it's why we have to do our jobs within the limits we're set."

"So we just turn a blind eye, carry on as if nothing happened?"

"No, we keep a watching eye. But, unless you tell me otherwise, they did you no violence. In Spain they would have shot you, so we need to keep it in proportion. Like all of us you must be careful what you have in your possession, information that could be misread, misused. But we have the law with us as long as we do nothing to break it."

Lorna shied away from argument with Bryan. It would make things too difficult and it was easier to swallow disagreements with the cups of tea that fuelled the day. But inside her head, her thoughts were suggesting that doing nothing enabled another police state to kill its citizens. And, inevitably, her thoughts came back to Harry, wondering where he was at that moment.

These sudden thoughts of Harry were vivid, like stones seen in glistening water. But just as the stone's colour fades when taken from its resting place in the stream, so the picture of Harry – one she could see, feel, smell – faded when she took it to the next office, to the street, to the bus. She wished she did have the letters that those men had searched for. She felt deprived of a means to summon memory at will.

CHAPTER 11

Routines establish themselves quickly. Lorna's second visit to North Stoneham was just one week after her first, but it now felt routine. She knew where she was going, she knew what to expect.

The one great unknown was Pepe. What should she expect from him? He was a mystery to be explored and Lorna looked forward with an edge of nervousness to meeting him again. She would have more time to spend with him as Diana had not joined her for this second visit. Diana considered her work done, having visited the camp. She would save her main efforts for the loftier campaign, getting reports from Lorna on any problems at the camp.

Father Chambers met Lorna again and there was something different about his behaviour. Relaxed by Diana's absence, he felt free to patronise Lorna. She in turn enjoyed this new game, exercising powers that were still unfamiliar.

"At the camp I would like to wander and see things for myself," Lorna announced in the car as Father Chambers drove.

"Is that wise? You might not understand what you are seeing."

"Their customs are not that strange."

"Sometimes they are. The children are not yet accustomed to this new life."

"I don't suppose they could be. But I would like to see how things are. And I want to see Pepe, of course."

Father Chambers considered as he drove the car into the camp. Lorna saw clearly, for the first time, that she was not welcome here. She might create trouble. The realisation strengthened her resolution.

"Less mud, as you can see. The weather has been better." He pulled firmly at the hand brake to park the car. "This is what I propose. You will meet Pepe again and he will show you around the camp."

Lorna nodded. It was an arrangement that should suit her, though she felt it might make use of Pepe in a way that caused her some qualms. For which side would Pepe be working and reporting?

She had come better equipped than before. An old pair of unfashionable walking shoes and the dried mud would make it easier to walk around. She could tuck her growing hair into the new beret that she had bought.

Father Chambers led her to the far side of the field, down the main path between the rows of tents. She smiled at the children who came out of tents to stare, but she had the feeling that she was no longer a novelty to be gawped at. Perhaps visitor fatigue had set in.

Half a dozen boys were standing outside one of the khaki tents. Lorna spotted Pepe in the middle of the group, and their eyes met. She was surprised to feel her spirits lift at the sight of him.

It seemed that they were already in the habit of greeting each other by clenching their right fists. Pepe's "*No paseran!*" was an exuberant shout. Lorna's was a wry smile, hesitating to suggest encroachment into Pepe's culture or affections. Despite her embarrassment Lorna enjoyed this moment, their eyes locked, their hands mirroring each other in a rehearsal of defiance.

"I did not think you would come again," said Pepe. "Thank you."

"I said I would come. You can rely on me. I will be here when you want."

Father Chambers explained that Lorna should be taken wherever she wanted to go in the camp, and he asked Pepe to escort her. Pepe replied with a bow and then the word "Please". Lorna accepted the offer of his arm, then stopped.

"First, can you show me inside your tent?"

Pepe held open the flap and Lorna entered. There were a dozen narrow beds, each with a straw mattress. Half a dozen crates, between pairs of beds, were used for tables to hold a few possessions. The paraphernalia of boyhood – pocket knives, neck scarves, pencils – mingled with the nostalgic souvenirs of home – a photograph, letters, a locket.

"Are the other boys your friends from home?" asked Lorna.

"No. I did not know most of them. Some of them have been moved now."

"Why is that?"

"It is always the same. Franco calls us all Rojos, we are just Reds in his eyes. But why, even here, do people see us as all the same? People here should know better."

Lorna noticed that Pepe had a black eye. It had not been obvious in the half light of the tent, with his face half-turned away. Now the bruising was clear under his right eye.

"Who did that?" asked Lorna, touching the skin below her own eye.

"I got this from an Anarchist. He's not a Red, and he laughed at the photo of my mother."

He painted your eye black and blue, thought Lorna.

"So, you had a fight."

"I won. He hit me with one lucky punch. But I made his nose bleed. Red."

He clenched his fist and laughed. "Now they decided that the tents will not be all mixed up. They now put the Socialists in this tent, Anarchists in another. And the Communists separate also. It's better that way."

Lorna did not know what to say. She was tempted to sigh, and to sigh loudly. But she needed to gain Pepe's trust before being critical.

"Come. Take me around the rest of the camp."

Tent after tent, row upon row. The smell of communal cooking. The washing lines loaded with clothes, raised high with poles, fluttering like makeshift flags. The ditches that were latrines dug, Pepe said, by Boy Scouts. "It's good, they teach me new English words."

"Such as?"

He shook his head, put his finger to his lips with a conspiratorial smile. "Words you will not like."

He stepped onto the end of a queue that was forming. Lorna asked what they were queuing for.

"We will find out. In Bilbao, my mother tell me, you see a queue, join it, you might get food. It's same here."

"Is there not enough food?"

"We are growing boys. We need food, there is never enough."

The latest batch of baked bread was being handed out in rough-cut hunks. Pepe took his when he reached the front of the queue. He insisted that Lorna should also take one. "You will be hungry. If not, I will eat it."

They heard the noise of an engine getting louder. Closer. Everyone looked up in the sky and an airplane was approaching the camp, flying low, close to the ground. The queue quickly broke up, the children scattering, running in many different directions, bumping into each other in their panic. Lorna, not knowing what the plane was up to, looked around, trying to work out what to do. She looked at Pepe, bread in hand, standing there with his eyes fixed on the plane as it droned overhead.

"Scare babies!" he shouted. "You're little kids. Scare babies! Stand still, it's nothing."

Lorna clung to Pepe's arm. He showed no sign of fear. Instead he explained calmly to Lorna that he had seen the second man in the airplane taking photographs.

"They're not dropping bombs, just taking pictures. This is not Bilbao, this is England."

He spoke those words to Lorna in English, then switched to rapid Spanish for the benefit of the children. The plane had now flown off into the distance, its engine whine fading as fast as its shape in the sky. The children who had thrown themselves to the ground, into tents, under tables, came crawling back to the comfort of the standing crowd. Pepe reassured them with words spoken loudly in Spanish, and Lorna observed the relief in the children's eyes.

Afterwards, arriving back at the admin tent, Father Chambers apologised. He had been told that a plane would fly over, taking pictures of the camp, but it had not occurred to him that it would be misunderstood by the children. It was simply a plane doing a job required by the government.

Lorna let it rest. There was nothing to be gained by pointing out the different way in which the children would view aircraft. She needed to gain information from Father Chambers and it would be easier to do that without antagonism between them.

"Tell me about what is going to happen next with the children," said Lorna. "The camp was meant to be temporary, just for a couple of weeks while more permanent arrangements were made."

"That is so. But it's been a little harder than we thought. Next week we will move out some of the larger groups we've placed. The Salvation Army, for example, can take quite a few into their hostels. And the Catholic Church will take a lot into convents. It will mean a few families have to separate where there are brothers and sisters, for example. Then there are the children we will have to send into colonies around the country."

Lorna produced her list. She wanted to update it and make it more complete. So for the next couple of hours Lorna went through the lists with Vera who was a cheerful volunteer. Father Chambers was happy enough to leave them to work he found tedious.

Lorna was keen to see Pepe's name on the list, both to find out more about his background and parents, and to see what the plans were for him. At last his name came up.

"You can't send him there," protested Lorna. "How will I be able to see him if he's in Yorkshire?"

"Will you need to see him? We thought, with his English, he'd be useful going with this big group to the priory. He'll be able to translate and make things easier for the others."

"Yes, I will need to see him. For what it's worth I have 'adopted' him. I'd like that to be more than simply paying for his food and board."

"Ah, I see," said Vera. "So where do you live?"

They managed to switch him to a small group that would stay in a colony in Finchley, just a mile or two from Lorna's flat in London. He would be staying in a large house, a total of sixteen of them together. As far as they could make out, the group would be like-minded in politics but, thinking of Pepe's black eye, Lorna wanted to check this with Pepe. Vera was not sure they could do this. Was it giving too much information to Pepe?

"Oh come on, Vera," said Lorna. "He is quite grown up. We can ask him to be discreet about it."

So Pepe was sent for and soon he arrived at the tent. Lorna explained that he would be sent to stay at a colony, a big house in London, with some other children. Did he know these names on the list?

Pepe read the names. Most of them were unknown to him. He did not object to the names he did recognise. Lorna got the impression that Pepe had not formed any strong friendships with others on this *expedicion a Inglaterra*. As he was older than most, the other children looked up to him and kept their distance. With his language skills he was seen as neither in one camp or the other, not Spanish, not English, but going between the two.

"Then Pepe, keep this information to yourself for now," said Lorna. "The camp leaders will announce these things soon. You will then move to London."

"I want to see London, that is good," said Pepe. "When will this be?"

Lorna looked at Vera. "I think very soon. In the next few days."

Pepe smiled and bowed his head to Lorna. "Thank you. I was beginning to think I must escape the camp but now I will wait."

Vera shook her head. "Escape? You must do no such thing. A little patience is needed. Then things will get better. You are not prisoners here. Think how much worse it would have been had you stayed in Spain."

"I could have fought. I am ready. Soon I would have persuaded my father."

Lorna needed to intervene. She understood how Pepe bristled when reminded of the situation back in Spain, with his parents in danger. "Is this their address, Pepe?" Lorna pointed to the list. "You should write to them, tell them about England."

For the first time Pepe was frosty towards her. "If I write, the fascists can open the letter. They can see who my parents are and that I am in England. It will be bad for my parents, especially my father. So I must not write."

Lorna groaned inwardly at her own naivety. She did not know what to say so she simply nodded. She told Pepe that she would think about this and see if there might be a way to get letters through without endangering his parents.

The afternoon had passed quickly. Bright sunshine was baking the mud on the pathways through the camp. It would not be an easy path for Lorna to tread, as she saw more clearly now. There would be much to think about on the train back to London but she was relieved that next time she would visit Pepe closer to where she lived. It was not home, it was simply where she lived, and that thought cast a shadow over her with the sudden realisation that she would have to do something about moving.

CHAPTER 12

The following Saturday Bilbao fell to Franco's forces. Lorna heard the news from Diana. They agreed that they should still present a positive face to the Spanish children, but Lorna doubted her own acting skills. She felt depressed by the news and dreaded the meeting she would have with Pepe next day.

She imagined that Sundays might accentuate the differences between Spain and England. Lorna was bored by English Sundays; she longed to return to work on the following day. Outside her flat the streets were often empty, eerily quiet, the silence broken mainly by church bells. People went to church in hushed tones, or they went out for other purposes as if going to church. Those staying at home nursed their boredom, convincing themselves as they turned paper pages that enforced inactivity was a well-deserved rest.

On this Sunday morning Lorna did an hour's work on the list before setting out to Pepe's new colony. Finchley was a long way away but Lorna did not have the patience for the extra waiting time of Sunday bus schedules. She was also able to buy a bag of boiled sweets from a newsagent's shop on the way.

At the imposing but dilapidated detached house in Finchley, Lorna knocked on the door. She was surprised when Pepe opened it.

"*Mi madre inglesa*," Pepe smiled. "Come in. We are going to have cakes. You know why? It is my birthday."

"I know. Happy birthday," said Lorna, handing him the bag of sweets. She had seen his birthdate on the list that morning. Seeing Pepe in this different setting, there was an incongruity in the childish present. Now Pepe was fifteen and he hardly matched the description of 'child'. In the house's communal area the half dozen other Spanish boys were clearly younger, perhaps aged eight to twelve, or so it seemed to Lorna. They were bright-eyed, respectful and seemed to look up to Pepe as a hero in this house.

"Mrs Willett gave us cakes. She cooked them herself. Would you like one?"

Lorna picked a jam tart from the plate. She did not really want one, but there are times when appetite has to be feigned in the cause of sociability or even solidarity.

Pepe spoke to her quietly in English, though it was unlikely that his words would be understood by the children. In any event they had accepted Lorna's presence in their space, so they chattered loudly in Spanish.

"They do not know," he said.

She looked at him sharply. "What don't they know."

"About Bilbao. That it has fallen. That Franco's troops are on the streets."

He spoke without obvious emotion. Lorna's impression was that he was shielding the children from upset. The news might mean danger, perhaps death, for those closest to the children.

"I'm sorry, Pepe. It's all too grim. When will they be told?"

"Later, I've agreed with Juan that I will tell them."

Juan smiled weakly towards them. He was one of the small number of Spanish adults, mostly teachers, who had accompanied the children from Spain.

"I would like to go out," said Pepe. "Already here is making me feel jailed."

For an hour they wandered the humdrum streets of that

London suburb. Theirs was a conversation of equals, not tilted by differences in age or nationality or language. "You are a remarkable young man," Lorna did indeed remark.

"Why would anyone want to be anything different?"

"Perhaps to merge into strange surroundings," suggested Lorna. "It might be best to be noticed less."

"No. I think that would be strange. I want people to notice me. I am nervous if I am left alone."

"You really are a big bonce," laughed Lorna. For her, Pepe's egotism was something to smile at with admiration.

"Bonce? What's that?"

Lorna simply gestured with her hands on either side of her head, indicating size. By now they were walking in a park, with trees and grass and a gravel road. And also, Lorna now realised, gravestones. They had turned into the gates of a cemetery.

"I'm sorry. I hadn't noticed. We shouldn't be here," she said.

"Why not? It's peaceful. I like these places."

So they wandered through the Victorian monuments to the dead, mixed with the more modest stone farewells of more recent times. Around them the leaves of the trees were dark as if in mourning. They sat under one of these trees, on a wooden bench. A crow, ragged and black, waddled with dogged steps in search of worms or scraps, bobbing its head repeatedly to the grass between the graves. Then, spearing its meal from the soggy earth, it flew off into the trees.

Pepe's mood changed. At first he had seemed calmed by the funerary location but then he began to seem more agitated, sitting on the bench under lowering skies. Lorna remarked on his mood, and asked what was the matter?

"The war is the matter. Today fascist troops march through

Bilbao. They will round up people and shoot them. Perhaps my father."

Lorna tried, through questions, to encourage him to speak. The ease of their earlier conversation had not been disturbed by thoughts of war and death. Now those thoughts were inescapable.

Lorna put her hand on Pepe's in a gesture of comfort. He put his other hand to his mouth, to bite his nails. They sat like this for five, ten minutes, the time passed slowly, then Lorna said "We really ought to go".

After she had returned him to the colony in Finchley, Lorna continued walking to her flat. Her own thoughts took her mind off the physical tiredness she now felt. She had walked a number of miles. As she trudged this final stretch along the main road, she went over the conversation in her mind. She marvelled at Pepe, his mingling of childhood and manhood, crossing and recrossing the borders between the two. *But, in the end,* she told herself, as if to put an end to the matter, *he is just a child.*

CHAPTER 13

The next week was difficult. Lorna was busy at work but intended to visit Pepe one evening. She did not manage it so she had to be content with another Sunday visit. Sundays now came with the accent of Pepe, with a Spanish lilt and the gurgle of laughter and chatter and sometimes melancholy that walked alongside her in Pepe's presence.

The week turned into weeks and they were always difficult. Little good news came out of Spain but Lorna was content with the way things were going at work. She was getting on top of the Spanish work, finding a comfort in the compilation of lists, trying to keep track of the movements of the Basque children to different colonies around the country. A late period was irritating but her bigger cause for worry was the lack of news from Harry. He had disappeared into a deep silence, the kind of silence that Pepe hated and filled with his own words.

She thought of Harry often, though she tried to exclude him from her working day thoughts. Bryan startled her one day by asking "Any news of Harry?" She flushed with emotion and had to lock herself in the refuge of the lavatory. An uncomfortable wave of warmth swept into her face, and she sprinkled her face with water until she felt able to return to her desk.

She longed for Harry when she allowed herself, but kept these thoughts like sugar lumps to sweeten her mood. Often they had the opposite effect and Lorna, alone, could not hold back the tears. She wanted to see him again, to speak with him and touch his face; there had been so little time.

Politically it was hard to come to terms with impending defeat. She went to an evening meeting to hear the latest news from Spain. There was no reassurance in stories of prisoners murdered or starved to death in prison. While the stories stiffened her political will, they weighed down her heart with foreboding.

Despite this, Lorna felt that she was changing. She no longer felt embarrassed in meetings she attended, she put herself forward instead of hiding in the shadows at the back of a room. Confidence was growing in her own ability. Months earlier she might have felt a young girl, hardly more than a child inside. Now she was mature and able to hold her own in the loud social circle around Diana. She looked for signs to affirm such changes, a surprised glance, a word of praise, but she found she could draw unexpected lessons from simply observing her surroundings and drawing conclusions.

She watched the pigeons in Russell Square one summery evening as she took a leisurely stroll northwards towards home. She increasingly avoided this home that no longer felt like home, so she frequently delayed her journey by public transport. On the grass under the plane trees in the square she observed the pigeons, slobbish in their waddling walks yet elegant in their flying. It seemed to confirm that you could be seen differently at different times, while still being true to your own character. There was a comfort in that as she contemplated the next committee meeting. She imagined the other committee members as birds of various kinds, and it made them less intimidating to shrink them to the scale of a sparrow or even a robin, to see them preening in peacock feathers.

She sat quietly by herself, her thoughts idle, reluctant to

leave the green setting, even as the evening dusk drained away colour. It was strange that summer to feel the absence of gooseberries. It was an unusual taste of hers to enjoy gooseberries most when they were at their greenest and sourest. She had developed this taste as a child, picking the wild gooseberries that grew in a local wood near her family home in the Kentish suburbs of London. You had to be quick to catch them at the perfect moment, before they started to swell, ripen and sweeten. But that summer in London, despite a sudden craving, Lorna was unable to find the gooseberries on the fruit stalls during their fleeting appearance. She wandered down the covered alleys of Covent Garden market, peering through the grilles. She asked one elderly porter who was sweeping up at the end of his shift about green gooseberries.

"Sorry darlin', the green 'uns are done. Best try at one of the stalls."

At a stall, looking at the available gooseberries, plump and tinged with a sugary pink, Lorna's stomach felt queasy. She was one week late and that time could not be turned back. *One more regret*, she told herself with a hint of bitterness that even cheered her a little. But she bought half a pound, feeling embarrassed to have asked. The woman scooped gooseberries into a brown paper bag, but Lorna knew they would not do. "Make lovely jam," said the woman.

It was almost dark so Lorna eased herself away from the comfort of the warm gloom that was wrapping around her. She made her way back to her flat, ready for the next day and the day after, in a suspended state of waiting, waiting.

Then, miraculously it seemed, the longed-for unexpectedly happened. A letter arrived for her one afternoon at work, and inside the outer official envelope was a letter from Harry, written by hand in a neat script. She started to read but found herself short of breath. Having read enough for reassurance of his safety, she put the letter away, blowing her nose to restore professional appearances. But the relief flooded through her and made her giddy. She intended to read the letter later, to savour it, to read any meaning between the lines as well as the surface meaning that simply stated 'I am alive'.

Lorna recognised that words could be a secret code, they did not easily yield their full meaning. Even 'my darling Lorna' might hold layers of ambiguity if you looked at the words in the shifting light of another hour, an altered mood. Sometimes you needed to read cryptic clues but could you ever be sure that you understood the full meaning? The chances were that words could leave you uncertain of direction, whether to take the path left or right, whether simply to follow instinct. Who could you trust? Certainly no one else's interpretation, these were not trustworthy times. You had to trust your own instincts.

Lorna spent the day distracted by thinking about the letter without knowing exactly what it said. She had scanned the first lines but the emotion had threatened to overwhelm her and she was strict about the need for devotion to her work. She needed somewhere to read the letter where she would not be surprised by the inquisitive kindness of others. Home would not do, she did not feel at ease there any more, but it remained the place where she kept her belongings. She took advantage of Bryan's early exit to a meeting in Kensington to leave work half an hour early.

She raced home by tube and bus, reaching her flat in less than an hour. Her stay was short in her Bonfield Court flat, allowing her simply to drop her bag on the table and extract the envelope from it. She then made her way swiftly down the stairs and headed across Archway Road into Highgate Wood.

Lorna loved Highgate Wood and its near neighbour Queen's Wood. She would miss it if she moved but she was resigned to moving. Her previous visit to Highgate Wood a week ago had turned resignation into determination, because it had been there that she had thought the decision through. After being caught in a shower, sheltering beneath trees but getting soaked, she had made her way back to her flat. There the smell and the steam of her mackintosh drying in the warmth by the window had been evocative of other times, other times when she had been younger and happier.

Now she went through the gate into the dark trees of Highgate Wood, absorbed in her thoughts, not noticing the black clouds above the trees once again. She walked down paths whose earth had been trodden hard by walkers over many decades. This place was a refuge to her, reminding her of the suburban woods of her childhood, a place to think, to muse, to dream. A place to read Harry's letter with no one to observe her except a few pigeons that might here be named doves, a rare squirrel, birds that she could not identify by their song. She saw magpies on the fringe of the field, scavenging for whatever caught their eyes, those eyes flicking from left to right, right to left, on the lookout for discovery or danger.

Deeper into the woods, Lorna sat on a bench that offered remoteness and privacy. It was a bench with ironwork supports at either end, making bookends for the wooden slats on which she sat. The metal was cool to her touch, making her aware of the clamminess of her palms, brought on by humidity and anxiety. She delayed no longer, unfolding Harry's letter to read it in the green light of the woods.

My darling Lorna

You find me back in Hendaye. It seems I cannot avoid the place as it is the last stop on the train line before Spain. I am nearly back at the country where I must go in the company of some new comrades met in Paris.

I miss you. I wish I could be with you. I would love to touch your hair to see how it is growing. You said you would grow it. Please do, I know it will suit you.

I cannot write anything of what will happen next and I have no idea when I will be able to write again. It's not the writing that's hard it's the sending. I am sending this thanks to my 'friend' Stevenson at the embassy here in Hendaye. He's the one that took me out of Gernika. He has been in Bilbao recently and only just got out safe.

I must tell you about the meeting I had here. I called at the house where the embassy is based, I was curious to see what they might say. Anyway, Stevenson was friendly enough in his civil service way. He asked me to meet the ambassador Sir Henry Chilton. I had never met a Sir Anyone before.

Chilton was a cold fish but Stevenson has some humanity even if his job does not allow him to show it at times.

"What are you planning here, Mr James?" Chilton asked me.

"I'm meeting some friends."

"I hope you do not plan to go to Spain. It is not our war, you know."

"How can you say that after Gernika?"

"We do not have the full account of it yet."

"You do. I saw it. I saw the bombs and what they did to the people. He saw it (me pointing at Stevenson). He brought you back the bombs, you must have seen the German markings. He saw the fires still burning after the bombing."

"Our Nationalist sources tell us the fires were set by the

Republicans as they pulled out."

"I saw the German bombers. Their bombs lit the fires."

"None of this is conclusive."

I was hopping mad but I had to stay calm. We stared at each other in silence, then he asked: "Do you have a passport? I could confiscate it."

"What would that achieve? You would only stop me getting into England."

Chilton pressed the fingers of his hands together in front of his face, looking at me over the tips. I was determined not to blink. I did not. I will not. The meeting just stiffened my resolve.

Stevenson showed me out. It turns out he is the consul so high ranking. He urged me to be careful. I explained that I wanted to write and send you a letter. I called you my sweetheart and I hope you don't mind. It softened him and he agreed, so later in the day I gave him this letter, sealed by my own tongue, which I hope you have been reading. I wish I could have a letter from you but I do not know how it would reach me when I do not know myself where I will be.

Someday, someday soon. The lips on this letter will meet yours again. I hope this letter reaches you and finds you well.

Your sweetheart

Harry

Lorna read it through, then read it again. There was so much both to lift and depress the spirits, and she did not know what to feel. She was glad to have the letter; it was a sign that their relationship was real. She could build hopes upon its reality, but she knew those hopes could be dashed in an instant. Her overwhelming feeling was exhaustion. The rush of so many conflicting emotions made for a hard struggle inside her head. And now she was suddenly and totally drained.

In normal times that bench would not be a place to contemplate sleeping, but now her eyelids closed and she fell into a deep slumber without realising what was happening. Sitting upright on the bench, letter folded into her fingers' grasp, she slept and dreamt. Her dream was vivid and disturbing, filled with falling buildings, explosions and people running with a ringing of boots on stone. The dream was short but intense and she woke from it with a sense of fear and panic.

Although now awake, the loud crashing noises continued. The thunderstorm had been building through the afternoon, and now it had arrived. Flashes of lightning slashed through the canopy of branches and leaves overhead. Seconds later thunder cracked like a fracture inside her head, and she held her ears in pain. Heavy drops of rain like lead pellets pierced through the leaves onto her as she sat on the bench, and her first thought was to slip the letter into her handbag to protect it from what seemed an assault. But then she realised she had come out without her bag, she had left it on the kitchen table. All she could do was slip the letter inside her frock, hoping that the rain would not seep through.

She stood up and started walking, then running towards the exit gates. By the time she reached them the rain was slowing, though it was still dripping steadily from the trees. Looking out into the Archway Road, she saw the sun light the scene as if a match had been struck. Sunshine always seems brighter after a storm, especially in that first moment of relief when it squeezes through the dark clouds scurrying away.

After the downpour, the pavements glistened. Thunder still rumbled in the distance but here the storm had passed. As the presence of the sun increasingly made itself felt behind the clouds, the mirror of the wet paving stones shone even brighter. Soon, looking along the hill as cars splashed through the surface water, the sky and the earth seemed to fuse together, wearing a relieved smile. Lorna's step lightened too. Without daring to hope, happiness might be within reach.

That feeling shrank back, as did the sun behind the clouds, when she turned into the road where she lived. The shadow of that dawn visit remained over the flat that she could not call home, casting its ominous cloud over her state of mind.

She let herself in with the key that she carried in the pocket of her frock. There was still a relief in being inside, in the dry. She reached inside her neckline where Harry's letter had stuck itself to her skin and she laid the damp letter on a towel she brought from the bathroom. The letter had many smudges but she could still read it. She kissed it softly and put it back on the towel, separating the pages so they could dry naturally.

Relief was welcome but it was soon replaced by a sense that something was not right. Something had changed, here inside the flat. She looked around, and she walked the few steps that were possible from the areas for sleeping, cooking and eating. Everything looked the same but intuition told her that there was a difference, a presence or perhaps an absence.

She looked at her handbag on the kitchen table. Had she left it standing upright? Her compact was inside, the lipstick she had bought earlier in the week, a handkerchief,, her purse. But there was no sign of the envelope she had brought from work with the list of the Spanish children. Lorna imagined a man in a trilby hat striding down the hill towards Highgate underground station.

CHAPTER 14

Lorna did not know what to tell Bryan but she knew she had to confess about the missing list. Even the word 'confess', the word she used to herself, implied a sense of guilt. But what could she have done to prevent the theft? She had been burgled, her own privacy had been breached as well as that of the children. *Keep it to that,* she decided. *No word about Harry.*

Bryan took the news calmly enough. In his eyes this was an occupational hazard, and Lorna had to try hard not to show her personal distress. This meant that she poured all her anger and fears into the children's plight.

"Do we have a copy of the lost list?" Bryan asked.

"One that's nearly up to date – just a few new changes to add," said Lorna.

"There we are then. We need not worry."

"But I do worry. They have details of the children and their parents. It's dangerous for the children's families in Spain."

"Who do you think 'they' are? If this is a Special Branch job, which it must be, they'll keep the information for themselves. Those people don't like sharing with anyone."

"If our government has the list, they might pass it on to Franco's side."

"No, I don't think so. They're not in league with them."

"I'm not so sure. There's a lot of information sharing going on. I know that."

"Really? How do you know? Ah," he looked at her with a quizzical face, "I don't suppose Harry has been in touch? Or some of his Party friends?"

"No, of course not. Anyway, what if it wasn't Special

Branch? What if it was a Spanish agent?"

"Lorna," a stare. "Lorna. Too many books. Though I would not have thought Mr Buchan was quite so much to your taste."

"How can you be so smug?"

"Lorna, you must think more like a lawyer. That is now your training. What evidence do we have that Franco has spies walking our streets? There is none, probably because there are none. All his resources are tied up in Spain, where the likes of your Harry are keeping him occupied."

Lorna realised this was an argument she was losing. Bryan had made up his mind, and in this situation he was the judge. He had decided that the theft of the list – or even its accidental loss, as he had implied – were of little importance. The thought occurred to Lorna that German or Italian agents could be at work in London, and the list might be even more dangerous in their hands. They had shown their ruthlessness in Guernica and Bilbao. She kept the thought to herself, knowing that she would feel even less secure in her flat.

"Harry," said Bryan, as if stating a legal precedent. "Seriously, have you heard from him? I heard that you might have."

Lorna could not help lowering her eyes. She felt that her face was pinkening. She forced herself to look Bryan in the eyes.

"I had a letter. He is about to cross back into Spain."

"Then I hope he looks after himself. And I wish him a safe return. Diana showed me his account of the Guernica bombing. Dreadful. We have reason to hate the fascists, wherever they are, there or here."

"There is conclusive evidence, do you not think?"

"Without doubt. Though our government of appeasement

is prepared to turn a blind eye to any amount of wrongdoing. As long as it means they can carry on doing nothing."

"Can Harry's account be published? I thought Diana would help with that. Did she ask you?"

"It's background information for the newspapers, no longer news apparently. *The Chronicle* will draw on it when they have a story about Spain. Parts of it cannot be published because it will get a D-Notice. The best route might be a private press, a pamphlet, say. Or a Chapter in an anthology once the war is over."

Lorna was upset, particularly on Harry's behalf. He wanted the facts to be more widely known. "Then there's not much to be done," she said, her voice catching in her throat.

"There is much to be done, Lorna. There is much more coming, I fear, and these are just the early days of our troubles. Spain is simply a dress rehearsal, as I'm sure Harry knows. We have to do what we can in the ways we best can. In your case, and in my case, that will not mean taking up arms."

I would, thought Lorna. There was a sudden surprise in realising that she had moved from a pacifist position to her current thinking in no more than three months. But events were forcing her to change. She felt that she now had firmer principles that she could trust, perhaps trust more than people, and she could be guided by their certainty. It was a small consolation too that she had not retreated to the comfort of making a pot of tea to share. At least, not till now, when she found herself gasping.

"Yes, please," said Bryan.

CHAPTER 15

Lorna made up her mind to write to Harry. She had no hope that a letter would reach him – where could she send it? – but she felt the need to write. One evening after most people had left the office, she sat at one of the large legal desks made of dark polished wood, furnished with a blotting paper pad. She unscrewed the top of her fountain pen and made sure there was ink in the china well, then laid some sheets of the firm's stationery in front of her. Deciding that this might not be right, that it might be incriminating in some way she could not specify, she fetched some sheets of plain typing paper. *At least I can practise on these*, she thought. She gazed at the blotting paper, thinking that she might need it to dry not just the ink but her own feelings, suspecting that she would gush too freely.

But the words would not gush. She found it hard even to get beyond the salutation. To reciprocate Harry's opening should be natural but it seemed too big a step to put 'Darling Harry' into ink on paper. She retreated to 'Dear Harry', mistrusting the abandon of 'darling'. She could not quite trust herself to keep her emotions level otherwise. Her letter-writing was still influenced by her father's formal style as well as by the daily practice of legal letters, so it seemed impossible to relax into words that she might not even have felt free to say in person.

'Thank you for your letter' was an easy enough start, but how should she continue? She wrote 'I love you and miss you very much' but it seemed a breathless plunge into the middle of things. How could she lead towards it less abruptly, without seeming (in her eyes as well as his) a giddy young thing. 'Work has been very busy and interesting' she wrote, then imagined him sitting with his back against a hillside boulder, sheltering from winds or bullets or the ribaldry of his companions.

'I have adopted a Spanish boy called Pepe. He is fifteen and was evacuated from Bilbao. Every time I meet him I think of you because he stands for the cause you are fighting.' Perhaps there was something in that but it sounded to her too close to a political speech she might hear. Although politics had brought them together, a different attraction had followed. 'I wish I could see you. I long to see you again and I fear that you might not return. You must. You will never leave my thoughts, no matter what.'

She signed off 'All my love, Lorna xxx' and agonised over that too. Reading through what she had written she knew she could never send it. It felt incoherent, a jumble of thoughts that did not say what she wanted them to say. What she wanted to say might have been deeper than her scrawled and scratched-out words could convey. She turned her words and pressed them into the blotting paper, which seemed to reinforce the feeling that these words were just the surface of her emotions.

Even so, she worried that the words 'love' and 'Lorna' could be deciphered on the blotting pad. She had no wish to be spied on at work, so she applied a blob of ink to the words, obliterating them on the blotting paper. The resulting spot of ink embarrassed her like a pimple on her face, but there was nothing she could do to make it look better.

"Are you all right, Lorna?" asked Trevor, one of the partners, who put his head around the door. "Working late?"

"Yes. Is it that time already?"

"I'm afraid so. I was just about to lock up."

Lorna put the letter into her handbag, not knowing what she might do with it. Outside, the Strand was busy with strolling couples on a warm, summer evening, with light fading from the sky as the theatre lights glowed brighter in the dusk. *Home and Beauty*, she read in neon. *One day, with Harry, that will be good.* But for now she made her way to the uncertain refuge of her flat in Highgate.

Some days later, on the Saturday, she had arranged to meet Pepe. It was a sign of his increasing integration that they had agreed to meet at Holborn tube station so that they could walk around places that Lorna knew well in the centre. Saturday had less of the frantic bustle of a weekday, and Lorna felt it would show London in a better light than a disconcertingly quiet Sunday.

Lorna was beginning to understand Pepe better, and to understand his complexities. She was starting to realise, despite his youth, the depth of his independence and the strength of his will. Of course, she had few points of comparison as a single child with no siblings, as a young woman with no children, and she had to make allowances for differences that came from his own culture. Pepe, it seemed to her, was a resister. Not just politically but socially. He resisted silence which meant that he was talkative, giving the impression of sociability. But he resisted other people entering or trying to enter his life. Which gave Lorna a challenge, even if it was one she could relate to herself.

Having met at the tube exit, they walked along High Holborn before turning into Drury Lane. Pepe complimented Lorna on the red beret she wore. Shops and stalls were open, mainly selling food. Pepe was fascinated by the eels in a stone bath wriggling and squirming beneath the swinging fan that circulated fresh air. Mostly there were fruit and vegetable stalls stocked with fresh produce from Covent Garden market.

"Colours," said Pepe. "At least London gets colour from this fruit."

"Did you think our fruit would be grey?"

"I did. At least a little bit."

Slightly offended on behalf of the city she now loved, Lorna bought Pepe an orange. He held it in his hands, marvelling at its brightness, sniffing at its zest.

"The best oranges are from Sevilla," Pepe stated.

"Why do you think that?"

"I was born there. There is where I first went to school."

At Lorna's urging, Pepe peeled the orange and broke it off a segment at a time. Lorna declined his offer to eat a piece, not because she did not like oranges but she preferred it to be enjoyed by Pepe. She fancied something sweeter, which was unusual for her, and all the fruits promised too much sharpness.

Walking through a courtyard – "these are lawyers' offices" Lorna pointed out – they passed a pub. Pepe spotted its sign with the sun painted on it. The prospect of a real English pub excited him but Lorna explained that he was not old enough to be served with a drink.

"Would you like a lemonade?"

Lorna asked Pepe to sit on the step while she went inside to buy the drinks.

"Can I try it?" Pepe asked, pointing at Lorna's glass of Guinness.

"As long as no one sees you."

Pepe made a face at the bitterness of the drink.

"That's good, you won't want any more. Guinness is good for you – for me anyway. How's the lemonade?"

Lorna was aware that Pepe's mood had changed again.

He had started out excited and bubbling with curiosity but it had slowly drained out of him. She asked him if anything was wrong. At first he shook his head, but Lorna allowed the silence to swell, filling the air between them. *Like a balloon, it will burst*, she told herself, and concentrated on her drink.

Before long Pepe began talking about his worries for his parents in Spain. He had received a letter from his father, which had been reassuring in that he knew his parents were alive. But he knew that all was not well by the lack of real news. They hardly mentioned the situation in Bilbao, confining themselves to small talk when Pepe wanted hard information. What damage had been done to places that he knew? What was it like to live in their city occupied by Franco's troops? Pepe was ready to read and to be outraged by the situation, but everything written was anodyne.

"They probably fear that their letter will be intercepted and read," said Lorna.

"I know that," Pepe replied, a little sharply.

The worst thing, he said, was a part of the letter where his parents talked about his grandmother. "It is quite crowded in our house. If you come back you might have to live with your grandmother. This is what they wrote to me."

"Oh dear, would that be difficult?" asked Lorna.

Pepe snorted, as if to say 'you should know'.

"Of course it would be difficult. Both my grandmothers are long dead, they are in graves. They are telling me, if I go back, I will get killed."

Lorna hated the way that sometimes she was made to seem naïve. It was one of her fears at work, in the presence of lawyers. Now it was even worse in the company of a 15 year-old boy. Her response was to be practical and defiant.

"Well, we will not let you be sent back. I will raise this in work next week and with the committee."

Even as she said this, Lorna was thinking that it would not be easy. When the Spanish children had arrived, the expectation had been for a three-month stay. That had never been realistic but even the committee had talked about three months as the likely duration, as a way of defusing criticism. "Only three months." Many of the children had the hope for a short stay because they wanted to be reunited with their parents. In Parliament, in government, there was pressure to abide by this timescale. The new prime minister Chamberlain was keen not to anger the fascist dictators in his desperate hope for peace. Members of the Conservative Party who had argued against the coming of the children were now arguing even more vociferously for their return.

Pepe was not appeased by Lorna's reassurance. He knew that it was hollow. Between them, on the pub doorstep, their glasses were half-empty. A heavy feeling of unease hung between them. Pepe was biting his nails, a distracted look on his face. "Don't, Pepe," pleaded Lorna. "Don't bite your nails, it makes you look nervous."

"But I am nervous."

"There's no need. We will sort it out."

"Everyone is nervous, it is life."

"Well, you don't have to show it. It's better not to seem nervous."

"That is pretending. That is being an actor."

"We all have to pretend. That's life too."

It was time to move on. Not because they had things to do but because they had things to avoid. Lorna did not, at that moment, feel equipped to provide what might come close

to spiritual solace. She could not take confession, she could
not bear the cross of Pepe's anxiety about life when she was
struggling to deal with her own anxiety. A thought of Harry
passed like a cloud across the sun as Lorna returned the empty
glasses to the bar.

They carried on walking, heading towards Aldwych down
Drury Lane. Lorna crossed the road because she saw a sweet
shop. Despite all the evidence, she clung to the notion that
Pepe was still a child and this view was reinforced when she
saw him at the sweet shop window. She observed his mood
shifting, growing lighter as he gazed longingly at the jars with
their boiled sweets of many colours. But it was the cloudy
whiteness of the acid drops that took his fancy, icy-coloured
inside the clear glass of the tall jar, like frost on a window.

"Grey fruits," smiled Lorna.

Inside the shop, Pepe studied the shopkeeper as he took
the jar down from the shelf, unscrewed its top and tipped out
the sweets until the scales reached the measured quarter. He
put them in a paper bag that he handed over to Pepe: "Here
you are, young man."

A sense of contentment was restored. The outing had
teetered on the brink of disaster but they had each pulled
back. Over tea and cake in a café, as Lorna spooned sugar into
her cup, Pepe mentioned his friend Angel. He explained that
Angel's parents now lived in a refugee camp in France. His
parents had sent for him as they now felt safer and relatively
settled, so Angel would be leaving England in a week's time,
catching a train from Victoria.

"Well, let's see him off. If you wish," said Lorna.

"I wish."

Feeling protective after the emotional turbulence of the

afternoon, Lorna took Pepe back to his colony house. She wanted to bring the day to a calm close, so she did not risk going inside the house in case that opened fresh difficulties. They smiled to each other as they parted on the doorstep.

"*Hasta luego*," said Pepe, re-entering his Spanish world.

CHAPTER 16

The next week passed with no further news of Harry. There was no real reason to expect any, but receiving his letter had raised Lorna's hopes. It seemed that everything she did revolved around Spain and this inevitably made her more aware of the dangers that Harry faced. There was no way of cutting herself off from these nudges of constant involvement and the fears that resulted. Her whole life now was political.

One evening she went to a meeting addressed by Jimmy Maxton. His rhetoric was stirring and she wondered what more she could do to show her support. She found herself arguing with Labour Party friends who accompanied her to the meeting. She found their approach too cautious.

But at work she had to be cautious, she had to adopt the persona of a lawyer, with a first reaction of reason and objectivity. At times she forced herself to smile when she wanted to scream. One day she attended a committee meeting at the House of Lords. The Duchess chaired it, reporting that parliamentary opinion was fluid. Appeasement was being questioned within the ranks of the governing party under its new leader Neville Chamberlain. "Winston in that way of his said that in time to come history would show that we were right." Lorna could not find it comforting to know that people who needed to act were still prepared to turn a blind eye.

"I agree with you, my dear," said Diana after the committee meeting, "particularly about the injustice and stupidity of the non-intervention pact. But we need to think how best we can change influential minds. We cannot do it by shouting protests and clenching fists."

It was a relief when the weekend came. Lorna looked forward to seeing Pepe again. This time he would have his friend Angel with him, and they had arranged to meet at Holborn again. Lorna wanted to take them to a photographer's studio in the Strand. She felt the need to record that these boys had been in her life, especially if they were to move on, as Angel was going to do, as Pepe might be planning to do.

She had not met Angel before. There was a foreignness about his appearance that surprised her. Pepe could almost pass as an English boy, particularly as he spoke English so well, and he dressed in clothes that allowed him to be one of the crowd – long gabardine trousers, black in colour, a white open-necked shirt, brown leather shoes. Angel was different; he looked exotic. He was younger than Pepe, twelve years old, but he was dressed for a special occasion. Obviously it was a special occasion because he was leaving the country and facing the prospect of being reunited with his parents at the camp in France. Perhaps Angel needed to wear these clothes, no doubt his best, to prevent them being spoilt from cramming into his cardboard suitcase. He looked incongruous in his light grey suit, with the high-lapelled jacket and trousers designed to reach down only to his knees where they met the tops of his woollen socks. The bright yellow cravat at his neck struck Lorna as the strangest item in this outfit, with its matching handkerchief peeking out from the breast pocket. And to top it all, his hair rose like a tidal wave above his forehead, carefully combed and gleaming, held in place by an overdose of brilliantine.

"This is Angel. He is ready to travel as you can see."

"I am pleased to meet you, Angel," said Lorna, holding her hand out for shaking.

"Hello. Very much," he replied.

Pepe explained that Angel did not speak much English, and that he would translate anything that needed to be said by Angel. Lorna presumed that the words he now spoke in Spanish were conveying the same message to Angel.

"A suitcase," said Lorna. "I should have thought. We cannot walk too far."

"It is all right," said Pepe. "See, I can help. When Angel needs a rest I carry," and he seized the suitcase, lifting it up to shoulder level. "It is not heavy. He does not have much."

Lorna explained that she intended taking them to have their photos taken. They would get a bus to the Strand. She checked the details of Angel's train – to Newhaven to catch the boat to Dieppe. They would have to arrive at Victoria in two hours.

Sitting on the bus as it wheezed its way down Kingsway, Pepe and Angel chattered in Spanish. Lorna asked what they were talking about.

"He says you look very beautiful. He likes your hat. He thinks you are very kind too."

Lorna blushed, caught off guard. She looked at Angel who was now looking out the window of the bus as it turned left into Aldwych, apparently without a thought for or about Lorna. Pepe returned her gaze with a smile, leaving Lorna to wonder how accurate his translation was.

"This is our stop," she dinged the bell and stood up. Pepe shook Angel's shoulder, and they all stepped down off the bus onto the pavement.

The photographer's studio had a shop window with individual and family portraits on display. Pepe and Angel giggled at the photographs for reasons Lorna did not quite understand. Telling them to behave, Lorna pushed open the door causing a bell to ring cheerily to announce their arrival.

The man in the shop was less cheery than the bell. Middle-aged and bald, with a thin cigarette hanging from his lip below an even thinner moustache, he exuded an air of reluctance. But Lorna was committed; she had decided that she wanted photographs and would not be deterred by his lack of enthusiasm or her excess of embarrassment. The two boys might not be convinced of this activity but Lorna had convinced herself.

"It's through here then," pointed the photographer, when the terms had been settled at the front counter. He pushed aside a black curtain, showing them into the rear of the shop where there was a raised platform, on which was a small table holding a vase of flowers, and arc lights pointing inwards.

"We can do different backdrops – hills, trees, waves in the sea, for example. Keep the flowers or move them. Depends what you had in mind."

Pepe laughed and set Angel off laughing. They found it hard to believe in a painted English landscape as the background to their lives.

"A plain background would be best," said Lorna quickly.

"As you wish, miss. Who will go first?"

Pepe stepped onto the dais. The photographer stood behind his camera on a tripod, directing Pepe to take his position, then he came forward to place him in a three-quarter pose.

"That's better. Now look at the camera, try to keep still. Ready?"

There was a loud pop and a flash of white light. This was repeated for Angel on the dais, then for the two boys standing together. They raised their right fists in a salute towards Lorna, which brought on a big smile from them both.

"Not sure about that one," said the photographer. "You want me to try again without the fist-shaking?"

"Oh no," said Lorna. "That was good. I liked that. We liked that, didn't we?"

Pepe and Angel were animated now. They seemed to be enjoying the chance to act a little, pulling faces for the camera that was now without its operator.

"Can we do another?" asked Pepe.

The photographer looked at Lorna. "It will cost. Extra, I mean."

"Then no. Come on boys, that's it."

"Can we see the pictures?"

Lorna explained that they needed to be developed, and that she would collect them another day.

"But what about Angel?" asked Pepe. "He won't see his picture."

"We'll just have to send it to him in France. I'm sure his parents would like to see his photograph from England. I'll post it to them."

Back in the reception area, Lorna filled in the form with her details and counted out coins carefully. She looked at the clock on the wall, realising that they would now have to head quickly to catch the train.

"But we must get you something to eat. Best get to Victoria first."

The Circle Line took them there fast, clanking through the tunnels. Back on the surface, they dived into a café and ate pies. In the station hall they met Manuela, the maestra who was accompanying Angel on his journey to France. They checked in with tickets and documents. They had their luggage searched. It had all been more of a rush than Lorna would have wished, but now she and Pepe stood by themselves on the platform while Angel peered out of the train window, waving with a mournful look on his face. Pepe got him to lower the window so that he could give Angel his last instructions in Spanish.

"It's all right, Pepe. Manuela knows what to do." Lorna pulled Pepe's shirt sleeve, tugging him back from the train as it whistled and started to ease forward. They stood waving beneath the glass roof of the station shed, a cameo of sad partings, like a scene from a film that would leave them searching for handkerchiefs to wipe away tears and regrets and the sharper pang of conscience.

Lorna felt Pepe's sorrow. It was like her own. She put her arm around his shoulder.

"He'll be OK, Pepe. In France, he'll be with his mother and father."

Consolation was no consolation. Tears were streaming down Pepe's cheeks. Instinctively he turned in towards Lorna's embrace and they stood facing each other, Pepe's forehead on Lorna's shoulder. For the first time Lorna realised that Pepe was now taller than she was – he was daily growing, shooting up even in the two months since their first meeting.

"Move aside there," shouted a porter. "There's people tryin' to do a job."

They made their way out of the station, with buses, taxis and cars criss-crossing on the streets around them. People hurried between, crossing the road through the traffic. Ahead of them stretched Victoria Street. A dingy café opposite seemed like a refuge from their emotions.

Over a cup of tea, into which he shovelled so much sugar

that Lorna wondered if his spoon might stand upright, Pepe started to talk. He had been unusually silent, his tears washing away the need for words.

"I am not sure if I will ever see my parents again."

"You will, Pepe, you will."

Pepe talked about the war. He was well-informed; it seemed he had been getting news from English newspapers and from visitors to the colony. He had few hopes remaining for victory. Lorna did not know what to say. She hoped that the war could still be won, all her political convictions were invested in that hope. No doubt it was bound up with the thought that victory would be the best chance of Harry's safe return. But…she felt with a piercing certainty that the obstacles to victory were piling higher with each passing day, with each new battle, with each defeat leading to further retreat.

When Pepe announced that he wanted to walk by himself and find his own way home, Lorna felt a little hurt. Had she been such an inadequate comforter? Pepe saw disappointment on her face and explained that he needed time alone. It was not because he did not like being with Lorna. He suggested that they meet again in a week, then got up from the chair saying "Sorry". He shot out of the café.

Lorna followed as quickly as she could but by the time she went through the door onto the pavement Pepe was disappearing into the distant crowd. She would need to walk fast to keep him in sight. Lorna felt uncomfortable about it but also felt it was her responsibility to follow him. She kept a discreet distance, some forty yards, behind him. She wondered where he might be headed in his quest to be by himself.

There was a throng of people walking in both directions along Victoria Street, and Pepe was moving faster than the rest of the crowd. Lorna hardly noticed the buildings and shops as she strode after him, keeping him in sight. He looked purposeful, as if he knew exactly where he was making for. But where was it? This was not an area of London that Lorna knew well.

Pepe took a sharp turn to the right and Lorna slowed slightly, just in case he had stopped around the corner. When she reached that point, she did not spot Pepe at first. She saw the red brick stripes of Westminster Cathedral looming before her, then Pepe going through the tall wooden entrance doors.

Feeling shifty, uneasy in her role of spy, Lorna slid inside, pausing to allow her eyes time to adjust to the relative darkness. She gazed down the aisle, seeing no one. To either side high windows allowed shafts of light through to the interior, casting patches of colour onto pews and stonework. The cathedral had few worshippers inside. There was no mass and no priest leading prayers, just a few individuals in isolated pockets of their own meditation, with heads bowed and knees bent. Despite herself, despite her own resistance to churchgoing and Catholicism in particular, Lorna felt moved by the solemnity of the place, its great echoing silence. She walked slowly and reverently between the marble pillars and the side chapels, aware of the ringing of her shoe heels on the floor tiles.

Pepe was unaware of her presence, even though she suddenly found herself standing almost within touching distance. She quietly stepped back, retreating into the shadows under an arch. From here she was able to observe Pepe kneeling, holding a thin white candle in his hand. The candle flame flickered in the slight breeze from an open side door. Pepe's head was deeply bowed in prayer.

Lorna felt that she had intruded enough on his privacy. She did not understand, perhaps would never understand, such an expression of faith. She knew, though, that she needed to respect it. It was not clear to her who or what the candle was for. Was it a prayer for his own family? Or for Angel's safety? She did not know but it was certainly an act of faith, and that was something she had not so far taken enough into account. She needed to allow Pepe his space and time to believe, recognising that their beliefs might not be shared.

She backed out, slipping quietly through the doorway into the summer afternoon daylight that now seemed painfully bright.

CHAPTER 17

Lorna didn't know why she felt bad that Monday. She had no particular dread of Mondays normally, no heart sinking at the weight of work in prospect. But she felt anxious lying in bed and, when she got up, she rushed to the toilet and was sick.

She sat at the kitchen table in the early morning half-light, willing herself to feel better. Her brow was cold and clammy, and she shivered at the morning breeze coming from the opened window, shivered at other life-changing possibilities that opened in her mind. She had no wish to miss work and started to feel better after ten minutes of sitting still. Pulling the curtains, she allowed sunlight and optimism to enter the room. *All will be well.* Cold water in the basin, brought to her face in cupped hands, cleared her head at least enough to get herself ready for work.

Outside she was relieved to feel a freshness in the August air. Summer had passed its carefree best and the trees were already showing the first signs of autumn's coming. The days were noticeably shorter than at midsummer. Yellow and brown leaves had drifted down from the woods near the bus stop, settling singly on the pavement and presaging the swept-together heaps of autumn. It made her feel a little sad, as the changing of the seasons sometimes did, a reminder that time and life were slipping past.

The lateness of her periods could no longer be ignored. If she were pregnant, what would this mean to her life? She shuddered, unwilling to face the consequences. Single parenthood. An exciting career aborted. The sheer embarrassment. *What will I say to mum and dad?* It made for an uneasy journey to work but once there she was relieved to immerse herself in work. After work, she told herself, she would face the situation and decide what to do. But for now there was a comfort in the familiarity of her surroundings and her growing absorption in the work she did. It was still something of a novelty, and a source of pride and wonder, that she was writing letters to government departments on behalf of others who depended on the effectiveness of her words. That day she made herself even busier than usual, choosing to work through her lunchtime, with just the clatter of her typewriter keyboard for company.

Later in the afternoon, Bryan asked her into his office. She noticed the teapot and two cups standing ready. Bryan motioned her to sit down.

"This is difficult, Lorna. I would rather not be the bearer of this bad news."

His pauses were making it difficult for Lorna. She stared at Bryan, trying to read his face, and he returned her gaze. She knew what he was about to say.

"I just heard that Harry has been killed. We have no body and no grave but we are certain that this is true. His troop was ambushed by Nationalist forces and only one man managed to get out of it alive. That man, a reliable source, has provided this information."

Lorna's face was blank. Inside her emotions were churning, struggling to cope with the information, believing it and not wanting to believe it. The image of Harry came into her mind, she saw him, conjured him up to be with her, his smile, a sideways look. But this would now be as close as she would ever be to him again.

"I'm sorry, Lorna. It's a terrible turn-up. Nevertheless we have to accept it."

Bryan was uncomfortable when the words went beyond the facts. He willed Lorna to say something but she sat there absolutely numb. He poured the tea and moved a cup closer to where Lorna was sitting, the spoon rattling against the saucer as his trembling hand placed the tea on the edge of the desk. The glistening of tears were forming in her eyes, the beginnings of grief that pierced through the deadness of shock. But anger was rising too, it was anger that threatened to burst.

Nevertheless. The word angered her, a lawyer's word, a word meant to reduce emotion, to weigh an argument in the balance when no balance could be found. *Nevertheless. Neverthemore. Never more.* Lorna wanted more but she had no rational sense at that moment what she wanted more of. Harry. Never again. She wanted Harry, she wanted the news retracted, disowned, sworn out of existence. She could not accept, nevertheless, despite any urgings, she could not face a future in which Harry would play no part, in which he would be no more than a memory. In which his seed might still grow without him, to produce a life that he would never see. *Why, nevertheless, was life so utterly cruel?*

She cried at last. The tears of grief, anger and pain burst out of her and her body shook with the convulsions of these swirling emotions. For the first time she thought of the foetus inside hers that was now the most real reminder of the man she had too briefly loved. It made her cling even tighter to his memory and, in doing so, sob even harder. She felt Bryan's arm placed hesitantly around her shoulder. Her sobs made her lean into him but she could sense his discomfort.

"I'm sorry," she whispered, as if to herself, but Bryan was close enough to hear.

"No reason for you to be sorry. War is to blame. This stupid war."

She was not ready for Harry's life, or his death, to have a label of stupidity attached to it. She felt like defending him, every thought and every action he had taken on his journey to the Spanish war; every act he had taken to fight for others, for his beliefs, his ideals. Surely that was good and beyond any hint of reproach?

"Do you know any more?" Lorna asked. Perhaps information would provide some kind of balm after all.

"Not yet. I'm sure he died a brave death."

"Of course. It was brave just to be there, to do something."

"We all try to do something. And we all must keep trying. But that is a hard thought at this moment."

Lorna's handkerchief was soaked through with her tears. Bryan handed her a big handkerchief from his desk drawer, and she blew her nose.

"I must look terrible," said Lorna.

"Not at all. Perhaps we should get you home? I'll ask Edna to take you in a cab."

"It's all right, I'll be fine. I'll make my own way home. I'd rather be alone." Lorna wanted solitude, she could not face the possibility of judgement that she felt would come from the company of anyone else. Edna was not one of her friends, they hardly spoke except on work matters, but there was no one else that she would entrust with her raw grief either. It would be best to deal with this by herself.

"Go home and you must not think about coming in to work until you feel able to. There is no rush, we can manage things around your absence. And of course we can get in touch with each other. If there is anything we can do – anything – just ask."

Kindness is apt to set off tears of gratitude. Fellow feeling, signs of common humanity, connect us through shared tears. To her embarrassment, and even more to Bryan's, she noticed that there was now a watery brightness in his eyes that he was struggling to suppress. He insisted on pressing two half crowns into her hand for a taxi.

"We must be brave, as Harry was. And we must go on. But these things take time, so take your time, Lorna. We will see you again only when you are ready. And I will be in touch with any further news."

She tidied her desk and swept up any belongings she could into her handbag. That afternoon she wore her red beret with an air of defiance despite the feeling that she was scuttling out of the office. The busy pavements in the Strand seemed surreal as she walked along in her solitary bubble. Finding herself next to an empty taxi at traffic lights, she got inside and took the long ride back to Highgate, with an anxious eye on the meter as it ticked over and a protective hand on her stomach as the cab went over bumps in the road.

Days later she would look back and wonder what she did during the rest of that day. She could not recall arriving home. She had no recollection of any of her actions, simply the memory of going to bed and crying into the sheet that she pulled over her head. She wept and carried on weeping, tears for Harry and tears for herself. Her tears flowed in streams of loneliness and anger into the pillow and into the fitful sleep that brought little relief until the first rays of the sun slanted through the inadequate curtains the next morning.

Lorna was inclined to stay in bed. There seemed little reason to get up. But a piercing pain in her stomach persuaded her otherwise. She turned to her side, doubled up, crawled in agony to the toilet, feeling a dampness between her thighs.

Sitting on the toilet she dabbed between her legs and saw the redness of blood on the toilet paper. The sight made her take a quick breath. A day earlier the prospect of a miscarriage might have been welcome, a solution to an unwanted problem. Now she desperately wanted to keep this child inside her. It was Harry's and it was hers; it might be the only tangible evidence of their relationship, when memories and the ink on letters inevitably faded.

She sat until the bleeding stopped but the pain remained inside, sharp like shrapnel in her womb. Very slowly, pausing between each step, she edged her way across the room to her bed. There she lay down as flat as she could, with a sanitary towel pressed tight between her thighs. The immobility made the thoughts in her head all the harder to cope with. Normally she would be active; it was her way of getting her thoughts into a manageable shape. Now the thoughts came at her from different directions, worries to do with work, her parents, her friends and the politics that came with them. Her thoughts were black and grey, she could find no way to colour them more brightly. But she lay under this dark covering, strong in her will to be as still as possible.

Hours passed. The sun crossed to the other side of the sky, far from the part that she could see from her bed. The sunniness of the day seemed to express hope even though it failed to match her mood. She had a sudden and vivid picture in her head of Harry on a hillside in the Pyrenees, with blood seeping from bullet wounds, with white eyes staring upwards at the same sun that she now experienced in another country. *Why, Harry, why? There might have been so much ahead of us.*

Later in the day she had to get up and go to the toilet. She could hold back no longer. She sat and started to pee but she felt a rush from inside her. Looking down into the toilet bowl she saw lumps and swirls of blood in the water. There was nothing to do but cry again, a second mourning added to the first. She sat there for a time that might have stretched into hours, unable, unwilling to rise until she was certain that it was all done.

Harry was dead. So was his child. The memories were fresh but they would disappear, even though she would try hard to hold on to them. She flushed the toilet, watching the water rotate in red, then be swallowed down the pipe with a harsh gurgle until still and clear water returned. The stillness was unnerving and she flushed the toilet again, at the same time turning on the tap in the basin. She spent a long time washing her hands and legs with the bar of Lifebuoy soap.

She slept. Her sleep was agitated but long. On a new day there seemed even less reason to rouse herself and get up, but signs of life in the outside world were reasserting themselves into her consciousness. The clink of milk bottles delivered by the milkman. The chiming of church bells. In the distance the sound of traffic; closer to, the singing of birds. The occasional car or van in the side street where she lived. The clatter of the letterboxes as the postman went on his rounds.

Her own letterbox rattled, and letters plopped onto the floor inside. Lorna forced herself to see what the postman had brought. She was surprised that there were so many letters. Her friends were rallying round, at least by post, and that was more welcome than their real presence. Few of them had ever met Harry so they were uncertain how to react. In the letters, from Diana and other friends in her political circles, people talked of Harry as a hero. *How would they know?* she asked herself, and she got little sense of Harry as a real person from what they wrote. She had no reason to doubt his bravery but she found herself doubting the standard phrases of grief and consolation that people put into their letters. There was a letter from Bryan in which he told her that Harry had been killed near Figueras. It was not a name or a place that would ever be in Lorna's affections.

By the weekend Lorna was on her feet again. Her larder was empty, and she had drained herself of tears. She was left with a void, the most complete sense of emptiness she had ever experienced. Since Monday she had hardly eaten, surviving on increasingly stale bread, cheese, milk and a tin of pilchards that only hunger convinced her to eat. She began to dress, picking out the darkest clothes she could find, readying herself for the short visit to the grocer's in Archway Road.

She was wanting to rejoin the world. Despite her occasional shyness she was naturally gregarious. She felt again the urge to be with and around other people, to connect with the moving mass of people that was beyond the walls of her flat. The flat that she had come to suspect and dislike had now become even more oppressive to her. A second letter from Bryan had given her heart: without mentioning Harry it addressed one of her greatest concerns. In the letter Bryan told her that he knew of a flat, just a walk from work near Holborn, that had become vacant; it could be hers for a reasonable rent. If she was ready, if she rang the phone number shown, she could move in a week. She made sure she had a couple of coppers in her purse, deciding instantly that she would ring from the phone box and accept.

There was a knock on the door. It was a loud, confident, even jolly knock. Lorna suppressed a first reaction of irritation then of fear as she walked to open the door. She was surprised to find Pepe on the doorstep.

"Yes, it is me," he said with a smile.

She did not know what to say. She had not expected him. "What day is it?" she asked.

"I know, it is OK. It is Saturday not Sunday but we have met on Saturdays the last few times. I have not heard from you this week so I worried that you were wrong."

"No need. But that's kind of you. Come in, Pepe, I haven't been well. In fact I was just going out to get some shopping."

"Then I can help you. I can carry bags."

Lorna thought that she might take advantage of Pepe's gallantry. She was still feeling weak and it would be handy to have someone carry the weight of any shopping. She put her shoes on while Pepe sat at the table.

"It is nice but small," he said. "And you have not made your bed yet."

"No, as I say, I've not been well. But I'm feeling better now. It's nice to see you. But let's go."

"*Vamos.* I teach you Spanish."

There was a phone box at the corner of the road and Lorna got Pepe to wait outside while she made the call. She put in the coins then pressed the button when a woman's voice answered. The conversation with the landlady was brief and friendly as Bryan had smoothed the way. The flat was hers and she would visit on Monday evening to see it and settle the details.

Pepe had wandered up the road a little, stepping on the paving stones without treading on the cracks between. It was a boyish game. The simplicity of it made Lorna smile for the first time in days. Now the shopping became another game as Lorna bought eggs, bacon, bread, potatoes, mushrooms, apples, milk, going from shop to shop on the street.

"Now I feel hungry too," said Pepe.

"Good. We have enough for both of us."

"I can make tortilla," said Pepe. "I am a good cook. Will you let me?"

Lorna could not stop herself crying. Kindness always led her to tears. She apologised to Pepe.

"You must think my cooking will be awful. I promise it will not make you cry."

She thanked him, and they walked slowly back to the flat. This was not the end to the week that Lorna had expected but it seemed an outcome better than she might have hoped.

CHAPTER 18

Lorna had a good feeling about the flat in Lamb's Conduit Street. It was a quiet street that ran between High Holborn and Coram's Fields. She would enjoy saying that she lived in Bloomsbury, with its recent artistic connections. Lamb's Conduit Street, though, was a working street, with its mix of pubs, tradesmen's premises, shops and flats above shops; it had fewer pretensions than the nearby squares with their Regency houses. The University of London was near too, on the other side of Russell Square, and Lorna liked the prospect of mingling with the higher education she had not received.

She veered from despairing thoughts about Harry and the world to moments of optimism and cheerfulness. She had been pleased to return to work – everyone had been so kind to her – and welcomed the chance to put her losses out of her mind. At the same time, work was full of reminders of Harry and most of the reminders came with thoughts of children. Every time she wrote an official letter it seemed to be on behalf of a Spanish child, and each letter stirred memories of her own lost child.

She sought both company and solitude more than she had previously, more aware than ever before of the fragility of her emotions and of her need to manage them. She was determined not to be known as suffering from her nerves, as they had said about her cousin Peggy. What had happened to her? She had quietly disappeared from family gatherings, never to be mentioned over the tea and scones apart from a whisper of regret that flirted with cruelty. So Lorna made the effort to be sociable, having a drink after work with some of the office girls, as well as attending a political meeting as if nothing had happened. Yet she felt in a strange way hardened by events, she was more convinced than ever of the right of her cause and the wrong of those she stood against. The news from Germany became more troubling every day, as Hitler changed from a figure of fun to one of menace. She visited a Jewish couple who had fled Germany and was horrified by their stories of persecution even as she was securing the legality of their status as refugees.

Much of this made her feel angry and powerless. Sometimes she could vent her anger with like-minded people, inside and outside work. But at other times she simply needed to be alone. While in the last days of living in her old flat she took refuge in Highgate Woods while she could, finding comfort in its unspoilt solitude. She would not have imagined, and her parents would never have allowed, that London could contain places like these woods.

At the end of a hot summer's day, reluctant to go to her flat, she went through the gates that led to the path through the woods. Once on the path, it was easy to make a diversion into deeper woodland without raising any fear of becoming lost. After a while she would find another path, and along the path she would sit down on a bench. Inevitably memories would flood back, recalling other times sitting in a similar spot, but there was something comfortably indulgent in this reconnection with the hopes and fears of another time, a deliciousness in the revived sadness that brought her closer to Harry. In doing so she found it easier to accept that he was gone and would never return. She must make the best of the life that remained.

We only have left what is left, she thought. *What remains is all that remains.*

As she looked around, as she took in the scene around her, those words were not as bleak as they first seemed because she saw that a lot was left. Life is rich and there is more to come. It might not be happiness but it was life. Perched on the bench she could appreciate the beauty in everything that surrounded her, even the insects flying in the dusty sunlight of the gathering dusk. The first leaves were falling, and there were hard red berries on the brambles that would swell to blackberries in a few weeks. But for now there was consolation in nature's ebb and flow. Lorna's only regret was that she was a dilettante with nature. She wished she recognised the songs of birds and knew the names of trees. If she knew more she would make a list, stretching beyond the easy grasp of plane tree, oak and horse chestnut that she identified around her. She loved the embracing cover of woodland, where she could observe and not be observed.

She made her way out of the woods when she heard the bell ringing for the end of day. Now she had to hurry to reach the exit before the keeper locked the gates, with the shadows thickening in the spaces between the trees. There was packing to do at home, and only two evenings left to do it. *Not that I have much*, she pointed out to herself. *Enough to fill a dozen boxes.*

Friends from the Labour Party helped her move on the Saturday. Les and Frank pulled up in a van that they had borrowed from work. By day, through the week, they delivered evening newspapers, dropping them off at the vendors' stands positioned on street corners and near bus stops. They were quick and efficient in loading the van with Lorna's boxes.

Pepe arrived late, finding that all the work had already been done.

"Never mind," said Lorna, "you can come with me. I'm getting the bus while the boys bring the van."

That became the plan. So Pepe became Lorna's first visitor to her new flat in Lamb's Conduit Street.

"It is bigger," he said. "That is good." He was able to help bring up the boxes from the van in the street below. Lorna was relieved to be in her new home, with renewed hope.

***

In the middle of the following week, three letters were delivered to Lorna at work, tied up in a bundle with a piece of string. When Lorna cut the string, she saw that each envelope was sealed but the sealing of the flap was crinkled. She knew that they had been steamed open, read and resealed. It felt like a violation. For the first time Lorna believed she was being treated as an enemy by her own country.

She read the letters at her desk in case her outrage at this intrusion of her privacy needed to be directed at Bryan. However, she was calm, in control, owing it to Harry to be the lawyer, to maintain balance even if the scales were tipped against her.

The letters were short, written by Harry in snatched moments. The first had been written on hotel stationery and sent from Paris before the previous letter, received from Hendaye, had been written. It simply reiterated what Harry called the 'state secret' that he did not want to be hidden. *"Those were German not Spanish bombs."*

The second letter was stark: *"Trust no one. I love you."* There was no indication where this had been sent from, nor how it had been delivered.

The third letter came from inside Spain, but with no location marked.

"My darling Lorna

This is hard. I see you as I write this. I see your face but seeing your face robs me of words. I hear your voice but the booming of guns silences my voice.

This war was always hard but now it is harder, now that I have the memory of you. Before – I had nothing much to lose. Now I have everything to lose, if I lose you.

I want to touch you. I wish I could feel your hair now, now that it has been growing – please tell me that it has. I imagine it as a cushion I could rest my head on. I am resting it now."

The letter stopped there. It was a single sheet, written by hand on both sides of the paper. There was no signature. Did he not have time? Or did he forget? Or had the following sheets of the letter been removed by whoever had opened the envelope?

Bryan advised her that there was no point in raising the matter – it would only draw attention to herself.

"No point in that. No point at all."

CHAPTER 19

"What is the point?" asked Pepe when Lorna wanted to update the details in his Alien's Registration Book.

"It means you can become a naturalised citizen. Without it, you can't. it keeps the choice open."

"I might not want to. I am Spanish."

"If you don't play by the rules, you will get sent back."

"Not if they do not find me."

It was the first inkling Lorna had that Pepe might be scheming on his own behalf. His life was now something he might gamble with, but he did not see it as such a gamble. He would simply become 'disappeared' until the times changed.

"What if they don't change?"

"They will. Or I will."

Lorna felt obliged to counsel him against doing anything illegal but she was silently cheering him on. He was fifteen and mature, at least compared to his English counterparts who would have been able to leave school and find jobs a year ago. Pepe was capable of that.

"Better not tell me, at least not officially," said Lorna.

When she visited Pepe at his colony, she discovered that the Spanish children were beginning to think about departures. They would disperse with mixed feelings to different destinations. Some would return to Spain, taking a chance that they and their parents would escape reprisals. Some would move on to other colonies in England, and some to refugee camps in France, hoping that one day they could return to Spain. Their home country was an emotional pull for many – *including Pepe*, thought Lorna – but for others this new life in another land had become safe and normal. Whatever the choices made, most were not made by the children, and all the choices involved uncertainty. Hoping to provide comfort Lorna gave Pepe a print of the photograph taken with Pepe; it made him laugh. "Who are these people," he asked.

All this meant that Lorna was busy, doing what she could to protect the childrens' rights. She found that it was a good way to deal with her own grief. When alone in her new flat she would cry at the memories of Harry and rage at the gap that his death had created in her life. It was best to fill that gap as best she could, through busyness, company and the occasional bottle of Guinness in a pub. Her nerves remained fragile though she maintained a serene outward appearance.

One day she visited the doctor, always a last resort for her. She resented paying for his lack of sympathy but felt that she had to listen to his advice. As a result, on doctor's orders, she took up smoking as a way to calm her nerves.

"Now you can offer one to me," Pepe pointed out, when Lorna brought out a packet of Senior Service. Her hand shook as she struck the lighter. She had explained to Pepe why she was smoking, and in doing so she had told him a little more about Harry.

They sat smoking together after a meal in a café. Pepe felt grown-up in this situation but it made him dogmatic and blasé, playing down the difficulties that might lie ahead for him. Lorna was keen to steer away from confrontation, breaking off a piece of bread that she did not really want. She gestured to Pepe to take some too but he was intent on his plans that Lorna had no wish to hear.

"There are jobs in the countryside," said Pepe. "I can do that work."

"Not at this time of year. Winter's coming."

"No, it is harvest. Anyway, I can work at anything."

"Not if you don't have papers."

"Better if I do not have papers. More work that way."

Lorna tried to sweep away the crumbs from the table and, she hoped, the conflict. She waved her hand across her face to waft away the smoke that was stinging her eyes. Smoking did not come naturally to her yet. But the tension clung to the table and, like tobacco smoke, to their clothes as they walked out of the café down Lamb's Conduit Street.

"I will make my own mind," said Pepe grumpily.

"I know you will." After walking another dozen steps she said: "I just don't want you to come to harm, Pepe. You are still young to be on your own."

Lorna unlocked the door to the house where she now had her flat and they walked up the staircase with its wooden balustrade. The glow from the gas mantle cast a warm light that Lorna preferred to the electric lighting in her flat, but she did not want to think critically about her new arrangements. *In every way,* she told herself, *this flat is better than my last.* If pressed, by Pepe or anyone, she would admit that she missed Highgate Woods – but the advantages of this location outweighed everything else. Here she was central, in touch with the life of London, she could walk the short distance to work.

Pepe's sulks never lasted long. They came and went like clouds across the sun. Before long he was telling Lorna about a special evening planned for next weekend at the colony in Finchley. Music would be played. Spanish music. Dancing. It would be fun. Pepe insisted that Lorna had to come.

"Some of the others are leaving," he explained. "It is a chance to say goodbye."

Soon after, Lorna showed Pepe out. She no longer felt any need to see him home. If anything, Pepe placed himself under a bigger obligation to look after Lorna.

She did not know what to expect the following Saturday, but she dressed in her smartest black dress. It was an autumn evening with the light falling; she wore an overcoat to keep warm. At the last minute she put on the silver ear rings that her grandmother had given her just before she died. They sparkled like diamonds as she turned her face from side to side to look at herself in the mirror inside the wardrobe door. Her eyes gleamed too as she looked; a sudden memory of Harry, a regret that he had never seen her like this, passed across her mind. She tucked her growing hair behind her ears. *Ridiculous*, she told herself. *Off to the children's party*. But she felt happy, perhaps excited. As she walked along she hummed a song to herself, *September in the rain*, everyone seemed to be singing it at that time.

She knocked on the door in Finchley and was ushered inside by smiles from one of the young teachers. He explained to Lorna that they had planned the evening as one of traditional Spanish and Basque culture. "Do you know this?" he asked. "We sing and dance. It will be nice."

Pepe greeted Lorna with a kiss on both cheeks. With black trousers and an immaculate white shirt he was obviously in his party dress too, obviously wanting to show himself at his best and most grown-up. He showed Lorna into the big reception room that was already busy with children and a few adults. The tables had been cleared out of the room, with the chairs pushed back against the walls, leaving space in the centre.

"This is where we dance," shouted Pepe above the hubbub. He smiled at her with a mischievous look. "You too!"

"I don't think so."

"Oh, I think so. You look so nice. That black dress, it is for dancing. And ear rings that sparkle."

The first chords of music strummed on a guitar hid Lorna's flush of embarrassment. She never wanted to be noticed and now she was pleased that attention shifted to the three couples who were starting to dance. They were boys and girls younger than Pepe but led by the young teacher and one of the senoritas from another colony. They raised a leg, like wading birds, poised and still, mirroring each other, then began an intricate series of steps and small hops in rhythm to the strumming of the guitar. Forward they jumped, then sideways, twirling, stepping backwards together. The dance was controlled, without a hint of frenzy, executed with the movements of recent practice and the inborn feeling of their own traditions.

"We call this *la jota*," said Pepe who stood next to Lorna. They clapped hands together at the end of the dance as the young people shuffled off, suddenly self-conscious. As soon as they did there was more moving around as other children gathered in one corner of the room, forming two lines, one behind the other in order of size. They began to sing and as they sang the audience clapped to provide accompaniment. Lorna recognised the folk song that was about a recent battle. There was an intensity to the singing that stirred Lorna's emotions and she clapped loudly, feeling herself carried along by the motion of the music, as one song flowed into another, with the choir becoming more and more excited as applause followed each song and led into the next. After half a dozen songs, there was a collective shout and a bow to the room.

Lorna knew that her face was flushed with the power

of the music. Her hands were red with the passion of her clapping. The guitarist rose to his feet and bowed then slid out of the room that was now filled with music from a gramophone. Dramatic music began to play and two couples entered the room to dance. *Paso doble*, Pepe called into Lorna's ears, brushing her ear rings with his fingers as he did so.

Lorna had never seen this dance before. It was beautiful and sensual and Lorna knew that she could never dance like this. She was happy to admire the couples who were moving so elegantly, then to applaud enthusiastically when the music finished. A voice behind her called "Encore" and she turned to see that it was Pepe. But the dancing couples had gone, their performance complete. Yet the music began again, and some of the children took to the floor to dance their own versions, nowhere near as expert but joyful in their attempt.

"We must try," said Pepe. Lorna shook her head but found herself taken by the arm. "I show you how. You follow me." Pepe might have been a good dancer but he was brought down by Lorna's awkwardness. "Just feel the rhythm," he said to her. "Let yourself go." But Lorna remained stiff, unable to relax naturally into the movement. Pepe drew Lorna to him so that they could dance more closely together and, in doing so, disguise Lorna's clumsiness. It was not the dance that Lorna had witnessed earlier but it was a dance, and she found herself becoming less self-conscious as she swayed in response to Pepe's movements. Then Pepe seemed to lose his own natural rhythm as they pressed together. Perhaps a stiffening in his groin as he held Lorna, perhaps the consciousness of people watching, he suddenly found it difficult to find the flexibility needed to dance well. The gramophone stopped playing, and it was a relief to both of them. To Lorna's embarrassment, all the Spanish children were clapping and shouting and smiling at them.

"There," said Pepe. "I told you. You can dance."

At some point, a little later as things were winding down, Lorna heard a request as if in a dream. She was intoxicated by the excited activity of the evening, and she could never quite recall the details. She knew that she had been thinking of Harry, his memory brought back vividly by the occasion. She remembered, or did she imagine, that someone had asked her to say a few words. She was not one to rush into public speaking. In her head she heard herself shouting words as spoken by La Pasionara, that she had read reported: "It is better to be the widow of a hero than the wife of a coward. Go proudly. You are history. You are legend. We shall not forget you."

That is what Lorna hoped she might have said but it was not possible that she said that, or that she would have been understood if she had. The imagined words touched a deep emotion inside her, and the depth of that emotion was expressed in a phrase as simple as "Thank you. *Gracias, gracias*" as she made her way towards the door, stumbling slightly and smiling as if intoxicated even though she had not had a drink.

Outside in the chilly evening air, she had to feel suddenly sober. There was a full moon in the sky with a hazy aura around it. She realised that the suburban street was empty and silent, a disconcerting contrast to the scene inside the house. She had said goodbye and good luck to so many people. But where was Pepe? She had not said good night to him.

"It is OK," said a voice behind her. "I will write."

"Don't forget," she called over her shoulder as she walked off down the street.

Next morning she could not picture how she had got home. Nor could she picture Pepe's face saying goodbye.

CHAPTER 20

Lorna had spent a few minutes every evening that week polishing Harry's boots. Harry had been dead now for more than a year. She had kept the boots for reasons she had not been clear about. It did not feel like sentimentality because Harry had hated those boots and they had nearly become an obstacle to keep them apart. But Lorna had carried them from the house in Camden Town to her flat in Highgate and then to Lamb's Conduit Street. She had kept them while Harry was alive and dead. The boots had been shoved to the back of the wardrobe, never to be looked at or handled until now.

Now was a wintry January in 1939. When the news was announced that Picasso's painting *Guernica* was going to be exhibited at the Whitechapel Gallery, Lorna knew that she must go.

The painting had become famous as a symbol of resistance to fascism. Picasso had painted it as a gift for his native country soon after the bombing of the town by German and Italian bombers. The bright light of attention that it had shone on the conflict was an important reason why the world now believed that the destruction of Guernica was a war crime by the German air force. Franco's propaganda had initially pinned the blame on Spanish republicans, claiming that they had set fire to the town. Picasso's angry painting exposed the truth through its jagged images in black and white paint. Hitler's invasion of Czechoslovakia had made it clear to all but the British government of Neville Chamberlain that he was bent on military domination in Europe.

Lorna wanted to see the painting for obvious reasons, to

make her own gesture of solidarity and defiance. She felt a small surge of pride when she remembered Harry and his role in bringing the truth to the world. Harry's account had been published in a pamphlet that was read in left-wing circles. *It did its job*, she thought, *in a small way. But small ways are important.*

Now those boots must do their job too, albeit in a small way. Lorna had organised the group from the local Labour Party, and the admission price to the gallery was to be a wearable pair of boots. Lorna dusted off the boots and prised off the lid of the Cherry Blossom shoe polish tin. With a cloth she rubbed black polish across all the leather surfaces of the boots, then used a brush to buff them to a shine. She repeated this on three successive nights until she could see the lights reflected brightly in them.

Lorna brought out her black dress, the only one that suited such an occasion. She had last worn it over a year ago at the party in the Hogar Espanyol, the last time she had seen Pepe. It had seemed right to retire it then and to bring it out of retirement for this occasion. She had bought a new hat – black velvet with a red lace rose – and now put on her pearl necklace and silver ear rings. That evening she took unusual care with her make-up, dabbing at her lips with tissue when she had applied too much red lipstick. Her hair demanded the most attention: it had a tendency to tangle, now that it had grown long. Lorna combed and brushed it, tried it in different styles, until she felt satisfied.

She had arranged to meet the rest of her party at Aldgate underground station ten minutes before the time stated on their invitations. First to arrive, Lorna stood waiting with a bag containing Harry's boots, jostled by people leaving work in a frantic rush towards home. One by one the people of her group arrived until all ten of them were there.

It was a short walk along Aldgate towards Whitechapel Road. The January evening was cold and damp, with a light flurry of wet snow falling from black skies. A wash of white light settled on the road surface that was gleaming from the drizzle. Not wanting to spoil her hat, Lorna removed it and put it in the bag with the boots until she was inside the gallery.

There was going to be a crowd; that much was clear from the queue to get in and the chatter they could hear as soon as they entered. Martha clung to Lorna, not at ease with the situation. Lorna put on her new hat, handed over the boots, and was relieved to have her hands free. She found Martha a seat where Frank could keep her company. She was determined to mingle and meet people, persuading herself that that is what she should do for work as well as for social reasons.

She took a glass of wine and set off around the gallery. She immediately bumped into a tall man who was cutting across the room towards the painting.

"Why, it's you. The girl from my studio. Whose name I have forgotten."

"Lorna Starling. And you are Vincent Hillyer, I remember."

"Of course. And what did happen to your young man?"

Lorna still found it difficult to talk about Harry, but Vincent left the pause for her to fill.

"I'm sorry to say he died. He was killed in Spain."

"That's a terrible shame. But I see why you are here. I long to see the Picasso. Shall we go together?"

It would not have been Lorna's choice but she felt unable to refuse without being rude. She felt uneasy around Vincent.

His piercing eyes seemed to challenge her to be different from what she wanted to be. He looked at her silently, assessing her, a man much possessed by painting and physical form, seeing the body beneath the clothes. Or at least Lorna felt so, uncomfortably. She could not hold his gaze, finding herself looking downward, made shy by his attention.

"Come, take my arm. We shall look at Picasso together."

Lorna was surprised by the scale of the painting, having seen it before only in newspaper reproductions. She did not feel able, particularly in Vincent's presence, to comment on it as a painting. *Why was there no colour?* She could not explain that in technical terms but it seemed right to her. There were areas of light and dark, almost giving the impression of colour. *Do you need the colour red to see blood?*

"What do you think?" asked Vincent.

She wished he had not asked. She felt foolish saying "I don't know."

"You have no response?"

"I find it difficult to put into words."

"Ah, that is different. I find words difficult too."

"Yet it speaks. Or it screams."

"It is magnificent, it is visceral. It makes my own work seem shallow."

Lorna stood still in front of the painting. She felt curiously cocooned in this crowd, allowing the pain and anger of Picasso's vision to enter her mind. The naked light bulb, the agonised horse with its silent scream, the noble head of the bull, explosions, rubble, fire, a mother and her child. There was a rawness of emotion, Picasso's inner hurt scraped and brushed onto the canvas in layers, blasted away by bombing then reapplied by the artist's need to show the depth of humanity and inhumanity, so that the world should see too, so that his voice could be heard.

"You are right," said Vincent. Words are not enough."

"Harry knew that. But now he has no words to speak. This speaks for him."

Vincent looked at her in his penetrating way. This time Lorna returned his gaze. She was tempted to raise a clenched fist.

"You are remarkable," said Vincent, still staring. "You understand that pain and paint are close companions."

Lorna laughed, then was not sure if he had really meant to make a joke. *Probably not.*

"I'm not sure we really understand pain," she said, to cover her reaction. "Perhaps only in those moments when we experience it."

"You can make it real. This painting shows it. We get closer to the reality of emotion through painting."

Lorna smiled, not knowing what to say. Vincent's next words were urgent, intense, directed straight to her. "I want to paint you. I must."

Lorna was startled and immediately shook her head. "It's not something I do. Or want to do."

"Say Yes. I am not used to saying 'please'. But please, I beg you, say Yes."

Their eyes were locked together, as if they were wrestling each other, will against will.

"Hello, you two," a woman's voice broke in. "I hope I'm not interrupting something."

Lorna turned her head to face Diana. She was no longer Diana's protégée in quite the way she had once been. They saw each other less frequently now, as the Spanish war received less attention. The more obvious danger came from Germany and Diana put her efforts into raising awareness of Nazism. Her soirees brought Jewish refugees into her circle with stories of escaping Germany.

"Not at all," said Lorna. Vincent said nothing, looked thunderous.

"It's been a while, my dear," said Diana to Lorna. "I hope you've been well. But I don't think you have met my companion Betsy. Betsy. Lorna. And Vincent, of course."

Betsy was a striking young woman with a powdery white face and jet-black hair with a fringe. A gash of bright red lipstick made her words seem to spit out of her face.

"We have not met. But Diana has described you. Not very well..." Betsy took Diana's arm and squeezed it.

"Not well? My words seldom do justice," apologised Diana, not sure for what.

"Clearly not. Though *she* is a woman of justice. And much more interesting than your description."

"Betsy. Enough. You must not tease."

Lorna did not know if she had been complimented or insulted. She suspected the latter because there was no warmth shown towards her by Betsy. Lorna wondered what was the nature of this relationship. Was Betsy a new protégée? Or more? What was meant by 'companion'?

"I am not teasing," said Betsy. "You know I rise easily to jealousy."

Before Lorna could say anything, a hush started to fall across the room. "Let's talk later," whispered Diana into the hush, then backed away, arm in arm with Betsy.

The reason for the quiet was the appearance of a bald man in a grey suit and dark tie. Apparently to his embarrassment, people were applauding Clement Attlee as he was ushered forward to speak.

He did not speak for long and his words were in no way poetic. He talked of his experience visiting Spain in the previous year and meeting members of the International Brigade. The visit had reinforced even more for him the need to resist fascism by every means. He would do so in Parliament, and through the Labour movement outside parliament too. Picasso's work provided a reminder, and a rallying call, for all those who understood the dangers facing Europe. As leader of the Labour Party, he was determined to fight for humanity and justice, and against the forces of fascism.

The crowd clapped him warmly. Lorna had heard many orators in recent times and Attlee was not one of the great orators. He had little charisma but then people said that Hitler had charisma. Perhaps it was a quality to be mistrusted. Attlee exuded trustworthiness, there was a solidity to him that Lorna admired, and she applauded with enthusiasm. Was it Attlee's words or the pile of boots next to the painting that brought a tear to her eye?

The crowd moved in different directions. Those who had not yet seen Picasso's painting joined what was now a queue to pass in front of it. Lorna needed to step away and to allow others to take their turn – in doing so, she managed to separate herself from Vincent. She picked out Roy from her group and joined him. Soon the other members, including Martha who had been persuaded from her seat, joined the throng. They stood around, like interlopers at a garden party, not really believing that they should be there. The Picasso baffled them but they all used words to praise it: "wonderful", "very good", "really interesting".

"And did you all hear Attlee?" asked Lorna. They responded to this more easily. It had made the evening worthwhile. Lorna was gratified by that: as political education officer in her ward, she wanted people to experience evenings like this. Even as she was thinking this she realised, at the back of her mind, how far she herself had come from a shy, nervous spectator of meetings to the committed organiser.

The crowd was breaking up. Lorna watched people squeezing out through the gallery doors. She noticed Diana and Betsy making their way out but she made no effort to catch up with them for Diana's promised chat. They had moved on, so would she soon, once the numbers were reduced.

Then Lorna noticed a figure several rows in front of Diana. There was something familiar about him, even from this view of the back of his head. He was tall, standing out a little above the rest of the crowd, and wearing a Basque beret. Several other men in the room were wearing similar berets but this one seemed to be worn more naturally. It had been a long time – fifteen months now – since Lorna had last seen Pepe but she was sure it was him.

"Pepe!" she shouted, one voice in a cacophony of voices. She started to push her way towards the door but there were too many people in front of her. The figure was already gone and outside the winter's damp darkness allowed people to slip away into the anonymous shadows of the night.

PART TWO:
1943–44

Drawing the lines

CHAPTER 21

People fall in love. *Even in times of war people still fall in love.* Lorna sat on a bench in Russell Square and watched, as discreetly as she could, the young couple on the bench nearby. In his army uniform he would have been granted latitude to misbehave but still they were careful not to make their display of attraction more open. After all, this was Britain in 1943 and this was deep into a brutal war. There was a need to keep feelings in check just in case an excess of emotion ceded ground to the enemy. Secrets needed to be protected, information kept close. Walls have ears, and they have eyes too. The trees in the square might be even more cunning spies.

Lorna's eyes told her that the couple were in love. It was making them visibly happy; a light was lit within and it shone through their eyes as they looked at each other. The simple holding of hands provided confirmation. British reserve prevented any more overt display, a kiss perhaps that might have suggested passion as well as love. But Lorna enjoyed the vicarious sensation, almost like soaking in a warm bath, of skin being placed on skin in a gesture of closeness. *A furtive edge, but the reticence deepens the feeling of love.* She had a yearning to feel something similar but her own life was not leading in that direction.

The war had changed the lives of everyone. Life was suspended, like a lost radio signal. "Normal service will be resumed as soon as possible," as the BBC announcer might say. But it was taking a long time to repair the broken wires of normal life. After four years, Lorna observed a greyness in the faces of her friends, the leaching out of colour from all the signals of life. It was partly a chronic lack of sleep, restricted even more drastically than the food specified in the buff ration books. Who could sleep when nights were filled with bombing? Quiet nights could almost be worse; imagination can always exaggerate reality. Bombs are at their worst just before they explode.

That was why Lorna had decided three years earlier, when the Blitz had begun, that it would be better to do something to reduce the number of nights spent alone and listening for a silent killer to drop from the sky. There were dark times when she did not really care if she came through this or not, but in daylight she resisted any surrender to fatalism. If a bomb was going to take her, then let it take her in a place where she could see it. Death inside the walls of her bedroom or under the roof of a shelter seemed more pointless than beneath the open night sky. So Lorna had signed up to be a watcher for bombs and fires from the rooftops as an ARP volunteer. Wearing a tin hat she could live a charmed life among the flames, explosions and falling shrapnel of German air raids.

For three nights a week Lorna did her duty at the tops of buildings and below in the streets near where she lived. On the roofs she kept watch for the fires that followed the bombs, reporting them to the firemen to put out before they became targets attracting more bombs. On the streets and around the squares of Bloomsbury she patrolled and made sure windows were properly blacked out. And often, when the incendiary bombs had fallen, she would be on the scene offering whatever help she could, dousing the fires with a stirrup pump, directing people away from danger. She hated the devastation that she saw all around her but when the light of day returned she took heart from the surviving people defiant in the rubble of buildings that had been homes. After a short sleep, she would wash and dress then walk briskly to work as she had done before the war, as if nothing had changed.

The nights were quieter now than they had been during the Blitz. After the relentless bombardment of that time near the beginning of the war, there had been relatively few raids. The focus of the war had shifted. People were always ready to praise the collective effort of resistance, from the fighter pilots in the skies to the citizens on the ground. Now the tide of war seemed to have turned, or so everyone hoped. The Allied troops had driven the Germans out of north Africa and were heading into Italy. News had come through of the bouncing bombs that had destroyed the Mohne Dam in Germany. The bombing that had been inflicted on British cities was now being visited on Germany. It was impossible not to rejoice but enough remained of Lorna's pacifist instincts to keep her celebrations muted. She could not allow herself to be happy at the misery of others, particularly when her own recent experience had demonstrated at first hand the pain of bombing.

Still, duty called. She had signed up to the ARP and now Civil Defence, and she was conscientious in her duties. On this June evening she had been told to report to Senate House. This had been the most visible building of London University, towering over the central cityscape before the war, a looming and strangely alien architectural presence. It remained a towering monument but the students had moved out since the Blitz, and the building now housed the Ministry of Information and the Royal Observatory Corps. This would be the first time that Lorna had been summoned to fire watch from this building.

She had left work early to walk home to Lamb's Conduit Street, a journey that took no more than fifteen minutes on foot. The signs of war were everywhere in the rubble, sand bags and half-repaired craters in the streets. In her own street, just three doors away, a terraced house had suffered a direct hit and been reduced to rubble. Anything that could be rescued from the house had been removed by the salvage teams. All that remained, a daily reminder of the dangers, was a gap in the terrace filled with a jumble of bricks, plaster and stone. The family living there had been lucky: they had left the house to go to a shelter just minutes before the bomb fell.

In her flat on the second floor, Lorna got ready for her night shift. Outside it was still daylight but inside she needed artificial light to illuminate the gloom. She kept the blackout curtains drawn even in daytime. It hardly seemed worth pulling them open when she was out all day. In any case the windows were boarded up on the outside as the glass had long ago been blown out. The flat had not seen daylight for a couple of years. *A bat would feel at home here*, she thought. By the harsh overhead lamp she put on her blue serge uniform, applied a little make-up and pinned back her hair with kirby grips. Looking in the dressing table mirror she adjusted her cap and gazed around the room, taking in the standard lamp in one corner, the row of books on the sideboard and the painted portrait of a naked woman above the fireplace. As usual she had a thought about the artist Vincent Hillyer when she saw it. The thought provided its usual shadow of discomfort that she tried to dispel by repeated confrontation, much like her now-ended relationship with Vincent. *It might have to go, it might just have to go.*

She walked around Russell Square on her way to Senate

House. Growing darkness and the possibility of encountering young lovers made her avoid the route through the square. Tonight she was not feeling at her most confident though of course she would hide this when necessary. At times Lorna felt she was two people inside. When she felt reserved, her 'twin' could become much more extrovert, to her own surprise. So she would talk to people – particularly about politics – in a way that was impassioned but at the first chance she would revert to the girl who wanted to hide in the shadows. She was never sure if this was individual to herself or was simply the nature of being human. At any rate it suited her to live alone, she had become accustomed to solitude and never confused it with loneliness.

She reported to the ground floor reception desk, was checked in and sent up to the watching station. There she was met by an elderly man in Civil Defence uniform.

"Evening," he said, giving a half-hearted, possibly ironic salute. "My name's Jack."

They put on their helmets and stepped out through the door onto the roof balcony. Lorna was used to seeing London by night from rooftops but this sight was beyond anything she had previously experienced. For some reason it reminded her of the time before the war when she had gone to a concert at the Albert Hall. Unable to afford a good ticket she had sat high up in the top balcony, swallowing up the vertiginous view as the crowd gathered in the seats below and as the orchestra filed into their places with their instruments. Looking out over London's skyline as the sun went down, picking out people making their purposeful ways through the streets below, the sounds of traffic were like the orchestral instruments tuning up. As night fell further and the sky grew blacker, the eery silver glint of the barrage balloons and the sweeps of searchlights finding their range, criss-crossing each other, became a soundless overture to the evening.

"It's quite a sight, Jack," said Lorna.

"It is. As long as it stays quiet."

"Let's hope. Is there any word? Are we expecting anything to go off tonight?"

"We always expect somethin'. Especially when it's quiet."

Lorna used her binoculars to scan the sky to the east. Despite the darkness she could still see the shapes of buildings at the horizon. Over time she had developed a kind of night vision, at least in her imagination.

"I've a feeling that something will happen tonight, Jack."

"Oh? Why's that?"

"Just a feeling."

"Try not to, my dear. It's not good, gives us the jitters. Seen too much of that. No alarm till the alarm, and then we keep calm."

"Sorry, Jack. I know the drill. I'll be all right, whatever happens."

The tin hat next to her nodded. He had a particular story in mind that he told Lorna, perhaps as a cautionary tale. He talked about being called to Bethnal Green tube station a couple of months earlier. "It was all a false alarm," he shook his head sorrowfully, "that's the pity of it. All set off by the jitters." He and others had pieced together the story afterwards: how the siren had gone off, how people had rushed in a panic to get underground to the platform as fast as they could, how someone must have tripped on · the stairs. With the siren wailing above ground, more and more had tried to barge in, falling over those who had already fallen. It had been mayhem but once started it was impossible to put things into reverse. People trod on people; men, women and children. When the All Clear had sounded – there had been no air raid – it was already too late. Jack arrived to help out some of the injured, but mainly to remove bodies. Nearly two hundred people had been killed; crushed and suffocated to death.

"Y'have to stay calm, no matter what," he concluded. "Nerves lead to more nerves."

Lorna nodded and accepted the cigarette he offered. "You're right. Of course. I read about Bethnal Green." She wished she could see his face more clearly in the darkness. "It must, well…it must have been awful."

They fell silent, staring fixedly ahead, contemplating awfulness or just the blackness of the thickening night. The lighter Jack struck for their cigarettes revealed a redness in his face that natural light might have toned down.

They heard someone making his way carefully along the balcony behind them. He identified himself as Captain Wallace of the Royal Observer Corps.

"All quiet so far. But just wanted you to know we are expecting something tonight."

He allowed a pause so that Lorna could supply the question "What? What are we expecting, sir?"

"We think Jerry is going to give us some stick. We bombed Dusseldorf a few days ago. 800 bombers. They'll want to pay us back. We've just heard they've crossed the channel, heading this way. So, eyes peeled, the party might start soon."

Lorna hated the lingo of war, with all its false notes, its desperate jollity. If the bombers came, it would be nothing like any party she had been to. But she bit her tongue and stayed quiet as the officer moved back inside with a "Carry on" waved towards them.

"Schtum," said Jack, reading her thoughts, "we're on the same side."

"If you say so, Jack. I'm sure you're right. You and me at least."

In the darkness they could not see each other smile.

"You're the Labour lady, aren't yer? I've heard of you. A troublemaker from what I hear."

The darkness could not hide the smile in his voice; they could feel it in the space they shared.

"When this is over, Jack, when this is over. We'll all need to visit the free doctors. A new health service for us all."

The conversation might have continued but it was cut short by the heart-sinking banshee wail of the siren. There was no other sound that could make Lorna's heart sink as fast. Repeated hearings made it no easier. It was not a sound that had the least bit of music in it, though it rose and fell, gaining volume by the second, sending a mournful dread into the ears and minds of all those who heard it. The only way to cope with it was to focus on the task in hand, so Lorna was quickly on the alert looking from the balcony across the sky to the east. The searchlights swept up and across, their beams cutting across each other, fading into the outer reaches of the clouds.

"Can't see nothin' yet," said Jack.

"Nor me," said Lorna.

And so it went on till they had to rub their eyes; eyes that were now smarting with the concentration. Yet Lorna found it companionable with Jack, even though they did not talk a lot. They needed to concentrate and talking would distract them. Lorna had heard enough to know that Jack was on her side, she would not have to quarrel with him about making a better world after the war. The prospect of change was what now kept her going; she was seeing a brighter sky once the war was finished and now, for the first time, she saw an end in sight.

"One more push, eh?" said Jack, as if reading her mind. "Bloody war will be over."

"That's the hope, Jack. That's the hope that keeps us going."

Captain Wallace reappeared to let them know that it had been a false alarm. Down below there was some movement in the streets. Behind them came the single continuous note of the All Clear. It should have been a joyful signal but it still managed to sound mournful even as it faded, as if the siren itself was dying.

"We're beatin' 'em, me dear. We've got 'em on the run."

"Steady, Jack. Let's not get carried away. They could be bombing us to bits tomorrow."

"Y'right. They says they might have a secret weapon still to come. But who knows? Who the bloody hell knows? D'you think they do?" gesturing over his shoulder towards the back of the departed captain.

"I guess we'll find out. We might be the first to find out. We'd get a good view from up here, that's for sure."

Lorna was starting to feel a little light-hearted. She and London and all its people had survived another night. "I could do with a drink," she said.

"You and me both. A nice pint."

"A Guinness."

"Guinness, eh? There's a gel. Not much chance, though. But the night's nearly done. And you go home and go to bed and say 'What am I goin' to do tomorrow?' And we'll do the same, no doubt, because it doesn't stop. Not yet. And you realise that years have gone past without anythin' happenin' 'cept more of this."

"It's going to end, Jack. And we can make something better after all this."

"That gets my vote."

It was time to pack up her things. A new pair of fire watchers came in to relieve them. Lorna was sorry she might not see Jack again as the following day she would have to report for duty much closer to the ground. She took a last scan of the sky, just to make sure it was still clear, but also to take in the view of London. It was dark still but there was a beauty in the darkness, serene and silent as a graveyard. *Fortunately*, Lorna smiled, *we avoided the graveyard tonight*.

It was a short walk back to her flat in Lamb's Conduit Street. As she walked through the blacked-out streets, a warden called out to her: "Mind how you go."

"Is that you, Charley?"

"It is, Lorna. A quiet night after all."

"We'll see about tomorrow. I'm on duty here tomorrow, see you then."

She needed to concentrate on finding her way through the dense blackness and quiet, but she knew the way so well and her night vision made it surprisingly easy. In less than ten minutes she was unlocking her front door and going up the carpeted stairs to her flat. Inside she just used a torch to get ready for bed, and then she lay there under the blankets with the torch flicking around the room. She allowed the beam to rest on the portrait of herself that Vincent had painted three years earlier. That seemed such a distant part of her life now and it was no longer painful. Switching off the torch she thought, as she often did, of Harry – so much further away in time, so much closer still in her feelings. It was a deep and abiding love, conjuring his image from the few memories she had to cling to. She touched her own skin, rubbing her hand over her shoulder in the darkness, imagining that this hand might still be his.

CHAPTER 22

The reprieve lasted only 24 hours. The next night began with the siren's wail that was soon followed by the searchlights and the ack-ack guns, signalling the arrival of a real bombing raid. Lorna was ready, in uniform, and she gathered with the other fire guards in their area post.

The noise became deafening. The anti-aircraft cannons were thundering rapidly from just a couple of miles away in Hyde Park. The searchlights like giant torches swept their beams across the sky, sometimes catching a glimpse of a German plane, sometimes locking their beams on to that plane as it rumbled through the blackness. This gave the gunners a target to aim at and once, almost miraculously given the speed and distances, they succeeded in hitting a German plane. The bursts of shellfire were constant, seeming to shake not just the buildings but the air itself. In percussive response the bombs fell from above, setting off explosions followed by the heavy rain of brickwork and shrapnel, then the finer drizzle of plaster dust.

"Messerschmidts," said Reg, one of the fire guards. "Focke-Wulffs," said Charlie. They were all plane spotters now, forced that way by the repetitive practice of their job. After years of bombing, even though it had come in waves across the years, they could notice that the big bombers were now replaced by fighter bombers, quicker, lower, nimbler, able to duck under the air defence more easily.

The bombs were landing away from their area. Inside the post it was relatively snug and calm. On quiet nights this could be a pleasant enough place to stay, with a darts board on one locker door and a shelf of books supplied by St Pancras

Travelling Library. Lorna had read all the books she wanted to read from the shelf but this was not going to be a night for reading. They heard a swishing sound, a heavy pattering, that they all recognised as incendiary bombs, and this acted as a call to action. They brought out the full water buckets and the stirrup pump, locating the incendiaries by their white flames. Like sparkling snow they settled on the roadway and the nearby children's playground in Coram Fields, but the houses had mainly been spared.

By this stage in the war they were skilled in their use of the pumps. Lorna remembered her embarrassment at her own clumsiness when she first used the contraption. With a nearly full tin bucket, a pump operated by hand and a hose that could direct a jet or a spray of water, it was not an elegant contraption but it worked. Flat on her stomach, lying on the pavement, Lorna doused the fires one by one by pointing the nozzle and streaming water onto them while her colleagues worked the pump.

"They're all done," shouted Reg. "Just that blighter up on the roof, but the Warden's onto that."

Lorna watched the figures on the rooftop; they were on top of the fire and flames were dying away to wisps of smoke and steam. Above them in the sky the searchlights were still piercing the blackness and the ack-ack guns were still firing, but the enemy bombers were moving away, heading back across the channel. Lorna persuaded her two colleagues that they should go through the gates into Coram Fields to assess the damage there.

It was dark but the darkness was suddenly illuminated by the flaring of an incendiary. They often took time to burst into flames, and it was startling to be caught off guard in this way. Lorna shone her torch on the area around the flame. The incendiary was burning in the middle of the children's swings. Lorna rushed forward while Stan and Reg followed with the pump and buckets. Stan pushed down into one bucket and the water started to flow through the hose. They managed to extinguish the incendiary quickly, then covered it with sand.

"Good job," said Lorna. "The children can still play." It was good to acknowledge small triumphs, to say that there is a purpose to their effort.

Her two colleagues went back to the post but Lorna stayed behind alone. She said she would finish clearing up and then go home. In the relative quiet she heard their boots crunching on glass underfoot where windows had blown out into Guildford Street. As their torches picked the way ahead the glass sparkled like frost on the ground.

Lorna lifted her gaze to the sky where the searchlight beams were fading one by one. At another time, in other circumstances, she might have treasured the scene for its beauty. *Perhaps there is a beauty in bleakness.* She shone her torch around her to take in the scene. Sitting on the wooden seat of a child's swing, with its clanking metal chain, she observed a slide, a sandpit and a roundabout like a witch's hat made of metal. It was easy to imagine sunshine instead of darkness, laughter instead of silence, activity instead of petrification. One day soon the world would wake and activity would return with the steps of the children, running and jumping into a time of peace. For now there were just future ghosts and she sat in a mood of accepting melancholy, feeling that her night's work had been worthwhile.

Time passed without her realising. Perhaps she had even dozed off in a state of childlike slumber. She realised that the glow in the sky was the spreading light of dawn not the distant blazing of fires. Now she could distinguish the play equipment and the low buildings around her as shapes that offered comfort. She got to her feet and walked around the playground, laying her hands on the metal bars of the seesaw, rocking it gently, perhaps for the first time in months. It creaked in welcome.

With the horizon brightening minute by minute, smoothing light across the sky above, she slipped through the iron gates onto the pavement. There was a small roundabout at the junction of Guildford Street and Lamb's Conduit Street. In the centre of the roundabout was a stone statue, covered with a film of brick dust. The statue was of a kneeling girl pouring water from a jug into the drinking fountain below. This fountain was there to quench people's thirst during the business of a working day. Nearby a horse trough of heavy stoneware provided a similar service for London's working animals. Beneath the roundabout was a public lavatory. These simple signs of public consideration moved Lorna to sudden tears.

Lorna decided to express her gratitude for these acts, and simply for being alive, by cleaning the statue of the girl water-carrier. She climbed onto the plinth and wiped away dust with her handkerchief; then she dipped the hankie into water before wiping it carefully, as if across the skin of a living person, over the girl's face, her fingers feeling the stone through the wet fabric, bathing the girl's downcast eyes and mouth and nose. Now these gleamed wetly in the first rays of the sun. It seemed, at that time with the new day brightening to a hazy, smoky dawn, the right thing to do before going home for a couple of hours' sleep.

CHAPTER 23

Lorna pushed the street door open. The door lock was broken again, a victim of the aerial bombardment that had distorted the doorframe. It was a running source of irritation to her that things broke but could not always be repaired during the war. You had to make-do and mend: it seemed unpatriotic to complain but it was yet another reason to long for the end of the war. Most of the locksmiths, glaziers, electricians, tradesmen were in the services so you had to rely on the more elderly odd-job men to patch things up. Lorna worried less about the lock – *I've nothing worth stealing* – than the lack of glass windows. But she had come to terms even with that, giving up the effort of getting blown-out windows replaced. She now lived without daylight, with boarded windows, without any great expectation of comfort, with a grim stoicism. With her ARP helmet on, she told herself *it made the blackout more secure*.

It was a time for introspection during the war's quiet moments. Despite everything, despite the desolation and devastation all around, Lorna's love for London had grown. It fitted her need to meet life on her terms, to dip in and out of situations when she wished. The natural reserve that she had had instilled in her through her parents, school and suburbs, gave way at times to gregariousness. London was a naturally gregarious environment, and Lorna found comfort in the feeling of being in a crowd whenever she wished. The war had not really thinned the crowd but it had changed its composition. She had not noticed at first but now, four years into the war, the absence of men near her age was increasingly evident. She did not depend on male company but there was a change in her expectations. It was a strange premonition of a future world, perhaps written in a story by HG Wells, where the human race had become a gerontocracy. She smiled grimly at the shop sign 'A. FRANCE – funeral director' that she saw opposite her flat, pulling the front door to behind her.

The house seemed to be empty, it had an air of abandonment. Mrs Hayes, her landlady, and the Gerrards on the first floor, must have spent the night in a shelter and were yet to make their way home. The attic flat above her had been vacant since the beginning of the year. Lorna unlocked the door of her flat and stepped inside with some relief, looking forward to sleep. On nights after bombing, Bryan accepted that she would be late for work.

Lorna was aware that she brought the smell of smoke into the room; it was steeped in the fabric of her uniform. As she removed it, ready to wash herself at the kitchen sink, she thought that she must get it clean soon. It showed too much evidence of her night-time trade. She looked at the discarded clothes with distaste, as she increasingly looked at all her clothes. She had acquired skills in darning, extending the life of clothes with sewing and patching, but it was not just the lack of choice as the lack of occasions that she found dispiriting. She had little incentive to dress with the elegance that had become her style before the war. She needed something new to happen in her life.

For two hours she slept deeply. Her dreams were unusually, unexpectedly serene. Exhaustion had made sleep necessary, however short it might be. She closed her eyes on the reality of war and dreams washed anxiety out of her system, at least for a while. The while might have been longer but she was woken by a sharp knock on the door.

"Mrs Hayes?" she called because she could think of no one else who might come calling at this hour. There was no answer. She dragged herself out of bed and put on her housecoat. When she opened the door, a familiar figure stood outside, but it was not her landlady. Familiar but not immediately recognisable. The figure in rumpled working-man's clothing raised his right fist then changed the salute seamlessly into a V for Victory sign. As he did so he smiled, and the smile was infectious. Lorna smiled back, remembering Pepe's smile from the time when he was a boy. It spread toothily across his face, bringing a sparkle to his eyes then to hers. His face was longer and thinner than when she had last seen it but now she saw, with a sense of joy reignited by the memory, that it really was Pepe's face.

"I said I'd be back," he laughed.

"No, you said you'ld write."

"Sorry, shall I send you a letter?"

They giggled like children, which perhaps they had been in their earlier time together, perhaps they still were. Lorna threw the door wide open to let Pepe come inside. The light was on overhead, an electric bulb hanging from a brown twisted flex, its low-watt austerity slightly softened by a cream lampshade with a rim of red tassles. Lorna became aware, slightly ashamed even, of the ordinariness of her surroundings. There was nothing fancy here *but we're in a war*. She might even have said those words out loud, in mitigation, as Pepe stepped inside. But he was interested only to see Lorna not her furniture.

"I dreamed of you," he said. "I could not stop. I had to see you."

She looked at him, quizzical, wondering what was really

happening here. "Really? Well, yes, you could have written a letter."

"I would. But it is easier for me to speak in English than to write it. I talk. That is easy for me. But not to write." He smiled seeking her smile in response.

"We have a lot to catch up on, no doubt," said Lorna. "It's been six years. Six years. And look at you."

"I know. I am sorry. I am a little dirty but I have been travelling. And not much sleep."

"Let me make us a cup of tea. We'll take things slowly. It's been a long time."

While the kettle was boiling on the gas ring, Lorna established that she would have to get ready and go to work. Without probing deeply she learnt that Pepe needed a place to stay before he had to return to the country. He had been living in Gloucestershire, working on a farm, keeping out of trouble.

"Glad to hear it," Lorna said. "You're welcome to stay, as long as you don't mind sleeping on the floor."

"That is what I did last night. I sleep on the landing up there. I knocked on your door but no answer. Then the bombs start so I can only stay."

The kettle had whistled and Lorna poured boiling water into the tea pot. She lit cigarettes for herself and Pepe, then cut some slices of bread. She put out her cigarette, as if rebelling against its taste. Pepe spread some jam on the bread and ate hungrily while Lorna drank tea.

"I hardly know where to start," she said. "So many questions. But they'll have to wait till later, once I've finished work. You can stay here but you'd better keep quiet. Are you legal? I have to ask. There's the bed, help yourself, have a good sleep. Then we'll talk as long as the Germans leave us in peace tonight."

Pepe thanked her, looking around the room. "It is like a night club in day time," said Pepe.

"I wouldn't know about that." Lorna resisted the temptation to apologise for her room with its boarded windows. "There is a war on. Even Gloucestershire must have noticed."

"They bomb us too," he said in a matter-of-fact tone. "But not as much as this."

Lorna knew that she had been defensive, even aggressive. That was not normally her way, but Pepe's arrival had taken her by surprise, a pleasant surprise at first, then one that led to apprehension. Pepe had stirred something that she was not able to recognise; she felt like welcoming it and rejecting it at the same time. There was so much to find out but now she had to leave for work. She smiled more gently towards him, then left the room to get changed.

"Help yourself to anything you fancy," she called out. "There's food in the larder."

"Thank you. You are very kind. That is what I remembered. That is why I wanted to see you again."

They stood facing each other, for the first time really taking in the differences in appearance since last they had met. What did they amount to? Were they different people now or did they just look different? Or did they really just look exactly the same apart from the superficial scratches of time? Her longer hair, his Brylcreemed hair, her ready-for-work office clothing with the white blouse, his farm worker's worsted trousers and brown boots, her face that seemed so beautiful to him, so beautiful, even more so than he had remembered.

"I'll bring in something to eat later," she said.

They kissed each other on the cheek, and she closed the door behind her with a quiet click and a quick smile. She was pleased that she had decided to wear her red beret for the first time in years.

CHAPTER 24

Lorna walked to work as usual. It was not that far and she had got used to walking everywhere. It just seemed easier when the buses sometimes did not run in the aftermath of a bombing raid. *In any case,* she told herself, *it's probably safer.* Safer to be free to run herself rather than be a sitting target for the bombers.

She walked through Covent Garden. The pavements were busy but she did not see a single child. It was becoming a form of brooding for her to notice and mourn the absence of children. Did this mean that the country areas were now packed with children evacuated from the cities? She wondered if this could be a propaganda mistake – *after all, we're fighting for a better future and children represent that future. But not if we cannot see them.*

When she arrived at work, she headed for Bryan's office. She had a small office to herself now – a partitioned rectangle with frosted glass in a wooden frame that stopped short of the ceiling – but she wanted to see Bryan first.

"Rough night," Bryan stated.

"It was. Just when we hoped we might be over the worst."

"Get any sleep?"

"A little. But then I had a surprise. Pepe turned up."

"Pepe? Who's he?"

"The Basque boy. The boy from Bilbao. But not really a boy any more. A young man of twenty-one."

There was a tap on Bryan's office door and Diana walked in without waiting to be called. Lorna had a working relationship with Diana. It had survived – out of practical necessity – the frostiness that had settled over them when Betsy had entered Diana's life. Lorna and Betsy were not rivals, though Betsy seemed to imagine they were. Through the gritted teeth and forced smiles of embarrassment, Lorna had tried to make her position clear and gradually, one brief encounter after another, the relationship with Diana had been restored. Which was necessary as some work continued on the cases of the Spanish children, particularly those who had not returned to Spain.

"Diana. You should hear this too," said Bryan, his eyes peering through the gap between the glasses on the end of his nose and the still luxuriant grey hair on his brow. "I think we're about to hear a story. But let's get some tea first."

The making of the tea gave Lorna a chance to adjust her story a little to the extra listener. Diana had met Pepe originally at the Stoneham camp but that now seemed an age ago. *It is an age ago, so much has happened since then.*

"There's not much of a story to tell," Lorna began. She sipped the tea to find the resolution she was seeking. She explained that after a night's fire-watching she had slept. Then been woken by a knock on her flat door. Finding Pepe there. Establishing the bare details of his life. Working on a farm in Gloucestershire. Leaving him in her flat. Coming to work. Needing to find out more later. But not knowing what to do.

"It sounds as if he's not been hiding," said Bryan. "But you need to find out. The Basque children, if they managed to stay, still have to report to the police. Even if they do, there is still the curfew. And travel permits. And permits for a bicycle. We don't make it easy to be here as an alien."

"Still, there are still many of them who seem to have settled in," said Diana. "They're scattered around the country. What a palaver could be made of this if we didn't manage to keep a lid on it. It's just as well Franco stayed out of the war – otherwise they'd be interned."

"What are his plans, do you think?" asked Bryan.

"I don't know yet." Lorna shrugged her shoulders. "I'll find out later. Right now I expect he's catching up on sleep."

"We need to be a little careful. As lawyers we cannot flout the law."

"He tells me he's legal."

"So has he been reporting to the police? You need to find out. It could be awkward."

There was silence. Lorna felt she should have asked more of Pepe, but she realised with a flash of surprise that she had been happy to see him, she had not wanted to frighten him off with questions. She was reluctant to send him scuttling away, for personal or legal reasons.

"Perhaps he's thinking of joining up?" suggested Diana.

Bryan raised his eyebrows towards Lorna.

"I don't know. Can he?"

"Some of the boys have," said Diana. "One or two anyway that I heard of."

"It could be the best thing." Bryan spoke, placing his teacup in the saucer with exaggerated care. "It could be a very good thing. The trickiest part of it might be his own conscience. Does he have such a thing?"

"I'm not sure I know what you mean by that," replied Lorna.

"Well, the only case I know, one of the Basque boys wanted to join the RAF. He really wanted to be a pilot and God knows we need them. So he filled in the forms, signed up, passed the tests, got a uniform. Then he had to take the Oath of Allegiance – to defend King and Country, in peace and war. That was a sticking point. He said he would sign up for the war but no longer. And he was adamant that he would not fight against Spain, if the war turned that way. The officer asked him why and suggested that, had he been old enough at the time, he would have fought in the civil war. He would have fought against Spaniards, whichever side he was on. But he was a Republican, of course."

"So he refused?"

"We talked it through. His position was that he would – in that situation – be attacking his friends and family who had not managed to escape from Spain. He could not do to them what the Fascists had done to him. He came from Bilbao, he knew about Guernica."

"I can understand that," said Lorna. "But surely we didn't send him back."

"No, of course not." Bryan laughed as if he had told an outrageous joke. "He saw sense. Now he's bombing the Germans to buggery."

They laughed. They had to laugh. The desperation of war made laughter inevitable, even as Lorna was thinking of her own recent pacifism. Listening to Gandhi speak in a London hall ten years ago, pacifism had seemed realistic not romantic.

"You're right, Bryan. Play the patriotic card, even if we don't believe in it," said Diana.

Lorna felt herself flushing with emotion. She had not discussed politics at work since the war began. It was as if she too had signed an oath of allegiance. But now she could not hold back.

"You can be patriotic without believing in all those ridiculous patriotic trappings," she burst out. "You can love your country without wanting to kneel before the King or mindlessly waving a Union Jack. You can love the land but not the landed gentry. You can love your country even more deeply without believing in those things. It's what we're really fighting for."

"You are right, of course," said Bryan. "Of course you are right. But the war makes hypocrites of us all. We have to know what we can say, when we can say it and where we can say it."

"Absolutely," agreed Diana. "We're still fighting for the right to oppose the system we have."

"Then what?" asked Lorna. "Then what do you want me to do about Pepe? Suddenly he feels like a double agent I've got in hiding."

"Talk to him. See what his plans are. We'll help him to do whatever he wants within the law."

Bryan spoke the words like a defence lawyer summing up. It was his habitual mannerism made all the more natural by the passing years. Lorna felt a small surge of gratitude, recognising that he was offering something of a gift, and knowing that she should not spurn it.

Lorna went out, closing the door of Bryan's office behind her. Walking through the corridor of partitioned cubicles, she was pleased that there was no one to witness her flushed cheeks. She could feel their colour so she went into the lavatory to splash her face with cold water.

She went to her own office and pulled out the files on the Basque children. They were still current but seldom opened in recent times. Even so, she felt a comfort in them, a nostalgic warmth: this had been an important programme for her, establishing her place in the firm. She spent an hour reading through the files in the unsettling quiet of the offices. Before the war there had been a bustle as people moved around, opened doors, made telephone calls, had sometimes animated conversations. Now there was not even a whisper, just the hush that comes from empty offices. Most of the partners, all the younger men, had switched from the law to the military, and there were few women employed as a result. Lorna was one of the few because she worked closely with Bryan.

She needed to go outside into the fresh air and the busy streets. The air was hardly fresh; it still had a smell of smoke from the previous night. There was a breeze blowing a light drizzle down the river. Under the now-false jauntiness of her red beret, Lorna's face was getting wet, but she felt in the mood for wetness. She lit a cigarette, her first since breakfast.

She strolled through Embankment Gardens, where the summer flowers were putting up a brave fight to be noticed. Stern statues of famous men stared down on them, not noticing, possibly disapproving. Lorna took a greater sense of pride from the men and women who still walked purposefully through the gardens, in mackintoshes, under cloth caps, beneath umbrellas, bent against the rain but still intent on doing the tasks they had to do.

Reaching the end of the gardens, looking up at Hungerford Bridge, it seemed something of a triumph that trains still clanged and clattered along the rail tracks into Charing Cross station. It was the background noise of a country still at work, not only at war. On and under the bridge there were columns and brick walls from railway structures that seemed to serve little purpose beyond the dismally decorative. Today, however, with the rain slanting down, they provided ledges and canopies for birds. Lines of pigeons were strung out, huddling side by side, sheltering from the wet.

There were black puddles here and there on the roads

and pavements, filling holes made by bombs or perhaps by more innocent wear and tear. Where trees overhung the puddles, leaves had fallen, even in summer, and they floated like nature's abandoned bodies in the water. It was all too easy to see death in everything because there were signs of destruction and decay everywhere. *It will pass*, she told herself. *It will pass.* She dropped her cigarette into a puddle and, in the extinguishing moment's wisp of smoke, she decided that she no longer needed cigarettes.

It was time to head back to the office to clear up some outstanding pieces of work. Later a conversation with Pepe awaited her. It was one she looked forward to with eagerness, anticipated with dread.

CHAPTER 25

Lorna found it strange – a glimpse of an unknown domestic life – to return home to the flat, expecting someone else to be there. And he was. Pepe got to his feet when Lorna opened the door. He had been sitting on a wooden chair facing the chimney breast where the large portrait hung.

"Are you OK?" Lorna asked. "Did you sleep? Find something to eat?"

Pepe answered the questions with an almost sulky nod. She realised he had been looking at the charcoal portrait on the wall. Caught in the act of looking at a picture of a naked woman, he showed his embarrassment.

"Don't you like it?" she asked. "It was done by a proper artist."

She stood in front of the portrait, studying it as if for the first time, hoping that she would convince Pepe to do the same. It was a nude portrait of a woman, and the face was unmistakably Lorna's. Dark shades of charcoal gave form and depth to her body in the portrait. She stood straight and staring, as upright as a pine tree, with no hint of stooping in her back or knees, breasts pointing forward. Black eyes were fixed on the viewer, unflinching, daring, no trace of a smile. *Defiant*, Vincent had insisted to her. She had been his reluctant muse, hating to be drawn or painted, but it was that discomfort he had found interesting. He wanted to capture her discomfort in charcoal, in pastels, pencils, oils and watercolours in a series he called *After the Spanish war*.

It was a quality that made Lorna unlike any other model he had ever had. Still her eyes stared their defiance at the viewer, even when that viewer was Lorna herself. The burnt charcoal black was smeared here and there, like markings left on the surface by a fire. She remembered how Vincent had rubbed his fingers across the flesh, moulding the skin into its contours. The overwhelming blackness of the medium dominated everywhere except, and this was the section of the work that Lorna loved, the midriff that was covered by an object painted in vivid colours. Her charcoal hands held a bowl of fruit in front of her stomach; the bowl rendered in green pastels of many tones, containing half a dozen spheres of bright orange. Lorna liked the contrast of black and grey lines with this area of deep vibrant colour; it allowed her to look at the portrait without shyness.

"Did you have to?" asked Pepe.

"Of course not. I agreed to. There were more but this is the only one I have. You might, in time, find others in galleries."

"Are you happy with that? Do you not find it shaming?"

"Why? It is only a woman. I hardly think of it as me."

"It is you. It is beautiful."

"Oh Pepe, come on," taking off her beret, "we have so much to talk about. Let's set this aside," walking up to the picture, lifting it off its hook, and turning it to face the wall.

Pepe looked at the blank hardboard that now leaned against the wall. The frame was minimal and cheap, but it held Pepe's attention.

"I look to see if I can see your back," he said. He turned to look into Lorna's eyes and smiled. She remembered the mischief in his eyes from the time when he had been a boy. They both laughed, a sound of shared relief.

"It's a work of art, Pepe, not a bit of pornography. Like your friend Picasso."

"My friend? I do not know him."

"But you went to see his work."

There seemed no answer possible; at least Pepe gave none. They sat down at the table, and Lorna laid out some simple food to eat, bread, cheese, a tin of spam, apples. She had got out of the habit of cooking at home, eating had become a function not a pleasure. Pepe ate hungrily then said "Tomorrow I cook for you." Lorna cleared away her "If you wish" with the empty plates.

"So, tell me. What have you been doing, Pepe? It's been six years – that's a long time. I want to know it all. And I want to know what you plan to do next."

It took a while. Pepe was hesitant. His English was better than ever but his mild Spanish accent was now spiced with a sprinkling of a rural burr. He had the vocal skills of an impressionist. *Give him a few weeks and he'll be a cockney*, she thought.

The story that emerged was simple enough, at least in the version Pepe chose to tell. After leaving the colony in Finchley he had made his way by begging lifts, jumping on the backs of lorries and walking long distances. He kept heading west, without really knowing why, with little knowledge of English geography. He simply had the belief that it would be easier to live invisibly in the west, away from London. He passed through Oxford, then Stroud, and found himself in the Cotswolds. This seemed like congenial countryside to him. He liked the green, rolling hills and the farms with cattle and crops of many kinds. This countryside seemed to offer a haven. He knocked on the door of a farmhouse and asked for work.

The farmer and his wife were in their early fifties. Sam and Doreen Hodges had two sons, a little older than Pepe, and neither had any interest in farming. They both wanted to join the army as soon as they could. So the Hodges took Pepe on as a farm hand. The work was hard and the pay was a pittance, but Pepe would not starve on a farm. He settled into the agricultural life.

Early on Pepe decided that it would be best to register with the local police. He had remembered a conversation with Lorna about the advantages of doing this, with the prospect eventually of becoming a naturalised citizen. He registered, got his book stamped and even became friendly with the village policeman. In rural Gloucestershire he was almost cherished as an exotic but useful creature from another world. He became absorbed into this new world until, after a time, he was no longer regarded locally as foreign. He was one of them and, as war overtook everything, his credentials in opposing Fascism stood him in good stead. When the Hodges boys joined up and went off to fight, Pepe was needed more than ever at the farm.

Years passed. Pepe began to tire of keeping his head down. He felt a great debt of gratitude and loyalty to Mr and Mrs Hodges. He could not contemplate leaving them when they had come to rely on him for so much. Their youngest son Wally was killed in north Africa and they grieved all the harder because their boys had arrived relatively late. Pepe shared their grief and dug even more potatoes, picked more apples, fed the pigs and chickens, took vegetables to market. The women of the Land Army helped share the work burden, and Pepe was now not just a labourer but a manager.

"I grew up," he stated. "I had no choice. They trusted me, they knew me. If I had left it would have been more difficult. People might think I was a foreign spy."

He told about seeing a train arrive at the local station. The train was packed with children evacuated from the cities. "They were like me and the Spanish children all those years ago. But it was horrible, worse than horrible, seeing the kids standing in the line waiting to be chosen. The people waiting on the platform – farmers like Mr Hodges but not as nice – looked at them like they was choosing cattle. Some just wanted the kids for their ration books."

The story reached the current year. Pepe's life had gone on as before. Then out of the blue a letter arrived from his parents. Pepe had met a Spanish exile in Cheltenham who arranged for letters into and out of Spain. So Pepe had written to his mother and father, the first contact between them for years. Months later, after Pepe had abandoned hope of hearing from them, he was handed the letter. He took it home to the farm and settled into a corner of the barn's loft for solitude. He knew it would be emotional. Reading the letter he was aware that his father was on guard. It was as if the letter was written in code. Pepe took out of it that his mother and father were alive but fearful and feeling threatened. "*Alguien llamó a la puerta anoche.*" He spoke the sentence, as he had read it, in Spanish. *Someone knocked on the door last night.* Pepe was convinced his parents were in danger from Franco supporters, whether official or unofficial. *We cannot complain about our life* seemed like a warning. *We have everything we need except you* seemed like a threat to Pepe.

"I need a cigarette," said Pepe, interrupting his story.

"Here, you can have these. I've given them up."

"Really? Your Player's are better than my Woodbines."

"Have them. I don't want them any more."

He lit a cigarette and drew on it deeply. It was one of

those moments that struck Lorna forcibly with the passage of time that it revealed. She had once before seen Pepe smoking but he had done it, surrounded by Spanish children, with the clumsy bravado of a boy experimenting with becoming an adult. Now he did it from habit and practice; it came naturally to him in a way that it never had for Lorna. She had taken up smoking as a prescription from the doctor but now she felt she had finished that course of treatment. She felt better, no longer in need of smoking's reassurance.

"I am different," said Pepe. "It is not just time. I have grown because I had to. But I never want to be a farmer, it just happen. Now more has come along. Wally died. He died fighting. I should fight too. I have been like a pig in a pen, everything given to me. Now I see the world, it is out there. I want to get back in it."

"I can understand that. You want to give something back. You want to help defeat the fascists."

"Yes. But not really. There is more than that, different from that."

"What? What more do you mean?"

"My parents. Things I believe in. My country too. But what is my country now? Is it here or there? Perhaps I need to do something to find out?"

"After six years? Is it not clear?"

"No, not really. But you make me confused. I am here because I want to see you. Because you are my best English friend. Because perhaps you can be more than that."

Lorna looked at him. Pepe turned away, then back; their eyes locked.

"I'm not sure, Pepe. I don't really know what you mean."

Meaning was fading with the light outside. With so much

dust and smoke lingering in the air, it seemed that dusk arrived earlier these days.

"I mean many things. But some things are hard to say. I want to feel part of the world. No more a refugee. I do not want to be outside things, I want to be inside. It will be better for me. I want this for me not for the good of the world."

Outside the world re-imposed itself through the clanging of an ambulance bell. Even in war ordinary accidents happen, natural emergencies occur, and life goes on in the territories around them.

"Night is coming," said Lorna. "And perhaps the bombs. It's time to take shelter."

"How do we do that?"

"Tonight I think it might be best underground. Have you ever sheltered in the tube? It's OK. We just need to take some things to make it more bearable."

She got to her feet with some relief. The conversation had become uncomfortably intense. Perhaps, despite everything, there could be comforts found in a shelter underground. She brought a thin, rolled up mattress from underneath the bed, and a couple of blankets.

"We'll need these. Though it gets hot down there on nights like these."

Pepe carried the bedding, while Lorna stuffed some emergency rations in a cloth bag. "We don't want to starve. Who knows, we might be there for days?" She smiled to let him know that this was unlikely.

"I can think of worse," Pepe said.

They walked through the darkening, wasted streets of Holborn until they reached the tube. Already the station was getting crowded and they had to squeeze through the narrow gap in the metal gates.

"Looks like a full house tonight," she said to the man in the peaked cap.

"Always room for you, love. I don't think they liked the show above ground last night. Through you go, you know the drill."

At the bottom of the stairs, there was a long corridor to walk down. "This way." Pepe followed Lorna through the low-roofed tunnel. He could hardly have imagined this scene when he had left the farm two days earlier. Although Cheltenham and the area around had been bombed, this brought home the reality of war in a way he could touch. He grasped the mattress and blankets tightly, pulling them close to himself, suddenly anxious that some in this crowd might snatch them from him. But Lorna was resolute, striding ahead, and Pepe had to walk fast to keep up. Their footsteps, his boots, her heels, the tramp of many other shoes, were amplified by the lowness of the tunnel.

"It is like cattle," said Pepe. "It sounds like it too."

"Don't exaggerate," Lorna called behind her. "It's only people."

The platform was a strange sight. Most of the floor space was covered by men, many more women and some children sitting down in a long row, backs leaning against the tiled walls of the platform, away from the tracks. Some of the people were already stretched out flat, sleeping or at least trying to sleep. One group at the far end was determined to have a good time, with singing lubricated by bottles of beer. Turning in the other direction Lorna stepped over reclining bodies until she found enough of a gap to squeeze into. She motioned to the mattress that Pepe was carrying: "Lay it down here."

This then became their bed for the night, in the company of several hundred others. If Pepe had imagined going to bed with Lorna, he had not imagined it like this. Lorna took off her coat and rolled it up to make a pillow; Pepe did the same with his jacket. They slipped off their shoes. Then Lorna lay down with Pepe beside her, and they covered themselves with the blankets. On either side were sleeping bodies. Underneath her blanket Lorna wriggled as if getting out of her beach bathing costume. She unhooked her suspenders and slid out of her stockings.

"How can people sleep? Just like that?" asked Pepe.

"If you haven't slept for weeks, it helps," she replied.

"I am not tired. I cannot sleep yet."

"Well, we can talk. Quietly."

So they talked. In the rambling conversation, like a walk through countryside woods, they moved beyond their immediate surroundings. Pepe talked about his life on the farm. It was a life Lorna knew little about and she felt less inclined to speak about London during the bombing. Touching on it, Pepe expressed anger and guilt at the destruction of war – and the death of Wally Hodges. Without guiding the conversation, Lorna started when Pepe talked about joining up.

"Are you sure?" Lorna raised herself on one elbow to look at Pepe. His head rested on the handkerchief he had spread over his pillow-jacket, to protect his clothes from the smear of Brylcreem combed into his hair.

"Of course. It would be good. Would make things easier. If I am in hiding, I come out of hiding. I live a normal life. At least once war is over."

She lay back again, her eyes dreamily looking at the ceiling above the platform, as if she was gazing at stars. "I think you might be right," she murmured.

She did not expect him to kiss her at that moment but it seemed natural to accept his lips on hers. He offered them tenderly then his tongue entered her mouth and she found herself returning the pressure.

"Oh Pepe," she sighed. "I'm not sure."

He lay back. "It is OK. It will come."

"Perhaps. Who knows?"

Beneath the blankets, Pepe's hand reached for and held Lorna's hand. She did not resist. After a time, it felt a natural thing to do, lying side by side in now dimmed lighting.

"This makes me happy," he whispered. "And you? I hope," turning his face towards her.

"Happy? There are some things that make me happy. Being with you, right now, much to my surprise, that makes me happy. But there's more to it than that."

"Really? That is enough for me."

"There's more. Has to be. Seeing a child and having the child return a smile. The thought, yes even the thought, that the war will be over at some point. But that puts happiness out of reach again. You have to be able to touch happiness, in the here and now, and the end of the war's still a distant prospect."

"I want to touch happiness too," Pepe whispered, turning towards her again. He laid his fingers on Lorna's face, stroking her cheeks with the back of his hand, tracing around her mouth. Then he returned his hand below the blanket, letting it rest on Lorna's stomach. She let it stay there, conscious that her breathing was lifting it gently like driftwood on a wave. They lay in silence, a silence that Lorna found companionable, freed from the pressure of speech. In the vacuum, she felt Pepe's hand move lower, snaking under her skirt, sidling towards her knickers. Then a finger lifting the elastic and entering the flesh beyond.

"No, Pepe. No. Not here." Her hand lifted his hand away from her, putting it down on his chest. "I think we should sleep. Everyone else is."

CHAPTER 26

Neither of them slept well. They tried but found themselves talking like schoolchildren under the blankets for much of the night. At least their conversation was a distraction from the sound of snoring that rumbled like tube trains through the tunnels. As soon as it would be light outside, they rolled up the mattress and blankets, then headed for the surface.

It was a relief to come out into daylight; even more so when Lorna remembered that it was Saturday.

"That was always our day," said Pepe.

"Unless it was Sunday…"

"Either was nice. Still is. What shall we do?"

"First…first we will take these back home, and I want to have a wash."

Lorna sneaked Pepe up the stairs, grateful for once that her landlady Mrs Hayes was deaf. She was not yet ready for an embarrassing conversation about a young man staying in her room. Best to postpone that confession, if she could, till times far into the future.

The bathroom was across the landing, and with the little flat above empty, Lorna had the bathroom just for her own use. She told Pepe she would be taking a bath and that she would not pull the plug when she had finished. Pepe would be able to use the water after her – "it will still be warm. But you'll need to be quiet – no whistling. I don't want Mrs Hayes prying about."

The bath tub took a while to fill but Lorna eventually relaxed in a hot bath. It was still a luxury, one of the few she had. She would have soaked longer but the water would cool if she took too long. Drying herself with a rough towel, she slipped on her house coat and scampered back to her flat to bring Pepe. Half an hour later, their skin puckered and reddened by water and scrubbing, dressed in clean clothes, they were ready to talk about the day ahead.

"We should go out – at some point. For a walk," said Lorna.

"OK. But I could cook."

"There's not much to cook." Lorna went to the scullery to see what was there. "I'll go out and get something. I've just got some vegetables here. And some sausages."

They had sausages for breakfast and Pepe said he would make a stew later if Lorna could get some mince meat to go with the vegetables.

"Any spices?"

She shook her head. "Just salt and pepper." Pepe rolled his eyes to the ceiling and they laughed. It was good to be together, enjoying that feeling, to feel young, to teeter on the edge of something unexpected, unforeseen. The day stretched out in front of them with its prospects to be explored. Lorna had not had a Saturday like this since the war began. She was bubbling with emotion, smiling without reason except the pleasure in that moment.

Pepe looked at her and returned her smile. He reached across the table and put his hand on hers.

"Aah," she sighed. "We should be serious for a moment. Or we'll find the time has gone, and nothing decided."

"What is there to decide? This is enough."

"We have to decide about you. We need to talk about your future. What are you planning to do? Not just the pipe dreams, but a plan."

"A plan? Tomorrow I have to go back to the farm or I'm

out of a job. I told Mr Hodges I will be back on Sunday evening."

Lorna was taken by surprise. Pepe had a plan and it had more detail than hers. It forced her back to reality, making her think more like a lawyer again. Saturday turned into Monday in an instant.

"Of course," she said. "That's right. But – but were you serious about joining up? Is that what you want to do?"

Pepe's hand lifted off Lorna's and reached for a cigarette. Lighting the cigarette he pondered in silence, looking at ash on the tip as if to read the future there.

"I do not know. To be honest I do not know what is possible. I went to get a form but it is difficult. There are parts where I do not know what to say – to lie or the truth."

"The truth is always best. You are not in a situation where you can afford to be caught lying."

Pepe shrugged. "I want to do…" he paused, looking at her. "I want to do what will please you. That is all. I will be a soldier for you. I will fight."

Lorna did not know what to say. She thought of Harry who had died fighting when she had not wanted him to fight. It seemed now that she had the power to send Pepe off to fight and perhaps to die. But this was not a power she sought.

"I cannot tell you to do that, Pepe. It's too much for me. It's like a sacrifice you are suggesting."

"No, not at all. I do it willing. If I am a soldier, I am English. I stay. And after the fighting – it will not be long now – I come back to be with you."

Lorna said nothing, not knowing what to say. She rose from the kitchen chair and moved away from the table. She sat on the edge of her bed and opened up a file she had brought from work. But her eyes could not read a word.

"Pepe," she said eventually. "I cannot send you into the army. You have to decide. You might get killed, I cannot send you to be killed and have that on my conscience."

"Why? I might live. I do not go to be killed. I want to come back and be with you. That will be easier if I have become like one of you, an English person. I will get an English hat."

"You make a lot of assumptions. About me. About everything. And I still feel responsible, in some way, for your safety. That is what I was supposed to do, to look after your welfare, a Spanish boy in a foreign country."

"And you did that. Look at me. Grown. But the time of looking after me has passed."

"Not really. You are still a Spanish boy in a foreign country. With no family to look after him. Make a false move and you could be locked up or deported."

"That is why I must join up. They will not deport a soldier on their side."

Lorna's elbows rested on her knees, her face in her hands. She stared at him but Pepe could not translate the meaning of that stare, whether rejection or resistance, defiance or love or longing. It might have been all of these. He moved across the room to sit next to her on the bed.

"Lorna, Lorna, look at me. I am not the small boy you knew before. I have grown up and I am a man. I have the feelings of a man. My feelings are for you."

Lorna's smile at him was wan, a low-wattage light bulb smile that cast little glow. She feared where the conversation might be leading. She did not want to make a commitment of any kind, emotional or physical, to a relationship surrounded by such uncertainty.

"We all have feelings," she forced herself to say. "But sometimes it's better to keep them to ourselves."

Pepe exploded in exasperation. "No, no, no. If we have feelings, we must show them."

Lorna's own feelings were in turmoil. She hardly knew what she really thought about Pepe. He had re-entered her life 24 hours ago after a six-year absence. She had always felt fondly towards him but it was clear he had thought more about her than she about him during those years. Could her feelings deepen now or in time? She looked at him. It was true, he was not the boy he had been before, but she had already made that adjustment.

"Lorna, I have to say. I love you."

He paused to look at her, and felt encouraged enough to put an arm around her. Bending close, he spoke quietly. "I want to fuck you."

Lorna gasped inside. The words shocked her. She had never liked crude language. It was not, in her eyes and ears, the way to behave.

"Your language is too coarse," she said. "You should not speak to me, or any woman, like that. That is a boundary you should not cross."

Pepe looked puzzled. "Have I used the wrong word? What should I say?"

"It's a bad word. Men might use it when talking on the farm and no doubt you heard it at your work. But not here. Not with me."

"I am sorry. I will never say it again. But what should I say?"

Lorna paused to think. "You might say I would like to make love to you. That would be acceptable language."

"Then I would like to make love to you. Because you are so beautiful and I love you."

"The words are better but the proposition is still not acceptable. We are too different, not least in our ages."

"Ages makes it no different. Anyway now it is my birthday. Last week. Do you remember? No. I am twenty-one. I can do all sorts of things legally."

"Legally? We have to see about that. You might not even be legally allowed to stay in this country."

'I am still here. No one has expelled me. And I want to fight for this country. I have decided. I even have the forms. See, here they are."

Lorna stood up, looked at the official papers Pepe held in his hand, took a handkerchief from her handbag and blew her nose.

"It will still not be easy. We have to play everything by the book. It might change everything, if we can pull it off."

"Everything? Everything. Everything is what I want. It means you."

"Pepe, no. Not back to that. Look, I'm going to tell you our deal. Are you listening?"

He looked younger again, chastised, a schoolboy in trouble for talking out of turn. He exaggerated his look of concentration for Lorna.

"It won't be easy. Getting you signed up to join the British army will not be easy. But I think it will be possible if we take all the right steps. I will talk to Bryan about what you want to do and I'm sure we can help. But I won't sleep with you. You can't have both, you have to choose, and you have already chosen. You want to join up. This is our deal. You will join up, be a soldier, fight the war."

"And after?"

"After you will be a British citizen. Then who knows? You will have more choices. Choices of your own."

Pepe wore his sulky look, eyes turned down to the ground. Then he raised his eyes and smiled.

"Deal. We have a deal."

The deal became their contract which, inevitably, had to be completed with the filling and signing of forms. In work mode, Lorna made them a pot of tea then settled at the kitchen table with her pen, poised to go through the forms for Pepe. She asked him questions about factual details, and they discussed questions that needed more complicated answers.

"So, you are twenty-one. Happy birthday."

"And you are twenty-nine. So young…"

She flicked at him in pretended annoyance, but smiled to herself. *In our twenties together. If not for long.* Then she returned to the form, copying down details from Pepe's Alien Registration document. Later that morning they had finished the forms, Pepe adding his signature and that day's date.

"This looks so good," remarked Lorna. "They'll probably make you an officer."

"Really?"

"No, not really."

Lorna realised that the biggest impediment to their meeting of minds might be a sense of humour not shared. *But even that,* she thought, *might be a source of amusement.*

"Pepe, I'll just pop out to the butcher's. You wanted to cook. I'll get some mince for later."

"Butcher's? I forget. That's rhyming slang, is it?"

Lorna shook her head, grinning to herself. "Only if you say so." She took the ration book from the kitchen table drawer and chuckled as she walked down the stairs. It was a relief to laugh.

CHAPTER 27

Lorna felt as if she was sneaking Pepe out of the house, although there was no reason why she should not have a visitor in the middle of the day. It just seemed to her that there was something clandestine in Pepe's presence. It would be too complicated a story to explain her friendship with a Spaniard in wartime to her landlady.

"We'll have a walk," said Lorna. "Just a wander."

They turned left at the bottom of Lamb's Conduit Street and made for Russell Square. In summer sunshine the square represented a peaceful haven despite evidence of the war all around. They walked past the British Museum, looking solid despite signs of recent air assault, into Bedford Square.

"So many squares," said Pepe.

"I love them. There's one more I want to show you."

Soho Square was just off Oxford Street, and they entered it from the north. It was a tiny square compared to the others and it was full of the clutter of war, not least the sandbags being stacked by men in Civil Defence uniforms. Lorna checked to make sure she knew none of them before leading Pepe inside the square. Right in front of them was a stone statue of Charles II – "the last Catholic king," explained Lorna – standing straight but with a face that had crumbled with the ravages of time and weather.

"I feel a bit sorry for him," whispered Pepe. "He had to stay true to his faith."

The stone king now faced, as if in penance, the French Protestant church outside the square. The church looked austere next to its neighbours, grand houses from the 18th century. The king's statue betrayed no emotion but an additional insult was heaped on its head by a squatting pigeon that seemed to have taken up residence there. Pepe and Lorna sat down on a bench, with their fingers intertwined.

"This is nice," he said. "Are you happy?"

"You keep asking. I'm not sure why. I can't really be happy with a war on."

"No, but you cannot win the war through what you do. You have to do what you can for yourself. We all have to look after ourselves and try to be happy."

"Are you? What makes you happy?"

Pepe thought, observing that the pigeon had finally abandoned its regal perch.

"Love makes me happy. There are many kinds of love. The love that I have for my mother and father – it would make me happy to see them again. And love for my country – if it will allow me to once more by becoming itself again. Other things, other kinds of love that are too difficult to say."

He stared at the statue in the near distance. The pigeon had returned.

"And, of course," he said, "you, Lorna, you make me happy. Or you could."

Lorna had always supposed that her own happiness was related to that of others. She felt selfish in the pursuit of personal happiness; she was more concerned to bring it about for others. Was she wrong, did Pepe show a different way? It seemed that Pepe might have more chance of achieving happiness by setting his sights lower.

They sat in silence with the warm sun on their faces. Their eyes were closed, providing shade for their thoughts and dreams.

"Let's walk on," said Lorna. "It's getting hot."

They took the eastern exit out of the square. Pepe seemed to be drawn to the building opposite the gate. The red brick tower of St Patrick's church summoned him with a ringing bell. Pepe guided Lorna by the hand through the portico with its tall wooden door into the lobby of the church. Once inside, Pepe let go of Lorna's hand.

Pepe was no longer aware of Lorna. If he had been he would have noticed her reluctance to enter. She resisted religion, almost feared it, and those feelings were intensified by Catholicism. She did not belong here, she felt like an intruder. Pepe, on the other hand, seemed immediately at home, asserting his security and independence in this space. Lorna hung back shyly in the lobby while Pepe strode purposefully forward, dipping his fingers in the stone bowl of water held by a statue of an angel. With holy water on the tips of his fingers he made the sign of the cross on his brow.

Lorna edged her way forward to the start of the aisle. Here the church opened up vertically in an unexpected display of space and light. Ahead of her was the altar beneath a half dome: halfway down the wall the lettering SANCTUS gleamed in gold. Individuals were on their knees praying in the pews, with side chapels and lighted candles to the right, and mahogany confessional boxes to the left. An aroma of candles and incense, sickly to Lorna's senses, hung in the air.

A couple of years earlier, as Lorna now remembered when she saw the scene, a bomb had pierced the roof, leaving a roughness in the once sumptuous floor and taking chunks out of a marble pillar. An air of solitary meditation permeated everything but Lorna's acceptance of that was undermined by the images of suffering everywhere, decorating the walls and the nooks around the church. She could not give herself up to a faith that gloried in, what seemed to her eyes, grief, pain and torture. The Pieta, with Mary cradling the dying Jesus, the reliefs of Christ with the cross, made her feel queasy. She turned around towards the exit door. In the lobby she read a notice from Father Reardon thanking God for the church's deliverance from destruction.

Her final view of the church's interior was through the archway, past the statues of angels, to observe Pepe in earnest conversation with a man in a dark suit.

She decided to wait outside until Pepe re-appeared. In her imagined scenarios of the future, including those conjured by the last 24 hours, she had never considered that religion might play a part. The Catholic church in particular had sided with fascism, sometimes covertly, sometimes overtly. In Spain the church had been squarely behind Franco. How could Pepe cling to this religion?

Thoughts and images rolled around in her head, revolving with dizzying frequency. The bleeding wound in the side of the dying Jesus. Mary's maternal tears. *Superstition*, she screamed inside her head. *Domine*, spoke the priest. The refuge of reactionary forces. A sprinkling of holy water. *Ora*, pray, prayers spoken on their knees and lifted up towards heaven through the hole in the church ceiling.

Lorna waited, agitated. Pepe was a long time, or so it seemed. Lorna did not want to go back inside to bring him out. She persuaded herself that she had to respect his faith even while fearing that this would separate them. She did not feel that she could pass over to his religious view of the world, if that was really what she had witnessed.

Eventually Pepe came out, blinking a little in the bright

sunshine so that he did not see Lorna at first. The man in the dark suit – bearded, she now saw, like an El Greco portrait – followed straight after. He and Pepe nodded goodbye to each other, and the stranger walked south down Greek Street deeper into Soho.

"There you are," said Pepe. "I am sorry to be long."

"What was all that about?"

"It is a long time since I go to church. It is the way I was brought up."

"How much does it...does it matter to you?"

Pepe took Lorna by the elbow and walked back into Soho Square.

"It matters," he said. "But other things matter too. You matter."

They sat down again on the same bench as before. "Who was the man you were speaking to?" Lorna asked.

"Funny thing," said Pepe. "He was Spanish. He works in London at the embassy. Spanish, from Madrid. Like most of us he goes to church. We talked a little. It was good to speak Spanish again."

Lorna decided that a change of scene was needed, and a chance to speak openly. It was a short stroll to Lyons Corner House.

Over a pot of tea they talked about subjects they had not touched on deeply before. This was a place where Lorna used to have tea with her mother. The trip from Kent had become more difficult in the war, and rarely undertaken. Lorna felt guilty that she made such little effort to see her mother, especially after her father died, but they now had so few things in common. Conversation was difficult, simply accentuating the divide that now gaped between them. She explained this to Pepe, feeling that it was part of being more open with each other.

In return Pepe talked about his mother and father. He missed them as much as ever, perhaps even more now that he had had the recent letter. He longed to see them again but did not know how that might be possible. But it meant that he felt the need to pray for their safety, to light a candle for them and keep their memory alive.

"You see, we will pray for each other. We do not need to write to know that. It is part of us, the way we are."

They walked back to Lorna's flat, with each saying little. Something had changed. Lorna felt something important had changed but, as the evening drew on, there was a gathering sense of relaxation and reconciliation.

Pepe had promised to cook. He enjoyed cooking and he used the mince and vegetables to make a stew as rustic as he would eat on the farm. Sharing a bottle of brown ale, they talked with greater freedom and they laughed together in a renewal of friendship. When it came to bedtime, Pepe joked about having to sleep on the mattress on the floor. He fell asleep in minutes, while Lorna lay, eyes wide open, in a room disturbed by the swelling of another's dreams.

CHAPTER 28

Pepe returned to the farm in Gloucestershire, and summer unfolded into autumn. In London there were hot days and rainy days but most nights were quiet for Lorna. The bombs were not despatched from Germany or they were directed elsewhere, so the leaves could fall at their own natural pace along with the spinning sycamore seeds and the heavier thud of conkers onto the ground. The war had become routine, humdrum, irritating for outstaying its time like the last incoherent drunk at a bad party. Locked into this routine, Lorna did what she would always do; she applied herself to work, part of which was shepherding Pepe's papers through the legal system.

"It all looks fine to me, Lorna. We should get those off right away." Bryan pushed the forms across his desk towards her.

"What are the chances?"

"I think he'll be fine. We need soldiers. That will probably outweigh our national distrust of foreigners."

"I'll let Pepe know."

"How does he feel about it? It must be strange for him. Think it's probably for the best that he's past 21 now."

"Why?"

"Less complicated. No parental permissions needed. Or perhaps I'm just showing the naivety of age – I find myself susceptible to that these days."

Lorna was pleased that another stage in the process was almost completed. Soon Pepe would be both British and a soldier.

Bryan's words clung to her. She wondered how Pepe really felt about all this. The Pepe she knew, particularly after that last weekend, was still a figure of some mystery. She felt uncertain of her own feelings towards him. She knew the surface details, as she would recognise the streets of London when looking down from a rooftop. But what was going on inside? She wanted to know more, and she realised that this in itself was significant. The wish to understand better was a step towards a feeling that might be deeper. But how could she know him better if she had no chance to see him?

She would have to write and encourage him to write back. Even as she thought this, she acknowledged its impossibility. Pepe hated writing letters. If forced to it, he would write "I am well. How are you?" Such exchanges would lead to irritation rather than understanding. But in thinking about writing, Lorna wondered if she could write for Pepe and about Pepe. She might explore his life and feelings in this way, even if they were not actually his in reality.

What she had in mind was a diary. "Some sort of a diary" as she put it to herself. But not written as Lorna, not words from her own mouth. She went to the stationery cupboard to take out a notebook that would be the diary. There was something in the wartime austerity of the rough paper that seemed to fit the need, as she thought of Pepe on his farm. Yet what did she know of farming? *Very little, but it will help me discover. And it will be better than silence.*

She was excited by the idea and determined to make a start that evening. Unusually for her she wished the afternoon away, finding it hard to concentrate on the work she had to do.

At last she could head for home, still in daylight. She was accustomed to the fifteen minute walk, and most days she hardly noticed the people and surroundings as she walked. It was a useful time to wind down and make the transition between work and home, and often she would be surprised to find herself already arrived at her doorstep. This evening, however, was different. She found her senses heightened by the wish to think and write about Pepe.

It had been a hot day in September, perhaps a last burst of true summer in the morning. The weather had turned throughout the day, and a late afternoon shower had freshened the air and soaked the pavements. In the evening sun the rain left a glistening dampness, like a cold sweat on the skin of the roadway. In those few hours the season faded from summer to autumn, and Lorna decided to walk through Russell Square, taking the small deviation to seek signs of the season's passing. She smelt the earthiness of the soil under the grass and the woodiness that was breathed out by the leaves that still hung in the trees. Bending down she picked up a handful of leaves beneath a tree, scrunched them between her dry palms and threw them in the air like confetti. She rescued one leaf from the path for the sheer beauty of its mottled red and orange colouring. Holding the leaf, like a pen between her thumb and index finger, she cut through Queen Square for home where she sat down to write.

September evening

The days of summer are gone. A farm worker fills the days, from dawn to dusk. How does he fill them? With work.

Look at my hands. Feel them. They are rough with daily labour. There is no cream that will soften these calloused hands. A labourer's hands are his most familiar, most unfamiliar necessity. They are the tool to use all other tools. Without them I can do nothing. I cannot dig for roots, for discovery, for victory. They are indispensable for my being.

Yet I look at them and they are strangers. Why do we so rarely look at our own hands? Why do we not look and ponder? We might notice the lines in the skin and read the stories of our past if not our future.

Lorna put down the pen, spent by the effort. She looked at the parts she had crossed out before reaching this version. She was not used to this kind of writing and the way it had drained her. *Oh this is hopeless*, she thought. But even as she thought it, there was a vestige of pride in what she had written. Pride and exhilaration; she had enjoyed the effort. Looking at the mantelpiece clock, she was surprised that so much time had passed unnoticed, disappointed that so much time had passed for such paltry results. But she determined to continue whenever she could; she felt closer to Pepe.

The working days of autumn were dropping behind her. Pepe's case was becoming clearer as she looked ahead. Dates were firming up in the naturalisation process.

"It's nearly there," said Bryan. "But you'll need to go through it all with our client, and you'll need his signature, of course."

"I'll post it off to him. He normally responds fairly quickly."

"Best to meet. For this last transaction. It will save time in the long run and it's always good practice."

"Who needs the practice?"

"Lorna, you know what I mean. I think you should arrange to meet him. Not in London, that will be too difficult. What's the town nearest to him?"

So it was arranged that Lorna would meet Pepe in Cheltenham. She would travel by train and meet him in the town. She felt a flutter of excitement inside, whether caused by the prospect of an unexpected journey or the chance to see

Pepe. *Yes, I'd like to see him.* That night, sitting at her kitchen table, she added another entry to her Pepe diary.

   October evening

The days are growing shorter, faster every day. Autumn comes in, blowing from the west. You harvest crops but as the weeks pass there is less to harvest. You fill the days still with work, and your days spill over into night. You lay down stores for winter. Apples, onions, potatoes. Mrs Hodges makes jams and pickles. The cattle eat their hay. The sun hardly shines. You get up before sunrise and go to sleep long after the sun has set. There is a natural rhythm to this life.

I long for winter to come and then to be done. My sap has fallen and it needs to rise. I pray to God that it will, come the spring.

Reading back through the writing, reading it again and again, it finally struck her that she had in some way fused herself with Pepe. She was not really writing as him. How could she? She did not know his life or thoughts, her attempts were guesswork or imagination but strangely not her own. These words appeared from somewhere that she could not locate. She was not writing as herself, she had never had such thoughts herself. Yet they must have come from within her and from her belief in such thoughts existing within Pepe. Her personality and Pepe's had drifted towards each other in this process of imagining, like two banks of mist that now mingled as one. She felt closer to him than ever before.

For the first time the 'adoption' of Pepe as a young boy became consigned to history. Everything had changed, everything was different now. They were starting again as two people brought together for reasons that were not the original reasons. She could look at Pepe through a different lens and see him more clearly as he really was, as she really was. This meant that she could ask herself questions that had seemed impossible to ask before. Did she love him? Could she love him? Did she trust him? To her surprise this last question was the one she found most difficult. Love and trust need not go together. People betray each other – why did she feel that Pepe was so capable of betrayal? Or would trust come inevitably with a full acceptance of love? Was the combination of love and trust essential for happiness?

He is and remains a friend, she told herself. *There is no need to venture further.*

So Lorna wrote to Pepe in her most professional tone, setting up a meeting in Cheltenham in a week's time and proposing that they could conclude their business in an hour. She set a time to meet him, in the hotel where she would be staying, stressed the importance and asked him to confirm without delay. Two days later, receiving his 'I will be there', Lorna bought train tickets and made arrangements to stay at the hotel in Cheltenham recommended by Bryan. She had worked out that, even if the meeting was business-like, it would be impossible to complete the round trip from London in a day.

Early the next morning, she wrote an entry in the diary.

October morning
I wake up in darkness. It is pitch black but time for my day to begin. Work needs to be done.

Opening the door, stepping outside, the first glow of light rises in the sky. My breath is like smoke before my face. There has been a hard frost, making the grass as white as snow. The soil will be frozen today but that will not matter. There will be no digging today, the ground will not be disturbed. Today's working tasks are to tidy and repair. To prepare the farm buildings for the approach of winter.

As my boots crunch on the frosted ground I think of those I love and those who may love me.

Lorna wondered if she were falling into fantasy or reality. Perhaps she would never know. but she felt that her life might have changed course.

CHAPTER 29

The train was packed. At Paddington Lorna was shown to her reserved seat but was surprised at having to squeeze her way down the corridor through people already spilling out of full compartments, making seats out of suitcases and bags. Peering through the windows into smoky interiors she saw men in uniform stretched out on the overhead luggage racks as if they were hammocks. The train seemed to be full of soldiers and the soldiers were of many nationalities.

"Yes, miss, the soldiers are heading for Cheltenham too. It's become quite the place to see the world."

"And there's me thinking I was off for a quiet time in the country."

She settled into her seat, one of six in the carriage. She had specified a No Smoking compartment, and she now realised that this meant her fellow passengers were not male and not soldiers. It would be possible to keep to herself and work during the journey.

The train trundled through the English countryside. Lorna allowed herself time to take in the scenery as they rattled along. There were still cows and sheep, hedges and trees, rivers and ponds, and an overall impression of greenness. It was all comfortingly ordinary, a landscape that had not changed for centuries. You could almost imagine that there had not been a war.

That impression was dispelled by arrival at Cheltenham. As she stepped down onto the platform, with her small suitcase in her hand, Lorna was nearly swept aside by British soldiers carrying kit bags, Indians in turbans, short-cropped Americans, a trainee army on the move. She allowed the porter to carry her bag and sneak her further up the queue for a taxi. Feeling embarrassed, she slipped him a couple of coppers as a tip.

Cheltenham was not what she expected. There were many more people and the streets were bustling. She had wondered whether she needed to book ahead for a hotel but Bryan had insisted she must – and now she was relieved that she had done so. The George was not a grand hotel but Lorna was not a connoisseur of such places. She assumed that this was what hotels were like, particularly in wartime: brown, overwhelmingly brown, from the painted doors and wainscots in the corridors to the heavy varnish on the wood panelling that covered the lower walls of the public rooms, an air of fatigue wanly illuminated by watery lighting, a feeling that time had stood still for many dusty years. But her spirits lifted when she entered her bedroom. It had the same faded look to it but she turned down the bedclothes to reveal clean white sheets and she peered through net curtains into the daylight of the park opposite. To her, after years of her boarded-up flat in bombed-out London, this was a touch of luxury. She might enjoy the trip as something of a holiday after all.

It was already getting late into the afternoon but Lorna decided to take a walk. She had never been to Cheltenham before and her knowledge of England beyond her familiar south-eastern corner was sketchy. *It will be good to see what we are fighting for.* So she wandered through streets that were elegant still, despite their ransacking in the cause of the war effort. The Regency houses had been stripped of their decorative ironware, to be melted down for military metal; so too the railings around public gardens. A smell of paraffin smoke permeated everywhere, becoming a taste in the mouth and a mistiness in the air. She found out that smoke pots were used frequently to shroud the town from the air, allowing its factories to hide from the bombers. Not only London had been suffering; and now the throng of soldiers from all parts of the world were gathering in Cheltenham for what might be a final assault to end the country's suffering.

Even as she thought this she was aware that she was making herself and her location as the centre of the war's activity. *Ridiculous*, she told herself. She was never comfortable taking too much attention. She was happier to hide herself behind the shelter of a personal smoke pot, carrying on working hard but unseen by others. Perhaps she could only be happy by making others happy.

That night she had a solitary meal in the hotel and that suited her well. She looked forward to the pleasure of a quiet room and ironed sheets to sleep in. And perhaps a vision of a brighter future that dreams sometimes offer.

The next morning she awoke refreshed but could not recall dreaming at all. Her sleep had been too profound. She felt a tinge of disappointment as she brought the reality of Pepe to mind, having expected him to be part of her night-time slumber. She thought of him as she washed her face, as she brushed her teeth, as she drew on her stockings. But she needed to clear her head properly, to rehearse and be ready for the meeting that she had set for 9.30 that morning.

She went out for a walk before breakfast, crossing the road to the park opposite. Mist lay on the ground, stirring gently, exhaled like the waking earth's chilly breath. It had not rained but water droplets hung like necklace pearls from the telephone wires that circled the park. Inside it looked uninviting and dark so she kept to the outside pavement where a flying leaf brushed her face then settled on top of the layer that was already making the ground slippery underfoot. There was not a breath of wind to disturb the leaves or the thoughts that were settling in Lorna's mind. As she walked the determination of her steps reflected a gathering sense of commitment to her 'client' as she persuaded herself she needed to think of Pepe.

The sun was now a gleaming presence behind the mist. The growing light encouraged her into Montpellier Gardens. Spiders' webs draped over the leaves of the shrubs, but she gradually realised that the shrubs were vegetables. Digging for victory, the flower beds had been turned over to vegetable patches, the utility of carrots and beans displacing the decoration of roses and dahlias. She scolded herself for not thinking enough where the food on her table came from.

Back in the hotel, breakfast was in a small room with tables set for two or four people. It was clear that single people were expected to share tables, so Lorna was not surprised when an elderly woman was shown to the place setting opposite. They exchanged words of mutual welcome. The lady's scarf tried to cover her awareness of anxiety, the bobbing of her Adam's apple behind the fabric that she pressed to her neck with thin fingers. Lorna poured tea for her. It was a good deed to be reassuring.

"No, I live in the countryside but I have to see my solicitor today."

"Really?" asked Lorna. "Not a big problem, I hope."

"That's what I hope too. I have to change my will."

Professional curiosity overcame Lorna's natural reserve, so

she explained that she herself was 'in the law'. This persuaded the woman opposite to open up and explain her situation. In no time at all Lorna was told of a husband recently lost to illness and of a son who was serving in the Navy. Now, worried by one death about the constant threat of other deaths, she feared for herself and her son, but most of all for her grandson. He was dear to her but her daughter-in-law was not, so she wanted to set up a trust fund for the grandchild and leave everything she owned to him in the event of her son's death in action. Anxiety throbbed in her temples and throat as she spoke. Lorna made understanding noises and dispensed toast, tea and consolation.

"I'm sure it will be possible to do all you want. Hopefully the war will be over soon and your son will return safe and sound."

"We all hope so. For everyone. But I will keep the arrangements for my grandson, no matter what. It is a responsibility I had not appreciated before. I love my son, of course, but I care more desperately for my grandchild. What world will he grow up in? I wish to see him frequently and I live near enough to make that possible despite my daughter-in-law's reluctance. But I had not expected that it would matter quite so much to me. I want to be a good grandmother so I need to see him and do my bit to look after him."

"Oh, I'm sure you will. You must be close."

The old lady's eyes were closed, contemplating the future, the day ahead and the years ahead.

"I'm sure you are right, my dear. Thank you for being such a good listener."

They rose from the breakfast table together, then went their separate ways to their rooms. Lorna needed to change from her flat shoes. She felt the need for the boost of an inch or two of height and confidence and perhaps even elegance before beginning her business meeting with Pepe.

CHAPTER 30

Lorna waited on the pavement outside the hotel. She was concerned that Pepe might find it intimidating to come inside in what she imagined would be his work clothes. She need not have worried.

A station wagon drew up outside the hotel and a young gentleman stepped out. Pepe was dressed in a shirt and tie with a dark jacket and trousers that almost matched. He wore a black felt hat tilted slightly over his left eye. He looked respectable enough and English enough for any of the day's possibilities. His kissing of Lorna on the cheek was his only betraying sign of foreignness.

"You look very smart, Pepe," said Lorna.

"And you look lovely, of course," replied Pepe quietly.

The reason for his whisper was the figure getting out of the driver's seat in the car. Lorna observed him over Pepe's shoulder. "Is this…?" Pepe nodded.

"I'm pleased to meet you, Mr Hodges. Thank you for your help in all this. We could not have managed without you."

Mr Hodges looked the gentleman farmer, awkward in the urban environment. His tweed jacket and brown cloth cap were worn with an air of defiance, as if daring anyone to object to his presence or his very being. He looked suspiciously at the doorway of the hotel. Lorna waved the way forward.

"We'll go inside as I have a room reserved for us."

"Do we 'ave to? Not so sure they'd welcome me in there. Might get mud on the carpets."

"It will be fine. You really don't need to worry."

"What d'you want me for anyways? It's Pepe you need to see."

"Mr Hodges, I'd like you to witness a document or two."

"Best be quick then. I have things need seein' to."

"It won't take long."

"That's more'n I've got."

Lorna checked that there was the hint of a smile on his face.

"Don't think me nettlesome," he said. "Just my funny ways."

"That's true, Joe," said Pepe. "Funny ha-ha and funny peculiar."

"You see," Mr Hodges nodded in a conspiratorial way to Lorna. "He's one of us now."

"No doubt about it."

Lorna led them up the steps and into the foyer. Pepe and Mr Hodges blinked at their perception of its grandeur, shuffled at their discomfort in these surroundings. The crystal chandelier glittered its resistance to the possibility of bombing, while the pastoral scenes in gilt frames gave evidence of peaceful days in the past and the hint of a promise for the future. Lorna took them through into a back room that was much smaller and plainer, sparsely furnished with a scrubbed wooden table and four chairs.

"I was sorry to hear about your son, Mr Hodges," Lorna began.

"Wally did his duty. And we don't forget 'im. Reason why Pepe's lookin' so smart is those are Wally's clothes. They fit 'im a treat, flummock that 'e normally is."

"Not true," protested Pepe. "I can't go wearing a suit to clean out the pigs."

"Thank you for that too, Mr Hodges," said Lorna. "He needs to look presentable."

"Rather the clothes get worn. Tommy's smaller than Wally so they won't fit 'im."

"Your other son? Is he at home with you now?"

"Nah, away in Italy. A corporal now. I need 'im to come back after the fightin' and run the farm. Specially as this lad won't be around. Though I keep tellin' 'im he could be a reserved occupation. A farmer. Tommy wouldn't listen to that neither."

"Tommy's English," said Lorna, "so things are more straightforward. We have to get things sorted out with Pepe," starting to spread out the paperwork on the table before them.

"Pepe's a different case, allright. Been like another son to me but blowed if I know 'im. Could be a spy for all I really know 'bout 'im. Doesn't really talk about his own country and things."

"Perhaps this is his country now."

"Doubt that. But 'e can fight for us."

Pepe seemed not to notice the conversation. He gave no reactions to any of the words; they were spoken as if he were not there; he hardly seemed to be there. That suited Lorna's way of getting this business done. She wanted to make it as impersonal and objective as possible. She felt that would give them a greater chance of speedy success. She got out a pen and talked them through the documents that needed signatures.

They were soon done and able to release Mr Hodges to his own business in town. He arranged to pick Pepe up at the end of the day.

"That's just the first part," said Lorna to Pepe. "Let's go and see what we can do about the army now."

They walked out into a weakly-smiling sun that was melting away the last of the grey mist. The smell of paraffin smoke still hung in the air and soldiers were training, running up and down the muddy ground of Montpellier Gardens.

"It's like the school PT class," said Lorna. "Lucky you. All this will be yours soon."

Pepe made a grimace of mock-horror and slipped Lorna's arm through his. It was done so nimbly that she did not resist. *There's no harm.* She enjoyed walking along the leaf-strewn pavements arm in arm with a young man.

"You won't be able to sign up on the spot. Just to be serious for a moment. These papers have to work their way through the system. But you might as well get things under way."

They were standing outside the yellowy-brown stone of the town hall frontage, with pillars behind and Union Jacks fluttering from flag poles. Pepe was silent.

"You're not having second thoughts?" she asked.

"No, no. I want to do this. But I need a little time."

"What? Minutes? Weeks?"

"Do not worry, Lorna. Just a short pause. It is just – this looks – well, it looks so English. English, yes. Look at those flags. See those soldiers. Who am I to be part of this?"

She squeezed his arm tighter, and reached out to take his hand.

"Don't worry. You're as good as any of us. You don't have to pretend. Just be yourself."

"I always have to pretend. I am not English. If someone asks, I say I am Basque. Not Spanish. That makes people less suspicious. They either do not know where Basque comes from or – if they do – they think I am on the right side."

"There you are then. You are on the right side."

"I think it is different, joining the army."

"It is. But it's what you want. What you need. You'll be able to be accepted."

She looked at him, almost imploring him. She realised that she was almost holding out a white feather to him, shaming him into joining up. Telling him to be prepared to sacrifice his life. Then feeling shamed herself, hating it and telling herself it was what she had to do for everybody's sake – her own, Pepe's, the country's. It was the patriotic thing to do, and her patriotism, suppressed for so long, was now firmly ingrained by the need to resist the Nazis above everything else. The war effort was part of the same thinking as taking a stand against fascism in Cable Street before the war. Inevitably she thought of Harry and she looked at Pepe with doubts in her mind. She had to have those doubts silenced. She brought Pepe's head down towards her and she kissed him, taking him by surprise.

After a few seconds they became conscious that they were in public. They moved their faces away, staring each other in the eye.

"I must then," said Pepe.

"You must. We have a deal."

Pepe's face, previously with no expression except one of worry, creased into a smile. He kissed Lorna's brow below the narrow brim of her hat.

"It is a good deal," he said. "Now I am ready. Let us go."

"You have to do this by yourself, Pepe. They won't take kindly to a surplus female."

Lorna checked that he had his identity card and paperwork. They went inside together, with Lorna prepared to wait in the town hall reception as long as it took. Pepe went to a desk and the process of seeing different people began. They had to shuttle between the town hall and municipal offices, opening and shutting doors on interviews that brought frustration, relief and, eventually, progress.

"I saw the Major," Pepe explained. "In his uniform, lots of medals, an old man really."

"I expect he talked about the Boche."

"He did. Who are they? He asks me if I am ready to bash the bosh. I could tell he want me to say Yes so I did."

There would be more to do, in due course. A medical. Another interview. These would have to wait until his naturalisation papers were processed but Pepe was beaming. He had done his duty. To the cause, to Lorna, especially to Lorna.

"We should celebrate. Let's find somewhere to have lunch."

They now felt more like a couple. They were easy with each other, strolling arm in arm along the promenade through the avenue of trees.

"Where shall we go?"

"Back to your hotel."

"You know that's not our deal."

"Do they not serve food?"

In the parade of Georgian offices and shops, with larger-than-life classical stone caryatids stationed at intervals like a guard of honour, they slowed to look at possibilities for lunch. A British restaurant announced itself on a sign inside one window. 'Lunch. Two courses. 1/9d' it said.

"One and nine. I cannot afford that, Lorna."

"No, but I can. Come on, let's have lunch."

The food was unremarkable. Next day neither of them would be able to recall what they ate. Food was limited by scarcity and rationing. At the heart of all food options were the National Loaf and National Cheddar, and meat came in processed versions of itself that might not have been recognised before the war. It did not matter. They talked excitedly, eating occasionally, looking at each other across the table for two. Lorna could not force down the food on her plate.

"Do you want mine?" she asked Pepe.

"No. It is horrible. But they will be in one of the pig clubs. All the waste feeds our pigs."

"I hope not. They'll turn the poor things into cannibals."

"No chance of that," said Pepe, looking at the left-overs on Lorna's plate. They laughed. It was a joke of sorts but mainly it was good to laugh for the joy of being together. Lorna paid the bill and they decided to continue their stroll around town.

They came to a photographic shop called Rose's. The shop window offered a variety of cameras for sale. It also offered memories that they shared of Pepe and Angel having their portraits taken in the photographic studio in the Strand.

"I still have the pictures," said Lorna.

"Do you? Show me."

"I can't. I don't have them on me. But I can tell you this – you've changed a lot."

"I hope so. I was just a boy then."

"Next time we meet in London, I'll show you. I'll put them next to the picture of me at home."

"Oh. That," shaking his head.

Lorna pushed the door open, making the bell tinkle in the shop. A studious-looking man, with half-glasses perched on the end of his nose, sat behind the counter, surrounded by shelves containing cameras and equipment. He was happy to talk. Customers were scarce at the moment.

"Do you know much about cameras, miss? Not to worry, I do. So we're in luck."

Lorna had entered the shop on a whim, feeling light-hearted by the day she was enjoying with Pepe. Through a series of questions and answers, demonstrating different kinds of camera he set out on the counter, he suggested a Kodak as the perfect choice for a person such as Lorna in this particular place at this particular time.

"I'll have it," she said. "Can you wind a film in so I can use it straight away?"

"Of course, but I'll show you how to do it. You'll need to know."

Through all this, Pepe was a spectator. He said nothing, just raising his eyebrows when it became clear that Lorna was going to buy the camera. When they got outside, with the camera strung around Lorna's neck, he simply said "You surprise me".

"In a good way, I hope," she smiled.

"It is always good when I am with you."

Turning into the High Street, they came to a tobacconists'. Pepe went inside to buy some cigarettes while Lorna waited outside. After her short period as a smoker, she tried to avoid any temptation to resume the habit. She stood near the doorway, next to a painted statue of a Highland infantryman wearing a tartan kilt, red jacket and bearskin hat. The Highlander was forever caught in the act of taking a pinch of snuff in front of an advert for Wills's Capstan cigarettes.

"Look, Pepe. Isn't he handsome?"

"I like his uniform. Do you think they will give me one like that?"

"Not unless you join a Scottish regiment."

Lorna got Pepe to stand next to the Highlander, shoulder to shoulder. She looked into the lens of the camera, lining them up side by side, then clicked the shutter. Just to be sure, she took another shot.

Walking on, without any particular direction in mind, they crossed and re-crossed the road, talking about whatever came into their heads. Lorna took a few more photographs of Pepe who was only too willing to play up to the camera, and he took one of her to finish the roll of film. They talked about holidays because this was, for each of them, as close to a holiday as they might ever have had.

"After the war, we go on holiday," said Pepe.

"Where shall we go?"

"I would like to take you to Spain. To show you my country."

"Well, a lot will have to change for that to happen. Are you going to ask Franco to step down so we can go on holiday?"

"Oh, if I could," he looked wistful. "I would like you to meet my mother and father."

"You really are running ahead of yourself. Besides, you have a war to win first."

The Regal cinema was showing news reels, and they decided to go in. They were shown by the usherette with a torch to seats in the side aisle. The cinema was crowded and the people in the seats were watching the black and white films almost in the spirit of a football match. Every so often they would cheer and clap as the pictures showed Allied troops making advances through one or other theatre of war, while the commentary jollied everyone along.

Pepe's left hand was holding Lorna's right hand. Then he placed his arm around her shoulder. Emboldened by these advances of his own, while British soldiers jumped down from a landing craft into shallow water, Pepe leant across to kiss Lorna. There might be advantages to a soldier's life that he had not imagined.

They left the cinema when they noticed the same commandos making the same progress up the beach again. Lorna realised that the day was also advancing, and it was hard to see the hands of her watch in the darkness of the cinema. Stepping outside, blinking in the gloomy daylight of an autumn afternoon, they had to think about bringing their day to a close.

"It's nearly four," said Lorna. "We'll have to get you back. Don't want Mr Hodges to be fretting."

"He might have forgotten. Or got caught up in a new bit of business. Or having a cup of tea."

"Either way, he'll have to take you back. There's no point blotting your copy book now. Things are looking better for you."

"You mean, soon I'll be going off to war and running up a beach with machine guns firing at me."

"Who knows? It might be over before you finish training."

Pepe shrugged. "Let's hope so anyway."

They had come together and now they would part, united by things they had in common. Perhaps they were fundamentally different as well as the same. Perhaps that was true of everyone. Events were pushing them together and apart, Lorna towards ever greater altruism, Pepe towards a deeper instinct for personal survival. It was not something to ask themselves, for fear of wrong answers, nor to ask Mr Hodges who was waiting in his car outside Lorna's hotel. It would be futile or possibly counter-productive to attempt more than a business-like farewell, so they shook hands to keep Mr Hodges' curiosity in check.

CHAPTER 31

Lorna spotted Pepe's letter among the Christmas cards. She hesitated to open it at first, fearing it might bring bad news. At least, thinking back later, this told her that her feelings for Pepe went beyond luke-warm curiosity.

She read his words with difficulty. He was not fluent with the pen as he was with his tongue but she soon discovered the gist: he was well and undergoing army training. The letter did not say, perhaps could not say, but she knew he was in Swindon. Next he would be sent for 'battlefield inoculation' to some remote corner of the British Isles, to prepare with as much reality as possible for real action in war. *He'll be seeing a lot of his adopted country*, she thought. *Parts I'll never see.* Then a shiver ran through her, the recurring realisation that she had channelled him closer to danger. She read the letter again, then again.

That night she returned to her diary, trying to think herself into Pepe's life. In doing so she might find her way into part of his mind.

November evening

My last days on this farm. I will miss it, as I still miss my homeland. But I never worked the land in Spain. These repetitive acts of tilling and raking, digging and planting, ploughing and scouring the soil till it is broken down to crumbs. At this time of year the ground is sodden; rain has made the soil sticky, it will not crumble as in summertime. I must not either, this is my life now. I know the words so I know the deeds.

For some, soil is sacred. Not for me. I would not fight and die for soil, neither here nor in Spain. The war raged across the Spanish countryside, its mountains and plains, but it was people who died. That is all you could or should fight for.

Here I hold the soil of Gloucestershire in my hand. I pick it up, form it into a ball, then allow it to drop between my fingers like muddy rain back to the soggy earth. This earth is just as much mine as Spanish earth, this rain is mine either here or there. Or just as little mine.

Lorna wrote it and felt some satisfaction even while thinking 'this is not Pepe'. *But who is?* She was conscious of knowing him too shallowly but did we ever know anyone deeply? She thought of the last time, only a week ago, that she had seen her mother. Another awkward conversation over a teapot in Lyons Corner House. She had come out of this woman's body but felt a stranger. *Yet the man who I say is a stranger, I feel close to this man.* She looked at the photographs on her mantelpiece of Pepe in Cheltenham and she smiled.

The next day in work she was working on a case of trade unionists who had been sacked for striking for higher pay. It was considered an unpatriotic act in wartime. Bryan and Lorna had no qualms about representing them on behalf of their union. "This is why we are fighting the war," Bryan said. "This is part of the fight." Yet Lorna thought of Pepe learning how to fire a gun with intent to kill. Life, mixed with emotion, became more and more complex. Bryan could see the disturbance in her face, like a film running at too fast a speed.

"We should talk about after the war. Because it will end," said Bryan. "With luck it will end soon."

"It's hard to talk about such uncertainty."

"Of course. But still possible. I don't wish to pry but will Pepe be part of your life after the war?"

She looked at him, not angry, not even puzzled. It seemed a reasonable question at that moment. It was one she had been asking herself.

"I don't know. I had not expected it. But something seems to have made that possible. Perhaps likely. But I cannot bank on anything when he is about to go and fight. And when I have made that possible."

"The law of unintended consequences. It seems there is a law for everything. But I suggest you plan for life with or without him. You need to think of yourself. We must get you properly educated and qualified as a lawyer."

"Oh, that's even more difficult to think about now. We are so far from that kind of normality."

"Not at all. You are still young. You know the obstacles but you have the fight to overcome them. You do a good job now but you could do a better one with a university education."

"There is no university. It's the Ministry of Information. There is no place for thinking."

"You show that there is. Even by saying that."

Lorna believed that Bryan was showing her an impossible dream. But it did move her away from thoughts about Pepe that might be fruitless. It gave her a renewed vigour for her work, stirred by the vague possibility of a perhaps in her life. *Why not?* The new year arrived without great anticipation but without the sense of dread that had accompanied recent new years. The news seemed to promise that 1944 would be better than any year since the start of the war. *As long as…* Every hopeful thought was brought to earth by fear and the prospect of fear. So she was brought back constantly to thoughts of Pepe and an exasperated awareness that her feelings were strengthening in his absence and the absence of any real contact with him.

February morning

It has been three months now. Learning to march, firing lethal weapons. This is a hand grenade, this is how to use it. Keep your head down, soldier. Keep your discipline or lose your life.

I moaned and groaned, but so did everyone. The shared pain, the communal torture that makes us comrades. You have to suffer so that others suffer less. The agony you feel today will be banked and you'll gain the rewards later on. This week they test us to the limit. We march in full battle order, a forced march, ten miles, two hours, boots and blisters. Shooting a rifle, infantryman, this is a Bren gun, you kill them or they'll kill you.

I want to do well. I do well. I survive. I will survive. I have everything to live for. I live for you.

At the passing out parade such a sense of pride, it took me by surprise. We marched past the Colonel, we saluted him, he saluted us, we felt ten feet tall. I had not expected this, Lorna, but I am doing this for you.

I want to see you.

CHAPTER 32

Pepe's letters said little. Lorna compensated by saying too much in her letters to him. She told him that she wanted to see him and she hoped it would be soon.

Still the weeks passed. Winter turned over, stretched, came awake as spring. In the London squares and parks that she loved, Lorna rejoiced in the tight buds of flowers and leaves that opened out towards the light. She took out Pepe's most recent letter and feasted on its sparse words.

London was rarely under threat in these days but she still found it difficult to sleep. She wondered if the whole nation suffered from insomnia. Her lack of sleep might be a way of showing fellow feeling.

There was little to do, and less to enjoy, by way of entertainment. The war added a sugar coating of patriotism to films, plays and shows; her patriotism was of a different kind. She occupied herself in the evenings by getting involved in political meetings. It was exciting to be talking about what might happen after the war, and the growing feeling in her circle that big changes might be possible. There were moments when she asked whether she was deluding herself but hope is a powerful need, and she desperately needed hope.

One day in early May she took a phone call at work. She asked the telephonist who it was but the caller was put straight through. "Lorna, it is me. Pepe. I am in London." Recovering from her surprise, establishing that he was on leave, she told him to come to her offices.

Bryan looked up from the papers he was reading, his eyes

above the half-glasses. He listened to Lorna's news with a sympathetic smile.

"Well, it will be good to meet him. I'm sure others will wish to too."

Lorna could no longer concentrate. She paced up and down then decided she would go downstairs to wait for Pepe on the steps. She was there for twenty minutes before she heard the metallic ring of boots on the pavement and saw a figure in army uniform walking down the street towards her. She recognised Pepe by his gait; but his face was quite changed.

"What have you done?" she asked, almost in horror.

"What do you mean? Ah, this…" and he touched his upper lip.

"Yes, what's that fungus? You have a growth."

"Don't you like it? I thought you would like a moustache."

They embraced. Lorna had anticipated this reunion for so long but she had not imagined it like this. She insisted that they go to the barber's shop before they did anything else. Pepe submitted meekly to her will.

They walked into the barber's underneath the twirling red, white and blue pole in the railway arches. Pepe sat in the capacious chair and was covered in a white sheet up to his neck. Then the barber used leather strop and cut-throat razor, brush and shaving cream and steaming towels, to remove Pepe's moustache while Lorna sat on a wooden chair behind him. There was talk between Pepe and the barber – not about the war as she expected but about the barber's trade.

"So you enjoy it?" Pepe asked.

"It's pretty good. Been doin' it forty years so must be somethin' good about it. You get to meet people, chat to 'em, send 'em away happy."

"Sounds good."

"How's that look to you?" gesturing towards the mirror. "Happy with that?"

"Lorna? You happy with it?"

She nodded, counting out coins from her purse.

"You're onto a good 'un here, me lad," said the barber to Pepe.

They left the shop and walked down the street. They ducked into the doorway of one of the buildings in the street.

"Here, let me have a look at you," said Lorna. She felt his face smooth under her touch, his skin still warm from the towel. She traced her fingers around his eyes as if to make sure he was real. Then she brought her face towards his and kissed him. It was what she had longed to do for weeks.

"Well…that was nice," he said. "I thought I'd done something terrible and you'd never do that again."

"Never do that again. I really don't like moustaches. They're not for people I like. And I want you to make a good impression."

Pepe gave her a puzzled look but decided to accept her judgement. He would have to do this now and perhaps for all the time they were together. So he told himself, at least for the present.

The lift was at the top of the building so they walked up the stairs to the offices of Thomas Brothers. Lorna was now suddenly conscious that she had been out of the office for a long time and people would be wondering where she was. The office was much slimmed down from its pre-war complement but there were still a dozen people. She knew because she could see them all; they had all come out of their offices and cubicles to see Pepe. Much to Lorna's embarrassment there was a round of applause. At the far end of the corridor Bryan was smiling in welcome.

"Come in, Pepe, it's good to meet you. It seems as if I've known you for a long time. You've become one of our famous cases, as you can see."

Lorna organised tea while Bryan started talking to Pepe. They filled the conversation with trivia about training and hope about the progress of the war. It became clear that Bryan was better informed than Pepe on the latter.

"The war is a state secret," said Pepe. "They tell us little but I know I am going to be part of something big soon."

"The invasion?"

Pepe shrugged. Iris brought in the tea and smiled. George, an elderly partner, came in for no apparent reason than to shake Pepe's hand. Roger, the messenger boy who had a club foot, put papers in Bryan's tray and giggled. In wartime, after so many years of business not as usual, the visit of a soldier was an event. An event that Lorna became anxious to bring to a swift conclusion.

"I think we should go," she said. "If it's OK to leave a little early, Bryan?"

"Of course. Take what time you need. See you after the weekend."

Walking home, London had never felt so precious to Lorna. She clung tight to Pepe's arm as she led him down Kingsway and into Lincoln's Inn Fields. She wanted to show him that London was damaged but defiant. The May blossom on the trees, the clusters of pink flowers, seemed to support that message and she almost shouted her feelings aloud.

CHAPTER 33

The first thing Pepe wanted was a bath. He complained so graphically about the poor conditions of hygiene at his camp that Lorna was keen to oblige. She ran the bath for him – "sorry, it won't be very hot" – and gave him a towel, then left him to remove whatever from his past or present might be easily scrubbed away. In truth she felt a little testy with him.

He reappeared a little later in civilian clothes: baggy trousers, a short-sleeved shirt, bare feet.

"So. A lot to tell me?"

"What do you want to know? I am in the army. I have finished training. I am ready to fight. Now I just wait for orders."

"The soldier's life. Waiting."

"A lot of that. It is boring but I do not mind. I am not gung-ho, as some say. I have no burning desire to kill Jerry."

"Jerry?" Lorna shuddered. "I wish you wouldn't. They're Germans."

"That is just the way we talk. It means nothing."

"It means a lot. It means you don't quite see them as humans."

"Perhaps they might not be."

"You have to take them seriously."

"We cannot. If we did, we would be more scared."

Sitting side by side on the settee, they fell into silence, simply looking at each other. After a while Pepe's hand reached out to touch Lorna's hair; the hair long and waved, unlike when he had first seen her, and perhaps he was now lost in recollection of that.

"You look different. I probably do too. But you cannot change me completely from what I am."

"I don't want to. Why would I want to?"

"Oh you always seem to want me as – I do not know. Something else. Something better than I can be."

She ran her hand through his now-short hair. "Those army barbers, eh?" Pepe's fingers combed Lorna's hair around her ear, and he bent to whisper in it.

"I have done my side of the deal."

"How do you mean?"

"I have joined the army. As you told me to. I have become British. As you told me to. And now I have to fight. Your deal was to help me, and you have."

"And all without a legal contract." Her smile teased him.

"You said we could not make love till that deal was completed. Now it is done."

"A new deal?"

Pepe nodded. "You are beautiful. And I love you. I cannot put that in words I write. And not well in words I speak. But you are everything to me. You are the reason why I am doing what I do."

Lorna kissed him. They were locked in a long embrace with their hands around each other's heads, cradling them. There was an element of wonder in their reaction to each other.

"Your face," he said. "I see it all the time when I am not with you. It is the face I love."

"You," she laughed, "you are a shameless flatterer. I know I'm not beautiful."

"You are. You are."

"We have a phrase – flattering to deceive. I'm sure you

know it. If you flatter me, that's one thing, but I wouldn't want you to deceive me."

"Never. Never."

They got to their feet, still clinging to each other. While still staying close they began undressing each other. Pepe cupped Lorna's breasts and nodded at the painting on the wall – "more beautiful, much more beautiful". Lorna unbuttoned Pepe's shirt and fingered the golden crucifix that hung down between his breast bones. Agricultural work and military training had made him well-muscled.

"Are you keeping on your Spanish cross?" she asked.

"Does it matter?"

"It might feel as if I'm making love to a priest. And that would not be right. Would it?"

He fumbled for the catch on the gold chain and opened it up. She took his hand and the crucifix in it, then laid the cross on the table. Then he kissed Lorna while his hands cradled the back of her neck, as if to close the clasp of a necklace there. But there was only skin, soft skin not resistant even as his hands slid lower down her body, as they moved together, skin against skin.

Afterwards they lay folded into each other, intertwined. They kissed each other with the softness of passion spent and Lorna set aside, at least for these moments, the doubts and anxieties that had dwelt inside her for too long. Pepe reached for his packet of cigarettes but Lorna placed her hand on his.

"No, don't. Don't spoil it. You smell too nice, of soap not smoke."

"Whatever you wish."

"I have had enough of smoke. The war is full of it."

They lay there talking, not knowing what they were talking of. They kissed each other's eye lids and the thought that they might share many moments like this in the hours, days, even years ahead. It was a thought to encourage dreams and Lorna fell into a deep, contented sleep.

When she woke she could sense that a summer evening was drifting through the gaps in the window boards. Her first thought was that she had needed such a refreshing sleep after so many deprived nights; her second thought was to panic at Pepe's absence. But she saw him, she felt him, resting on an elbow, next to her, gazing at her with a look that could have been devotion. She kissed him, as if to reassure herself of his reality, and relished even the smoke on his lips.

Later, not knowing if it was evening, mid-night or that dark hour before dawn, he caressed her and used the scissors he had found to snip a lock of her hair. He put the hair in a locket that was next to the crucifix on the kitchen table.

"I have never done anything so romantic," he said, as if amazed at himself.

"Foolishly so," she laughed, and spread herself on top of him, with her fingers in his and their arms outstretched horizontally. "I can't cut any of yours, it's too short. And I wouldn't want you to lose your strength, Samson."

"Ha, you even know the Bible now."

"Not as much as you. And I never will."

In the morning, they were reluctant to rise in case the spell was broken. But Pepe slid out of bed eventually to bring a glass of water. They shared it, Pepe brought another, then asked:

"I have two questions for you. First, are you happy?"

His eyes showed a disappointment that she seemed reluctant

to give the impulsive Yes that he craved. Lorna smiled and mumbled "Of course".

"Second question. Are you hungry?"

"Definitely. Ravenous. But we'll have to make do with toast. National Loaf toast at that."

Half an hour later, with the room pleasantly smelling of toast, Lorna opened the door to a tentative knock. Pepe positioned himself in the scullery, away from the sight of the landlady, Mrs Hayes, who stood at the door.

Lorna met her with an unusually fulsome smile, but Mrs Hayes did not return it. She had steeled herself to deliver her message.

"We don't allow gentleman visitors who stay overnight."

"Really?"

"No, we don't. You know that."

"That gentleman is my husband. You might not know that."

Mrs Hayes shook her head. "No, I didn't." She stared then asked "A bit sudden?"

"Life can be. Particularly in wartime."

The landlady looked dubious still, then backed away. "Well, I wish you well, then, Lorna. And what's your husband's name?"

"I'll introduce Pepe to you later. He's a soldier and will have to return soon to his regiment."

The words cast a shadow of reality across them as she closed the door. It was true; Pepe needed to report back to barracks. After her public proclamation of a union that had taken by surprise both herself and Pepe, their next steps would be as separate as they had ever been.

CHAPTER 34

Lorna became obsessed by the news. She had always followed it closely, particularly in the newspapers, but now she became obsessive. She listened to the radio at work and at home, she watched news reels in picture houses, but her hunger for information was never satisfied. The commentary voices ranged from jovial to sombre but the suspicion remained that there might be a reason for sobriety behind the jollity, given a slight shift towards greater frankness.

Every day her walk to work took her past the towering Ministry of Information that in peaceful times might have housed her aspirations towards education. Now its purpose was propaganda, a reminder that she needed to be wary enough to filter the news in the pursuit of reality. In the Ministry's shadow the British Museum offered the promise that history could still provide a corrective to the present. But rather than look on these works and despair, Lorna walked past, only occasionally finding moments to stop and reflect. The siren call of that day's news was always stronger.

When the news came through that Rome had fallen to the Allies, Lorna thought of the ancient city and she saw its ruins in black and white images. She sifted the news she heard and read but still concluded that the reported capture of Rome had to be true and had to be good news. Within days it was followed by announcements that the invasion of France by Allied troops was under way. She hardly dared believe or hope. The voice of the BBC was more sombre, more guarded, as if there was bad news behind the good. There was no premature claiming of victory but the tide of war did seem to have turned decisively. Churchill's voice was most familiar of all. She was ready to fight with him on the beaches but against him through the ballot box. He did not always speak to her when he spoke to the nation. She was angry when she heard him say: "The internal political problems of Spain concern only Spaniards. We must not interfere in those matters." *Why else were we fighting the war?*

There was no news from Pepe. Lorna read nothing sinister in that as he was not an enthusiastic letter-writer. She wrote almost daily to him but it felt like dropping pebbles into the depths of a well, waiting to hear the sound and timing of their arrival. She read the D-Day landing reports line by line in the newspapers, then she read between the lines. She was convinced that Pepe was an active part of the invasion, and this conviction brought both comfort and anxiety. *Pepe would pray to God. What can I do?* She could not face the task of writing in her diary for Pepe, her imagination at the moment was unlikely to release a stream of consolation.

The news reports became mixed, at least in her eyes. The talk was of success and of fierce fighting. With every mention of casualties, Lorna feared the worst. She dreaded and longed for the arrival of the postman, constantly relieved and disappointed by the absence of a message. She checked daily that Pepe's letter was still safe in her drawer at home. This was a letter that Pepe had written, sealed and entrusted to Lorna on his last visit. The envelope was marked with his parents' names *en el caso de mi muerte*.

Despite her fears, Lorna allowed herself some optimism about the war. *The end might be in sight.* The Germans were in retreat in Italy and France; it seemed just a matter of time before victory, but time had to be counted in casualties. The count kept rising. She read lists of names in *The Times* but knew these were not the full lists; she became a connoisseur of obituaries; she read with tears in her eyes and a scream in her throat.

Then there was a turn for the worse. After a time of relative relaxation there were many reports of explosions, officially described as 'gas mains incidents'. Rumour soon turned these into 'doodlebugs' and in this case rumour was true. Whispers had been circulating for a long time that the Germans were working on a secret weapon. It seemed that this, the V1 rocket, had now arrived and was capable of great destruction.

Yet people carried on. The Blitz had been worse, more sustained and more intense. The V1s caused fear but their destructive power was less than the worst fears. Bombs, or unmanned rockets like the V1s, brought down buildings but they did not always take away lives. And morale seemed indestructible. The possibility of a doodlebug attack was simply another factor to take into account in everyday life.

Lorna, on civil defence duty, arrived at the scene when one building had been struck and reduced to rubble. She scrambled over the stones, bricks and timber that now filled this gap between standing houses. A ghostly figure, white-faced with a film of dust, emerged from the smoke and powdered stucco. It was an old woman, stepping gingerly on the shifting stones of her ruined home. Lorna moved towards her and grabbed her by the arm and shoulder, leading her out to what remained of the pavement.

"How are you?" she asked.

"How do I look?" the old woman's voice was sibilant, wheezing.

"You look lovely. Course you do. You're alive and that's the main thing. Let's get you safe."

"What about me teeth? I've left me dentures inside. Let me go an' get 'em."

Lorna laughed, hoping it would help the woman to laugh. "I wouldn't worry about them, dear. They're not going to be dropping food parcels for you to eat."

The doodlebugs came mostly in the daytime but were strangely invisible. Few people saw or heard anything until the impact on a building. Lorna was briefed at a civil defence meeting, under instructions not to divulge information as it might spread panic.

"But what do they look like? How do we recognise them?"

"Like a steel cigar shape, flying low with flame trailing behind it. But listen first. It makes a put-put sound, like a motor-cycle, then the engine cuts out. Silence for many seconds. Heads down, take cover, hope it doesn't hit near you."

Even the official briefing documents had an ominous sound to them, a mechanised drone of facts. Lorna dreaded, day by day, the rising possibility of an official communication. Then a letter arrived, which she opened with trembling fingers. Inside was familiar handwriting in the midst of what looked like a coded pattern of thick black lines, the lines made by the military censor to obliterate 'sensitive information' such as place names. But enough of the handwriting remained to reassure that Pepe was alive and well, and apparently the following words were untouched and not considered 'sensitive information': MARRY ME.

CHAPTER 35

There were two front lines for Lorna that June in 1944. The one where she was based in London under enemy attack by V1s; and the one in France where she imagined Pepe, rifle in hand, attacking the same enemy. At the end of the month her birthday came not as a release from this intensity but as a chance to allow herself a momentary respite.

For one thing she now considered herself engaged to be married. This had taken her by surprise but it made the passing of another annual milestone – this birthday marked 31 – a little easier to bear. Without admitting it to herself she had feared that the war had been consuming the important years of her womanhood. She had been denied so much that might otherwise have been her natural right: relationships, motherhood, entertainment, education. At least she now felt she had achieved in one of those areas, and this was a reason to accept if not celebrate her birthday in the working company of others.

Through the morning at her desk her colleagues brought her cards, most of them hand-made. "It's the thought that counts" were the words on everyone's lips or sometimes unspoken in their heads. It was true; the thought did count. Thoughts add up to create a warm feeling of gratitude without obligation. Bryan arranged to take her for a drink after work, as he had a lunchtime appointment. She shared a pot of weak tea and stirred cups of stronger hope with the girls who gathered around her desk.

Lorna was tempted to share her secret but felt too uncertain. Did she trust Pepe? *Yes*, but she was reluctant to rely on the evidence of two words in a censored letter. Even though she had replied "Yes, if you mean it, I do." So she went out at lunchtime for a stroll alone, doubtfully happy about the future yet not quite believing in it. She walked towards St Mary-le-Strand, which stood like an island in the traffic, then she turned left into the broad curve of Aldwych, heading towards Drury Lane.

In the sunshine it was possible to believe in the possibility of better times. Such thoughts can be fleeting, as Lorna knew well, and hope always shone with the caveat, even the expectation, that it might be extinguished in a moment. So it proved again.

There were crowds of people out, their busyness, their laughter suddenly turned, swiftly galvanised by the urgent melancholy of the air raid siren that keened around them. Inside the big buildings on either side of the road shrill alarm bells were ringing without stopping, and people raced inside and out in search of shelter, places to stop and be safe. Lorna stood still under the canopy of the Waldorf Hotel, listening to the clanging of bells inside, mixed with the gathering rattle of the approaching doodlebug. She saw it, with its burning exhaust trailing orange flame behind, above the huge stone pillars of Bush House opposite, thinking grimly in that moment that *the BBC will not have to go far to report the news today*.

Then the noise of the sputtering engine cut out, leaving an impression of silence despite the alarms sounding all around. The absence of the engine noise created an eery sense of dread and anticipation. Seconds passed, a menacing shadow, seconds were counted, one, two, the rocket could be seen overhead now, three, four, five, then it plunged vertically, six, seven, eight, a screaming nine ten of people not machines eleven twelve boom a sudden ball of fire. The blast was close and ear-shattering, sending a wave of hot air and debris down Aldwych, knocking Lorna off her feet. All around her, on the roadway and pavements, were people lying flat on the ground, faces pressed against the surface. Fragments of building stone rained down in a soundless storm, through a glowing cloud of dust. In the aftermath, hearing lost to the percussive power of the blast, there was a deep silence and a scene that was animated only by the slowest of human motion.

Lorna had the strange sensation of shouting words that she could not hear. Perhaps others were shouting at her and hearing only the same silence that turned into a monotonous buzzing inside the head. In this collective deafness, in the silent film before her eyes, the buildings were moving more than the people, shimmering in the after-shock. A large segment of balcony crashed to the ground in a storm of dust. Bodies were strewn across the road, unmoving, twisted, lifeless.

She forced herself to her feet, having been pinned against the wall by the physical shock of the explosion. She started walking on unsteady legs through the mist that brought a bitter taste to her mouth and nostrils, making her choke and cough. She wiped her face and around her eyes with the tail of her blouse, instinctively taking off her jacket then draping it over her head. As she walked she studied the bodies on the road, searching for signs of life. Bending down to a young woman close to her own age, she held her hand at the wrist, for comfort, to feel a pulse. The woman stirred and cried out "My baby!" Lorna tore off her own jacket, pulling it over her head and forming it into a pillow that she slipped under the woman's neck and shoulders. Blood was streaming from her temples. Even as Lorna lifted the woman's head, she felt a final shudder run through the body and escape with a gasp.

Lorna spotted the young girl nearby. She and her mother might once have been holding hands in innocence, but they had been blown apart by the force of the explosion. Lorna crawled across the rubble ridges and low walls of stone and concrete that littered the road. Sound had returned to her world, she heard the clatter of broken masonry that shifted under her knees and the rising din of people screaming, screaming like animals snared in traps, screaming with pain, screaming at the injustice of being in that place at that time.

The little girl was six, perhaps younger, impossible to say in her bomb-blasted condition. She lay five yards from her mother, flat on her back, her chest pinned down by a rock that pressed on top of her. Lorna was able to lift and shift the rock to one side. *This rock*, she thought, *might have been torn from that building and flung at me. Like an unequal fight with a giant.* It had crushed the girl's chest and Lorna knew she could not survive such an impact. *Why not me? Why her not me?* The girl was barely breathing but her mouth called quietly for her mother.

"She's all right, love. Don't worry. And you'll be right as rain too."

Lorna felt she had to do what the mother would want to do. She wiped dirt from the girl's cheek, she smoothed her hair away from her face. She sought medical help with desperate eyes, desperation all the greater for knowing that nothing could be done. But she must do what she could, bring what succour she might be able to bring.

"What's your name, love?"

The girl's whisper sounded like 'May'. She repeated it, each breath an effort, each word an agony to utter. This time Lorna thought she heard 'Pray'.

"Pray? You want me to say a prayer?"

Lorna could tell from the girl's eyes that she had discovered the right meaning: she wanted to say a prayer. It was what her mother would have done. But Lorna was not sure she could do this – it had been many years, in those first school days, since she had last said a prayer. But childhood memories, the teaching of her Church of England school, flooded back, even if imperfectly. She held the child's hand and bent low towards her so that together they might attempt the prayer.

"Our Father," began Lorna and she saw the flicker of recognition light the girl's eyes in almost a smile, "Which art in heaven," squeezing her hand gently. "Hallowed be thy name. Thy kingdom come. Will be done. On earth as it is in heaven. For ever and ever. The power and the glory. Forgive us our trespasses. Deliver us from evil. Amen."

The unfamiliar familiar words passed between them. The girl had sighed on the last word. *Our last action in life is to sigh.* Had she done enough to comfort the girl? The question might never be answered for certain. Lorna comforted herself that she had tried, she had at least done her best, then she closed the girl's eyelids.

"Are you OK, my dear?" asked the ambulance man.

Lorna nodded but could not speak for crying. The ambulance man put a blanket around her shoulders and helped her to her feet.

"Have you been hit? Any pain?"

Lorna shook her head. The truth can sometimes be close to a lie. She allowed herself to be led away through this landscape that was now animated by people walking across it in every direction, carrying stretchers, loading bodies on the stretchers, taking them away, the living and the dead. Lorna could make out the junction where Kingsway met Aldwych, and she saw the lines of ambulances waiting to receive their human cargo.

She suddenly remembered that she had left her jacket under the dead woman's head. She had worn it that morning for the first time, a birthday present to herself. But it was gone, and she would not miss it. It had served its purpose, it had served a purpose.

CHAPTER 36

Lorna could not say she was happy but at least she was alive. And at least Pepe was alive, though he had been wounded. The news took her breath away but then she felt relief that it had not been worse. "Nothing to worry about," he wrote. "I might even get a leave to recover."

Lorna had been following the progress of the war as closely as possible after the Normandy landings. Not everything was reported but it was possible to build up a picture, like that painted by any number of armchair generals in the shires. Caen was captured in July, then the battle moved on to the Falaise Gap. Even the official reports talked about casualties, so the letter from Pepe might even be a cause for celebration if it meant he was spared the worst of the fighting. "Only a piece of shrapnel in my leg," he wrote.

Lorna had quickly discharged herself from hospital after the V1 bombing. Her work colleague Biddy had brought in clothes to the Elizabeth Garrett Anderson hospital in Euston Road, and they had been able to walk home from there. Physically she was unharmed; the true test would come in the next bombing raid but she was defiant that she would not give in. Bryan offered her as much time off as she needed but she refused. Work was therapy.

Walking was another therapy. She had always enjoyed walking and she explored London on foot. It gave her a close connection, in these times, to the plight of other Londoners. The buildings all around had a battered air, even the ones that had not been bombed; the association with derelict neighbours rubbed off. Yet, despite all the damage, the essential shape of the city remained, as she could observe from the civil defence maps that plotted where bombs had landed.

Lorna loved maps: they went with her addiction to the news. She could imagine scenes on the ground beneath those big arrows on a map signalling an advance. She could certainly imagine the human stories where a cross marked a bomb strike in London because she had been witness to so many. Maps worked with the grain of her mind, and she found it easy to follow a trail or navigate a route by studying a map and committing it to memory like a pedestrian taxi-driver. It was part of the reason why she had always taken to life in London. With the sinuous bend of the river through its centre it was made for interesting maps that she carried in her head not her hand.

Her walks, which she took when needing to calm her mind and plan her thoughts, had a labyrinthine quality. She could divert from the main roads to find alleys and courts that revealed more intriguing lives than the big thoroughfares. Like Daedalus she could create a maze out of buildings and not need a thread to find her way back.

She needed time to think and had always been inclined to trust her own counsel. Her independence went hand in hand with a desire to help others, and there was no contradiction for her in that. But now she needed to think about herself, with the prospect of a husband who might be taken from her at any moment – and, as the weeks went by, the growing certainty that she was expecting a baby, his baby. *This baby could not be blasted out of me. This one will stick.*

Her walk had taken her through the Temple and its gardens, with the legal chambers that Dickens would still have recognised. Inevitably thoughts of her own career arose here. Would she ever become a lawyer? Is that really what she wanted to do with her life? Other aspects of life were more pressing. She was now determined to marry Pepe soon, not least for the sake of her unborn child. The concept of legitimacy mattered to her and to society, and her free spirit was still constrained by unwritten social laws.

Passing by St Mary-le-Strand, she crossed the road to the church. She had often seen it, wondering at its height and narrowness, but had never felt inclined to enter. She feared religion; she believed in its potential to do harm while claiming a desire to do good. Yet she understood its influence over so many people, and she had recently been moved by the little girl's need to say a prayer even as she was dying. It stirred memories of her own childhood when she had, at her father's suggestion, read to herself a passage of the Bible chosen randomly each day.

The church was on an oval island in the road, and she pushed open the iron gates. Even from the outside St Mary's gave the impression of being compact. Would it open up into a vast expanse of space inside, or would it remain as cramped as it seemed? She walked up the stone steps with some trepidation, urging herself on with the thought that the church doors were shut and she would not be able to go inside.

When she reached the portico the door opened, and a grey-haired priest in a dog collar stepped through it. He smiled at her.

"Would you like to pray?" he asked, holding the door open, his voice plummy. His face seemed very familiar. "I'm afraid we cannot offer too much else at the moment. The war affects everything, and I have to visit some parishioners."

"No. No thanks. I was just curious."

"A quality well-known to God. You can enter and satisfy your curiosity."

"Actually I am curious about you. Do I know you?"

"Perhaps you have seen me on the streets. Or perhaps you have been inside?"

"No, I've never been in."

"Well, we do welcome people. We need volunteers to help the poor. Those who are hungry and without homes."

"I think," she paused as the memory clarified, "I think we have met in another place. Were you at the camp for the Spanish boys and girls? Before the war?"

Father Chambers turned his head to one side and looked at her. "I was. But I cannot remember you."

"I visited once or twice. Then adopted one of the Spanish boys."

"A good deed. God will thank you." He searched for the next sentence. "What happened to the boy? Did he return home to Spain?"

"Oh no, he stayed. England is his home now."

"Really? He must miss his homeland."

"No, not at all. In fact he's in the army, fighting against the fascists."

"Oh? Good for him."

"In fact we are getting married."

The priest stared at her. He was almost certainly calculating dates. "Time flies by. He is a young man now. What was his name?"

"His name still is Pepe. Do you remember him?"

"Perhaps. One of the older boys."

"You will have noticed him at the time."

"Indeed. I often think about those children. What became of them."

"Most went back. To live under a dictator."

"But the bombing has stopped for them."

"The fight continues. There is no freedom. The country is ruled by fear."

The priest was reluctant to venture into politics. It became obvious that he wished to get on, but duty obliged him to explore one channel. "Where will you marry? Our church could be yours."

"No. No, I don't think so. Though Pepe is religious."

"We are Anglo-Catholic here. He would feel at home. As would you, I hope."

"No. Thank you. A registry office is what we planned. Something simple, particularly as we would need to do it at short notice."

"The offer stands. Or you might want a service of blessing afterwards. To seal your union in the eyes of God."

Lorna shook her head vigorously. "I'm sure you mean kindly. But no. and now I must go."

She turned away from the wooden door and walked briskly down the stairs. As she crossed the street to the pavement, she looked back to see him locking the church door. She felt a twinge of regret but she was not sure for what.

A couple of weeks passed slowly and there was pain in their slowness. Then time accelerated, with the news that Pepe had compassionate leave. Arrangements were quickly made for a wedding at Caxton Hall. Bryan and Diana would be witnesses. The Government minister Duncan Sandys went on the radio to declare that "the battle of London is over" – which was a relief until a V2 struck Chiswick next day, the news suppressed by a security blackout that kept few people in the dark. *Take nothing for granted, certainly not peace*, thought Lorna.

Pepe arrived, still in uniform, walking with a slight limp. Lorna borrowed a wedding dress from Biddy and everyone admired her broad-brimmed hat. The few guests threw torn-up pieces of newspaper instead of confetti. As she did so Diana called out "Be happy!"

PART THREE:
1947

Over the borders

CHAPTER 37

Pepe wanted to get married.

"Pepe, we already are married." Lorna's reply was a weary one.

This was not a legal matter. They had been married in the eyes of the law; now Pepe wanted to be married in the eyes of God. This statement had not taken Lorna by surprise but she still found herself irritated by the frequency of Pepe's agenda.

Life was hard enough, without this additional irritation. The war had ended two years earlier, and the nation experienced the euphoria of victory. The war might have changed the country in a way that could bring happiness to Lorna. The newly-elected Labour government suggested that peace, not only war, might be won. It offered hope of a country that would bring pride to her, her Spanish husband and their young son. The little boy, named James and called Jimmy, had been born in the final February of the war, with bombs still falling on Germany. When Lorna campaigned for political change, she did it for the future of her son, hoping for a peaceful world.

The reality was not living up to the original optimism. At the beginning of 1947 the coal mines had been nationalised but were not providing enough fuel to prevent electricity blackouts. One of the harshest winters ever had brought blizzards that laid snow over everything. Jimmy's second birthday arrived in an icy, white world, where the reflected light of the snow provided an unnaturally blinding brightness. Food was in short supply, winter vegetables frozen into the ground, sheep buried under snow drifts.

In the midst of this crisis Lorna, Pepe and Jimmy moved into their new flat, giving them more space and the prospect of greater comfort in time. Simply keeping warm – keeping a young child warm – was the preoccupation of those early weeks in the new flat. For weeks they struggled to survive with the minimum of furniture and appliances, until, eventually, the thaw would come flooding in.

They now lived in Levita House, on a council estate between Euston and St Pancras stations. The estate was regarded as something of a model for new public housing when it was built in 1930. Its architects had been influenced by modernist styles from Germany and Austria. *Part of the post-war reconciliation*, thought Lorna, not really believing herself. But she remained pleased with her new home even as she stared from her balcony towards the bank of snow that had been shovelled from the pavement against the high redbrick wall that ran along Ossulston Street. Behind the wall the trains were still not moving in the station goods yard.

All this had not diverted Pepe from hankering after a church wedding. Lorna could not see the point but Pepe was persistent. His ties to his native land, religion and parents nagged at him daily; and he in turn nagged at Lorna. She was sympathetic to his parents' situation but this would never be stronger than her antagonism to Spain and Catholicism.

"Your man Manny is no good," said Pepe, knowing this would annoy his wife. Manny Shinwell was the Minister for Fuel and Power who was being blamed for coal shortages and electricity cuts. Pepe was pointing to the photograph in the newspaper he was using to light the fire in their grate. He added a few pieces of wood from a broken crate, then some lumps of shiny black coal before applying a match to the newspaper.

"He's doing his best," replied Lorna. "We've never had weather like this before."

"He doesn't have a baby boy to keep warm."

"Jimmy is no longer a baby. He's two. And he's healthy."

They huddled around the fire for warmth as its bright orange flames leapt up towards the chimney. It seemed they could provide each other with more than enough fuel for unnecessary arguments but they were short of everyday necessities. They sat on packing crates in their overcoats; gloves covered their hands even when they later used the cooker to heat some soup.

"It is barmy, this life," said Pepe. "I do not know what my mum and dad would think. Even in Spain it must not be as bad as this."

"It's a barmy world. Spain is suffering bad weather too. I heard in work. And they are suffering worse from Franco. At least here you can say what you think and not be put away in prison."

Pepe's grunted "huh!" was not reassuring to Lorna. There were times when she suspected that his political commitment had become as cool as the weather. At those times she steered their talk away from politics; it seemed a necessary compromise that went hand in hand with their marriage.

"Look at that," she said. She was standing at the window, looking down into the spacious circular courtyard, above which rows of balconies made horizontal dark stripes in the panorama. Children were playing in the snow, building a snowman that was already taller than them.

"It can't be that cold. The kids are playing."

Pepe put his arm around Lorna's shoulders. "We will be all right. Children are tough," looking back at the sleeping

Jimmy. "It is just that the cold is not good for my leg. It makes me bad-tempered. I am sorry."

The wound in Pepe's leg was something to be ignored at times or used in mitigation at other times. The shrapnel that had damaged his left calf could be passed over or moaned about. Lorna never doubted the reality of the pain that Pepe experienced but could not decide if it caused or resulted from his dissatisfaction with life. Even a slight wound can tip the psychological scales towards unhappiness. Pepe came to resent the pain that he blamed for his limping life. Where should he direct his resentment? There were many possible targets including those closest to home. Too often his resentment was channelled towards Lorna. *Why can't we be happy?* she asked herself and sometimes Pepe.

"I am happy," he insisted, hearing or reading her thoughts. "Or I will be when I have a proper job. You have a job. And a lovely boy. And me." He stretched his arms wide and laughed at his own unexpected good humour.

Pepe was not lazy. He wanted to work but he did not have the skills that were recognised in a big city; nor did he have the native privileges to enter working class occupations that were generally reserved for friends and family. So he picked up work and money here and there, whenever he could, but it was piecemeal, precarious stuff in markets, stations and back doors. He desperately wanted to be, and be seen to be, the family breadwinner.

The pressure was on Lorna to work and bring home money from working. In truth, setting aside the finances, Lorna wanted to work for her own independence and satisfaction. She did not consider herself a natural mother, having little interest in the domestic trivia that went with caring for a young child. She found herself wishing Jimmy's babyhood away, and was bored by the times she had to spend alone with her son. Despite it all, the boy was contented enough and rarely asserted his wishes in a tantrum. So Lorna worked as much as she could, every morning until lunchtime, consoling herself that Jimmy would be happier and better looked after in the nursery that she had found for him in Drury Lane.

Bryan, and everyone at Thomas Brothers, was willing to support her. She was efficient at her job although its nature had not changed as much as she might once have hoped. There had always been talk of what she might become, with more education and qualifications, but those possibilities had been shelved by the war. The war – with the Allies' commitment to four freedoms – had shifted the legal landscape in the firm's eyes. Freedom of speech, freedom of religion, freedom from fear, freedom from want: these were causes to which Lorna could pledge her personal commitment. It seemed to her that human rights could become her lifetime dedication.

For the time being, with Jimmy so young, Lorna recognised the need to cherish what she had. Now, looking out at the boys and girls playing in the snow in the courtyard, it was a scene in black and white that Lorna believed could develop into full colour. *I have so much to cherish*, she told herself. She bent down and kissed her son.

CHAPTER 38

After the snow the clouds the rain the thaw came a stream of clear nights with no cloud cover at all. Lorna was bringing in washing from the laundry drying room at the end of the balcony, sheets folded into her arms, when she noticed stars that she had never seen before in a London sky. She called Pepe out to take a look.

"They're so beautiful," she said. "Have you ever seen so many stars?"

"Of course. More than these. In Spain at night you see many more stars. There is not so much light from the city there."

"They're all the more beautiful because it's unusual."

Pepe shrugged and went inside. Lorna stayed to continue staring at stars. She had often done this during the war but then it was always with an undercurrent of dread – to see stars from the ground meant that the bombers could see the ground from the sky. Now she made out the Pole Star and the Plough, and in doing so exhausted her knowledge of the heavens. There were so many constellations; so much knowledge to gain; she doubted that she would ever acquire more than the basics.

After ten minutes she went inside when Len arrived from the local Labour Party. They had things to discuss but these days her political commitment ran more easily towards supporting jumble sales than participation in marches and meetings.

"I think we're doing good things, Len, but my time's limited. I'm working and there's Jimmy, it doesn't leave a lot."

"Why don't you come along to the meeting on Thursday? We've an Indian gentleman from the high commission. He's going to talk about independence, what's going to happen now that Attlee's announced it."

Lorna looked at Pepe. "You should go," he said. "If you want to go."

"I'm so tired. It would be rude to fall asleep while he's speaking."

It was true, she was tired, physically and mentally. Lorna had discovered that the condition of constant tiredness was not confined to wartime. She longed for the energy that had been hers before war, marriage and childbirth had intervened to douse the flames inside, one by one. Yet she remained outwardly the same as she had ever been, a young woman with a presence that made people warm to her. Appearances can disguise the internal process of aging, those changes inside are subtler, deeper; invisible and rarely noticed until they have already taken hold.

"Not this time, Len. But I will get back to it soon. I promise. I need to for my own sake. I don't want to go mouldy."

"Hey, Lorna, you are not mouldy," called Pepe from his newly-arrived armchair by the fire. "But it is true, Len, she is a busy woman. It is not me stopping her."

"What about you, then, Pepe? Why don't you come along? You'll find it interesting."

"Think those days might be done for me. Once I had a fire inside. But this is a luke-warm country, it takes away the heat."

Len left. Lorna finished clearing away the laundry, putting some in the pile for ironing, hanging the sheets over chair backs to air them, sorting underwear into drawers. She did not resent the house work; she loved her home. It meant she had a reason for reduced involvement in the world, her excuses were already made for her. As she cleared away she thought about this: had she grown up? Had she become middle-aged?

Were her best days done and, if so, why did this not worry her? Should it worry her? *Maturity kicks in, changing eagerness into confidence, experience into wisdom, fearfulness into knowingness. It's easier to be protective of youth, but maturity defies protection, it allows itself less vulnerability. Oh such pompous excuses, such retreats from life. I must find a way to connect again to the excitement of life.*

"I do not want to hold you back, Lorna. You must do what you must do."

"What? Oh, it's nothing. I just want to have life a little easier for a while, not have to fight the world."

"Fair enough. I will do what you want me to."

She looked at Pepe. She recognised that he had changed; so why would she herself not have changed too? Yet she longed for something of what he had been, the fiery young boy who raised a clenched fist and stood in defiance of those more powerful than himself. Now they were sinking all too early into a comfort that she would have despised back then. Her middleness worried her, despite her rationalising. The political centre of gravity had shifted with the Labour government. Now she had the prospect, and in some cases the reality, of real change: a free health service, public ownership of industries, the end of empire, better housing, internationalism. Causes that stirred her blood, once. Did they still? She had evidence of this progress as she looked around her. She had the child who was in his cot sleeping. *I have so much, not least this perfect child. But where is the excitement?*

Pepe had dozed off in his fireside chair. The embers would cool in the grate, the orange glow would fade to grey ash and he would wake at midnight and wonder where she was. By then she would be asleep in bed where she would try to dream of stars.

CHAPTER 39

"These are my friends," said Pepe. Lorna had said that she wanted to come with Pepe to see him play football in Regent's Park.

"There will not be much to see," he said. "I play in goal. Because of my leg."

"That doesn't matter. It will be nice to see your friends."

Pepe's weekends were increasingly centred around football. On Saturday afternoons he would watch, either Arsenal or Tottenham. On Sunday mornings he would play with Spanish friends, the remnants of those who had come over on the *Habana* and never returned to Spain.

Lorna did not understand football. She knew the rules – but she did not understand its appeal. It was a masculine club but unlike other examples of such things, she had no real wish to become a member. However, she sensed that she needed to try, to grow closer again to Pepe.

"Was it a good match?" she asked Pepe when he came home with a copy of the pink evening paper. "What was the score?"

"Good game. A draw."

"At Arsenal, I guess."

"Yes, Spurs next week."

"Is it OK to do that?" asked Lorna. "Shouldn't you choose one or the other?"

"What for? I go for the football game, not the wish for winning. There are many people do this."

"Really? People I know – the football fans – wouldn't dream of supporting both teams. You have to be one side or the other."

"No point. I do not worry if my side gets beat."

Pepe played with a similar attitude. He was not a good goalkeeper. His bad leg restricted his mobility but, compared to the other players, he put little commitment into his play. At the end of the match – a kickabout with coats and bags for goalposts – Pepe's jumper was still clean whereas everyone else was covered in mud.

"OK? Lorna, this is José. And Alberto, Luis, Josep. They are grown up since you last saw them. You will not remember."

Lorna did not recognise or remember these boys, if she had met them before in Stoneham or Finchley. That was now a long time ago.

"I remember you," said Luis. "You were always kind. And you did this…" he clenched his fist.

The old reflex asserted itself, and Lorna raised her right fist back at him. There was laughter all round.

"Different times, eh? But we don't forget."

Pepe took Lorna aside. "Better not to do that," he said. "That is past."

"Oh? Not for me. Not for them either. Else why would they still be here and not returned to Spain?"

Jimmy was cold and starting to get restless in his pushchair. It was too muddy to get him out to run around, so Lorna got ready to move off.

"You go, Lorna. I will catch up. I have to talk to people here."

Lorna nodded to Pepe and moved the pushchair forward stickily through the mud. It took her a while to reach the path that would lead out of the park. When she got there she was a little out of breath so she stopped and looked around. Most of the Spanish lads were moving off together in the opposite direction, but Pepe was talking to a man dressed in a black suit, clearly not one of the footballers. There was something familiar about him, particularly his black beard. She seemed to remember him but none of the Spanish boys would have had a beard ten years ago.

Pepe caught up with her ten minutes later, at the gates of the park near Camden Town.

"Shall we get a bus?" asked Pepe.

"No, let's walk. Jimmy's asleep."

They walked briskly side by side.

"So, you met my friends. They are good lads."

"Who was the older one? The one with the beard."

"Oh, he does not play. He sometimes comes to watch."

"Who is he then?"

"Not sure what he does."

"So you were talking about the weather, just like English people?"

"Yes. Exactly."

They walked in silence down Delancey Street. Lorna was suddenly uneasy, realising where they were. She kept her head down underneath the fur hat she had worn for warmth. They passed the house of the artist Vincent Hillyer, and Lorna said nothing.

When they reached Chalton Street, Lorna asked again. "I wish you would tell me who that man was. It seemed as if I must know him."

Pepe sighed. He pulled his overcoat tighter around himself, shivering a little as he was still in his football kit underneath.

"I must tell you then his name is Antonio."

"Good. And why would I know Antonio?"

"No reason. You do not know. He is just a Spanish man, from Madrid, and he lives in London."

"And? And what does he do?"

Pepe shook his head. He did not want to say anything more. Lorna looked expectantly at him. Pepe suddenly brightened.

"It is this," he said. "Antonio is a priest. That is why I know him."

"So. You go to church. I do not mind. But I want you to be open about it. No secrets."

"Of course. I have no secrets. Actually Antonio would be happy to get us married."

Pepe had discovered a way to bring the inquisition to an end. This was a subject Lorna no longer wished to discuss. They walked in silence in what had now turned into the bright sunshine of an early evening in Springtime.

Soon they were home, back in Levita House. They were all in need of a bath. First Pepe, then Jimmy, then Lorna. The hot water was running luke-warm by the time it was Lorna's turn so she boiled a kettle to add to the bathwater. For her a bath was one of the essential treats that peacetime had made possible.

There were other little luxuries now that the privations of war, some self-imposed, were past. Even if the bath tub was in the kitchen, covered by a wooden worktop when not in use as a bath, it represented luxury to Lorna. She added other treats such as Nivea cream, shampoo and a cube of chocolate every other day. The eking out of chocolate was reinforced by rationing, but the self-massage of her face with Nivea was something she could extend into a soothing pleasure. It completed bathtime.

Except that her hair was still wet. And her hair was getting long. She sat brushing out droplets of water onto the towel that she draped across her shoulders.

"I need to get my hair done," she said.

Pepe looked up. His hair was still damp but neatly combed – he spent a lot of time combing his hair even though it was quite short.

"*Que piensas, Himmy?*" he asked the boy sitting on his lap and bent his head, pretending to listen for his reply. "Jimmy says you should let me cut it for you."

Lorna laughed. "So you want mummy to look funny, Jimmy, eh?"

"No, it would not look funny…I cut people's hair in the army. I can do it."

Lorna looked doubtful. "What with?"

"Scissors, of course. We have scissors. I will do it well. I will just shorten it a little so no need to worry."

Lorna agreed that Pepe would cut her hair. She conceded partly because she was annoyed at herself for being irritated by him speaking Spanish to Jimmy. Rationally she knew it was a good thing – for Pepe and for Jimmy – but she was a little worried that Jimmy had not yet begun to speak much in English or Spanish. Perhaps he was confused by the two languages? She let it pass, and went to sit near the fire that Pepe had lit when they had come home.

Pepe knelt behind Lorna and took first the brush, then the comb, from her hands. Then he picked up the scissors he had taken from the kitchen drawer and began to snip snip at the sides and lower fringes of her hair. He cut in a quick snapping motion, occasionally drawing the hair across the blades of the scissors, shaping the hair not crudely cutting it. While he did this he was intent on the task. Lorna refrained from asking constantly "is it OK?" He seemed confident. After ten minutes he gathered up the hair that he had cut and wrapped it in a newspaper to throw away.

"Enough to fill a hundred lockets," smiled Lorna.

"True. Let me see." He used the comb to hang layers of Lorna's hair over his fingers, then leant back to take a look. "It is good. Now just stay there and let it dry properly. I will clear away."

Later Lorna declared herself happy with the results. She looked in the mirror, noticing her face shining pinkly with the effects of the Nivea cream. Her hair had dried and it had more shape and bounce to it. "Just like a proper hair dresser," she said, coming back smiling into the room. Pepe hardly looked up as he was sitting on the floor playing with Jimmy, using a saucepan and wooden spoon as a drum and stick. As Jimmy hit the metal, Pepe shouted "*Muy bien! Bien!*" And Jimmy shouted "*Be be be*". Suddenly she was filled with a feeling of love towards her son now speaking a recognisable attempt at a word, and with gratitude towards Pepe for his part in this. *We do have love.* She felt her hair with the tips of her fingers, patting it gently. *Amor*, she said to herself, one of the few Spanish words that Pepe had taught her.

CHAPTER 40

Pepe did not have a job but he found work. He became friends with people locally and ingratiated himself with some of the market stallholders. There was a street market in Chalton Street, particularly on Saturdays, and Pepe offered to do more, helping them set up in the morning and clear up at the end of the day. This meant he was no longer able to watch football on Saturday afternoons, but he shrugged and told Lorna that it did not matter to him.

There was so much he was missing. What was one more privation? He tried to stay outwardly cheerful in the face of so much that he resented. He had no proper job. Now trying to do a job, he had to give up football. He was missing his language, his parents and his native land.

"It is me. I have gone missing," he announced to Lorna.

"What on earth do you mean? You are just starting to make your way, soon things will get better."

"And I am missing other things. Church, my religion. Getting married."

Lorna did not know how to cope with the marriage question. In her eyes, and as far as she was concerned in the eyes of everyone, they were married. *Why even question it? It is not a proper question.* Lorna hoped that more regular market work would help Pepe's self-esteem and make the question fade away. So he began early on Saturday morning, pushing a wheelbarrow down Chalton Street and helping set up stalls, mainly fruit and vegetables. At the end of the day he received a few shillings and a bag of produce. He prized the oranges most of all.

"They remind me of Spain. Sunshine. Market days at home."

It emerged that Pepe's father now worked in a Bilbao fish market. He was not able to work as a teacher under a regime that placed little value on education, and even less value on a foreign language such as English. Pepe now seemed to receive regular letters from his parents, though they were never delivered by the postman. He must be writing regularly too as the news he spoke from Spain suggested there was dialogue between parents and son.

"I have friends," said Pepe when Lorna asked how he managed to get letters. They seemed to arrive on Sundays after the football match in Regent's Park. Pepe's friends divided into the English and the Spanish ones, centred around either the market or the park football. Lorna imagined there must be some arrangement, probably clandestine, to keep letters crossing the borders. She did not mind that; it seemed to be cocking a snook at the fascist regime.

"Why do people call you 'Bill'?" she asked, because she had heard him addressed by this name on the estate and in the street.

"They call me Bill because it is easy."

"Pepe is not really difficult."

"They know I am from Bilbao. So, Bill. Bill Barrer in full. Because I push the wheelbarrows." Lorna looked quizzical. "It is funny, I do not mind. It is only a name. It shows they like me."

"I don't like it." Lorna was quick to take offence on behalf of those closest to her. It meant that she would sometimes be seen as a bit of a snob by the people she most wanted to accept her. She had aspirations for herself and her family, and she thought that those aspirations might be undermined by names and words. She tried to correct Pepe when he slipped into slang, whether he picked it up from his old army days or now in the market. Pepe was something of a ventriloquist, able to speak in another's voice, picking up words and phrases easily. So he talked about being 'borassic' when he had no money, 'taking a butcher's' when he looked at anything, stacking the stall with 'spuds'. Lorna winced a bit inside when she heard him talk like this. To her ears this Spanish–cockney voice made him sound like a spiv.

"It's phony, Pepe."

"It is me, Lorna. It helps me fit in."

She shrugged and let it pass, again. But each time these words grated a little more.

"At least you cannot correct my Spanish. Though I feel I am losing my language a little. I have not enough chances to use it."

Lorna knew this was true, and she sympathised. She determined to be easier on Pepe, aware that she was making too many petty criticisms. She encouraged him to speak Spanish with Jimmy, putting aside her previous reservations. *It will be part of his culture, language is important.* At the same time she told herself that she really must make more of an effort with both husband and son, to speak to them more. That evening she read a story to Jimmy. The three little pigs might be a little advanced; of course the boy would not understand every word but she realised that this was important, to encourage him to speak.

Talking to Pepe was also important, though there was little need for encouragement. Talking was Pepe's favourite activity and she would often pass by in wonder when she saw him with other people. She envied his ease in conversation. That Saturday evening, after Pepe's market stint was done and after Jimmy was asleep, Lorna suggested that they should go out for a drink to the local pub, the Coffee House. Despite the name, that went back to the neighbourhood's French refugees in history, it was a pub that sold mainly beer and absolutely no coffee. Lorna looked forward to a rare evening out, taking the chance to talk about many of the things that they found too few opportunities to discuss. They asked Lorraine, the daughter of their neighbours, to sit with Jimmy so they could go out to the pub for a drink.

After a day working in the market, Pepe was limping slightly. Inside the pub, with its Saturday night crowd, he brought their drinks carefully from the bar to a seat in the corner. He had a couple of conversations along the way, with people he knew from the estate. Lorna groaned inwardly at the use of 'Bill'.

"Cheers, Pepe," said Lorna, perhaps to make a point, perhaps in relaxation. They clinked glasses, a pint of bitter to a Guinness, then they began talking, easily enough. They talked about Jimmy and the way he was changing, making that sly change from baby to boy. Pepe talked about wishing his parents could see the boy.

"I wish they could too, but we can't go to Spain, you know that. If they let you in, they wouldn't let you out."

"Perhaps. And perhaps there are ways. Ways to meet halfway."

"Find a friendly border guard? One with a popgun."

"Things are possible. I have friends."

"It's a dream, Pepe. They would shoot you."

"Surely not if I read Karl Marx to them. Then they would

understand…." His smile showed that he was joking. It pleased Lorna as they rarely mentioned politics these days, and never in a tone of levity.

"You could slip across while they were sleeping then."

"So it would be a dream."

Pepe talked about his mother and father. Lorna knew little about them and had no expectations of meeting them unless the regime changed in Spain.

"It is a waste. My father is an intelligent man. A good teacher. Now he carries crates of fish in a market."

"Pepe, you are an intelligent man. And you carry crates in a market."

"I know. But I am not trained to teach others."

"I'm sure you could. If you set your mind to it."

"Huh, not everything is possible 'if you set your mind to it'."

"You'll never know if you don't try."

Lorna had never thought of Pepe as a potential teacher, but *why not?* she thought. *He could teach Spanish.* Lorna always had higher aspirations for herself and, especially, for others. It was part of her mission in life, to help others reach higher, climb higher. If she had such aspirations for Pepe, it would be easier to have them for Jimmy.

Pepe went to the bar to get some more drinks. Lorna had slipped him a pound note from her purse. She told him to buy a round for his friends at the bar. "Cheers, Bill," they said. Lorna smiled under the influence of Guinness and friendship. Such influences come and go. She supped at the new drink that Pepe had brought, limping across the room.

"Your leg seems bad tonight," she said.

"It is. I worked it hard today and now it hurts like a toothache."

"Perhaps you need to see a dentist."

"Not funny," he winced at the pain of his leg and the joke.

"I'm sorry for your wound, Pepe. But I don't know what I can do to make it better."

"I have it for you. It is what I did for you."

Lorna drank some more, disconcerted by this new front opening up in their relationship. Pepe had not previously raised this.

"Pepe, don't rewrite history. It was your choice to join up. You wanted to fight fascism, you wanted to do your bit."

"My choice? You told me it was what I have to do. Become British, join the army, marry you. Boom boom boom, easy. And I paid the price."

"There was nothing to pay."

"My leg was the price."

"Oh, Pepe, come off it, you hardly notice it."

She knew he would sulk, as soon as she said it. But words slip out, like greyhounds at the starting gun; before you knew it, they were away, chasing down, tearing apart. And sometimes they were followed by silence.

They sat without speaking, sipping at drinks they no longer enjoyed, hoping their spirits would be restored. One or two people, a few drinks ahead of them, were starting to sing in that way brought on by alcohol and the slurred hope of ignoring the world's reality.

"We mustn't turn into that, Pepe," Lorna nodded at her neighbour Emmy singing over the top of her beer glass.

"Seems OK to me, Emmy does her job. She buys flowers,

makes funeral wreaths. Then forgets about the memories over a drink."

"And that's it?"

"At least she is honest. She knows where she stands."

"We know where we stand. We live together and support each other. And we have a lovely little boy."

Pepe paused, stared. "I stand on a bad leg. Which my wife does not care about. So why would my son?"

"This is just nonsense. Drink up. We might as well go home."

They both wanted more from their lives, and this was the real ache that they felt. A need for more was eating into them, like a worm into an apple. The problem was that they could not agree on what **more** meant. Perhaps, in Pepe's case, a job, the sense that he was contributing, valued for what he did for his family. In Lorna's case, she wanted to be happy but she felt that would come only if she helped others. The main thing they now held in common was Jimmy. *But I cannot be with him every minute of every day.*

They walked home, they thanked Lorraine and gave her thruppence, they went to bed and made love to make peace, relying now on Marie Stopes principles, fearing that love-making might not be love itself. A fear that was almost the same as knowledge, a fear that might in time become an acceptance.

CHAPTER 41

On the following Tuesday Lorna started for home from work, collecting Jimmy from his nursery, in a good mood. She stood at the bus stop in Kingsway where the woman paperseller as always screeched "*Star! News! Standard!*" With no bus in sight Lorna bought a copy of the *Star*. It was a light news day but Lorna's mood was light because of her work.

It had been a day of progress in the case that she was most involved in. Thomas Brothers were representing a warehouseman and his union; the man had been offered employment then had the offer withdrawn because of a criminal record acquired when he had stolen a bicycle at the age of 11. The case had personally outraged Lorna and she had vested a lot of her own faith in fighting it. She had marshalled her arguments well and made a compelling case that everyone said would win, perhaps even forcing a small change in the law. Soon it would go to trial.

When she got off the bus, she walked down Ossulston Street, entering the furthest courtyard. Pepe met her there, in a state of excitement.

"I got a job!" he shouted.

"What? What is it?"

He explained that it was at the barber shop in Eversholt Street, right next to Euston station. There were many advantages: regular money, tips, no Saturdays, just a short walk from home. Most of all, a job.

"But can you cut hair? Do you know how?"

"Of course. I cut yours. And I did a couple of trials. I am good at it. And I will get even better."

Lorna was pleased and disappointed at the same time. It was a job, and the money was useful, but it did not match her aspirations for Pepe. The thought of him becoming a teacher had wormed its way into her thinking, even though Pepe himself had shown no interest.

"Well done," she said, grudgingly but trying not to sound that way. "Let's hope it all works out. When do you start?"

Pepe decided to tell Lorna more once he had started the following week. The labyrinthine network of connections was too complicated to explain now, involving both English and Spanish friends. Lorna might not like all those connections, but she did not need to know. Deception is part of life's everyday exchange. Small deceptions keep people together; bigger ones can drive people apart. Pepe was hopeful – and so was Lorna once the news sank in properly – that this change in circumstances might bind them more tightly together.

Pepe was happier to be working. It meant he had an income and no longer needed to ask Lorna for money. No longer being 'borassic' he no longer needed to say the word. They grew closer together again, enabling Pepe to raise one of his difficult subjects one more time, many haircuts, many tips and a few weeks further on.

"I want my mum and dad to meet you, Lorna. I want them to see Jimmy."

"Pepe, we've talked about this. You know it's impossible."

"I do not think so. There must be a way."

"Not without you losing everything. You've no rights in Spain. They see you as an enemy of the state."

"You know all about rights – except when it is your own family. My parents have rights. Jimmy has rights. The right to see each other."

Pepe had shifted the argument onto quasi-legal grounds, so Lorna felt she should establish exactly what the position might be. She spent some time in work talking to Bryan and others, doing research. She arranged a meeting with Pedro Escobar, a Spanish lawyer in exile.

"I am not sure, Lorna, what you wish me to say."

"The truth," she answered.

"Really? Often the truth is built on shifting sands, not least for those who claim most firmly to speak it."

"Meaning? Meaning yourself? Or me? Or Franco?"

He smiled. "Perhaps all of us. Perhaps for everyone. Mr Attlee and his ministers seem less inclined to stand up for anti-fascist Spaniards than before the war."

"I know that. And I'm not trying to bring down the Spanish government – though I wish I could. I just want to know what would be the position of someone like Pepe if he chose to go back for a visit."

"I would not recommend it. Certainly not. Things would have to change much more, even to think about it."

"Explain it to me, so I can explain it to Pepe."

"Pepe is a *profugo*, a refugee would be too nice a way of saying it in Franco's eyes. He is seen as a traitor to the state. In theory he can apply for an *indulto*, a pardon. In practice he will not get it. They have no wish to give pardons. It is a process of humiliation, not a real legal process. If Pepe went back he would be arrested, he would be put in prison. Then he would have to do military service, three years. I doubt if a bad leg will get him off that. They see it as re-education."

"But he is now a British citizen. With a British passport."

"It counts for little when you have a bad-tempered *Guardia Civil* at the border. Those people have more power to do harm than one of Franco's ministers. It will not matter if there is a passport, it will not matter if all the papers are correct. What matters is what they think of who they see in front of them. So a British passport is good anywhere but Spain – if you were born in Spain, it gives no immunity, it simply gives an incentive towards revenge. They look up his records, they know which side he was on."

"And what about me? I am married to him. Our marriage must give some protection?"

"I think not. I believe you were married in a registry office. This counts for nothing in the eyes of the Spanish state, in the eyes of the Catholic church. To them you are not married at all."

Lorna was not surprised. It stirred some of the original spirit of opposition to Franco that had not been fanned to life since the war. It suited too many people, including the government, to live with the status quo in Spain. The Spanish government was still fascist but, in the post-war world, usefully anti-communist. *What would Harry think? Did he die in vain?*

What would Pepe think? When Lorna reported the conversation, she was not sure if Pepe believed her. He reacted as if this did not matter. There are ways, he said, there are ways.

Lorna felt better for knowing the truth but she did not report the information about marriage to Pepe. It made no real difference to the argument in her eyes.

CHAPTER 42

It was an evening like the first time Lorna had walked up that hill in Hampstead towards Diana's house. Then she had been Lorna Starling, a diffident if determined young woman, apprehensive at the evening in prospect. Now she was Lorna Calderon, ten years older, a mother, still feeling a flush of nervousness at the thought of an evening in company outside her area of comfort.

Then she had met Harry, only to lose him all too quickly. Now she was accompanied by Pepe who seemed to be looking forward to the evening rather more than she was. Lorna rarely talked about Harry to Pepe but tonight it would have seemed deceitful not to have mentioned him.

"It's ten years, almost to the day, since I met Harry here."

"You still think about him?" Pepe's words seemed more a statement of fact than a question.

"I do. I think about him often."

"I know. It makes me a little sad."

"A lot of people died. Harry was just one more. One that I happened to know."

"And love. That is what makes me sad."

Pepe felt a sadness that was close to jealousy. This was one reason why Lorna talked about Harry much less than she thought about him.

"We met and weeks later he was gone. RIP Harry James." She spoke his name almost under her breath, like a private prayer, but loud enough to be heard by Pepe.

"Harry James. His name was James? I did not know."

"Oh yes. But of course there was never a gravestone I could show you."

"Perhaps one day. One day we go to find it in Spain."

They were nearing Diana's house in sombre mood. When meeting Diana, particularly when it was a *salon* with many other people, Lorna always felt under pressure to be as bright as possible. Diana had a reputation for bringing together people from different backgrounds, even though from the same range of the political spectrum. Her gatherings were lively, intellectually stimulating, with no place for wallflowers. Lorna's heart sank further.

"Pepe, let's just walk on a bit. I don't want to go in till I'm ready."

Pepe shrugged and they carried on strolling up the road, past the house with the columns. At the end of the road they would reach Hampstead Heath. The road leading up the hill at the side of the heath was crowded with people making the most of the late sunshine. Couples strolled arm in arm, reminding Lorna of the evening ten years ago, the same sense of trying to escape the shadows hanging over peace. Lorna linked her arm into Pepe's and he smiled at her. They passed an elderly man wearing a sandwich board. "Where will you spend eternity?" the board asked in bold letters. *You might be finding out soon*, Lorna thought to herself grimly.

"That looks heavy," said Pepe.

"It's no weight," replied the old man, staring ahead unsmiling. "REPENT!" shouted the back of the sandwich board.

Lorna whispered to Pepe, when they were out of earshot "I was just thinking he might not have to wait too long to answer his own question".

"Perhaps not. But I think he believes. So it is real for him, not a joke."

Lorna felt a little chastened. She had been thinking herself into the smart kind of conversation that appealed to Diana, where irony could replace feelings. But old age is the last thing that should be mocked.

"I'm sorry," she said. "I didn't mean to be cruel. We ought to go inside now anyway. Before we're the last to arrive."

The door bell was answered by a young woman with a hairstyle as severe as her East European accent.

"Lorna. And Pepe. Yes, Diana has talk to me about you. Please to come in."

They were waved ahead into the imposing room where Harry had spoken on that night still vivid in Lorna's memory. The room was full of people and Lorna scanned those who were there, picking out familiar faces. But she found herself first facing George Robb just inside the doorway.

"Lorna, my dear. How nice to see you. Let's grab you a drink."

George's star was in decline. These days he was invited to Downing Street for old time's sake, not because his opinion mattered. Lorna had heard this from Bryan and felt fortified by the knowledge.

"George, this is Pepe."

"Pepe? And where are you from, young man?"

"Me? I am from Somers Town. And I am from Bilbao."

So the story had to be told, with the connection to the evening ten years ago when Lorna had paid her ten bob, and the subsequent visit to North Stoneham, meeting Pepe.

"Well," said George. "Isn't life strange? I can't work out if that means you got a cheap husband, Lorna – or an expensive one. Anyway, I'm pleased for you both."

Lorna tugged at Pepe's sleeve, wanting to move on, away from George. She had always felt patronised by George Robb, and her feelings against him were stronger than ever. She slipped away, pulling Pepe with her, as George greeted trade union friends arriving. Working through the crowd, stopping here and there for brief conversations, getting drinks topped up, they found themselves in a corner of the room in front of a bookcase.

There was a familiar figure, leaning on the bookcase, pretending to read a book he had taken from the shelf. Lorna's eyes met those of Vincent Hillyer and no retreat was possible.

"This is a surprise," he said.

"I suppose so. Though I might have expected it."

"Might you? Why?"

"Oh, life plays tricks."

The awkward silence might have lasted just seconds. Then Pepe made his presence felt, unlocking their eyes by waving his arm between them.

"Pepe, this is Vincent. Vincent is an artist. Pepe is my husband."

"Your husband? Now you have surprised me. And mortally disappointed me," putting his right hand on his heart.

"Why is that?" asked Pepe. "Am I a disappointment to you?"

"Oh no, my dear man. I mean that now I have to put aside my still frequent thoughts of Lorna. I find your wife ravishing."

Pepe did not know how to react. He felt puzzled and angry and defensive. He looked at Lorna for explanation or rescue.

"Pepe, it's all right. You must not mind Vincent. He's an

artist, a Bohemian. He thinks he moves on a different plane from ordinary people like you and me."

"Ordinary? Never. Lorna, you were always extra-ordinary. That's why I painted you."

Pepe looked from one to the other, finding it hard to break the intensity of gaze between them.

"Are you....?" He asked.

"Yes, Pepe. It was Vincent who made the portrait of me that you dislike so much."

"You did not like it?" asked Vincent of Pepe, sounding amused rather than disappointed.

"No, I did not. It was gross. You did not capture Lorna's beauty."

"Ah, there you are right, I'm sure. How could I? Look at her face. Those cheekbones. Look at her," and he stepped back to appraise her from top to toe.

"I'm afraid the portrait is no longer on the wall. It made Pepe uncomfortable," said Lorna.

"Well, some portraits are best kept private. They can be like acts of love."

Lorna laughed. It seemed the only response that might defuse the situation.

"Pepe, you must understand that Vincent is hardly ever serious. He never means what he says."

Pepe was not convinced. He could not laugh at Lorna's words or Vincent's stares or his own thoughts. "There will be no more portraits. I forbid it."

"Pepe, don't make yourself sound so pompous. Don't be so...Spanish. Only I can forbid myself from doing such things."

"*Olé*," smirked Vincent.

Pepe had moved away, unable to bear the conversation any longer. Lorna looked at his departing back, knowing that she must follow.

"That was bad of you, Vincent. Now I will have my work cut out to make up."

"No, no. You will find me forgiving," he said, looking hard at her face. "You are still extra-ordinary. I still want to see you, to *paint* you."

"That's not possible."

"Are you sure? I am serious. And I do mean what I say."

Lorna turned away in pursuit of Pepe. She found him next to Diana, talking as if nothing had happened.

"Lorna, dear Lorna," said Diana, kissing her on the cheek. "Pepe has been telling me he has a job."

"Yes. He does. It will tide us over until something better turns up."

"I like the job," said Pepe.

"Of course. And here's to you both." Diana chinked their glasses. "I'm sure you don't need anything better to turn up."

Lorna felt ashamed of her own shame at Pepe's job. Words were slipping out, beyond her control. She wanted to take them back, to take back the whole evening. But the only remedy, for now, was to drink up quickly and leave; to go home, to try to make things better, to make sure Jimmy was sleeping safely.

To her surprise, Pepe was happy to stay. So she had to plead a bad headache and lead him down the stairs outside, then down the hill towards the tube station. It was a silent journey back to Levita House. She was pleased to get home and find Jimmy fast asleep, happy in the care of Lorraine.

CHAPTER 43

Life's natural events, like birth and childhood, might have been reduced but not replaced by war. There were still babies, still children, and children still wanted to play with other children.

Their parents also wanted them to play. Parents never quite relinquish the wish to play themselves, even if they seem to join in games with reluctance. Lorna played hide-and-seek with Jimmy, and they all laughed when his teddy bear appeared to say 'Boo'.

Adults play adult games too. Lorna had a growing desire for play, the kind of play that she was not getting from her everyday life. With Pepe she had settled all too swiftly into a domesticity that she recognised from her parents' lives, a domesticity that she had resisted and fled many years earlier. She yearned for more, a frisson of excitement whose absence was becoming a bigger and bigger gap to fill. She tried to fill it by buying herself a new frock, with colourful patterns unlike her usual style, but when she wore it at home it did not seem to fit her situation even if it fitted her body. Pepe acknowledged it only with a passing smile. *Does he like it? Or not?* Lorna had little personal vanity, but she did want to be noticed as a woman.

"Pepe, what do you think?" Her open hands made clear what she was asking about.

"It is nice. Unusual."

"Does it suit me?"

"Of course. It makes you look very nice."

Lorna wanted more. Much later that day she went out to the balcony and looked down at the courtyard. In the early summer evening, on a day after school, the children were playing. There were mainly groups of girls; the boys were roaming further, into the land marked by 'Keep Out' signs, the bomb site opposite. Only one adult was in sight, a woman with her hair tied back in a scarf, on her knees, scrubbing her doorstep on the ground floor at the far end of the courtyard.

Lorna enjoyed watching people, young and old, living their lives all around her. She became an observer, as if at a cinema with the film setting the scene. Perhaps something would happen? It rarely did; ordinary life was enough, children at play; only squabbles that became the dramas of childish jockeyings for dominance. *They learn it so naturally*, thought Lorna.

Lorraine emerged from her flat next door. At the age of twelve her maternal instincts were already in full bloom. "Can I take Jimmy down to play?" she asked. "We'll stay where you can see."

Lorna carried Jimmy down the three flights of stairs, and Lorraine took his hand at ground level.

"Play nicely, Jimmy," called Lorna, half-wishing that he might be reluctant to leave his mother. But the boy was already in a world where grown-ups were uncalled-for outsiders. Lorna walked back up the stairs to lean over the balcony to watch.

Jimmy stood out in Lorna's view, as any child will for a mother. But his curly blond hair was different, bobbing like a buoy among the waves of the girls' brown hair. There were five girls in the group, with Lorraine the eldest, and a couple of them just of school age. Lorna knew their parents. She thought she recognised the clothes they were wearing from the local jumble sales that raised Labour Party funds. They also had some clothes borrowed from their mothers' wardrobes, particularly high-heeled shoes that were much too big for easy walking. Lorraine tied a scarf around Jimmy's neck and he did a little jig of excitement.

Lorna was surprised to see him so happy. Her gaze wandered beyond the courtyard to the bombsite where the boys were playing. She could not make out the 'Trespassers shall be prosecuted" notices, but she knew and understood that these represented an almost irresistible challenge to the boys. Half a dozen of them were wandering up and down the rubbly slopes of the ground, turning over anything that might be of interest for being different and perhaps usable in a game. They extracted short planks of wood and wheels of various sizes, with bits of string and cord. They carried or dragged these over to the corner where a couple of boys were assembling the found objects to make carts that they would use for racing on the pavements.

The railway yards were to the right, behind the high walls with the bricked-up Gothic arches, and behind them the sooted windows that allowed only darkness to penetrate. The height of the brickwork meant that the trains could not be seen, only heard as they clanked their way along the tracks. With Euston, St Pancras and King's Cross stations within walking distance this was railway country, the estate a residential pocket in between the coming and going of locomotives carrying freight and passengers somewhat wearily to and from London and the north. Lorraine's dad Roy worked on the railways, as did many neighbours, and soon everyone would have a stake in the publicly owned system. *That's progress*, Lorna assured herself, rehearsing an argument for another time.

Lorna's gaze returned to watch the group of girls and

Jimmy. She was pleased that he was not yet absorbed into the company only of boys. Jimmy was trying to join in with the new games that the girls had moved on to after dressing up, but he was still proudly wearing the scarf. Imitating two of the younger girls Jimmy was riding a broomstick as a horse and making clopping sounds. The other three girls were taking turns with the skipping ropes.

To the left, at the end of the courtyard was Chalton Street. Lorna thought of this as Pepe's territory because he still spent time there with the market stallholders on Saturdays. He would help set up the stalls at the edge of the road in front of the permanent shops like the Co-op, the fish and chip shop, Fred Field's the hardware shop that sold vinegar from barrels. At the end of Saturday, he would still come home with a bag of fruit and vegetables as his pay.

This is idyllic, Lorna thought as she took in the scene below, making a reckoning. But still there was a need for more, a feeling that she needed excitement, even interest, that went beyond children's games. She got more from her work but was increasingly resigned to never becoming the university student of her dreams, perhaps of Bryan's wishes as he still kept the prospect alive in their conversations. But it felt as if he was stringing her along, trying to keep her happy. Looking at Jimmy, aged only two, Lorna was determined that he would one day have the chance to go to university.

Motherhood, work, politics, more. What about life? The effect of the war was that she now felt that life should offer more to herself and other women. She had thoughts and feelings that might have been suppressed by low expectations before the war. Music, theatre, art, more. She had an interest but no knowledge. Could she feed that interest?

She thought of Vincent and immediately tried to banish the thought. Thoughts of him brought guilt. Even the fact of thinking about Vincent brought guilt. But she could not head off the daydream that spun through her mind. She had gained something from the contact with Vincent that no one else supplied in her life. He had hands and eyes like no one else; she was frightened by them and drawn to them in equal measure. The portrait now out of sight on the top of the wardrobe, the sitting and standing in front of him, the being observed by the intensity of his penetrating gaze, his fingers blackened by charcoal, perfumed by turpentine. The realisation that he could already see her body beneath her clothes so there was no point in being prudish. The swelling pride and confidence in her body that she received from his eyes upon her, the awareness of her sensual potential that had taken her by surprise, the pleasure that she felt in it. The coming together of hands and eyes, flesh and hair and skin, the contours traced by fingers.

Lorna was shaken from her reverie by the sight of Pepe entering the courtyard. She glanced at her watch to see that it was getting late. She called down to Pepe to bring Jimmy up with him.

"So, what a big boy, playing out with the big children. That is good."

Pepe lowered the boy to the stone floor of the balcony so he could totter towards his mother.

"Sorry," said Lorna. "I haven't done anything about tea yet. I'll go and see to it now."

She wanted more than just their tea – more than lamb chops and boiled potatoes and peas because it was Thursday. Her hunger was of a different kind. She wanted life to take her off guard and make her see things through another's eyes.

"I got a letter from my dad," said Pepe. "The situation is very bad, he says. They do not have enough food to eat. At least we have that."

"Except for the rationing."

"A little rationing is not bad."

Lorna could only agree. She understood and supported the need for rationing. But the guilt of wanting more was eating into her from the inside.

"That frock," said Pepe. "It is very good. Too good for doing the cooking in."

CHAPTER 44

It was Spring Bank holiday, just a few days later at the end of May. Pepe wanted to go to Hampstead because there was a fun fair. He insisted.

It would not have been Lorna's choice. She had no interest and Jimmy was too young, but Pepe would not consider other options. So, believing that she had been too harsh on Pepe recently, even feeling a little guilty, she went along with the plan.

Hampstead is a good place to spend a bank holiday when the sun brings the crowds out. So Lorna told herself. Heading up the hill alongside the heath, they were in the company of many other families with young children. The war was becoming a memory now, but it was still close enough for there to be a slightly desperate air to the collective need to have fun. Pepe was childlike as they skirted the pond, his eyes seeming to shine more brightly at the sight of the rides and stalls ahead of them. He carried Jimmy in his arms and '*Mira, mira*' he shouted, joggling the boy higher to see better.

The crowds were so dense that Pepe had to carry on holding Jimmy, at least until he could no longer resist having a go at some of the side shows. He managed to win a doll by knocking empty cans off a shelf, then a goldfish in a bag by hooking a plastic duck with a long rod.

"No more, please," shouted Lorna, competing with the noise of talking and music. "What are we going to do with this stuff? I'm not taking the goldfish anyway."

"It is fun. Enjoy yourself. Look at Jimmy."

It was true, Jimmy did seem to be enjoying himself. Perhaps

it was simply being carried by his father after a few weeks of seeing less of Pepe because of work. They walked further into the centre of the fair, with Pepe looking at all the rides, laughing along with the people who were being bumped in dodgem cars, twirled around by carousels, with fairground music blaring out all around them. He was particularly attracted to a circular swing ride, like a giant maypole with ropes attached to wooden seats. At the flick of a switch it swung round, starting slowly then getting faster and faster, sending the people further out in their arcs around the main pole.

"Look at that, Lorna. I love that. I am going to take Jimmy on it."

"What? You cannot. They won't let you anyway, he's much too little. Look, there's a sign saying 'no children under five'."

Pepe stood watching. A new group of people took the places of those who had stepped off at the end of the ride.

"OK, not Jimmy. How about you? Take a ride."

"Oh no, not me. I hate that sort of thing."

"Let me then. I want to have a go."

So Pepe paid out the coins and took his place at the next change-over. Lorna now had to carry Jimmy but found a metal barrier to sit him on, a spot where they could see, where they could wave and be waved at.

"See daddy," Lorna pointed at the swing beginning to pick up pace. Round and round, faster and faster, at dizzying speed, with the riders almost horizontal at the top of the circle, locking their jaws into tight smiles or opening their mouths to scream. *Why is this fun?* asked Lorna. There was no answer from the screamers or from the little boy sat on the bar in front of her. After a couple of minutes the ride had slowed to a halt and everyone jumped off.

An exhilarated Pepe came running over. "Did you see?" he asked Jimmy, lifting him up into the air and swinging him round. "That was fun." Jimmy squealed his agreement.

They had no money left to spend. Lorna had set a limit in advance and she was in no mood to relent even when Pepe started chanting 'mummy is a spoil sport' as if from Jimmy.

"Come on," she said. "We're done here. Let's go and have a drink."

They crossed the road to *The Freemasons*. Lorna decided that she would not mention coming here on that night with Harry, but it cast a further shadow over her mood. Meeting Vincent again at Diana's was another shadow, and she definitely could not mention the letter she had received from him at work, marked 'Private', urging her to visit his studio whenever she was free. It seemed that in recent times everything was conspiring to remind her of earlier times, and those times were resonating with the ring of regret. Lorna was relieved to take Jimmy into the pub's garden, sparing herself the memory of the bar where she had drunk with Harry. Pepe brought the drinks out into the garden, with a bag of crisps for Jimmy. He opened the bag, took out the blue wrapper of salt, and held out a crisp to his son. Pepe was talking cheerily in Spanish to the boy on his lap, while Lorna sipped at her Guinness. She felt she had something to say, and must say it.

"I'm sorry, Pepe. I am sorry."

"What for?" he asked.

"I've not been very nice lately. Begrudging you things. Like this, your first day off since getting a job, and I've not been good about it."

"No need," he said, "no need. But I just need to catch up with someone. I just recognised someone I know."

He got up and was away as Lorna's voice trailed "Pepe?" after him. "Be back in a minute," he called over his shoulder.

Lorna stood up and watched him leave the garden and cross the road. She recognised the man with the black beard that Pepe was speaking to and, she saw, giving a letter to.

Pepe came back quickly, as he had said he would. "It was my friend. Antonio. The one I told you. Sorry to rush off."

"We're both saying Sorry. And both not being honest? Perhaps?"

"No. I am honest."

"Why didn't you ask Antonio to have a drink with us?"

"Oh, he was in a hurry."

"And what did you give him?"

There was a pause. Pepe shifted a little, uncomfortable.

"It was just a letter for my father."

It took a while for Pepe to explain because he was reluctant. His story was that Antonio arranged letters to go both ways between England and Spain, between the refugee children and their families. Letters using the postal system would be intercepted and read, bringing risks to the families in Spain, so this alternative channel worked well for Pepe and others. At least it meant there was communication with his parents.

"But can you trust him? What if your letters get passed into the wrong hands? You told me he's a priest, and the church is not on your side."

"The church is on the side of all believers. I trust him. Anyway I do not think he is a priest really. Just a good man."

Jimmy was getting restless: he needed more than crisps and a lemonade. So they gathered their things together to head home.

"What did you write to your father?"

"Just news. My job. To say things are good and hope not too bad for him. To say we try to get to see him, one day soon. To say you are a good mother and his grandson is a good boy."

What to do? Lorna felt uneasy. She was made anxious by Pepe's confession because he had not been honest before about what was happening. Was this now the truth, or was there more to be discovered? She felt he had been deceiving her. But had she been deceiving him? Perhaps deceptions cancel each other out. She knew that could not be true and she knew that Jimmy would be the reason to keep honesty between them, would be the object of love to keep them together.

In a strange way she felt that she too had confessed and been absolved by saying Sorry. She had admitted to fault and that made future fault admissible. Perhaps as a result things would start going better in their life. In her life.

So it was worrying a week later when Jimmy became sick. She collected him from the nursery in the early afternoon, and they told her that he seemed irritable. "Not like Jimmy." He was very hot when Lorna felt his brow.

She got off the bus a stop early so she could drop in on Pepe at his barber's shop.

"I'm sorry," she said. "It's just that I'm worried about him. He's not right and I don't know what it is."

Pepe was embarrassed at being visited at work and he tried to play down the trouble. He whispered reassurances to Lorna that did not reassure. The situation was unusual enough to attract the attention of George Marcoullis who owned the shop.

"I tried to cock a deaf'un but I see you have some trouble," he said with a voice as oily as brilliantine and an accent that veered between cockney and Cypriot. His own hair was plastered down flat to his scalp, with a straight parting down the middle. He wore a suit with a watch on a chain in his waistcoat pocket, to give him a managerial look – or so Lorna assumed. Her first impressions were not favourable but she had to deal with the man to reach a satisfactory conclusion. Pepe introduced them to each other, and then Lorna explained that Jimmy was poorly, laying her hand on his brow.

"Oh dear, poor little mite. I can see. Not well, is he? That's a fever, all right, you mustn't let it go."

"So what do we do? I can't see a doctor just like that."

"Take him to the hospital. This one, just off the Euston Road. Elizabeth Garrett Anderson. You can walk there in two minutes."

"Of course. Thank you."

Lorna stood up, taking out her purse to check she had money if needed.

"I don't suppose they'll charge you," said George. "Not if you take him, and it's an emergency. But here, take this, I'm sure it will help the boy get better." George slipped a ten shilling note out of his waistcoat pocket into Lorna's hand. She was so surprised and so flustered by the word 'emergency' that she kept the money.

"Thanks so much. You've been so kind."

"Not at all, my dear. I just remember when my boy had a fever. Didn't know what to do. We was too late by the time we got 'im looked at. Lost 'im, no bigger than yours."

"No. I hope not."

"Lost 'im, just like that. True, I'm afraid. So don't hang aroun', get there quick. Bill can follow in a while, he can finish early today."

Bill? Pepe. Lorna had almost forgotten him in her anxiety but now she saw him buttoning Jimmy's cardigan up. "Keep him warm," he said. "George, I am just going to carry him there, to be quick, then I come straight back. OK?"

It was their first health emergency with Jimmy. Other people, including George, suffered worse emergencies, but Lorna was not well-schooled in children's diseases. There were no handy grandparents around. For once Lorna wished that either her own or Pepe's mother were close at hand, to explain what might be happening, what to do. She was surprised at the strength of her anxiety, faced with the reality of her child's illness, and seized with a terror of losing him.

In time everything is put into proportion. Measles, so frightening at these first signs, became a disease that came, was unpleasant and departed with the future status of a childish rite of passage. The women doctors at the hospital were calm and matter-of-fact and instantly comforting, persuading Lorna to let Jimmy stay until he was better again. He would have his own bed in the children's ward and she could visit him to see how well he was doing. She told this to Pepe with some relief, because Jimmy would be well looked after and even because now, guiltily, she would have some more time to herself. She would take time off work, be a good mother and also grab the chance to do more, at least for a while, to be free.

CHAPTER 45

His fingers pressed, roughly at times, then gently, a caress that smoothed the skin to a deeper colour. Submitting willingly, eagerly, reaching out while trying not to move, her eyes watched as the tips of his fingers plucked the surface, squeezing, forming a ridge, laying his palm softly with a sure imposition of his will. Pushing upwards, exaggerating the ridge of the cheekbones, then sliding his finger lower, further, inserting it into the slit he found, yielding to his touch, enlarging the crack, then running a finger along one lip, lips opening, parting the folds to find a depth within, swelling voluptuous as Lorna had never felt or seen herself before. Vincent manoeuvred the oil paint while it was moist and malleable, working like a sculptor more than a painter, his hands moulding life into the face that responded as clay to his manipulative touch. His hands moved almost tenderly, against previous expectations and experience, yet with a concentration entirely on the subject of their close attention, feeling exultantly the rises, shudderingly the falls transmitted through this caress.

Lorna was sitting next to Vincent on a stool while he sculpted the paint onto the square of canvas. He stood there at the easel with Lorna's living face within touching distance to his left and the forming portrait of her face to his right, holding them both within the same field of vision. Lorna, by a slight shift in her eyes, could see the portrait shaping. She knew the portrait was of her but could see little connection to the face that she saw each day in a mirror. Yet it was her, she felt it was her, she felt the connection that Vincent was making with his hands through the medium of paint. She started to say as much but he silenced her with a 'shush' putting a finger to her lips. He continued scraping, stroking, pressing, now with his index finger, now with his thumb, bringing the paint, she imagined, into the flesh-like life that he imagined. Then sighing, withdrawing, turning his head aslant to look at her, at the portrait, with his eyes flicking from one to the other, as if with a tongue trying to supplement his vision through other senses, tasting her, drinking her, smelling her, the perfume of her on his fingers as paint.

"Oh," he stepped back, wiping his fingers on a cloth. "It is nearly there."

"Really? So soon?"

"I will work at it more later. When I have only the memory of you."

"Will that be enough?"

"It will have to be. But you leave a powerful memory. Let me see."

He stared at her and she returned his stare. It felt like a contest, and Lorna would not blink first. Two pairs of eyes fixed on each other, keeping the memory vivid, storing it fresh for future use.

"Enough," he said, snapping eyes away from hers, back to the portrait on the easel. "You are extra-ordinary. As I keep telling you. As you will not believe."

"Because it's not true." Lorna hunched herself inside the towelling robe Vincent had given her to wear, shrinking herself in the face of his exaggeration.

"This is the truth," he pointed at the canvas with its layers of paint. "And this," he pressed his fingers against her cheek. Finding no resistance, expecting none, he smiled and slipped his hand inside the robe. His fingers, smeared with paint, fondled her breast, its hard nipple.

"No!" she said sharply, as if waking suddenly. "Don't. Not now. Not again."

Vincent's eyes did not move from hers. It seemed he was still painting her, observing her face and the thoughts that hid behind it. There was the ghost of a smile on his face as he withdrew his hand.

"Are you thinking of your boy?" he asked.

"Soon, I must get back to see him soon. It will be visiting time."

"No…nooo. Not your son, he is in good hands. I was thinking of the other boy. Pepe, is it?"

"He is not a boy. He is a good man. As you are not."

"Oh, I know that. I was never much drawn to goodness. It's always more interesting to be bad. But you know this."

Lorna shook her head, and drew the robe tighter around herself, turning away from Vincent.

"Tell me, does he know? Does he know you are here? Did you tell him?"

"No. I don't want him to know. I can cope with deception. But not…not with betrayal."

"Oh? Does he know what you want to do? Is that what you call betrayal?"

"I won't go there."

"It's a fine line," said Vincent. He looked at the canvas, the portrait with cavernous eyes as they now seemed to Lorna. "I no longer do fine lines."

He walked across to the porcelain sink in the corner of the studio, turned on the tap and rubbed the bar of soap up and down over his hands till there was a lather. Rinsing it away, he dried his hands on the towel then lobbed it across to Lorna.

"You had better remove the paint. Tell-tale signs I'd have thought. Pepe might suspect a nipple coated with Burnt Sienna."

Lorna strode across to the sink, brushing past Vincent. She now felt her moment of danger, of temptation, had passed, she was proud and confident and defiant again. That quality he had always claimed to see in her but understood so little. Renewed pride in her body, tautened by his attention as she removed the robe, meant that she washed her breasts without shyness. She had never felt any shyness under his gaze, he had banished any such thoughts from her early on. *Perhaps I ought to thank him*, she smiled to herself. She turned to face him to dry herself, then to put on her bra, before rubbing the towel between her legs.

"So, we're done," she said.

"If you say so," he spoke with slow reluctance. "I have more to do. Later." He held the canvas in his hands, at the full stretch of his arms in front of him. "One of my best, I think. Let's hope critical eyes are not as cruel."

"Will you show it?" Lorna studied the painting with its colours that now seemed to bear no resemblance to her own.

"Yes. Of course. It needs a title though. 'Lorna in recline' I think."

"Oh no, not my name. Use another name."

"What name would you suggest?"

"I always liked Rebecca. If I'd had a daughter, she would be called Rebecca."

"Good. That will be our secret. Rebecca."

Lorna, fully dressed again, felt more business-like. She glanced at the paintings and drawings on the walls, much changed from visits made years earlier. There were paintings leaning against the wall in wooden racks, and she started to lift them out to look at them more closely.

"My work changed in the war," Vincent explained. "It seemed pointless, perhaps foolhardy, to do pictures of people who might not be here tomorrow. But that is always the problem with people, war just makes it worse. A random act can always strike, obliterate. Such a waste."

"So, no portraits."

"No models, no muses, no portraits. At least not of people, but portraits of places. They seemed to have a better chance of survival. The ground would still be there after bombing. The curve of a hill, the broad line of a street. And it meant I didn't have to go too far."

Lorna's eyes swept over the panoramas all around her in the studio, stacked against walls, looking inward at herself and her creator. *It's extraordinary*, she thought, *that word again, our eyes were only for each other when I arrived this morning*. Now, studying the pictures, she did not recognise the places; but, stepping closer, she read from their labels that the green and earthy colours were Hampstead Heath; the wildly exuberant ones were Camden Town.

"Why so bright?" she asked. "I can't see this as the Camden Town I know."

"No? Perhaps you are not looking at it right? Perhaps you are too close, or too closed in your mind? Perhaps our minds are not meeting."

"Perhaps not. Almost certainly not."

"That can come, given time."

"The time is past. It's done. And you have moved on. You will find another model."

Lorna stared at one canvas, attracted by a familiarity in it she sensed through the slabs and strokes of subdued colours, greys and browns and brick reds. There was something childlike in the simple monotony of the colours inside the heavy black lines that, she supposed, delineated the shapes of buildings. A glow in the top corner, rising above a slanting rooftop, gave the sense of a scene set in early morning, a scene revealed by the drawing aside of bedroom curtains. Lorna recognised enough, more and more as she continued studying it, to identify the view from the window of the room upstairs where she had slept with Harry.

"I like this one," she said.

"You have simple tastes. I like that too."

Lorna slipped on her jacket and checked her handbag. All that remained was to put on her hat. She had decided that morning to wear a black velvet hat with a peacock feather. It was one she had bought recently from Little Edie who worked in a Soho hat factory and lived in the next courtyard of Levita House. The hat had vested her with a strength of emotion that she had felt in need of when setting out this morning, uncertain what she was about to do. Now it was right for this time, this place, with its memories and ghosts. Had she kept them away with such a display of style? Or had she summoned more ghosts to haunt her in another time, another place?

She closed the heavy door behind her, remembering even the solid feel of it from an earlier time. Walking down the steps, turning left along Delancey Street, she headed to the hospital to see the convalescent young boy whom, she now realised clearly, was the one she loved more than anyone else.

CHAPTER 46

Jimmy was recovering well; he seemed to be enjoying his time in hospital. When Lorna visited him she noticed that, for reasons she could not fathom, his language skills had improved. He was now saying, and trying to say, many more words. Lorna could not make out all of these and suspected that many had Spanish origins, learnt from Pepe. She hoped language would not become another boundary: it might become a crossing rather than a barrier. The simplest word worried her most. Was Jimmy calling her 'mummy' or 'mama'? She argued to herself that either meant 'mother' so it did not matter. But she hoped this would not lead, in time, to a linguistic compromise, a retreat to the safety of formality behind the wall of 'Mother'. She felt a sudden need to hug him, to take him back home, to let him know how much she loved him.

The hospital had said that they wanted to keep Jimmy in for one more day. Lorna thought they were being too protective but did not resist the suggestion because the time to herself was a welcome respite. *Perhaps the hospital recognises that.* So Pepe went off to work next morning, looking forward to seeing Jimmy at home later in the day.

It was a blustery day of early summer. Lorna decided to head for what now seemed to her the countryside. She had enjoyed living in Highgate ten years earlier but had hardly visited it since. She was curious to know how it now seemed to her, so she took the underground northwards with a feeling of curiosity.

First she made for Bonfield Court. It was a long trek up the hill and when she got there she felt strangely disappointed.

Was she disappointed with the place or with herself? She remembered the place well enough, the flat facades and rounded corners of 1920s architecture had a style that aged well with the passing of time. But that was a matter of aesthetics; her stronger feeling was that this place did not compare well with the real life of her current home. Levita House was more connected to people she wished to be connected to. Her recent concerns about her 'middleness' seemed to be more relevant to this flat in Highgate, in a street where people were happy to live their lives out of sight. She wondered, but only for a moment, about knocking on the door of her old flat, to see if anyone was there.

She went back to the main road and crossed it to enter Highgate Woods. She was surprised, as if for the first time, by the depth of the woods. Within minutes the sound of traffic could no longer be heard, replaced by the sound of birds and the rustling of wind through the dense leaves. She stood on the path, looking at the expanse of a playing field, the green grass vivid before her eyes. Trees stood like guards around the field and the breeze ruffled their tops. After each gust, the trees settled back into shape, ignoring the intrusion of this tousling like a young child shaking off the attention of an irritating adult.

She told herself that she really must bring Jimmy here. It was a place for a London child to discover nature, to explore colours that were not just those of man-made buildings, to discover animals that would never be found in the courtyard below the balconies, to see living creatures that might otherwise be seen only as cartoon pictures on the nursery wall. She must bring Pepe here; it would stir memories for him too, so close to places where they had first got to know each other. *Do we know each other?* Lorna did not know if you ever get to know a person properly. Perhaps the problem was believing that you ever could.

There was so much of Pepe's life and thinking that she did not understand. She had stopped making the effort, thinking that it might change her own life in ways that she did not welcome. Why was she so resistant to his desire for those elements of his past that still had such a strong hold on him? It was no sin, no human failing, to wish to see his parents, to revisit places where he had been born and grown up. She could understand that his parents might also wish to see their grandchild. Those were natural desires – even if she had no such hankerings herself for any such reconnection in her own life. She should be more open to the possibility, though there were so many practical obstacles in the way. Getting to Spain might be difficult, getting out again impossible. Yet she should countenance the prospect because it mattered so much to Pepe; and therefore it needed to matter to her.

A chunky black setter was nearby, on the edge of the sports field, struggling to carry a branch in its jaws. The branch was as long as the dog's body. The dog was determined to do the task it had set itself, clamping the wood tighter into its mouth, then trotting after its owner who just as determinedly ignored its efforts. Lorna felt like objecting on the dog's behalf but knew it was harder to intervene with pets and their owners than with children and their parents. *Perhaps I just don't understand why people keep pets.* She walked past, onto the green stretch of grass, and did not look back.

The corvids are out in force; she smiled to herself at the name she had dredged from childhood memory. It was years, or so it seemed, since she had seen crows, since she had seen any birds but pigeons and sparrows. Now she saw barrel-chested ravens, the muscle-bound black crows strutting around. The crows swaggered, rolling their shoulders from side to side, natural bullies, while magpies walked purposefully, knowing how to outsmart bullies by ignoring them. Lorna loved the iridescent blue among the black feathers of the magpies, observing the birds as they bobbed then hopped as a short prelude to flight. She watched as two of them flapped easily, rapidly away, then landed on branches of a nearby oak.

She would talk to Pepe about this later, and suggest a visit to these woods one weekend soon. They would talk about Spain too, though she had no idea what she might say, except that she wanted to make it a subject that could now be discussed.

CHAPTER 47

Lorna was at work when she heard that the government had lifted the restrictions on foreign travel. Bryan brought the news: "But I still would not recommend a visit to Spain".

"Don't worry. I've no intention."

She and Pepe had been talking about travelling. The lure of his homeland, or perhaps his parents, was strong and Lorna was as sympathetic as she could be without, as she saw it, betraying her principles of opposition to fascism. It was impossible for her to visit Spain but they talked about it properly. She recited the reasons given by Pedro Escobar the Spanish lawyer – solid, practical reasons that she felt ought to deter Pepe. There was Jimmy too – how could we take a young boy of two all that way? This was the argument Lorna herself was least convinced by. There was part of her that felt it would be good for her son to experience travel, to see another country, at an early age. *But not Spain.* Now the removal of foreign travel restrictions had taken away one obstacle, but it was just one plank in a barrier that remained impossibly high. So they talked about it that evening.

"The travel changes mean that we can go to France for a holiday – but not to Spain for a visit."

"France is nice," said Pepe.

Actually it is – or it could be. Lorna took refuge in the comfort of renewed fidelity. It was a relief to set aside the shiftiness, the threat of questions, to take things on trust. She had never been anywhere with Pepe, perhaps they could go across the channel to France, Jimmy's first visit to the seaside. It would be a way to show, to herself, that she was committed to her family life with Pepe, putting aside recent doubts.

"France might be possible," said Lorna. "We can think about it."

Pepe was worried about his parents and Lorna understood that completely. She knew their life must be hard and the snippets she heard from their increasingly regular letters confirmed that. Pepe had brought home the latest letter from them, delivered in the way that she now understood was the usual channel.

"Another knock on the door at my father's house," said Pepe. "This is bad. And little food on the table. I will talk to Antonio about it."

Lorna let it pass. What could Antonio do about it? He might be a good friend, as Pepe claimed, but he could not influence the actions of the government in Spain. Even if he was a priest, which Pepe now said he was not. So what is he?

"Just a friend. He has contacts. I will find out more about France."

At work Lorna was researching the owners of the railway companies for the firm's trade union clients. The nationalisation of the railways was getting closer. Her research gave Lorna some interest that she had not expected to find in the lives of the wealthy. One of the owners had a villa in Deauville, which made her smile. *French coast. We can go there.*

One midday a parcel arrived for Lorna. It was a large, flat oblong package, wrapped in brown paper and tied up with string. The delivery caused a stir in the office; this was more than the daily post, more intriguing than just a letter. Lorna tried to empty her space to open the parcel quietly but some people simply remained as spectators as she snipped the string with a pair of scissors. *What is it?* She tore away at the brown paper to discover a frame and, with more paper stripped away, a painting.

She recognised the painting right away, not needing to spot the signature 'Hillyer' at the bottom with its horizontal line leading from the 'y' to underscore the first syllable of the painter's name.

"Who's that, Lorna?" asked Doreen.

"What's that?" asked Bryan.

"It's a bit glum," said Eric the postboy who had stayed for the unveiling of the package he had brought in.

Lorna's first reaction was one of relief that the painting offered nothing more incriminating than the view of a street from a window. But perhaps even that interpretation was obvious only to herself. She had turned pink in anticipation of greater embarrassment, and now the brightness of her face seemed to stand out against the sober paint colours.

"What's it called?" asked Bryan. "Dawn in grey and brown? I thought Vincent's work was more colourful than that."

Lorna turned the painting around, to see if anything was written on the back of the canvas. She read 'Seen from Rebecca's window', and read the title out in response to Bryan's question. Underneath, in smaller lettering, she read to herself : 'The view will always be yours – a gift from Vincent'.

"Well, Lorna, that's a turn-up," said Bryan. "What brought this on?"

"I know him a little. I met him at Diana's parties a couple of times and we talked about his painting."

"He must have been impressed – no doubt by your enthusiasm for his work. Must be worth a bob or two. But who's Rebecca?"

"Someone he knows, I guess. It's all as big a surprise to me as it is to you."

"How are you going to get it home? Pepe will be surprised too."

Lorna flushed again. The public unveiling of the painting brought back a sense of guilt. *No reason for that*, she told herself. But Bryan was right, it would be difficult to get it home and she had no idea what to say about it to Pepe.

"I think it should stay here," said Lorna, pointing to the wall above her desk. "It will go quite well just there."

So Eric was despatched for a further task. Returning with a hammer and some nails, he bashed away at the wall till he could hang the painting. Lorna stepped back from it, putting herself in the position of a visitor entering the space. *It will do.*

Over a pot of tea in Bryan's office they talked about the unexpected gift. Bryan did not press her to disclose more, seeing the red blush returning to her face as she tried to answer a question about Vincent.

"I did not expect it," she said. "I hardly did anything. And he's not the kind of man to give anything away – at least I don't think so."

"I think you're right about that. Though he might give more to women than men. I've never managed even to get a smile out of him. Do you like him?"

Lorna looked away again before mumbling "No, not much. But he's a comrade, sketched the Spanish children all those years ago."

"Perhaps he should have given you one of those paintings?"

"No, they were just drawings. I don't think he ever made any paintings of them. Not that I saw anyway."

"Pepe might have liked one all the same."

She shook her head. "Definitely not. They don't get on."

"But you obviously do."

Lorna was quiet, thinking. Then she turned to look at Bryan. "Yes, we do. Pepe and I are getting on all right."

"Ah, not what I meant, but good. Is he still talking of Spain?"

"Yes, but I'm trying to persuade him that France might be a better place to visit."

Lorna found it useful to bring Bryan up to date on the conversations she and Pepe had had recently. Bryan was forceful in ruling out a visit to Spain – "Impossible. Dangerous. A betrayal."

"I know. Perhaps France will divert him."

"You should take a week off. You've not really had a holiday since you came back to work. Go away in August or September. It will be good for all of you. There are nice places on the French coast, and it'll be good for the boy too. Get away from all this English grey and brown."

Extra-ordinary. The thought raced through Lorna's mind, a confusing blur of France and Spain, Pepe and Vincent, Camden Town and French seaside. She would talk again with Pepe later.

CHAPTER 48

Later that week Lorna met her mother for tea. She took Jimmy with her to Lyons' Corner House at her mother's special request.

"Oh look how he's grown. Say hello to grandma."

Jimmy said something, though it was impossible to make out exactly what. It was enough to satisfy the needs of the situation. Lorna had counted that this was only the fourth time that grandmother and grandchild had met. There seemed a distance between them greater than the train journey from Orpington.

"You look well," said Lorna to her mother, though she was surprised how much she had aged since her husband's death during the war. Lorna had never been close to her father but now her conscience felt a stab of regret. The meetings between mother and daughter had been infrequent in the war, but that had seemed natural and inevitable at the time. Now, with a grandchild as part of the consideration, Lorna determined to see her mother more often. *At least to try.*

"What will he eat?" Doris Starling asked.

"He can have a bit of toast with me, and a glass of milk if we can."

It was an awkward conversation. The public room did not allow for expansive emotion even if such a thing had been felt. Mrs Starling had visited Levita House once, but had shown no particular wish to return there.

"How is your husband?"

"Pepe. Pepe's fine. He's at work, otherwise he'd be here too."

"Cutting hair? I suppose it's a useful thing to do. And I suppose he must like it though he might not be able to be too choosy. It's good that he's bringing home a wage. Are you managing?"

There was a pause, one that Lorna had not anticipated as she settled into listening mode once her mother got into her conversational flow.

"Managing? Of course. Why do you ask?"

"Well, I don't suppose a barber earns an awful lot. Not exactly a steady profession, is it? Though I imagine he gets tips, as long as he does a good job. Does he do a good job?"

Lorna was realising why she limited her meetings with her mother these days. Conversations turned into interrogations, and behind the questions was a demonstration of irretrievable difference. Was the difference social, political, cultural? *We have so little in common any more.*

"Of course he does. And so do I. Between us we make enough to give Jimmy everything he needs."

"The main thing, I agree. As long as the boy's happy. He seems to be a contented little chap. Does he want some more toast? He can have some of mine."

"He's got enough here."

"Does he talk much? Doesn't seem to, but perhaps he's shy. Not used to seeing me, which is a shame. I would like to see him more but, well, I'm sure it's difficult. Travel, work, expense. But before you know it he's grown up and doesn't recognise his grandma."

"Mum, I know you don't see him much."

"Hardly at all. But always happy to see him – and you. But I've become a bit of a spy, trying to find out information."

"Not at all. Anyway, think yourself lucky. Pepe's parents

haven't seen him at all."

"No? I'm surprised they haven't made the effort."

"It's not a case of making an effort. They're in Spain – they can't get out, we don't want to get in."

"But the war's over. Surely you can do something. Though I think you should come to Orpington first, it's a lot nearer. I'm sure the boy would enjoy the train."

"You're right about that. We've been thinking about a train trip, then getting the boat across to France. Just for a little holiday."

Mrs Starling retreated into her teacup but kept her eyes on her daughter. Eventually she said: "I wish you wouldn't. It's a long way for such a little boy."

"Not really. Children are able to put up with anything if you expect them to. I think it will do him good. Look, I bought him a toy train and he loves it." She brought the wooden train from her handbag and gave it to Jimmy sitting on her lap. "He'll love the real one."

"I wish you wouldn't. But I don't suppose you'll listen to me, you never do."

"I do. But we've already started making plans. Looks like we'll be away for a week in September."

After that, the conversation dried up and Lorna became more distracted by keeping Jimmy amused. Lyons' Corner House had aspirations of refinement. It was not a play space for children and Lorna started to hear, or just imagine, the tuttings of those taking tea on the tables around her.

"Children. They won't sit still. *You* never would."

"I'd best be off."

"Already?"

"Well, we can walk together if you like."

Lorna watched her mother shake her head and felt a surge of disappointment that was close to irritation. Disappointment and irritation seemed to mark these meetings between mother and daughter, but *what can I do?*

She looked at her mother sitting there, perhaps to sip disappointment in her tea, certainly to pay the bill. "Is that all right? Can you manage?" She felt mean for saying it but she had her own child to look after now, while retaining the expectation of her own dependent status as a daughter to be treated. She had her bag closed, Jimmy's train inside it, ready to leave.

"I will bring him down to see you," she said under the influence of guilt. "Perhaps one weekend when Pepe can come too."

"That will be nice."

"Good. But it will have to be after we get back from France."

She waved from the doorway, and tried to get Jimmy to wave too. Her mother was pouring hot water into the teapot, beyond a wave.

Emotions were churning inside Lorna as she waited at the bus stop on Tottenham Court Road. She decided that it was the time for a decision. She had not confirmed with Pepe that they would go to France, but now she was sure and she wanted to tell him so. She rang the bell to get off the bus in Hampstead Road and walked past Euston station to the barber shop where Pepe worked. He was surprised to see her, but first she went to speak to George in his booth where he collected money from customers.

"My dear," he said, "how lovely to see you. And I see the little boy is doing well now."

"Yes. He is, and thank you for your help before. I wanted to ask one more thing because Pepe might not have mentioned it, but we would like to take a week's holiday in September. I'm sure that will be all right, won't it?"

George looked a little startled, Pepe a little embarrassed, but it was all soon agreed. Lorna left the shop with another wave, and turned right towards Levita House. In the narrow alleyway that was Churchway, with small shops on either side, she entered the Chemist's shop. She bought some travel sickness pills. *This will make it all real.*

Later that evening Lorna asked Lorraine again to sit with Jimmy when he was asleep. He had had a busy day and was exhausted by meeting his grandmother, by walking, by the emotion. Or so Lorna told herself.

In the Coffee House pub, over their drinks, they started to make proper plans for their trip to France.

"There are lots of places near Calais," said Lorna.

"I think it will be a little cold in September," Pepe replied. "I have been looking into it. We should go further south, it will be warmer, better for Jimmy to have fun on the beach."

"Are you sure? It must be a long way. How will we get there?"

"By train, of course. We said Jimmy likes trains. And there is a place Antonio recommends."

"Really? What is he now, a travel agent?"

"No, just as a friend not an agent. He says we should go to a French town called Hendaye. It is near Spain. I can see Spain from there. It is a nice place."

Lorna felt a mixture of emotions. She felt manipulated, cheated even. It had never been her intention to go so far. Yet there was also a shiver of excitement when she recognised the name of the town. She had a letter that Harry had written to her from Hendaye. The prospect of seeing this place where he had been and where he had thought of her, setting his thoughts down in that precious letter, was a large part of the reason why she agreed to the trip, albeit with a show of reluctance.

Inevitably all sorts of practicalities started to arise. Pepe would save all his tips; he would stop smoking to save money. Lorna would put aside half her pay. They would have enough, with other savings, to make the trip. The train and ferry would be booked. Pepe would tell his parents how close they would be; he could imagine them waving from across the water.

They had another drink, then Pepe insisted on another. His exuberance was rarely shown these days, and Lorna was glad to see it. She herself felt excited but in a more restrained way. She was thinking of Harry and the memories could not be acknowledged to Pepe – she kept them inside, like the letter in its envelope. Tomorrow she would reach to the back of her underwear drawer to retrieve the letter. She looked forward to rereading it, being touched by it again.

Later, in bed, they made love with Lorna making the mildest of protests: "I wish we didn't do this only when you've had a drink". By then Pepe did not hear because he was already asleep but Lorna's mind was still unnaturally active. It would take a long while to drop off to sleep. On the balcony, outside their window, she listened to Emmy, who lived next door, rolling home near midnight. She was singing 'Nellie Dean' with the slur of too many gins on her lips – singing to herself and to everyone who was still awake nearby but singing for the sake of deadening her melancholy. In the morning Emmy would make more funeral wreaths, as that is how she made her living from the dead. Lorna turned over her pillow, hoping to shake away morbid thoughts and to slake her living turmoil in sleep.

CHAPTER 49

The English Channel was choppy in mid-September. The ferry from Dover was not the pleasant cruise that Lorna had expected and, as the boat pitched up and down and side to side on the waves, she was pleased to have bought travel sickness pills. Jimmy was stoically quiet on her lap and she hoped this inertia was not the prelude to sea sickness. Pepe's face had gone pale with nausea and flashbacks, as he leant on the rail in the blast of sea air. "This is like that boat I came on all those years ago."

"Hopefully it won't take as long."

The French coast was already in sight and soon they could make out the grey facades of houses on the sea front. Their spirits were further buoyed by the stillness of the harbour and the alluring sense of foreignness. This was Lorna's first trip abroad.

"It's exciting," she said. "I feel like a little kid."

Pepe squeezed her shoulders. "You see. Another country is good."

"Look at the people. The cars. The cafes. All different but not that different."

"I tell you it is different. Very different from when I landed in France the first time. Then I was scared to see people because they might be German soldiers."

The memory of war, suppressed in everyday life in London, was sharper for both of them here. Lorna had hardly given a thought to Pepe's wartime experience of France, mainly because he rarely spoke about it. She realised that there would be little nostalgia yet, if ever, in revisiting scenes of carnage;

she felt unexpected relief that they would be heading further south, away from the battlefields of two world wars. Watching him go down the wooden gangplank, carrying a pushchair and a big suitcase, it seemed that Pepe was more troubled by his leg wound than he had been recently. He limped under the burden of the luggage and Lorna's expectations.

Lorna had fallen naturally into the role of organiser. She carried all the travel documents, passports and travellers' cheques in a leather wallet that Bryan had insisted she take with her from work. He had been so helpful with passports and arrangements – *must bring something back for him*. For now she smiled in a forlorn attempt to pass swiftly through the border controls.

The train to Paris was a short walk away. She grimaced at the thought that their overnight stay there would be just the next stage in the journey, with the final leg to Hendaye on the following day. The excitement that had been in prospect was all but extinguished by the tedious reality of travel. She clenched her teeth, aware that she might need to keep them clenched for another 24 hours.

The time passed. A grubby hotel with a shabby room in Paris near the Gare St Lazare. A tatty compartment on a train clattering through the French countryside. Moving from overcast skies hemming them inside the carriage to wide blue horizons spreading outside the window. Pepe talking to Jimmy in Spanish, playing games to keep the boy amused. Eating baguettes, cheese and ham. Enjoying the strangeness of it all, even the water in bottles. Imitating the clanking and chuffing of the moving train, stopping at too many stations until, finally, with a hiss and a whistle of shared relief they pulled into the terminus at Hendaye.

Lorna was glad to have arrived but immediately apprehensive at what lay before them next. They had nowhere to stay. It had been impossible to make such arrangements from London but Pepe assured Lorna that his French was good enough to sort things out on the spot. His first attempts at speaking French on the train had not been reassuring.

"It is just like Spanish. There is no problem."

Reading an ancient guidebook on the train (another loan from Bryan) Lorna had been disconcerted by the discovery that there was also the Basque language to contend with.

"Not a problem. I know a few words. And anyway people will speak French. And who knows, Spanish too."

Lorna's reading on the train had also revealed that Hendaye station had been the scene for a wartime meeting between Hitler and Franco.

"Look at that, Pepe. Franco was late arriving. By train. Then he made all sorts of impossible demands. So Hitler stormed off and Spain didn't join the war."

They speculated, in their English-speaking bubble, what might have happened if the fascists had reached an agreement.

"More battles. A longer war."

"A better peace."

They had learnt to ignore the suspicious looks from French travellers as they spoke in a foreign tongue. But Jimmy had been a consistent breaker of barriers. It seemed that there was a universal language of childhood. As they gathered their luggage from the racks, once the train had juddered to a halt, an elderly woman pressed a sweet into Lorna's hand.

"*Pour le garçon.*"

"Thank you. *Merci.*"

Struggling down onto the platform, Lorna was imagining

the earlier scene, history now, with the fascist dictators standing there. It seemed to spread a chill through her. This was, to her, a closer and more foreboding encounter than when the bombs had been falling from the night skies over London. The rawness of that emotion, the dread and anger, swept through her unexpectedly and she began to cry.

"What is it?" asked Pepe.

"Nothing," she said, also thinking of Harry standing on this *quai*, wondering what his feelings might have been as his boots tramped on towards Spain. She blew her nose and found a bench to sit on beyond the ticket barrier, pulling Jimmy onto her lap.

It was late afternoon and they needed to find somewhere to stay. They decided that Pepe would go off alone to search for a hotel or guesthouse. This suited Lorna because she and Jimmy were exhausted; it suited Pepe because he could negotiate without supervision.

Lorna was getting anxious and Jimmy grizzly when Pepe returned an hour later.

"Come, I have a place."

"Where is it?"

"Not far. A little walk. *Un petit pas.*"

Lorna suspected that Pepe's words might be misleading in either language. Her fears were increased when he led them across the road to climb a steep stone staircase. At the top, after much heaving of luggage, they entered a narrow street with shuttered houses. With the exertion of climbing, Lorna was uncomfortably aware that the temperature was much hotter than she was used to. Heavy rain earlier had been followed by evening sunshine and humidity. Now as the daylight grew denser, clouds of mosquitoes hovered above the gutters on the roofs. Lorna shuddered at these sinister swarms clearly visible against the orange wash of the sky. Nothing had seemed quite so alien to her since arriving in France.

They came out into a square. Trees and flowerpots gave a more welcoming look. Lorna was able to return Pepe's smile even though she was struggling to carry Jimmy another step further.

"We are here," said Pepe, pointing to a large house on the right. The sign above the door said *Pension*. "It is OK, I have spoken to the landlady. She expects us."

Pepe led the way up the steps and through the front door into the hallway. Inside it was dark, lit by a lamp on a dark-varnished sideboard. The house smelled of times gone by. "It is French," said Pepe in a whisper as if that would soothe any misgivings Lorna might feel. "And it is not too much." Silence lay like a thin film of dust over the faded furniture, broken only by the clicking of the brass pendulum swinging in the grandfather clock. Pepe dinged the bell that rested on the sideboard.

After a while, in no great hurry, a middle-aged woman in black clothes arrived. "*Monsieur,*" she nodded in recognition to Pepe. "*Et Madame avec l'enfant.*" She motioned them to follow her up the stairs.

Inside their room the furnishings were few. Lorna sat on the large bed with a lumpy mattress and a cot at its side. The landlady – "*Madame Loti*" she had announced, with a hand laid on her chest – opened the door of the wardrobe that dominated the room with its size and dark wood. It seemed as if the room had been built around it many years ago and no one had dared to move it since. There was a dressing table with drawers to either side and an oval mirror on top. They were shown to a bathroom down the hall. Nodding replaced the need for words and Lorna handed over their passports for registration. Exhaustion and the wish to be left alone replaced any further questioning. Madame Loti withdrew with the merest hint of a smile.

"Is it OK?" asked Pepe.

"It will do. We came to experience something different."

For reasons Lorna did not understand she began laughing, throwing herself backwards on the bed, and her laughter was echoed by Pepe and Jimmy. They had arrived, and now they could sleep.

CHAPTER 50

The lumpy curvature of the bed brought the couple together in the early-morning light drifting in through the curtains. "See, I do not need a drink," said Pepe, meaning her to take meaning from his words. Lorna lay silent and contented, enjoying the holiday state of not having to get up, watching motes in the brightness of the streaming shafts of light, listening to Jimmy's breathing in the cot nearby. Soon Pepe also fell back to sleep.

After an hour, Lorna woke them both because she knew Madame Loti would be strict about breakfast times – not that there was anything elaborate about the breakfast of bread, coffee and warm milk. It added to the sense that they had arrived safely and the time could now be spent as they wished to spend it – doing very little, as Lorna expected.

They went out to get their bearings, but Lorna's instinct was to find the beach for Jimmy. However, they soon established that it was a walk either to the river shore or the beach facing the Atlantic.

"We'll take it slowly then. There's no rush and the sun's shining."

They were in the centre of the little town that was Hendaye. In the town square was the *Mairie* and official buildings, cafés, houses, some shops and, at the far end, a church. *Another day*, thought Lorna. *Pepe can go to church if he wants.* For now they visited the *épicerie* for food to see them through the day.

Pepe was pleased to find the post office. "Let me just go in here first," he said.

Lorna sat with Jimmy in the sunshine, waiting for Pepe

to re-emerge, telling herself that they were on holiday, there was no rush, no reason for irritation. To make the point to herself, and to keep the little boy amused, she softly sang '*Sur le pont d'Avignon*' to him from her paltry French repertoire of songs. Her white hat with its wide brim shaded her from the sunshine of early autumn, and she made sure that Jimmy kept wearing a similar one. Just as she was wondering what Pepe might be doing, he came out with a letter in his hand.

"*Poste restante*," he explained. "My parents have written here." He sat down on the step and began to read. Looking pensive, he passed the letter on to Lorna.

"What does it say? It's in Spanish."

"Of course. But it is good news."

Lorna looked at him, waiting for the answer that was slow to come. Pepe pulled the brim of his cap down further and read the letter again. Eventually he was ready to say what the letter contained. Knowing that Pepe would be in Hendaye, so close to Spain, his mother and father had travelled to Irun, just across the border from Hendaye. From there they would be travelling on Tuesday to the bridge at Hendaye. They could get a frontier pass that would allow them to make a one-hour crossing to meet Pepe.

"Tuesday?" asked Lorna. "That's tomorrow."

"Yes. Not long to wait."

Lorna was puzzled, Pepe was nervous but excited. "I really want to see my mum and dad."

"But I don't understand. How is this happening? Did you plan this?"

Pepe looked uncomfortable. He pulled at the peak of his cap, as if to deflect questions.

"Nothing can happen without planning. But I did not

know if this might work. I still have to see. Perhaps it will not happen on the day. But I want it to. I want to see them."

Lorna was sympathetic to his wish but still suspicious. "So, what have you had to do? Have you had to make a promise? Or give guarantees? I can't believe that Franco's mob will let this happen."

"That is up to my parents. They will give some extra money to the border guards. A little bribe. But they will have to go back in one hour."

"*They* will. But what about you? You could be arrested."

"No. I stay on this side of the border. It is safe."

Lorna felt she had been deceived. No amount of explanations would dispel that feeling. She had understood that Pepe wanted to come to Hendaye because it was close to Spain but she had not imagined that such a meeting would be part of the arrangement. It seemed to her a danger, and danger sank her spirits. This was no longer a holiday.

When she said as much to Pepe, he protested that Lorna was being unfair. They were still on holiday, they would still have a good time. It would simply be one hour when he was absent – absent to see parents he had not seen for ten years. That was only fair and reasonable. Lorna felt she had, in some sense, signed a contract to return Pepe to his mother. She remembered the feeling she had had when she first met Pepe in the refugee camp.

Lorna backed away from an argument. They were in a public place. "Let's take a walk. Find somewhere for Jimmy to play."

They walked down the hill towards the water, with Pepe steering Jimmy in the pushchair. The boy seemed contented enough but Lorna was struggling to let go of her bad feelings.

She did not know if she trusted Pepe. His machinations, as she saw it, had undermined trust.

Things looked a little better from the waterfront. She stared out at the sun glinting on the rippling waves of the estuary as it met the sea, and past that was the dark green hilly line that was Spain itself, almost in touching distance as it must seem to Pepe. To the right on this side of the water, beyond the promontory half a mile away, was the Atlantic. Lorna could imagine its immensity and crashing waves, but here there was a tranquility to the water that soothed her. It was like nothing she had experienced in England. The trip could be worthwhile after all.

It seemed so to Pepe. She watched him as he walked along the waterfront path. Below them was the estuary of the river Bidassoa, with one shore in France and one in Spain. It was possible to see the mud of the riverbed in the shallow water through the reeds that thrust out of the shoreline. You might believe that you could walk across the estuary on a fine day. Here on the path that wound around the slopes leading up to the town, with the sheltering trees and the lush vegetation growing over the stone walls, you could believe in a peaceful world. Pepe's eyes were fixed on the view to his left, staring into the near distance that was the coast of Spain.

The impression of peacefulness could be scratched at; just below the surface history had other memories to intrude. Lorna stopped where a round stone tower jutted out into the bay. Finding a stone to sit on she examined the ancient rusty cannons, relics of even older wars, pointed across the stretch of water. In earlier times soldiers of Napoleon's army might have stood at this spot, *face à face*, France eyeing Spain, *cara a cara* as Pepe now whispered to himself. Lorna sensed that he was in his own world of thoughts, and those thoughts were increasingly Spanish. The stirrings for his homeland were getting stronger, like the tide of water flowing into the bay from the sea to the right. Lorna left him to gaze longingly while she dug into the bag of groceries she had bought in town, sharing a biscuit and an apple with Jimmy. While she remembered Harry and thought that perhaps he too had sat here, gazing at his destination for fighting, with what might have been dread or foreboding or simply a sense of destiny.

"It is beautiful," proclaimed Pepe. "What a lovely place."

Lorna nodded but said nothing. Words seemed dangerous, so it was best to keep them locked safely away. Pepe was so engrossed in the view of his homeland that he was unusually content with silence. When the apple was finished Lorna decided it was time to move on. They walked further around the bay, keeping the shallow water to their left, away from the old walls of the border-hemmed town. Pepe veered off, while Lorna and Jimmy stayed on the path. He found the ground squelching under his feet so, keeping out of the reeds, he skirted the marshy area where water and land merged. This was a place for the coming together of natural elements, water and land, river and sea, sea and sky, flowing and lapping against each other in the changefulness of tides. Further out in the bay a couple of shallow fishing boats, with nets trailing over the sides, drifted in the currents.

When Pepe rejoined his family, they continued along the path around the bay until they reached the headland. Turning past this, they saw a different landscape: a straight stretch of sandy beach where the waves were rolling in.

Lorna was pleased to have found the seaside. This seemed more like the holiday she had envisaged. So for the next few hours they sat in solitude on the beach and Pepe, faced with a view of seemingly limitless ocean, turned his attention to his young son, building castles and canals in the sand.

It began to cloud over in mid-afternoon and the wind blew in more strongly from the ocean. They gathered their belongings for the long walk back to the *pension*, retracing their footsteps along the waterfront. *It is beautiful*, Lorna admitted. *Perhaps we shall do all right.* The changing currents of the estuary's tide meant that there were now sandbanks visible. Jimmy was asleep in his pushchair, so Lorna and Pepe no longer had the excuse for not speaking. They talked about what they were seeing: the low houses of the Spanish town opposite, the pirogues in the bay, the big, long-legged birds with lazy wing flaps as they landed in the reeds.

"What do you call those?" asked Pepe.

"I'd guess they're cormorants," Lorna replied. "Perhaps they're on their way to somewhere else."

Not for the first time Lorna wished she knew more of the natural world: all those trees, plants, birds, animals that she could not name. for now it would have to be enough to watch and admire.

The rising wind and the clouding skies meant that Lorna took off her hat. By now they were nearing the steep lane that led up to the centre of the town and the square where they were staying. Large drops of rain began to fall, one by one onto the roadway, making dark spots. Then the rain fell more heavily from the black clouds above. Scuttling through narrow alleys, they felt the rain soaking through their clothes as they raced for the *pension*. Jimmy began to cry as the pushchair rattled over rough roads and pavements. They had to jump across rivulets of rain flowing down and across the streets.

Water rushed through the storm drains, down the pipes, over the gutters. It seemed that many years of wartime and austerity had led the town's drainage system into disrepair.

They reached the town square then pushed their way noisily into the hallway of the *pension*, panting heavily, to be met by the disapproving tutting of Madame Loti. They carried their bags and bedraggled son up the stairs to the bathroom.

"A big day tomorrow," said Pepe. "I hope it will not rain."

CHAPTER 51

The peacetime of Lorna's sleep was disturbed by the aggressive drone of a mosquito. It dived and swooped across the landing ground of her exposed body. She wrapped the sheet tighter and tighter around herself, covering as best she could the surfaces of skin, leaving only her mouth and nose open to the night air to breathe. Still she felt under attack. *Jimmy too.*

All this after years of being bombed, growing used to attacks from above. *Do your worst. Perhaps in time you get used to attacks from the outside. You build resistance inside.*

The doodlebugs, hovering with intent then dropping abruptly, had been like giant mosquitoes with engines, she told herself in a state of irritated wakefulness. She tossed, turned the pillows, closed her ears to the snoring of other sleepers, trying to force dreams into sleep, but summoning only images of war and destruction and the vivid, present image of the man she had loved who had died not far from here. She stared into the dark room, letting her eyes rest on Pepe and Jimmy, willing their reality to lessen the presence of Harry in her mind.

Perhaps. Perhaps not. Nights can seem interminable without sleep, they stretch beyond the limits of a body's stretching. In the half-waking delirium of her restlessness, beyond the next landscape of her revolving imagination, she longed for the first glimpse of daylight. Her thoughts swirled like last night's storm and eventually, at an unconscious moment, the turmoil passed. She slept. She slept enough, till daylight, and awoke to an awareness of having been bitten on her cheek, her arm, her thigh. Waking simply brought greater sensitivity to an itchiness that would last through the day and, she thought, probably, through the rest of the time in France.

A few insect bites were not going to spoil Pepe's day. He woke rested and excited by the day's prospect.

"Today I see my mum and dad. After ten years. It has been a long time."

"I'm pleased for you, Pepe."

Over breakfast, they discussed the morning's plans. Pepe would go alone to the bridge. Lorna and Jimmy must stay out of sight. He had permission only for himself to meet his parents.

"Permission?" asked Lorna. "Who from?"

"Do not worry. It will be fine."

Lorna's misgivings were strengthening. It seemed to her now, beyond any doubting, that this 'holiday' had been planned in advance detail by Pepe. She felt she had been duped but she was powerless to resist his scheme. If its objective was to see his parents, she could think of no possible objection – not if she wished to maintain her relationship, her own humanity.

She excused herself from breakfast to calm her thoughts and to gather her necessities for the day. The morning would be taken up by Pepe's solitary meeting. She would not be part of that but she was determined to be at least an observer to the scene. After that there would be time for an afternoon on the beach.

She set out on the bed the few essentials that would be needed for the day. Her summer frock would receive its first outing even though, in this place, it seemed quaintly alien. A pattern of pink English roses did not seem at home on the borderlands of France and Spain. *Too bad*. She looked at herself in the mirror. In this room that had once seen better times, the dressing table mirror was a place to look at yourself and wonder how you and your life had ever got to this point. It was a place for reflection of the most honest, uncomfortable kind. The mirror, particularly in the room's gloomy light, would not flatter. She was 34, she had given birth, she was getting older.

"There is so much to look forward to," said Pepe, coming into the room with Jimmy. "Today I see my parents. Another day I hope you see them too. And Jimmy."

Pepe was keen to be at the bridge before the appointed hour of 11 o'clock. They set off on the short walk. Ahead of them was the bridge, a short bridge, and a bridge is such a basic construction in human existence. *Why then do I feel such dread? Why do I feel threatened by complexity? Because I want my life to be simple.*

There were signs of activity, with queues forming on the Spanish side of the border, and smaller groups of people on the French side. From the hillside road above the bridge, Lorna looked down and saw border guards in Spanish and French uniforms. She could not help ascribing to them an air of pomposity, a divide between different ways of looking at the world, the feeling that we should have nothing to do with these people. But Pepe, at her side, was determined.

"It is time," he said. "I will go now. I will be back as soon as I can, after one hour."

"I'll stay here. Or nearby. Take care."

"Wish me luck."

"Will you need it? It's all planned."

Pepe nodded. He hoisted his bag onto his shoulder then turned back towards Lorna, as if remembering something.

"It will be OK," he said. "Antonio has helped."

With those words he was off down the slope towards the bridge and the French guard post. Lorna watched intently with Jimmy on her lap, delving deeper into her tiny French songbook and drawing out *'Frère Jacques'* from her own childhood memory. A trickle of people started to make their way across the bridge from the Spanish side of the border, with shuffling, apprehensive steps, not wanting to break into a run that might be misinterpreted.

Pepe remained standing on the French side. She had seen him speaking to the French border guards, handing over something to them. Now he leaned on the railing of the bridge, his eyes fixed ahead. Many people made the crossing, carrying no more than small bags in their hands. Often they were greeted on the French side by hugs and kisses. Lorna found herself longing for the same for Pepe. *Come on, show yourselves.* Lorna had not counted but as many as a hundred people must have made the crossing, and still Pepe stood waiting. She saw the Spanish guards stopping those who were still waiting. No more would be let through.

At the back of the throng of those who had passed the barrier, a couple made their way nervously over the bridge. He was a balding man with brown trousers and jacket, she was a stooped lady with a black shawl across her shoulders. They looked uncertainly ahead at the small group of people beyond the French barrier. They passed through into the booth, spent five minutes having papers checked, then emerged on the other side to be greeted by Pepe. Lorna found herself weeping at the reunion. "Look, Jimmy, look, it's your granny and granddad". She wiped away tears but she continued to follow with her eyes as the reunited family went down the side of the bridge to the riverbank below.

Lorna was tempted to follow but did not want to jeopardise the arrangement. Pepe had insisted that she would not be permitted – *that word again* – to join the party. She sat there, quiet and intent until Jimmy became restless after half an hour, so she picked him up and carried him the short distance down the hill to the roadway that led on from the bridge. She found a place, next to a bush, where she could see the three people – three among many – on the riverbank below. She caught Pepe's eye and he, with a surreptitious air, directed the attention of his parents upwards to where Lorna and Jimmy were sitting.

The hour passed. Pepe's parents rose to their feet and made their way up the riverbank to the bridge. At the border post they embraced and held up their hands in a farewell wave. Pepe waited until they were out of sight on the other side, spoke to the French guard and collected what looked like his passport, then walked over to join his wife and son.

"How was it?" she asked.

"It was wonderful. I am so happy to see them."

They embraced as a couple, then as the three of them as Jimmy could not be left out. "I'm so pleased," said Lorna. "You must tell me more. But let's get away from this place. It feels like we might be arrested if we hang around."

There was much more to tell, though ten years of life cannot be compressed into one hour's conversation. Once they were back into the town square, sitting at a table in a café, it was nearly time for lunch and Pepe was in celebratory mood. His parents were alive, they were as well as he might have hoped; aged by ten years (or perhaps more in appearance) but delighted to have seen him. And to have recognised him, despite the passing of time from adolescence to manhood.

"And, my God, they were so pleased to see you. Even from all that way away. And to see Jimmy."

"I know. I could tell."

"They want to see you properly. To meet you properly. And to see their grandson."

"Of course. It's only natural. Let's hope it will be possible soon."

In a gesture that Lorna had not made for some years, she lifted her right fist and shouted, oh so quietly, "*No paseran!*" Pepe did not return the gesture but leant across the table and kissed her.

"Who knows what might be possible?" he said, looking hungrily at the *menu du jour*. It seemed he had an appetite.

CHAPTER 52

"I am hungry," said Pepe. "Hungry for food and for happiness."

"So – aren't you happy?" Lorna asked. It was an unusual question for her to ask. She knew how she distrusted it when people asked her the same question. You could only be fleetingly and forgetfully happy, in those brief moments when you could shut out the rest of the world. *We should seize that moment.*

Slowly through the rest of the day, and the following morning too, more details emerged. More plans too. Pepe seemed over-confident of his wishes but nervously uncertain of Lorna's reaction. So he released his intentions slowly, drip by drip.

He wanted to see his parents again. He wanted Lorna and Jimmy to meet them. Because they wanted to meet Lorna and Jimmy. This would make everyone happy. It was hard for Lorna to disagree with this logic but it ignored the reality of the situation that she saw every time she raised her eyes and stared across the estuary at the country on the other side of the border.

"My parents were numbers 99 and 100. The border commander had said only a hundred people could cross."

"You were lucky then. I hope it didn't cost them a lot."

"They say it was worth it. I hope so. But still they want to meet you. And the boy of course."

"Some things are not possible. Not at the moment anyway."

Hesitantly Pepe explained that it might be possible. Lorna listened, conscious of wishing not to appear negative. It came down to this: Pepe said his parents could hire a boat and stop at one of the sandbanks in the estuary at low tide.

"And what do you want us to do? Shout at them across the water?"

"No…. No, it is easy. We hire a boat too. One of these fishermen's boats, very safe. We meet on the sandbank for an hour."

Lorna stared at him. Was he being serious? He looked back at her and he did not look away. He meant what he said, he regarded it as a feasible plan. Not just feasible, but desirable and essential.

"Others have done it. Myself, I asked. People turn a blind eye, and anyway it will be night-time so we will not be seen. At low tide everything is calm."

Lorna shifted Jimmy on her lap. They were sitting at a café table in the square having a coffee and sharing a *croissant*. Her main concern was her son.

"I want it for Jimmy," said Pepe, anticipating her doubts. "He should meet his grandparents, and they should meet him. If we wait, if we wait till Franco is gone, it will be too late. My parents will not live that long."

Lorna's hopes for Spain had faded over the years. She felt Pepe's assessment of Franco's longevity was realistic, particularly as her own Labour government had shown no signs of wanting to live up to the ideals it had proclaimed in opposition. Spain had become an accepted *status quo*, cemented into the wall of the cold war that was now in place.

"I feel you have deceived me, Pepe. You haven't been straight with me."

"Why? I have done nothing to deceive you."

"You have brought us here with this plan in mind. But you didn't tell me that this was what you had planned."

"No, I did not plan this. It just came about. It is just that –
look, there is Spain, that is my country. There are my parents.
They are so close. It would be mad not to see them."

"You have seen them."

"Jimmy has not. They belong to him too."

Lorna could see Pepe's hunger for this final desire. She
understood how much he must have missed his parents and it
was that understanding that had brought them together in the
first place. It would be cruel to deny it now.

"Tell me, is there more? You are not holding back on
anything more with this plan?"

"No, of course not. I want this for Jimmy. And for you too.
I love you, Lorna, and I am proud of you. I want my mother
and father to meet you."

"I know that. But it's still a big risk. All sorts of things
could go wrong. Spanish soldiers will be on watch, and they're
soldiers with guns."

"But that will be OK. I guarantee. We will be safe."

Lorna found little reassurance in that statement; it was
more a cause of further suspicion, but she felt she could not be
too sceptical without endangering their relationship beyond
repair. She wanted this to happen, she could see why Pepe
wanted it, so she felt she had to accept.

"Let's get something to eat," she said.

It was one of those days forever on the cusp of the weather.
"We need the weather to be good," said Lorna. Pepe agreed
and cast his eyes anxiously at the sky. The sun hid behind
clouds and it seemed a touch too chilly to Lorna. Then
the sun came out in a sudden unveiling, and its rays were
now a little too hot. She saw everything from Jimmy's point
of view. The temperature variations did not matter to her but

they did to her son who was now playing with his floppy white hat.

"The weather is fine," said Pepe. "The fishermen told me it is going to be clear this evening."

So it emerged that Pepe had already sounded out the owner of a boat that would take them out to the sandbank at low tide that evening. He really had planned this. Lorna was irritated that he had, but would have been irritated if he had not. She felt things were beyond her control; all she could do was to go along with the situation.

Lorna was content for a while as they ate bread and fish in the café, watching the pigeons and sparrows. Pigeons waddled, with an air of dissatisfied entitlement, between the tables and chairs that were mainly unoccupied. The sparrows made more of their lot, hopping from chair to table in search of crumbs. She held out a piece of bread to one of the sparrows that hopped expectantly forward, then flew nervously to the side, returning with greater boldness to peck the bread from Lorna's fingertips. Jimmy squealed with delight at the sparrow's game, not knowing that it might be a game of survival. Lorna brushed crumbs off the table and birds hopped and flew towards their meal, fluttering wings. Pepe laughed that she was like St Francis.

They moved on. The Eglise Saint Vincent was a large, white-painted church at the top of the town square near the *mairie*. Pepe hovered outside, hearing the sound of an organ playing. He looked expectantly at Lorna and she nodded that he could go inside. Lorna followed with Jimmy, reluctantly passing through the wooden doorway. She stayed at the back of the church while Pepe entered the aisle and dropped to one knee before taking a seat on one of the pews.

The priest was speaking to the congregation, mainly children, in Spanish.

Lorna walked around the edge of the interior, stopping at a wooden statue of Joseph and Mary holding the infant Jesus. Further along, hung on the wall, there was another statue of a large, muscular figure carrying a baby across water. She had a vague memory, from her childhood churchgoing, that this might represent Saint Christopher and Jesus.

To her surprise, looking up, she saw that the gallery above was full of people looking down on the children below. Light sneaked into the church through the stained glass windows, illuminating the darkness a little without changing the overall crepuscular effect. Lorna understood none of the words that were said by the priest but took meaning from the responses. The devout intensity made her uncomfortable and she tried to catch Pepe's eye. He was too locked into prayer to notice her, so she went out into the daylight with some relief.

Lorna sat with Jimmy on a bench outside the church. After a while people started coming out, first adults, then a large group of children, finally Pepe.

"What was all that about? Was it a special service?" Lorna asked.

"It was for these orphan children. They are like me, from Spain, but they have lost their families. The town has taken them in."

Pepe was subdued but not unhappy. He seemed quietened by the experience of church and prayer. Lorna was content to see the effect even though she herself had not experienced it.

"It is a beautiful church," said Pepe. "Did you look at it?"

"I did. I liked the wooden statues on the walls. Saint Christopher, I think."

"You are right. I love that story. Carrying the holy child to safety across the water. I will tell it to Jimmy, it is such a good story."

Pepe picked up his son to carry him and, while they walked, he spoke gently to Jimmy in Spanish. Lorna understood that he was telling the story of Saint Christopher to his son. She smiled, thinking that Jimmy would not understand a word but happy that he seemed to take comfort from the closeness to his father. By the time they reached the park on the edge of town the child was asleep and Pepe stood upright to hold him, anxious not to disturb his necessary sleep. It would be a late night for the boy.

Lorna sat on the grass under the shade of a tree. Behind her, stone walls were overgrown with honeysuckle and ferns, and there was a pleasant, soporific perfume coming from them. Just before her eyelids closed in a doze, she looked along the bay at the marshy reeds where two fishing boats were drawn up on the strand. *One of those*, she thought, *must be our vessel this evening*.

CHAPTER 53

Later, at the hour when the change from day to night seeped over the wide sky, with the sun sinking sleepily below the horizon, the bay of Txingudi showed the beauty of its colours like a painting. A rainbow had followed a shower on the Spanish side of the estuary, arching over the river Bidassoa, bridging the countries on either shore. Spain looked warily at France beneath wispy clouds and France returned its gloom with brightness. Gradually the light thickened and grew dark, the rainbow disappeared like a magician's illusion, and the sky merged with the sea far out to the west. All was quiet. The bay was a calm mirror, reflecting the darkness overhead. The colours that had danced in daylight, as if singing with the natural joy of their being, muddied as they mixed on the border between sky and earth, day and night.

Pepe walked with a spring in his step despite carrying his son who was heavy with sleep. He was excited if slightly apprehensive about the meeting towards which they were heading. Lorna, trailing slightly behind, felt the same emotions but in opposite proportions. She could find no way to extricate herself from this situation without destroying so much that was important to her. Like a heavy anchor, she was slowing Pepe's progress towards his stopping point, and he kept looking over his shoulder to check she was still there.

As they walked around the curve of the bay towards the reeds the moon showed itself white and unusually bright. It was beautiful though Lorna was in no mood for the contemplation of beauty. *Let's get this over*, she thought, *and all will be well*.

If she had hoped for the intervention of weather, her hopes were dashed. There was hardly a ripple on the surface of the water, no rain in the air and only the most soothing breath of wind. Their boat was not large but there was room enough for the three of them plus the boat's owner who would row them out to the sandbank. The boatman nodded at Lorna and discreetly switched the money that Pepe slipped into his hand from his palm to his pocket. They seemed to understand each other in a mixture of French and Spanish.

"He says we have to wait about half an hour, then the tide will be right," Pepe reported back. Lorna sat down on a stone at the water shore. Pepe remained on his feet with Jimmy still asleep in his arms – he wanted him to rest as long as possible so that he would be awake and lively for his grandparents. They felt as if they were on a secret spying mission, even though Pepe had continued to emphasise the safety of what they were doing. Still, if they spoke at all, they spoke in whispers.

The boatman, naturally taciturn, simply nodded when it was time to go. They settled into the boat and Jimmy stirred awake without crying. Pepe talked to him in Spanish, repeating the story of Saint Christopher. It seemed to calm them all. The only sounds were the gentle ones of Pepe's murmuring, the dipping of oars into the water and the slapping of tide against the keel of the boat. Any clouds had completely blown away and it was a full moon, a night of clear streams in the bay, with the stars shining more brightly and more numerously as the minutes passed. *Stars I have never seen before.*

Lorna, entranced by the stars overhead, was still not able to allow that the trip might be worthwhile for such a spectacle alone. Beneath the boat the water was hardly stirring now. Ahead they could see a white strip in the water. Their boat ran into the whiteness of the sandbank and the boatman got out to demonstrate that it was safe to disembark. Jimmy grizzled for the first time but, sensing his parents' expectations, made little noise. Pepe placed him carefully on the sand and knelt down to start making a mound that, with enough time, might have turned into a castle. Lorna wrapped her shawl more tightly around herself and wondered if the cardigan and jacket would be enough to keep Jimmy warm.

Their eyes tried to pierce the darkness around them, then Pepe pointed to a white triangle a few hundred yards away. The sail of the boat came closer and closer until it bumped into the other side of the sandbank. Pepe got off his knees and strode across the sand to help his parents out of their boat. Lorna stood up and brushed sand off her hands but did not move away from Jimmy and their boat, aware of the proximity of water all around.

"*Buenas noches,*" Lorna tried when the old couple walked towards her.

"I am very pleased to meet you," the school teacher's memory brought to his lips, but the old lady simply put her arms around Lorna and kissed her on the cheek while talking in Spanish. Lorna felt tears on her face, then realised that Jimmy was pulling at her skirt. She lifted him up. "*Abuelo, abuela,*" she had learnt from Pepe.

Lorna realised with a sense of shock that this old couple must still be relatively young, in their fifties. Yet they did seem genuinely aged, inclined to stoop, their faces in the moonlight deeply lined with the wrinkles of years and hardship. The momentousness of the meeting suddenly seemed overwhelming, and Lorna's history with Pepe flashed through her mind, taking her back to the days when they had first met at the camp in Hampshire, making her think that then these parents had been left childless and anxious without their young son. Had she recognised that enough? Had she given enough thought to Pepe's deprivations, torn apart from his parents, his country and the things that were familiar to him in his life. She cried all the more, wiping her eyes with a handkerchief while the old lady smiled benignly at her, patting her arms in comfort.

Pepe had stood back from the scene, allowing it to take its course, but now he stepped forward to pick up his son. In the way of grandparents, they made noises that hardly counted as words, so no translation was needed. Lorna heard Jimmy called 'Hamez' but the old man said "I think you call him Jimmy, yes?"

"Yes," smiled Lorna, "we call him Jimmy. James is only on the birth certificate."

They stood together in a close circle on the sandbank, with the silver light of the moon shining on them. For a short time, perhaps for an hour if the tide allowed, they could unite as one family.

CHAPTER 54

Lorna stood there on the sand, as if isolated in a silver bubble of moonlight. The sand was damp, flat, white as snow. You could easily run on it, if you chose, at least for a 30-yard sprint. At one end of the visible sand was the boat that had brought Pepe's parents, and the boatman was lowering the little sail. At the other end was the boat that had carried Lorna, Pepe and Jimmy. Each boatman took a seat inside his boat, while the family group with Jimmy as the centre of attention clustered in the centre of the sandbank. Except that Lorna stood a little apart. The white piping on her navy blue coat seemed to have a luminous glow.

Pepe's mother – *abuelita*, said Pepe to Jimmy by way of introduction – had come prepared for a midnight feast. She set the canvas bag down on the white sand and spread a cloth that she took from the bag. Then she started to lay out the contents on the cloth: bread, cheese, ham, olives and oranges. The oranges looked extraordinary in the moonlight, their orangeness transformed into a colour Lorna had never seen before. This drew her into the circle and she began to say a few words, her language limited by the consciousness that the old lady might not understand a word she spoke. *It doesn't matter.*

"I am so pleased to have this chance to greet you," said the old man in a formal tone.

"And me," replied Lorna, smiling at him. "You speak very good English."

"No, no, not like Pepe. He is the student better to the teacher. This was always so."

"You were a good teacher," said Pepe. "Now I can teach Jimmy."

"We say he swallow a dictionary. The words, he ate them."

"Eat," said the old lady, spreading her hands to present the food, as if offering the hospitality of her own house. Lorna felt obliged to eat a little; Pepe took the food as if he had not eaten for days. *Abuelita* had something specially in mind for her grandson. She cut one of the oranges in half with a knife, then squeezed the juice of the orange into a tumbler. She did it skilfully and the juice all fell inside the tumbler which she handed to Jimmy. Lorna took the juice with a *gracias* and held the rim of the tumbler to Jimmy's lips. The boy shook his head and pushed the cup away with his hands.

Pepe spoke in Spanish and his parents laughed. "I explained that he is not used to oranges. Only when it comes in a bottle from the doctor."

This was not really true, Lorna told herself, but she said nothing to contradict it. It was easier to laugh and keep the atmosphere as relaxed as possible. But she felt the pressure to say something, to contribute a question to the conversation even if she could not offer her own food.

"How are you managing to live?" she asked. There was no way of calling back the awkwardness of the question once it was spoken, but she wanted to know the answer.

The old man looked at her, and she could see the creases in his face as he nodded his head in thought. He was forming the words, limited by the constraints of language and honesty.

"We live," he said. "We live. It is not easy. But I have work. In the fish market, not as a teacher. It is enough."

"It will pass," said Pepe. "One day soon. There will be work again."

His father shrugged. "Perhaps. I am not young. You are young. There is work for young men."

"But you have to ignore everything," said Lorna. "Everything that is good. You live under a dictatorship."

"Of course. You are right. But after a while you get used to it. It does not matter so much no more."

"You see," said Pepe directly to Lorna. "People find a way to live. There is no need for lawyers if you keep out of trouble."

Lorna felt she was being attacked by Pepe's words but the situation did not allow her to defend herself – or to fight back. They had planned to be here only for an hour; most of the time had already gone, so she must keep her words to herself, gulp them down with the crustiness of bread. She looked behind to make sure the boat was still there.

Pepe was talking to his mother and father in Spanish. His words were tumbling out faster and faster, the volume rising like the wind that was now beginning to stir. Lorna noticed the first gentle movements of the tide on the turn.

"Pepe, look," she said. "We need to make a move soon." She pointed at the boatman who was preparing to step out of the boat.

"Yes, we will go soon."

He carried on talking in Spanish. There was a lot of gesticulating between father and son. The old man shook his head vigorously and often.

"What are you saying, Pepe? It's time to go. Let your mum and dad say goodbye to Jimmy."

Pepe's face was turned away, still looking at his parents, still waiting for an answer from them. But what was his question? Lorna's sense of unease grew, a cold sweat of fear felt clammy on her forehead.

"We can go with them," said Pepe. "It is possible. We can live with them."

"Are you mad? You know we could never do that."

"We could. We could be a family, living together."

She dismissed this with bitterness in her dismissal. "What has got into you? You know you would be arrested. They are hardly going to roll out the red carpet for you, with Franco's special pardon."

"It is not all politics, Lorna. You can live life without politics. That is all I want to do, I just want to be left alone to live. And we can do that."

"We cannot. You are wrong. You are deceived and you have deceived me."

"I have not. I just try to do what is right for my family."

"This is not right. It is wrong, wrong, wrong."

The old man could understand enough of what Lorna was saying. He seemed anguished, not wanting to take sides, while his wife packed away the bag, pushing inside the uneaten food, the disappointment, the pain, the uncertainty.

"It is for you to decide," the old man said. "We will offer you a home."

Lorna shivered her refusal. "Thank you. But impossible. It is everything I have always resisted. You are not a fascist but *they* are" pointing with her finger across the estuary towards Spain.

Both the boatmen were now out of their boats and signalling that they must make a move. Water was beginning to well up around their feet. The black water in the estuary was starting to ripple with wavelets.

Pepe picked up Jimmy. "Come, Lorna, let us go. We will not have this chance again."

Lorna stood straight, deliberately making herself taller, then strode towards Pepe and snatched Jimmy out of his arms. Fury made her strong. "You go. If you must. But you go without me. And without Jimmy."

Pepe was angry too but trying to stay calm. "Lorna. Think. Be calm. It is OK. We have been given a safe passage."

"What? Safe passage? Who by? By Franco, I suppose."

Pepe nodded, reluctantly. "In a way, yes. It has been arranged. I will not be arrested."

Lorna clung tightly to Jimmy. Her eyes shone brightly in the moonlight. They blazed with an anger that was close to hatred. She could not say another word but turned away from Pepe and walked to the boat where the French fisherman was waiting. She climbed inside with Jimmy, sat down and said "*Allez!*" to the boatman.

"*Et lui?*" the boatman pointed at Pepe.

She shook her head. "*Allez!*"

The oars struck the water and the boat began to pull away from the sandbank, making for the shore that was only a few hundred yards away. Lorna's feet were wet and cold but she wrapped Jimmy tight inside her coat, holding in whatever warmth she could for him. She kissed the curly hair of his head while looking down into the darkness of the water alongside the boat. Her emotions were spent. She felt no grief, no anger, no hatred, no bitterness. There was only numbness and a desperate feeling of love for the young life in her arms. She looked up to the black heavens spotted with bright stars, and the stars seemed to offer the comfort that, just as she held Jimmy, the universe watched over them both.

The boat started to glide through the reeds that fringed the shoreline of Hendaye. She could see the land – the stone walls, the trees, the houses of the town behind them, lit only by the dimmest of street lighting. In the other direction, across the estuary, Spain was a black outline, impenetrable and hostile, or so it seemed to her at that moment. She gazed into that blackness, failing to see the boat that was taking its human cargo to the other shore. Then, where the dark land of Spain must be, she saw sudden tracks of orange fire, she heard the rat-a-tat of machine gun fire. Lorna stared at the bright points of light that soon faded into the darkness, swallowed up like refuse thrown overboard into the ocean. A shiver of freezing cold ran through her, she hugged Jimmy close for comfort, his and hers. An overwhelming silence enveloped them, broken at last by the thudding of the boat as it came to a halt on the sandy shore. The boatman stepped out and handed Lorna onto the beach with Jimmy still in her arms.

"*Merci,*" she said, with as much dignity as she could muster. She handed the boatman the packet of cigarettes that she had brought to give to Pepe after their mission.

Back on the firm ground of the path, she lifted Jimmy into her arms then began to walk up the hill into the shadowy streets of the old town; aware that it was late but with no real idea of time. Then the church bell struck twice. Half the night was still to be endured.

Carrying Jimmy her progress was slow but eventually she arrived in the town square and walked up the few stairs to the doorway of the *pension.* The house inside was dark, with not even a night light visible. The windows of her room were black; the wooden door was heavy and firmly closed. She tried pushing it but it would not yield, and she had no key. She could not face the prospect of trying to rouse Madame Loti by ringing the bell or banging on the door in the middle of this silent town in the middle of this strange night. She settled down on the doorstep, cradling the child in her arms, taking care to wrap him in her coat, tucking him into his own clothing as tightly as she could. She pushed her red beret tighter to her head, tucking in stray strands of her hair. Overhead the stars made bright pinpoints of light in the inky darkness, like the night lights that she had no wish to extinguish. *Shine on, look after us.* Thoughts tumbled inside her head now that she had reached a place of relative rest, but she entered an unquiet sleep.

She became aware of the noises of the town waking. Early risers were starting to go about their business. An old lady came by with a poodle, and the poodle sniffed curiously at the mother and child on the doorstep. The woman spoke to Lorna in French but Lorna gave no answer, she simply closed her eyes again, as if to say she wanted to sleep some more.

As she dozed in the doorway, she started planning her new life. She had to accept that this would be so. She had almost certainly seen the last of Pepe. His memory would be encouraged to disappear, left in the distance of a night scene across a dark estuary. That tide had gone, and she was surprised how casually she felt able to let it go. He was cast off, a memory set adrift. Betrayal – or the sense of being betrayed – encouraged her forgetting. He was dead to her, whether or not he was dead in reality. She had the precious leavings of her relationship, she held the child breathing softly in her embrace. For him she would provide all the comforts of life as well as the essentials of a mother's love. And, she would console herself that, in the end, she had made happiness possible for him, if he would allow it, in his own way.

It was daylight and it promised to be a fine day, with clear skies. She flicked away a persistent fly that buzzed around her ears but, like other unwanted things, it would return. There was no option but to live with this fate. *Not now, we will do.* Caught by an early bluster of breeze, that had a touch of warmth even at dawn, fallen leaves in the square seemed to hop like sparrows in a vain attempt to fly. They settled back on the paving stones. Lorna listened to the real birds whose song came from all around. She had a feeling she could not identify. It was neither happiness nor unhappiness, simply acceptance.

Behind her the front door creaked open and she looked over her shoulder. Madame Loti stood there with an expression of surprise on her face. Lorna struggled to her feet, unravelling from her cramped position, causing Jimmy to wake. He began to cry but quietly, as if to himself, not wanting to upset his mother if he could help it. *Will you always be like this? I hope not, for your sake.*

"*Où est ton mari?*"

Lorna understood the question but suspected she might find no answer more satisfactory than a Gallic shrug. Her face was blank. "*Mort,*" she mumbled, whether from belief or convenience, uncertain of facts and language.

Madame Loti saw them up to their room and helped them into bed. She covered the woman and child with a sheet and blanket, and instantly they fell asleep, exhausted by the emotion of their night. They slept for several hours and, when Lorna opened her eyes, she saw Madame Loti sitting upright in a chair at the bedside, watching over them.

"*Je te laisse maintenant. Dis moi s'il y a quelquechose que tu veux.*"

Madame Loti closed the door quietly behind her. Lorna was touched by the unexpected kindness of a woman she had thought a stranger. Down below in the hallway the grandfather clock struck twelve times. Half the day was done. Next day they must take the train and begin the long journey back to London.

Jimmy was still sleeping peacefully and she wondered what he might be dreaming. She hoped sleep would repair any damage that might have been inflicted by the events of the night. She was determined he would feel no loss of a parent's love even though she knew this role did not come easily to her. *Dream on. We will live our lives and hope to be happy together.* Lorna feared she might have cast away her chance of happiness but she could devote herself to making her child as happy as possible. *It's what any mother aims to do. So why not me?*

She fell back into a reverie that might pass for a sleep. Certainly she fell back into fresh dreams, and in her dreams she was still staring at stars.

EPILOGUE
September 1985, Spain

We mark the passing of people by anniversaries. Even those of us without religion have a reverence for the sacred significance of dates. So it was that I returned to Spain exactly one year after Mother died, wanting to be in that country to mark the anniversary. I intended this, not certain of my purpose, simply feeling the need to follow in the footsteps of those who had walked there before, wishing to make a connection with my family history.

When the idea first occurred it seemed clear that I would be seeking traces of my father. Mother had spoken little of him, there was always a resistance to the subject, but she had never said anything to prejudice me against him. She resisted with sadness not bitterness. It had become normal to speak of the 'disappeared' and I had been led to think of Pepe among those ranks. In my imagination, lacking the real presence of a father, I had painted his portrait with eyes staring resolutely forward, intent and determined and heroic. Mother had said nothing to contradict that image; nor had she affirmed it, which left a doubt hanging like mist. But it was what I wanted to believe and perhaps this visit could dispel the mist.

Such are the commonplace deceptions that comfort us. The reality was that when Mother died I had lost my last chance to ask the only person who might answer questions about Pepe Calderon. With Mother's passing, Pepe joined the shuffling ghosts of the disappeared forever.

Yet something unexpected happened instead. As her only child it became my duty to sift through Mother's personal effects. She had shown the diligence of a lawyer in making her will easy to find and administer. Everything came to me – it was not much in terms of money but she had worked hard for it. There were boxes of papers that had been stored away in wardrobes and cupboards. At last, I thought, I might discover more about my father.

There was little about Pepe Calderon however. I knew the name from my birth certificate but Mother and I had been known to the world as Lorna Starling and her son James Starling. I found documents recording Pepe's military service and even three campaign medals with striped ribbons, but otherwise it was as if the moths had reduced his memory to the dust that I blew away from the objects in the boxes.

If Pepe disappeared, another man fleshed more vividly into life. Mother had mentioned Harry James – indeed she always became more animated when talking about him – but I had not expected these boxes to contain what seemed like a shrine to Harry's memory. There were photographs, newspaper cuttings, obituary notices from union journals, letters and even a pamphlet. From the pamphlet's cover and introductory information Harry James was the author whose eye-witness account followed. That account was of the bombing of Guernica (or Gernika as he wrote it in its Basque form). Through these relics, preserved in amber plastic folders, Harry came alive to me, almost as if he had been the father I never knew.

So I decided that I should set out to discover this lost father. There were some tantalising clues in the paperwork, and it seemed clear that Harry had died in Catalonia. If he had been granted the dignity of a grave it was probably unmarked and unknown.

On our final trip Mother had talked about the possibility of visiting Bilbao and Guernica and Figueras, but there had been a reluctance to move on before she was ready. I had assumed that these were places associated with Pepe. But it now became an obvious certainty in my mind that I had been named James to honour this fallen soldier of the International Brigade. It also became clear that Mother had had a secret plan during her final weeks of life. Perhaps those sometimes desultory walks around Madrid and Seville were delaying tactics, while she steeled herself to tell me more. In any event she had been thwarted by her own death, cheated of her journey of remembrance, her private plan to follow in the footsteps of Harry James, to tread the same tracks that he had taken many years before I was born.

It was hopeless, of course, and unrealistic to expect that I might find him, but I felt that I owed it to Mother. I had no names of people, no addresses for places to visit; in any case history would have swallowed them. I wandered the streets of Bilbao disconsolately; I sat in gardens in Guernica in the rain under the shelter of an oak tree; and I walked on grey pavements around Catalonian towns. They yielded no secrets. There was nothing to make a connection to Harry. Mother had made me a good walker but not a discoverer. With some relief I headed out of Figueras, thinking the fields of the countryside might connect me to the battlefields where he had fought and died.

Some five miles out of town I stopped by a farmhouse as the sun was sinking. I talked to the shepherd there because I needed somewhere to stay the night, to eat some simple food. The shepherd and his wife were obliging and probably thankful for the money that I paid in advance for my stay. Later that evening as we ate mutton stew, I broached the subject of the civil war. We were wary of each other. This was not a subject that allowed easy conversations in Spain. But sentence by hesitant sentence it emerged that our sympathies leant in the same direction. I told them what I knew of Harry James.

The shepherd got to his feet and put on an outdoor jacket. He beckoned me to do the same and to follow him.

On the hillside it was easy to see because the moon was full, the sky was studded with bright stars, and there was no trace of a cloud. As we walked up the hill, with the shepherd tapping his stick on the rock-hard ground, stepping from stone to stone, sheep scuttled out of our path. Those animals must be tough to survive in such barren land. Yet there was something beautiful about the silver light that reflected off the grey rocks and that pointed the way ahead like a lantern.

Making our way around the brow of the hill, we came to a hollow on the other side. A rock overhung the hollow, like the entrance to a cave, and in that entrance was a small mound of stones on the bare earth. The moonlight fell on the mound and it seemed to glow with an internal light.

The shepherd said nothing; neither did I. This cairn might or might not be Harry's grave. How could anyone ever know? The shepherd gave no opinion but pointed with his stick, then crossed himself. This was a land where it had been forbidden to mark resting places for the defeated; here one grave had to stand for many, and to do so patiently, silently. One grave for one body and for thousands of bodies, a single individual or an army, it did not really matter which.

From my pocket I took out the artificial pearl necklace that I had discovered next to Harry's letters. When I had seen it, I had decided on a whim to bring it on this trip, perhaps as some kind of comfort because it reminded me of Mother. There had seemed something deliberate in their side-by-side placement, and that thought made me now deliberate in my own movements. I bent over the mound of stones, carefully removing the top three or four until a gap was revealed by its deep blackness. I dropped the necklace into the gap, then placed the stones back as I had found them.

Above, the stars were shining like pearls in the moonlight. There were more stars than anyone could ever count, more stars than anyone would ever want to count, in that black immensity of night sky. Each one was beautiful, however bright or dim, and it seemed to me, that night, every night, that each one counted.

ACKNOWLEDGEMENTS

Place is always important for the writing of any book. The places you write about and the places where you write. Wherever possible I brought the two closer together during the writing of this book, making visits to Guernica and Hendaye to see the places myself and at least to start to write there. But the bulk of the book was written in north London as near as possible to the places where the novel is set. I live in Muswell Hill and wrote there but I also found productive refuges for writing in the British Museum, the RA Academicians Room and the Somers Town Coffee House. I had the additional advantage of having grown up in Levita House in the post-war years. These places, and memories from my family history, provided the sanctuary and the inspiration needed.

Books were important too, in particular *Only for Three Months* by Adrian Bell, the story of the 4000 Spanish children evacuated on the *Habana* in 1937. My daughter Jessie discovered that book and passed it to me, and it proved the catalyst for this novel. Jessie also took interest in the stories of my mum and dad's connections with the Spanish Civil War. That proved a fascinating exploration as a background to this novel, leading me to organisations like the Basque Children of '37 Association UK and the International Brigade Memorial Trust. There were so many examples of serendipity, not least the discovery by my daughter Jessie that she was living two doors away from the address in Lamb's Conduit Street where my mother Jessie had been born.

Places, books and people. The two Jessies in my family inspired this book, though they never met each other. My wife Linda and son Matt were always encouraging me throughout the writing and were the novel's first enthusiastic readers. My cousin Joanna Wilmot also added to the shared family stories that gave me the impetus for the book.

The look of a book always matters to me, and David Carroll has designed the cover of *Spanish Crossings* as elegantly as ever – I'm proud to have been able to use the image by Wolfgang Suschitzsky for the cover. Wolf died last year at 103 years old, a survivor who fled the rising tide of 1930s European fascism to enjoy an amazing photographic career in this country. Photographs have been vital to the nurturing of this novel, and Wolf's helpful curator at the Photographers' Gallery, Anthony Hartley, deserves a special mention for being the conduit between me and Wolf's work over many years.

My publisher Matthew Smith is a great supporter of writers through his independent company Urbane Publications, and Matthew has now published both my novels. He is a joy to know and work with, and I value his support more than these words can express. This book would not have happened without him.

I'm grateful to Mathilde Caron and Rosa Cryer for checking my French and Spanish. Through Rosa (more serendipity, she lives next door to me) I met some survivors of the 1937 Basque evacuation, children who had stayed on to make their lives in England. Thank you Paco Robles and Agustina Perez San Jose for telling me your stories.

My biggest debt is to my parents Jessie and Frank who in 1937 'adopted' one of the evacuated Spanish boys, Jesùs Iguaran Aramburu, who returned to Spain in 1938. My thanks go to Carmen Kilner of the Basque Children's Association for tracking down his name and details. I feel as if Jessie and Frank might have been witnesses to many of the scenes in this novel, but they do not figure as characters. Their example and stories from my childhood inspired me to write this, sadly many years after the time when I could have asked them more about the people and events they witnessed in the 1930s and 1940s.

John Simmons
London, 2017

John Simmons is an independent writer and consultant. He was a director of Newell and Sorrell from 1984 until the merger with Interbrand in 1997. He headed many large brand programmes with companies as diverse as Waterstone's, Royal Mail, Air Products and the National Theatre. He established Interbrand's verbal identity team before he left in 2003. Since then he has continued to work with the widest range of companies and organisations on branding, consultancy and writing projects.

John has run "Writing for design" workshops for D&AD and the School of Life. He also runs "Dark Angels" workshops, residential courses in remote retreats, which aim to promote more creative writing for business www.dark-angels.org. uk. He has written a number of books on the relationship between language and identity, including "The Dark Angels Trilogy" – *We, Me, Them & It*, *The Invisible Grail* and *Dark Angels*. These books are now published in updated editions by Urbane. His books helped establish the practice of tone of voice as a vital element of branding.

He's a founder director of 26, the not-for-profit group that champions the cause of better language in business, and has been writer-in-residence for Unilever and King's Cross tube station. In 2011 he was awarded an Honorary Fellowship by the University of Falmouth in recognition of 'outstanding contribution to the creative sector'. John is on the Campaign Council for Writers' Centre Norwich as Norwich becomes the first English City of Literature.

Other books are *26 Ways of Looking at a Blackberry*, about the creative power of constraints, and *Room 121: A Masterclass in Business Writing*, co-written with Jamie Jauncey as an exchange over 52 weeks. In June 2011 John's first work of fiction, *The Angel of the Stories*, was published by Dark Angels Press, with illustrations by the artist Anita Klein.

He initiated and participated in the writing of a Dark Angels collective novel *Keeping Mum* with fifteen writers – the novel was published by Unbound in 2014. And in 2015 he published the novel *Leaves* with Urbane Publications. Spanish Crossings is John's second novel to be published by Urbane and he is currently working on a new novel, *The Good Messenger*.

ALSO PUBLISHED BY URBANE PUBLICATIONS

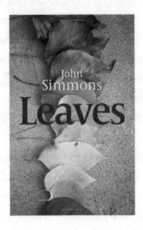

LEAVES
by John Simmons

ISBN – 978-1909273771
£8.99, pbk, 224pp

John Simmons is the best writer you think you haven't read. In fact he is one of the architects of the language of our daily lives. With his novel Leaves the secret is now out.
Caroline McCormick, former Director, PEN International

Ophelia Street, 1970. A street like any other, a community that lives and breathes together as people struggle with their commitments and pursue their dreams. It is a world we recognise, a world where class and gender divide, where set roles are acknowledged. But what happens when individuals step outside those roles, when they secretly covet, express desire, pursue ambitions even harm and destroy? An observer in the midst of Ophelia Street watches, writes, imagines, remembers, charting the lives and loves of his neighbours over the course of four seasons. And we see the flimsily disguised underbelly of urban life revealed in all its challenging glory. As the leaves turn from vibrant green to vivid gold, so lives turn and change too, laying bare the truth of the community. Perhaps, ultimately, we all exist on Ophelia Street.

Urbane Publications is dedicated to
developing new author voices, and publishing
fiction and non-fiction that challenges, thrills and
fascinates.
From page-turning novels to innovative
reference books, our goal is to publish what
YOU want to read.

Find out more at
urbanepublications.com